Farzana Moon

Poet Emperor
of the last
of the Moghuls

Bahadur Shah Zafar

Editions Dedicaces

POET EMPEROR OF THE LAST OF THE MOGHULS:
BAHADUR SHAH ZAFAR

Published by:
   Editions Dedicaces LLC
   12759 NE Whitaker Way, Suite D833
   Portland, Oregon, 97230
   www.dedicaces.us

Library of Congress Cataloging-in-Publication Data
   Moon, Farzana
   Poet Emperor of the last of the Moghuls: Bahadur Shah Zafar /
   by Farzana Moon.
   p. cm.
   ISBN-13: 978-1-77076-435-4 (alk. paper)
   ISBN-10: 1-77076-435-6 (alk. paper)

Farzana Moon

Poet Emperor of the last of the Moghuls

Bahadur Shah Zafar

For Rehana
My Loving Sister

Chapter One
Coronation of the Poet Emperor

The East bowed low before the blast
In patient, deep disdain
She let the legions thunder past
And plunged in thought again

If there be paradise on earth,
this is it, this is it, this is it.
AMIR KHUSRAU

These words engraved on the wall of the Diwan-i-Khas across from where Bahadur Shah Zafar sat on his Peacock Throne were a blatant reminder of the Moghul splendor, usurped and fading. Even Peacock Throne was replica of the lost glory since the magnificent Peacock Throne of Shah Jahan was carried away by Nadir Shah of Persia and lost to the world in briny waters of the ocean.

The coronation of the sixty-two year old Bahadur Shah Zafar twentieth in line of the Moghul emperors lacked the pomp and pageantry of the previous emperors since the coronation of the first great Moghul emperor, Babur. But the event was royal no doubt; Diwan-i-Khas with silk friezes, damasked drapes framing the marble walls in motifs of floral designs embedded with jewels. The Peacock Throne dripping with velvets was hosting Bahadur Shah Zafar in royal attire of gold and purple. Bejeweled and crowned, he was wafting the aura of wealth and majesty.

High decorum was lending this state occasion the air of festivity. The emperor alone was the one seated, the rest in attendance were standing, offering felicitations or presenting the written documents of court proceedings for the benefit of royal perusal if the emperor deemed it necessary. Lord Aukland's secretary of East India Company William Machaghten was standing in the front row to the emperor's right along with the newly appointed governor of Delhi, Ahsanullah Khan.

Bahadur Shah Zafar sensitive to the observance of etiquette and decorum in his court was happy to notice that his sons were standing most royally. They were impeccably dressed in Moghul style robes of gold, broidered with silk and studded with jewels. Crown prince Dara Bakht was the most handsome amongst his brothers with ropes of pearls around his neck and his turban stitched with agates. Prince Fakhroo standing next to him was no less handsome, a swath of emeralds in his turban matching his green robe was lending his features the glow of sunset. The eldest, Prince Mirza Quaish appeared to tower over his brothers, being the tallest, almost six feet two, gaining a couple of more inches with a large plume in his red turban. The youngest amongst them was Prince Abul Bakr the grandson of Bahadur Shah Zafar.

William Machaghten was mesmerized by the cool stream called Nahr-i-Bhisht—meaning literally the river of paradise, flowing smoothly in the middle of Diwan-i-Khas. Tearing his gaze away from this architectural wonder he was thinking of gaining the king's attention, but the king was communing with his sons Prince Mirza Mughal and Prince Khizr Sultan as if initiating them into the arena of ceremony and protocol. Makhund Lal—the secretary with his hands folded was standing along with the poets Zauq, Ghalib and Momin, waiting patiently for his turn in announcing the titles of the King. The King was dismissing his sons with a wave of his arm and granting Makhund Lal the permission to speak with his gaze alone.

"Zil-e-Subhani." Makhund Lal curtsied with a quick sweep of his arm, bending low to the floor. "His Divine Highness. Caliph of the Age. Padishah as glorious as Jamshed. He who is surrounded by Hosts of Angels. Shadow of God. Refuge of Islam. Protector of the Mohammedan Religion. Sultan son of Sultan. Greatest of the emperors. Emperor son of emperor. Offspring of the House of Timur."

"The House of Timur, Makhund Lal, is no more. It is buried under the dust of zeal and invasions." Bahadur Shah Zafar's gaze swept over all slowly and thoughtfully. "The mighty of East India Company who for years begged for trade concessions from our great ancestors are now our masters. I am not the emperor, not even the king of kings, only the King of Delhi."

"For us you are the emperor incarnate, Zil-e-Subhani." Shah Nasir—the court poet curtsied thrice with a long sweep of his arm. "Without your patronage our inspiration would expire. No one to string the pearls of poetry into some poem most beautiful."

"Ah, my tutor knows the art of flattery! Though, the expense of patronage also comes from the rich coffers of East

India Company getting richer from land revenues." Bahadur Shah Zafar waved his consent for the usual privilege of open parlance or discussion."

"Zil-e-Subhani, the Governor General of East India Company, Lord Aukland regards you as his Divine Highness and respects your wishes of decorum at the court." William Machaghten whipped this harmless lie, more so to satisfy his own sense of justice than to mitigate the mettle of harsh instructions heaped upon him by Lord Aukland. "To honor the memory of your father Akbar Shah an eighty-two gun salute was fired from the ramparts of Fort William. You yourself commented, Zil-e-Subhani, that your father died at the age of eighty-two."

"And with him died the custom of offering gifts—Nazr to the emperor." Bahadur Shah Zafar suppressed a sigh. "I recall vividly that when I was a prince the Governor General Amherst presenting my father a variety of gifts at his court. One hundred and one trays of jewels. Shawls and robes of silk most exquisite. Also elephants richly caparisoned and horses with velvet trappings. And now even tributary offerings are missing. You stand here empty handed by the orders of Lord Aukland most probably, who deigns not to come and pay his respects?"

"He is afraid, Zil-e-Subhani, that if he came here he would be besieged by some sort of demands." William Machaghten construed another lie of half jest, half truth. "I have heard Lord Aukland tell his officers, there is no worthy gift for Padishah who is as glorious as Jamshed."

"I have yet to get accustomed to the shafts of mockery." Bahadur Shah Zafar closed his eyes. "An emperor reduced to the status of a king can only request, not demand. If I was half as wise as Jamshed with his Jam-e- Jam my only treasure I would lack nothing, but the will to conquer and subjugate."

"For us, Zil-e-Subhani, you are the Caliph of the Age." Momin curtsied low. "Without your guidance we would be deprived of the gifts of spirituality and inspiration. No ideation or poetry sessions, but discussions about wars and intrigues if you didn't guide us in pursuit of love for learning and versification."

"Poets are the best and the worst of flatterers." Bahadur Shah Zafar chided kindly. "Best in a sense that they don't mean what they say and worst because they aim toward staying in the clouds, yet barely rise above the clouds of dust. The era for the Caliph of Age is past gone, now only sovereigns in name or tyrants without kingdoms rule in rapport with the needs and greeds of time."

"By contemplating the past, Zil-e-Subhani, we might be able to tame the tyrants and learn to avoid the mistakes our ancestors made which benefited only the fortune-seekers from lands alien and distant." Ghalib stole an accusing glance at William Machaghten. "Emperor Akbar consented to the pleas of the English to open trade routes between India and England. After the death of emperor Akbar, his son emperor Jahangir consented to open more ports for free trading. A century later, not until the emperor Farrukhsiyar was constrained to grant eight villages to the British that the troubles began."

"I was going to appoint you tutor to Prince Fakhroo as his poetry teacher, but you might as well be his history teacher." Bahadur Shah Zafar commented amusedly.

"Prince Fakhroo's mentor, Zil-e-Subhani, in poetry as well as politics is his father-in-law, Ilahi Bakhsh." Ghalib laughed.

"History needs to be rewritten, Zil-e-Subhani. Many flaws which need to be addressed?" William Machaghten commented.

"English history of the Moghul splendor if the author is not imported from London." Bahadur Shah Zafar arched his eyebrows, his look piercing.

"In any language, Zil-e-Subhani." Was William Machaghten discomfited response.

"East India Company minting its currency in the name of the King of England and with the English monarch's image embossed." Zauq could not help but voice his bitterness.

"Since English has become the official language of our country, I am going to learn it properly and thoroughly." Prince Mirza Mughal was quick to breathe low his own wish-comment.

"Learning English would be of great benefit to royal princes, Zil-e-Subhani. They would become great mediators between us and the natives of India." William Machaghten tossed in his own swift appeal-comment.

"If India indeed could stay intact as one nation?" One whiff of a prophecy escaped Bahadur Shah Zafar's lips, falling into the cauldron of future. "Kabul the Jerusalem of the Moghuls to be torn asunder by the policy of divide-and-rule of the Britons. Lord Aukland himself siding with Ranjit Singh and exiled Shah Shuja to ousted Dost Muhammed." He eased himself up from his throne as a signal of dismissal. "I am wearied of rivalries and intrigues. Come Ahsanullah Khan, take a stroll with me in the garden."

The afternoon sunlight glinting over the two bisecting channels of water in the garden of Hayat Bakhsh—life bestowing garden appeared to be shimmering like the confetti of gold. Bahadur Shah Zafar and Ahsanullah Khan strolling over the red-gravel path edged by square flowerbeds of roses in full bloom were lulled to silence by the pulse of warmth and fragrance. Marble pavilions with jets of water fountains were left behind, only serenading of the bulbuls magical and mysterious. Bahadur Shah Zafar's gaze was reaching out to the gardeners busy pruning topiaries, but his thoughts were dreamy on the verge of a passionate explosion. Since his chance meeting with Zeenat Begum not too long ago at the mansion of her brother Nawab Quli Khan, Bahadur Shah Zafar had sloughed off at least twenty years, feeling young and vulnerable to the charms of this beautiful maiden. Even now his thoughts were brewing a volcano of desires, ravaged by doubts that the lady of his love might never accept his proposal of marriage.

"As many times as I have been married I should be content, but I have fallen in love." Bahadur Shah Zafar murmured as if to himself. "At my age, for the first time in my life I have fallen in love, truly and hopelessly in love. I need your assistance Ahsanullah Khan."

"At your service, Zil-e-Subhani. You but command and I obey." Ahsanullah Khan breathed eagerly, trying his best not to sound too curious.

"I need to request, not command! Especially to the Lady and her parents." Bahadur Shah Zafar demurred aloud.

"Any lady would be happy to marry the emperor of India, Zil-e-Subhani and any parent honored to claim Zil-e-Subhani as their son-in-law." Ahsanullah Khan could barely suppress his agog on the verge of delirium.

"Now! I am only the King of Delhi and that too in name alone. Too old to be seeking young brides." Bahadur Shah Zafar sighed.

"Who is the fortunate bride-to-be, Zil-e-Subhani?" Ahsanullah Khan couldn't contain his fever of curiosity.

"Zeenat Begum, she is the sister of Nawab Quli Khan and the daughter of Nawab Samsam-Daula." Bahadur Shah Zafar murmured tenderly as if savoring the taste of her name upon his lips.

"She is beautiful! I have seen her, Zil-e-Subhani." Ahsanullah Khan declared suddenly, his heart burdened with the weight of envy and presage.

"You are to go to her parents' home, Ahsanullah. Take several trays of jewels as gifts for her family, and request her hand in marriage for the King." Bahadur Shah Zafar's feet were coming to an abrupt halt at the path leading toward the Pearl Mosque.

"I would be honored of the privilege to carry this message, Zil-e-Subhani." Ahsanullah Khan stopped beside the King, both facing the white marble façade of the mosque in utter silence. "When do you want me to start, Zil-e-Subhani?" He was the first one to break the spell of silence.

"If not this evening then early next morning." Bahadur Shah Zafar stood admiring three-arched screen over the courtyard of the mosque. "Their mansion is by the Red Well, not very far from our palace. You know that, I am sure."

"Yes, Zile-e-Subhani, I have had the honor of dining there at one of the Eid festivals."

"Tomorrow noon then you would go to their mansion with several trays of jewels." Bahadur Shah Zafar retraced his steps, Ahsanullah Khan following. "With that settled my thoughts turn to Afghanistan. A daring explorer I have heard by the name of Captain Burns has arrived in Kabul. He is no explorer I am afraid, but an agent of East India Company to cause rifts in Afghanistan."

"This is not his first visit, Zil-e-Subhani." Ahsanullah Khan Reminisced aloud. "His first mission was six years ago in eighteen hundred thirty-one by the very command of the King of England to make a survey of the Indus Valley. King William 1V had dispatched him with a gift of six dapple gray dray-horses to Maharaja Ranjit Singh to win his favors, addressing the Maharaja as the Lion of Lahore."

"Now I remember. His intelligence-gathering trip landed him in Kabul, over the Hindu Kush to Bokhara and from there, enroute Caspian and Persia, back to India." Bahadur Shah Zafar chuckled suddenly. "A great flatterer though, he was proficient in Arabic, Persian and Hindi. It was duly reported to my father that his first meeting with the Shah of Persia he addressed him as the *Center of the Universe*, saying, *what sight has equaled that which I now behold, the light of Your Majesty's Countenance. O, Attraction of the World."*

"He also wrote, Zil-e-Subhani, that England and Russia would divide Asia between them and the two empires would enlarge like circles in the water till they are lost in nothing. And future generations would search for both of us in those regions as we now seek for the remains of Alexander and his Greeks."

"Ah, the political imposter posing as tourist must have met the Russian agent Count Simonich in eighteen hundred thirty-four, urging the Amir of Kabul Shah Muhammad to capture Herat." Bahadur Shah Zafar's memory was taking a swift stroll down the rungs of immediate past. "Herat—the Pearl City has become a battleground for fortune-seekers, including the British, the Persians and the Russians. Didn't the Shah of Persia two months ago gather his forces at the borders of Herat? And now Peshawar is becoming the seat of contention. Dost Muhammed appealing to Lord Aukland that if Governor General would help him regain Peshawar, he would break off his negotiations with Russia. He would hold it in fief from Ranjit Singh and transmit the customary presents."

"Ranjit Singh doesn't trust Russians either, Zil-e-Subhani." Ahsanullah Khan began exigently before the king could disappear behind the palace gates. "A young Cossack by the name of Captain Vitkievitch tried to make contact with Ranjit Singh, but he refused to admit him."

"Maybe he didn't bring presents?" Bahadur Shah Zafar commented amusedly.

"Maybe, Zile-e-Subhani, but the presents he got from the King of England years ago didn't amount to much. The gift of horses which the King sent, one died during the journey and the rest few perished in the stables of Ranjit Singh due to excessive pampering and unfamiliar fodder." Ahsanullah Khan stood still, watching the King mount the vast steps leading toward the palace doors.

Rang Mahal the southernmost pavilion of the Red Fort Palace was hosting Bahadur Shah Zafar and his royal family in the luxury of its opulence and splendor. Its gilded ceiling with a large chandelier was enhancing the silks and the jewels of the harem ladies seated regally on velvety davenports. Across from them sat Bahadur Shah Zafar on a chair studded with jewels, while his sons and daughters occupied the couches all quilted with beads and brocades. Persian carpets graced the marble floors and tables of ivory and gold were laden with a variety of books and oriental artifacts. The middle of this chamber displayed a large pool fed by the waters of Jamna. It was decorated with fresh floral arrangements, their reflections shuddering deep under the clear waters.

"I have heard, Zil-e-Subhani that after your coronation you bestowed upon Captain Fane and other officers robes and silk scarves. The scarves they tied over their cocked hats?" Ashraf Begum sought Bahadur Shah Zafar's attention, her eyes radiant like the set of diamonds she wore in her hair and around her throat. "They don't deserve such favors, Zil-e-Subhani. Remember how William Fraser handed his ceremonial robe to a beggar which your father had bestowed upon him so generously?"

"Ah, my Beauty! The mother of our Crown Prince Dara Bakht." Bahadur Shah Zafar teased, divesting himself of his jeweled crown and setting it down on the ornamental table beside him. "You didn't know, my Beauty, but William Fraser was reprimanded most severally by Governor General personally. Greed of East India Company is multiplying, but so far they have maintained respectful behavior in the face of our customs and court decorum. Where is our Crown Prince?" His gaze was fluttering form one face to the other with a searching intensity.

"He has gone hunting, Zil-e-Subhani, along with the eldest Prince Mirza Quaish." Ashraf Begum smiled.

"Prince Fakhroo should have gone with them." Taj Mahal Begum shot an apprehensive look at her son who was sitting by the pool. He was drinking while playing chess with his half brother, Prince Mirza Mughal.

"I am glad Prince Fakhroo stayed. A worthy opponent to my son, for he loves to play chess." Akhtar Begum sang happily.

"Chess and drinking don't mix well together." Bahadur Shah Zafar murmured disapprovingly, shifting his gaze from his sons to his wife. "You would be happier, dear Akhtar, if he chose his older brother, Prince Khizr Sultan as his chess companion. Prince Fakhroo, as dear he is to me tends to lose his head while Prince Khizr Sultan keeps his on his shoulders." His gaze was wandering again. "Our princess' have learnt the art of discipline and propriety." His gaze was lingering over his daughters where they sat lolling against the satiny pillows playing a game of cards called Chandal-Mandal.

12

"I am very good at Chandal Mandal, Zil-e-Subhani, and I am winning too." Princess Fatima Sultan the youngest of Bahadur Shah Zafar's daughter chortled with glee. "Can't wait for next month when we go for a Flower Walk at Mehrauli. The Jahrna at that palace is my favorite to play cards."

"You would love it more, my Dear, since I have ordered an impressive gate to be erected at the entrance of that palace and now the palace at Mehrauli would be called Zafar Mahal." Bahadur Shah Zafar indulged cheerfully.

"Every year, Zil-e-Subhani, I have enjoyed that Flower Festival, and it's just now I am curious to know how it all started?" Rabeya Begum the eldest daughter of Bahadur Shah Zafar ventured forth thoughtfully. "I guess I was not interested until recently with all the rumors floating around that British Resident might stop our yearly excursion of going to Mehrauli."

"No one has the power to put an end to this Flower Festival, my Dear, as long as I live." Bahadur Shah Zafar intoned emphatically. "Citizens of Delhi look forward to this festival every year and hold this event in reverence. I would never allow it to be stopped by any British intruders even if they break their pledge of maintaining the kingdom of Delhi. And how they maintain it is from the funds which they receive from the revenues of lands they have purchased or acquired due to internal warfare amongst the rajas and nawabs of princely states."

"I too am ignorant about this Festival of Flowers, Zil-e-Subhani." Zamani Begum the younger sister of Rabeya Begum confessed cheerfully. "Could you please tell us how it all started?"

"A long story, my Dear, but I would make it as short as possible." Bahadur Shah Zafar began reminiscently. "Wonder why any of you never asked about this before?" His gaze was sliding down the marble pillars with floral pietra dura patterns as if cherishing their beauty before commencing. "It all started a long time ago. I was almost thirty-four year old then, a young prince my friends would say. My older brother Prince Jahangir the heir apparent was annoyed one day by the behavior of the British Residents who began asserting their authority by saying that they should be allowed to be seated with the emperor on equal terms. They were becoming rude and interfering as I recall. Dictating as to who should be named heir apparent amongst the sons of the emperor. Not too long ago Hawkins was reprimanded for causing affront to the House of Timur when he refused to present the trays of sweetmeats and turned away the gardeners who brought the offerings of nosegays. Well, I digress." He sighed, his gaze gathering his sons and daughters in one wistful embrace. "Back to my brother Prince Jahangir, who didn't get along with Resident Seton and nicknamed him Looloo, meaning dumb. Since Seton didn't know the meaning of Looloo he didn't care, but he kept offending Prince Jahangir by not dismounting from his horse while riding through the gates of the palace and Naqqar Khana where royal etiquettes were observed strictly by all as a token of their courtesy and respect for the emperor. As chance would have it, Prince Jahangir one day was standing on the roof of Naqqar Khana and espying Seton riding out of Red Fort without dismounting aimed a shot at him from his rifle. That shot only hit the hat of Seton, but it struck his orderly who was killed. Prince Jahangir was exiled to Allahabad by the orders of Seton. Queen Mumtaz Mahal his mother was grieved beyond consolation and made a solemn vow that if her son was allowed to return to Delhi, she would make an offering of a four-poster flower-bed at the shrine of Qutubddin Kaki at Mehrauli. When the Resident finally relented and recalled Prince Jahangir from Allahabad, Queen Mumtaz Mahal fulfilled her vow by offering an exquisite flower canopy at the shrine of Qutubddin Kaki. To which the local flower sellers added an intricate flower fan. Almost sixteen years since my unfortunate brother passed away, but the Flower Festival is still alive."

"A great Flower Festival it is, Zil-e-Subhani, lasting seven days of merrymaking!" Prince Fakhroo exclaimed suddenly, placing Prince Mirza Mughal's queen under check. "Kite flying, cock fights, bull baiting, wresting and swimming. Don't understand though, what's the significance of offering flower fan at the temple of Devi Yogmaya?"

"Since the temple is in Mehrauli, my besotted Prince, only half a kilometer from Qutub Minar, my father wanted to honor the shrine of the Hindus in a similar way as honoring the shrine of Qutubddin Kaki." Bahadur Shah Zafar expounded genially.

"My favorite during those week long festivities is going to the mango grove and sitting on the swing." Taj Mahal Begum murmured dreamily.

"Now that our princes and princess' have learnt about the history of Flower Festival, Zil-e-Subhani, it would greatly benefit them if they could learn about your royal lineage?" Mubarak Nisa the youngest of Bahadur Shah Zafar's wives requested avidly.

"Yes, my Beauty. You probably are keener in refreshing your own memory than anyone else around here." Bahadur Shah Zafar intoned amusedly. "Yet I want to test my own memory, so I would indulge a little in this charade of names and patrimony. Three hundred and eleven years with eighteen emperors in between separate me from the first Moghul emperor of India, Babur The Great. If I remember correctly, here are the names of the emperors in succession. Babur; Humayun; Akbar; Jahangir; Shah Jahan; Aurangzeb; Bahadur Shah 1; Jahandar Shah; Farrukhsiyar; Rafidud-Darajat; Rafi-ud-Daulah; Neku Siyar; Muhammad Ibrahim; Muhammad Shah; Ahmad Shah Bahadur; Alamgir 11; Shah Jahan 111; Shah Alam 11; then my late venerable father Akbar Shah. I am glad his grave is next to the shrine of Qutubddin Kaki where Flower Walk would lure us year after year as homage to his reign and remembrance."

"Wasn't emperor Jahandar Shah the one who suffered a violent death, Zil-e-Subhani?" Prince Mirza Mughal looked deflated after losing chess game to his brother, but his eyes were shining. "I just finished reading the accounts of the Moghul emperors, but I can't remember the events.

"You are correct of course, my Prince." Bahadur Shah Zafar's eyes were spilling compliments. "His rule lasted barely a year since he was defeated by his nephew Farrukhsiyar in a bloody struggle for crown. Farrukhsiyar was the one who sent stranglers while Jahandar was sleeping with his wife Lal Kunwar. The stranglers forcibly separated the husband and wife, then brutally killed Jahandar, and sent his severed head to Farrukhsiyar. Aside from being cruel, Farrukhsiyar is remembered for his folly in granting duty-free rights to the British East India Company in all of Bengal for a mere pittance of three thousand rupees a year. His penchant to please the British and to neglect the interests of his own subjects exposed him to more brutal end than he had concocted against Jahandar Shah. Two Syed brothers deposed him, starved him while imprisoned and then blinded him with needles before strangling him to death."

"Such a violent history, Zil-e-Subhani. I shudder to think how Crown became the emblem of cruelty and murder." Taj Mahal Begum shuddered visibly, her features washed by sadness.

15

"No such violence was present in the beginning of the Moghul history." Bahadur Shah Zafar was trying to envision the beauty of Zeenat Begum to expel the demons of the past. "Violence became rampant during the reign of Aurangzeb. He murdered all his brothers and imprisoned his father. Alas, violence was sanctioned by the sword of victory and released into the ocean of greed, ambition and ignorance. That was the inception of the crumbling of the great empire of the Moghuls."

"Real blow came to the Moghul empire, Zile-e-Subhani, almost thirty-two years after the death of Aurangzeb when Nadir Shah conquered Delhi." Prince Mirza Mughal couldn't resist flaunting his newly acquired knowledge of the Moghul Empire."

"Yes, my Prince, and a sad time it was when the Persian monarch Nadir Shah gloated over his conquest of Delhi. It has been recorded that he massacred thirty thousand civilians. Not to mention that he carried away the most valuable of treasures, the Peacock Throne and the diamond Koh-i-Noor. Although Koh-i-Noor keeps coming back to India, no one knows how? It was in the possession of Shah Shuja, now Ranjit Singh has it I have heard." Bahadur Shah Zafar was falling prey to his own sad ruminations. "Later during the reign of Ahmad Shah Bahadur, Durrani invasions cut deep into the roots of the Moghul Empire."

"India, the golden bird of the world! Though resisting capture, is almost crippled. Its jeweled eyes plucked out of its sockets, its golden wings clipped, and still the greed-mongers hover above to kill and mutilate." Shah Nasir broke his silence, his look distant and dreamy.

"Ah, the poet of the age speaks!" Bahadur Shah Zafar was startled out of his reveries. Realizing afresh the presence of his poets and musicians in this pavilion of Rang Mahal. "I was expecting to hear couplets, instead I hear laments of the past. A beautiful comment I must admit, but rigged with the poetry of tragedies. What made you say that?"

"I was remembering, Zil-e-Subhani, the most aggrieved of the sovereigns amongst the entire line of the Moghul emperors, Shah Alam 11." Shah Nasir breathed profoundly.

"How so, my venerable Poet? Refresh the king's memory?" Bahadur Shah Zafar's mind was gathering the mists of pain and nostalgia.

16

"Shah Alam 11 was the most ill-starred heir apparent ever as you know, Zile-e-Subhani." Shah Nasir obeyed promptly, sensing the emperor's mood of sadness. "After the assassination of emperor Shah Jahan 111 by Ghaziuddin, the emperor's vizier Feroze Jung had kept the heir apparent under guard. But Shah Alam 11 contrived escape and went straight to Bengal to recover his territories of Bihar and Orissa, but was defeated at the battle of Buxar by the British who were favoring the puppet king Mir Jafar. After his defeat Shah Alam 11 took refuge in Allahabad, asserting his right as an emperor, but without any means to protect himself. In despair he sought the protection of the British, signing a pact called the Treaty of Allahabad with Robert Clive of British East India Company, which granted British the authority to collect revenue from Bengal, Bihar and Orissa in exchange for annual tribute of six million rupees. After this treaty Shah Alam 11 returned to Delhi to reclaim his lost throne where his loyal friend and vizier Najaf Khan had restored some sort of order against the warring clans of Sikhs and Marathas. But after Najaf Khan's death, Ghulam Qadir of the Rohilla Clan forced his entry into Delhi palace with the intention of plundering. He was so enraged and disappointed in not finding any treasure in the palace that he blinded Shah Alam 11 just for the sake of brutal pleasure, before fleeing in utter madness. Mahadaji Scindia the close ally of Shah Alam 11, upon hearing this outrage chased and captured Ghulam Qadir, tortured and mutilated his body before killing him. Blind and broken in spirit Shah Alam 11 stayed in Red Fort in utter destitution until the French threat in Europe jolted the British to action. Fearing that the French would overthrow the power of the Marathas and befriend the Moghul Emperor to further their trade and stronghold in India, the British envoys headed for Delhi and came to Red Fort palace to pay homage to the emperor. Though finding him blind and decrepit under a tattered canopy, they decided to restore him to the status of the emperor. New coins were minted in his name and Friday Sermon read in his name at all the mosques in Delhi. The payment of annual tribute to the emperor which was discontinued under Warren Hasting was restored and Shah Alam 11, though he stayed under the surveillance of the British until his death."

"That ill-starred emperor is also is buried next to the shrine of Qutbuddin Kaki." Bahadur Shah Zafar sighed without restraint. "Tragedies vast and boundless happen all the time. No refuge against their assaults." He got to his feet. "Somehow the evening shadows are calling me to the luxury of a solitary walk and solitude. Feasting I might miss, but poetry session till midnight I would surely attend." He sauntered out of Rang Mahal into the sanctuary of his gardens.

The evening shadows, pale and gossamer were trembling through pipal and poplar trees as Bahadur Shah Zafar promenaded below the terraces. He could hear the gurgling of fountains left behind, still serenading his thoughts as he approached closer to the marble pavilions in the center of Hayat Bakhsh garden. His gaze was reaching out to Bhadon Pavilion gilded by patches of sunshine, but his feet were carrying him toward his favorite pavilion, Sawan Pavilion.

Bahadur Shah Zafar could feel the weight of sepulchral hush in this garden as he drifted along somnambulantly. An overwhelming sense of sadness gripped him suddenly, his heart longing for something pure and subliminal, though he didn't know what he wanted. Everything around him seemed allusive and surreal. He almost stumbled as he reached Sawan Pavilion, dazed by the shuddering of light-beams in the water-tank, reflecting candles in hundred of niches which were carved into the four walls of the rectangular tank.

How strange and beautiful! I have never noticed the beauty of this tank before. All candles lit to full refulgence—fireflies swimming in a pool? Bahadur Shah Zafar stood fascinated by the ripple and dance of flames in clear waters. *But then I have never been in love before. An old man, in love, the height of absurdity.* His heart was young, leaping out of his breast to fold Zeenat Mahal in one thundering embrace.

Suddenly, Bahadur Shah Zafar was transported back into the garden of youth, enjoying the carefree days of splendor and opulence with his brothers and sister. He stood watching the play of light in the pool as if trying to divine secrets of the past, but his thoughts were a whirlwind of contradictions. His brother Mirza Nali had fallen out of favor from the ruling elite of British East India Company. Later Mirza Jahangir was exiled to Allahabad due to his own violent behavior. British East India Company had begun exerting their power of supremacy, minting their own coins, replacing the Persian text with English and obliterating the emperor's name from the currency. They were finding means to

18

diminish the esteem of the emperor by urging Nawab of Oudh and Nizam of Hyderabad to assume the titles of royalty.

Nizam of Hyderabad had refused to do so, but the Nawab of Oudh had complied. Taking the liberty of reminding the emperor that since the emperor was receiving annual tribute from the British East India Company he should allow the British envoys to be received on equal terms, not as subjects to the sovereign. Suddenly, Bahadur Shah Zafar was remembering the anger of his father-emperor at the audacity of that particular request and at this memory his own thoughts were fleeing. He stirred, his heart aching and somersaulting for the love of Zeenat Begum.

This young heart in old body. Bahadur Shah Zafar sighed, bewildered by the urgency of his need to possess the youth and beauty of his newfound love.

The old king with young heart was fleeing his own garden, smitten by the beauty of the sunset, all heliotrope and tremulous. His heart was filled with some longing nameless and for one magical moment of bliss and agony he thought the entire garden had burst open into a shower of wedding songs, welcoming his beloved. The scent of Damascus roses was making him giddy as he glided past the canopy of Bougainvillea. A whiff of breeze and Rat-ki-Rani was wafting its own sweet perfume while Bahadur Shah Zafar sought the sanctuary of his palace.

Zeenat Begum, the houri of this age and I don't even have to die to possess her. Bahadur Shah Zafar's feet were guiding him toward his royal library, though he had intended to seek the company of his wives.

The great library with gilt ceiling and wall-to-wall book shelves all lacquered and illumined was Bahadur Shah Zafar's sanctuary. He drifted toward his favorite couch and almost flung himself into its cushiony depths. Closing his eyes he surrendered himself to the wildness of his heart.

I must marry Zeenat Begum lest I die of sheer misery and despair. Bahadur Shah Zafar's heart was a volcano of anguish and hopelessness. *Is this my heart? My old body, churning an ocean of agony I have not ever encountered before within me. But then I had not ever loved before. Is this love, madness? Pain supreme and insanity sublime! Oh, torment of my heart, Zeenat, Beloved—*

Chapter Two
Poetry of Love

Wedded to poetry all his life, Bahadur Shah Zafar now was about to espouse love as his true bride, no other than Zeenat Begum, the newly found cynosure of his sight and senses. He was to be married this very evening, but right now he was seated on his Peacock Throne in Diwan-i-Khas, receiving morning embassies. It had been three years since his coronation and his poetic heart was heavy with a strange mixture of sorrow and rejoicing, lamenting the loss of real power usurped by the British, yet grateful for the luxury of decorum in his court, no matter how empty and artificial. Though, the protocol for decorum today was relaxed in honor of the wedding celebrations. The hall was decked with colorful friezes in anticipation of the royal wedding, but the hearts of the occupants were burdened for the past few years by untimely deaths in the family and by sporadic tides of unrest in Delhi. Bahadur Shah Zafar's thoughts this particular day were restless, rising in defiance against the authority of the British Resident, so very irksome and arrogant. A sudden stab of grief cut through his wandering thoughts at the recollection of his son's death the Crown Prince.

Almost a year ago Prince Dara Bakht had died suddenly and the British Resident was still exerting his authority to choose the next Crown Prince. Bahadur Shah Zafar's thoughts were lifting more shrouds of deaths, but his attention was claimed by his vizier and confidant.

"You have not ceased to mourn the death of Prince Dara Bakht, Zil-e-Subhani, it is obvious." Mahbub Ali Khan commented aloud. "I can tell by the light of sadness in your eyes. Though, today is the auspicious day of your wedding."

"The happiest in my long life of struggles, ringed by the noose of deaths, tragedies and invasions." Bahadur Shah Zafar smiled wistfully. "As to my lost Prince, yes, he has been in my thoughts lately. The same year Ranjit Singh died and the war in

21

Afghanistan commenced. A year before that Herat was invaded and a year after Ranjit Singh's death Kabul was suffering the pangs of invasion. Russia and Britain fighting for supremacy in the land of the Moghuls, or to be precise I should say, in the land of the Hindus. How did it all start I don't seem to remember? Can't remember much these days, anyway. Refresh my memory, Mahbub, so I know where things stand."

"A sort of stalemate, Zil-e-Subhani, yet the map of Hindustan is dyed with the blood of the Afghans." Mahbub Ali Khan began rather histrionically. "Ranjit Singh, may God bless his soul, was reluctant to a tripartite alliance with the British, but did agree to one alliance urged by the British to ousted Dos Muhammad and to secure the throne for the exiled Shah Shuja. Even the emirs of Sindh were forced to sign a treaty to help put Shah Shuja on the throne, practically losing their independence. Twenty thousand troops by the orders of Lord Aukland marched to Afghanistan. After a great fight and countless casualties Shah Shuja was installed on the throne. Dost Muhammad surrendered and was exiled to Calcutta. Apparently Shah Shuja rules, but everyone knows Afghanistan is being governed by William Machaghten. Ghazni and Kabul were captured too, but then Ranjit Singh died suddenly, the rest you know, Zil-e-Subhani."

"Yes. Kabul, Jerusalem of the Moghuls, ravaged and plundered." Bahadur Shah Zafar half lamented, half reminisced. "Ranjit Singh, poor soul, may God grant him heaven as his eternal abode. He did like Shah Shuja I believe, but extracted Koh-i-Noor diamond from him as a price for protecting his life and interests."

"Shah Shuja is not going to last long, Zil-e-Subhani." Zauq prophesied, edging closer to the throne and curtsying. "When British Army entered Kandahar, bringing back exiled Shah Shuja, he was confronted with icy indifference by the citizens of Kandahar. Rumor has it that most of the time Shah Shuja sits idle, watching through telescope the wives and daughters of Kabulis who happen to enjoy fresh air on the flat roofs of their homes. And if he likes any of them, he summons them to his presence."

"Ah, my venerable court poet prophesies, besides indulging in canards!" Bahadur Shah Zafar declared with a sudden whiff of cheerfulness. "Since Shah Nasir has left Delhi, rather abandoned me, you would guide me in realms of poetry and I would become your disciple."

22

"You are our spiritual guide, Zil-e-Subhani. You yourself are greatly accomplished in writing Ghazals than any of the poets in your court. I myself would be your slave if you but permit me this great honor?" Zauq sang beamishly, his eyes shining with gratitude.

"First and foremost we are enslaved by foreign invaders." Ghalib breathed disdain. Envy cutting through his heart like sharp knives since he deemed himself better poet than Zauq. "Zil-e-Subhani, the corpse-strewn gorges of River Kabul tell many tales of wars and tragedies. British troops are comprised mainly of Indian soldiers as we all refer them as sepoys and sowars. And they are the ones dying for killing Indians, a paradox most horrifying. Sepoys dying in droves while the casualties on British side are only a handful."

"Can the pen of a poet mitigate the sting of those tragedies?" Bahadur Shah Zafar challenged.

"Half of those reports are not true, Zil-e-Subhani, and the other half exaggerated." Captain Fane took the liberty of defending his countrymen before Ghalib could respond.

"Even half the tragedies in this world taint the minds and hearts of countless millions than millions of lies multiplying every blink of an eye. And exaggeration, paradoxically, tempts all to dig deep into the roots of the truth." Bahadur Shah Zafar chided. "William Machaghten thinks that he can win Afghanis over with money, but he is entirely mistaken in this respect for Afghanis are a proud and chivalrous race. The reports are confirmed that after conquering Kabul William Machaghten offered Dost Muhammad's brother Jubba Khan ten thousand pounds worth of jagir if he would leave Afghanistan and would move to India as an exile. Jubba Khan was incensed by this offer, telling William Machaghten that he felt so insulted that he would spare his brother the shaft of such an insult by not even mentioning this offer to him."

"William Machaghten is inexperienced, Zil-e-Subhani, and is still in the initial stages of learning." Captain Fane chuckled to conceal his embarrassment. "Muslims should be more wary of Wahhabis than the British, Zil-e-Subhani. Are Wahhabis not the ones who desecrated the tomb of Prophet Muhammad in Medina?"

"That was thirty-six years ago. How did you know?" Bahadur Shah Zafar was impressed and fascinated.

"Because I am studying Wahhabi religion, Zil-e-Subhani." Captain Fane boasted proudly. "Besides, they are filtering in into Hindustan and preaching hatred and intolerance. Well, Shah Waliullah of Delhi and Al-Wahhab of Nejd were contemporaries. Both studied in Medina before returning to their native countries to implement radical thoughts."

Bahadur Shah II enthroned with Mirza Fakhruddin. Opaque watercolor, ink, and gold on paper H. 12 3/16 × W. 14 3/8 in. (31 × 36.5 cm) The Art and History Collection Courtesy of Arthur M. Sackler Gallery, Smithsonian Institution, Washington, D.C., LTS1995.

"That is correct, Zil-e-Subhani." Ahsanullah Khan couldn't stay behind to flaunt his own knowledge of Wahhabism. "Almost nine years ago a Wahhabi by the name of Syed Ahmed started teaching in Bengal the cult of war and hatred. He and his followers were noticed by Hindu and Muslim neighbors by their long beards and plain dress, their women completely veiled in a long shroud called burqa. Syed Ahmed incited five hundred men equipped with clubs to attack a village in the name of Jihad. They killed a

Brahmin priest, cut the throats of two cows and dragged them bleeding through a Hindu temple."

"The same Syed Ahmed who died fighting Sikhs in the village of Balakot? The same one, upon whose death Ranjit Singh fired gun salutes from every fort while ordering that the whole city of Amritsar to be lit up for celebration." Bahadur Shah Zafar reminisced aloud. "I recall snippets of conversations in my father's court about Syed Ahmed, how he was distorting Islamic laws, and preaching self-made laws of hatred and intolerance. The most hated of his laws is to declare war on so-called *infidels*, not even knowing that he himself is an infidel if there is such a thing as being infidel. Deviating from the precepts of Islam where war is forbidden, permitted only in self-defense, or when all negotiations of peace-treaty are foiled. With his death, hopefully Wahhabi cult would be finished and forgotten."

"Not likely, Zil-e-Subhani." Ahsanullah Khan pumped his quivers of Knowledge to fullness. "Wahhabi cult is flourishing afresh more than ever before since the disciples of Syed Ahmed are successful in circulating false statements that he was not killed. Weaving a web of sanctity around his disappearance that he didn't die, but was lifted up to the heavens. Ascribing saintly virtues to him and saying that Syed Ahmed himself foretold of his disappearance. He is well and alive, his disciples claim, hiding in a cave in the Buner Mountains. He disappeared because God was displeased by the faint-hearted response of the Indian Muslims to his—Imam's call. When his followers would prove their faith by uniting once more to renew their vow of Jihad he would return and would lead the men to victory against the unbelievers."

"Lies grand and fantastic. Those would-be martyrs would be the downfall of Islam." Bahadur Shah murmured sadly.

"May I add, Zile-e-Subhani, that the death-wish mentality of the Wahhabis has exalted the status of martyr as the ultimate goal of every Jihadi. Of course with the great gift of temptation—Paradise." Captain Fane couldn't resist his temptation to expose the fanaticism of the Wahhabis.

"You have succeeded, Fane, in distracting king's attention from the feast of poetry." Bahadur Shah Zafar eased himself up from his throne thoughtfully. "No more talk of Wahhabis. I must commune with my poets in Roshanara Garden." He dismounted the throne slowly. "Sad, passing sad that your Company is setting its own standards of fanaticism, dictated by greed, discourtesy and heedlessness. The customary gifts to me are altogether stopped, though revenues from our states that the Company collects are doubled."

"You didn't accept the terms, Zil-e-Subhani, suggested by the Company, which caused the cessation of gifts." Captain Fane stood there flustered and embarrassed.

"Those crafty terms with the reek of arrogance, demanding that the king abandon all his rights and renounce all claims on his sovereignty!" Bahadur Shah Zafar exclaimed with a sudden burst of passion. "My father didn't accept those terms and I honor his decision as my own now that I am the king, though emperor no more. Remind your rulers or schemers, Fane, that my ancestors ruled supreme in India. And now I as their progeny are compelled to subsist on a dependent existence, exposed to penury with inadequate means even to maintain the dignity of a nominal sovereignty. The main income of your Company comes from taxes they impose on the revenues from the states they themselves collect, labeling it euphemistically Pax Britannica, which is nothing but tax Britannica." He strolled through the files of his courtiers, acknowledging their curtsies silently, his look distant and unseeing.

The afternoon sun was lowering confetti of gold over the royal procession as Bahadur Shah Zafar with his poets and courtiers promenaded down the gravel path toward the garden. In the distance he could see the pavilions decked with friezes and colorful pennants where poetry session was to be held in honor of his pre-wedding celebrations. After breakfast he had decided to visit the royal stables to commune with his favorite horse Hamdam. Also, commanding his mahout to bring his elephant Maula Bakhsh so that he could share his joy with the pet royalty that the king was getting married this very evening. Now that the stables were left behind and waterfalls edged with roses coming into view, Bahadur Shah Zafar's heart was longing for the feast of poetry and profundity. Marble terraces and fountains gurgling not too far were claiming his attention, but his steps were guiding him toward the garlanded pavilion under which Persian carpets and brocaded pillows awaited the royal occupants to unleash their talents of poesy and inspiration.

Sawan Pavilion was coming alive with gems of poetry from the lips of the poets as Bahadur Shah Zafar made himself comfortable on his makeshift throne of gold and brocade. A tall candle was being passed from poet to poet for recitation or impromptu versification. It was now placed in front of the youngest poet by the name of Mustafa Khan Shefta who began to recite ecstatically.

> *"Indian soil is a luxury laved*
> *Even the pious indulge unfazed*
> *The mystics grow wild with wine*
> *Those on vigil sleep till day*
> *Not to talk of drinkers merry, even the priestly class*
> *Partake of sensuous feasts, amorous games play*
> *In this world of gay abandon*
> *Who will think of the Judgment Day*
> *The poor are daring like Farhad*
> *The beggars live in royal grace*
> *Joy here has come to stay*
> *All grief has fled the place*
> *Except of course, the grief of love*
> *Which gives delight, though irritates."*

"Sweet wine of poetry! No wonder I have no taste for wine of the grape." Bahadur Shah Zafar applauded, the rest cheering and applauding. "Your talent, Mustafa, would be shared by millions now that lithograph press has been introduced in Delhi. Pray, sing more of love and of Delhi. Poetry is the only treasure left in our court to boast of abundance."

"Your praise, Zil-e-Subhani, is my inspiration." Mustafa Khan Shefta's very eyes were spilling the wine of poetry.

> *"My moon of love went back home as the morn arrived*
> *The sun tore my collar cloth with its talons bright*
> *Who has cast a sizzling glance on my love's tender face*
> *Why with a rosy tint my teardrops are dyed*
> *Don't compare the vale of Nejd to Delhi's alleys wild*
> *Nejd was Majnun's desert, Delhi is my wandering wild*
> *While he was beheading me he turned to me and said*
> *'That I can keep my word, you should now realize'*
> *He hasn't even visited my home, nor graced my bier*
> >*or grave*
> *None of my desires, alas, has ever fructified*
> *O my kind, consoling friend, how can it stay untorn*
> *Remember, it's my collar slit, stitch it as much as you like*

27

If I don't engage my thoughts with her coiling locks
Who will then take care of me in this severance night."

"Sublime, sublime! My heart is breaking." Bahadur Shah Zafar cheered amidst applause while the candle was placed before Momin.

"Do not for God's sake quit such a fine resort
Let heaven go to hell, hug the beauties lane to heart
The lovers know no cure for the ills of heart
Abandon not the wails and sighs, though they profit not
Why find a new beloved and restart the game of heart
Alright, do no change, O love, retain your temper rash
and hot
Do not, O nightingale, leave your glade for the lane
Where even the morning breeze cannot easily blow
and waft
The tavern is a wondrous heaven, Momin leave it not
In this hell you can find houris blooming hot."

"Young stars are shining in my court today as if touched by the finger of God." Bahadur Shah Zafar complimented generously.

"I do feel the presence of God here today, Zil-e-Subhani." Momin sang cheerfully, spilling an impromptu couplet.
"I feel as if you are with me
When company I have none."

A great applause and Zauq was claiming the candle of inspiration.

"See how God bestows greatness on things small
The pupil of the eye enfolds the sky big and vast
Let heavens hurl a thousand bolts, I'll not complain
But save me God from the pain of parting, this will break
my heart
They'll never say on their own, no more, thanks thee, Lord
Never will they be content, the greedy human lot
I am that captive who would fall into the trap again
Even if the hunter kind liberates me from the bars
If you want to see His sight without veil or mask
Go get a clear view through the window of your heart"

"Divine, divine!" Bahadur Shah Zafar exclaimed, a thunderous applause following. "I don't drink, yet I am getting drunk without drinking." His gaze was alighting on Ghalib who sat contemplating the candle before him with a smile almost caustic.

"The world to me is a kindergarten where children sport
and play
A show goes on before me, be it night or day
Solomon's throne to me is a bauble commonplace
The miracles of Christ are just a trivial tale
The world to me is a mere phantom, without a solid core
The worldly things are to me, mere illusive shades
The desert hides itself in dust seeing me approach
The river rubs its brow on earth, fallen prostrate
Ask me not how I fared in your absence, Sweet
Rather see, how you blossom before my eager gaze
I am self-conscious, true, and self-adorning too
Why not, when a mirror-like beauty stares me in the face
Place a peg of wine before me, should you like to see
The blossoming of my tongue, the flowering of my prate"

"Ah, sublime, verses sublime." Bahadur Shah Zafar clapped, signaling the informal mode of versification.

Taking advantage of this sanction, Zauq was the first one to commence the art of bantering. Though patient and courteous, he genuinely disliked the style of Ghalib. The prime reason for his dislike besides others was that Ghalib deemed his poetic compositions much superior than from any of the court poets. So feeling a sudden prick of arrogance from Ghalib's recitation, Zauq shot this teaser.

"Keep yourself away, O Zauq, from the daughter of the Grape
Taste it but once and you become its slave"

"We are the connoisseurs of art and not Ghalib's
advocates
Let's see who can produce a marriage song of better
grace."* Ghalib quipped promptly.

"Those who flaunt their poetic claims, tell them to
their face
This is the true prothalmion, let them emulate."
Zauq flung this impromptu retaliation.

"My intent is to convey what I truly feel
And not to show my expertise in the poetic field
I am true to my word, lies repel me deep
God is my witness, truth is my creed."
Ghalib spilled his poetic genius with a haughty toss of his head.

"Talent runs in rivulets of rivalry, it is becoming obvious." Bahadur Shah Zafar chided. "Zauq, are you willing to take the challenge of Ghalib and construe a few lines in honor of this age and time, if not the paeans of our marriage?"

"Your obedient slave, Zil-e-Subhani. Poetry to me is like breathing. Where does it come from and where does it go, I remain completely unaware.

Gladdened by the happy news all the poets and bards
Are engaged in singing paeans of their king and lord
Let me also join the chorus, sing a song of praise
That even she should sing encores, the painted nightingale
What an auspicious day has dawned on earth today
If crows and kites lay their eggs, phoenix will they deliver today
Life-restoring is the news of your health restored
Even the dead would come to life with its healing force
Your life, O lord, is linked with the life of the populace
It's a fount of drink immortal, ah, your royal grace
From the drops that slip and fall when you wash and bathe
Precious pearls are seen to form, pearls in their shine and shape
If these pearls are used in making tonics for the weakening age
The new drug will rejuvenate the bone gone dry with age."

"This portrait of poetry in inspiration, Zauq, has earned you the title of poet-laureate." Bahadur Shah Zafar announced happily.

"I am overwhelmed, Zil-e-Subhani." Zauq gasped for breath, his eyes shining. "My breath is sucked out of inspiration and poetry no more."

"In faith then, we should turn to Ghalib to conclude this poetry session." Bahadur Shah Zafar laughed.

"In faith, Zil-e-Subhani, a sad and bitter conclusion. My apologies in advance." Ghalib's eyes were lit by the fire of jealousy as he sang feverishly.

"Faith tugs me back, heresy goads me on
Kaaba lies behind me, in front the temple gate
I am a lover given to fooling simple-hearted dames
Laila speaks ill of Majnun when I instigate
Men rejoice at union, but do they ever die
Lo, the wish of severance night has blown into my face
May it prove to be the last, the spate of blood I see
Who knows what dreadful sights await my gaze
Though life has fled my hands, it still flickers in the eyes
Let them lie before me, the cup and flask of ale
He shares my faith, he has my trust, is partner of my trade

How dare you malign Ghalib, right in my face."

"Beautiful, sizzling verse!" Bahadur Shah Zafar complimented profusely, getting to his feet.

"This poetry session is not complete, Zil-e-Subhani, until you recite one of your poems." Ghalib requested suddenly.

"Yes, Zil-e-Subhani." Zauq chimed in, others joining in a chorus.

"To escape this din, I must recite." Bahadur Shah Zafar waved away the candle, not willing to sit. "Also, I am afraid, my wedding ceremonies would be delayed." He began to recite dreamily.

I do not need the kingly crown, not the hermit's coarse cloth
Grant me, God, enough sense to love you like a maddened hart
There is nothing precious in the books, I wrote so many to discard
It is Your word that stands engraved in the tablet of my heart
Deem it a blessing great the moments spent in a spirited way
Do not, O promise-breaking Saqi, hold back the foaming glass
I'll welcome my path that leads me to my cherished goal
Be it the path of piety pure, or the way of cup and flask
It is the ebb and flow of breath, stop it, and the world is dark
The hallelujahs of a heartless priest are not as effective as the calls
Of a drunkard who, withal, has a kind, compassionate heart

I better get to my bride's house before she refuses to marry the old emperor."

Bahadur Shah Zafar sauntered out of Sawan Pavilion, followed by his poets and courtiers.

It was late afternoon when Bahadur Shah Zafar decided to visit his stables once again, neglecting his siesta after lunch since he was restless. He had summoned Ahsanullah Khan and Mahbub Ali Khan, but they were standing far behind him while he was busy communing with his pet elephants. The royal horses decked with gold and silver ornaments were claiming his attention, but his gaze was returning to the painted forehead of his pet elephant.

"Ah, Maula Bakhsh, how the mahout spoils you. Look at you, the silk scarf, steel shield and garlands of flowers." Bahadur Shah Zafar let Maula Bakhsh wrap his snout around his arm playfully. "Look at Khurshid Ganj and Chand Marut as gaudily dressed as you. All three of you so vain and coquettish." He turned abruptly, facing his viziers. "You should drag me away from here, my friends. I must not be late for my nikkah ceremony at the home of my future in-laws."

"That would be breech of etiquette, Zil-e-Subhani, we dare not be disrespectful." Mahbub Ali Khan spoke for both since Ahsanullah Khan stood there discomfited.

"I would be disrespectful to the parents of the bride if I am late for the wedding ceremonies of my own wedding." Bahadur Shah Zafar smiled. "Make sure that the feast at our palace when we return is grand and opulent." He headed toward the palace gardens, arresting the swath of colorful roses in his gaze, his senses catching the gurgle of fountains in the distance.

"Your grand wedding procession is ready, Zil-e-Subhani, waiting for you whenever you are ready." Ahsanullah Khan broke his silence, staying a few paces behind.

"A few more jewels to color me young and I would be ready." Bahadur Shah Zafar intoned cheerfully. "Meanwhile, any news of importance that I should be aware of."

"Nothing much of importance, Zil-e-Subhani, but news just the same, an unusual piece." Ahsanullah Khan appeared to think aloud. "Almost three years ago during the famine a Muslim boy by the name of Azimullah and his mother managed to enter a British compound, begging for food and shelter. One priest by the name of Reverend Carshere adopted them. Besides food and shelter, Azimullah received free education, becoming proficient in French and English while his mother was employed as a nursemaid. Now Azimullah is in the service of Brigadier John Scott at Cawnpore, working as a language tutor and a translator. He is quite a character, has learnt to play Mozart on Broad wood Piano, performing the parlor trick of reciting Shakespeare in Urdu."

"Zil-e-Subhani, if I may?" Mahbub Ali Khan began exigently before the king could disappear behind the palace doors. "This is what British officers are singing in Cawnpore.
For dancing and dressing
For sky-larking and caressing
No Indian station could vie with Cawnpore."

"They are singing much more than what I have heard." Bahadur Shah Zafar paused at the vast steps of his palace. "Ahsanullah Khan, tell us what was that snide verse which the magistrate Robert Thornhill recited in open court?"

"If I remember it correctly, Zil-e-Subhani." Ahsanullah Khan pumped his lungs for a powerful recitation.

With a turban on his head and a saber on his thigh
The stinking nigger mounts his gat to turn his back and fly
Then let the conches blast
To the loud tom-tom reply
A nigger must his hookah smoke
As without his hookah die."

"Scum of London! Thieves and beggars. Calling Indian, *nigger*." Bahadur Shah Zafar's comment heavy with disgust was tossed over his shoulders before he disappeared behind the imposing portals.

The much-awaited evening had arrived for Bahadur Shah Zafar with a fanfare of wedding celebrations, his bride-to-be only seventeen years old and he on the rungs of sixty-five. A large hall in the mansion of Nawab Samsam-Daula was lit to refulgence with gold and silver candelabras. Bahadur Shah Zafar seated with Zeenat Begum on the velvety davenport was receiving felicitations, the brocaded canopy overhead dripping with gossamer gold creating the illusion of magic and mystery. Yet magic was real in the dreamboat eyes of Zeenat Begum, sparkling in the grey pools of their own youthful serenity. She was dressed in bridal fineries of red silks, displaying clusters of rubies and diamonds stitched with gold thread. Her fair features were aglow with the warmth of curiosity and her large eyes catching each color and nuance from floral bouquets to Persian carpets, from tables of ivory and rosewood to the chests gleaming with koftgari designs. A Muslim priest was being escorted toward the bridal couple amidst the tunes of bridal songs from the lips of the ladies. These ladies were seated not too far from the royal couple, one of them playing a two-sided drum with both hands while another lady tapped the top of the drum with a spoon to balance the rhythm. A group of royal guests as turbaned men and bejeweled ladies were making way for the venerable Mulla so that he could perform the nikkah ceremony with all due propriety.

This Mulla was no other than Mulla Majasi, the spiritual guide of Bahadur Shah Zafar. He was hugging a green copy of the Quran, though he had no intention of reciting any verses. Instructed in private by Bahadur Shah Zafar to perform the nikkah ceremony simply and succinctly, he was most obedient to the instructions of the king. Besides, he was sad, rather feeling guilty

33

that he was leaving the king and settling in Rangoon since his son had found a lucrative trading opportunity over there, entertaining great hopes of helping other family members once that he was settled. Two witnesses were not far behind, also from the retinue of the king. One witness was Mirza Qaiser, a prince related to Bahadur Shah Zafar's wife Taj Mahal Begum and the other was Hafiz Muhammad, a scholar of theology. Nawab Quli Khan was making room for Mulla Majasi who stood poised for nikkah ceremony, two witnesses on either side of him waiting reverently. Suddenly voices faded to whispering and the music stopped as Mulla Majasi opened the Quran. He was overwhelmed by this sudden impulse to read one short verse from the Quran, but he closed his eyes, reciting from memory while avoiding the piercing gaze of Bahadur Shah Zafar.

> "In the name of Allah, the Beneficent, the Merciful
> Praise be to Allah, Lord of the worlds
> The Beneficent, the Merciful
> Owner of the Day of Judgment
> Thee alone we worship, Thee alone we ask for help
> Show us the straight path
> The path of those whom Thou hast favored
> Not the path of those who earn Thine anger, nor of those
> who go astray." 1: 1-7

Mulla Majasi kissed the Quran and procured an illumined document of nikkah-nama written in Arabic. Still not meeting the gaze of Bahadur Shah Zafar, he began the ritual of nikkah ceremony.

"Malika-i-Zamani Nawab Zeenat Begum is willing to accept Zil-e-Subhani Bahadur Shah Zafar as her husband. In the presence of two witnesses here, if you consent Nawab Zeenat Begum to marry Zil-e-Subhani, then sign your name to the left of the margin." Mulla Majasi handed her the nikkah-nama on a velvet tablet, while the witnesses merely bowed their heads.

Bahadur Shah Zafar's heart was somersaulting to catch Zeenat Begum in one eager embrace, but master of propriety always he sat there smiling ardently. Two witnesses were now signing under her name and nikkah-nama was passed to him, Mulla Majasi once again poised for continuing the ceremony.

"Zil-e-Subhani, Bahadur Shah Zafar in the presence of two witnesses agrees to pay a haqq mahr of fifteen lakh rupees to his bride Zeenat Begum. Of which one third is payable forthwith and two-thirds at any time during his married life. If you consent to this, Zil-e-Subhani, then sign in the box to your right."

Bahadur Shah Zafar signed impeccably and the two witnesses followed suit. Suddenly, the dancing girls converged from all four doors, carrying silver trays heaped with sweets. Two-sided drum came alive again against the nimble hands of one woman, while another one tapped it with a big spoon. The wedding songs soared high through the lips of the women singers in unison. Bahadur Shah Zafar sat there bewitched by the beauty of his young bride, worshipping even her feet shod in velvet shoes, studded with jewels. Zeenat Begum herself looked enchanted, her eyes bright and sparkling. The dancing girls were offering sweets to the guests while tumblers were being filled with wine or sherbet from the flagons of the stewards in gold turbans and red jackets. After sharing sweets with his newly wedded bride, Bahadur Shah Zafar got to his feet. He clapped his hands to gain attention amidst the jubilations of dancing and singing.

"I bestow the title of Zeenat Mahal on Zeenat Begum and fix an allowance of five hundred rupees a month and five hundred rupees for her relatives. My Queen." Bahadur Shah Zafar assisted his bride to her feet. "A great feast awaits us at our palace." He turned to his hosts and the guests, his heart somersaulting again, this time against some pincers of presage nameless.

"Zil-e-Subhani." Nawab Samsam-Daula edged closer. "The jewelry my daughter is wearing is worth ten thousand rupees, a part of her dowry." He stole a loving glance at her daughter who stood there blushing as if suspended between ether and sky.

"Your daughter is priceless, Samsam-Daula, worth countless times more than all the jewels in the world." Bahadur Shah Zafar flashed his bride an ardent smile, his old heart wild and implacable. "Don't think Samsam-Daula that I am not aware of what else you have given your daughter. Bolts upon bolts of silks, a great bed with brocaded pillows. Fine china and utensils of gold and silver, not to mention horses and elephants, all caparisoned and bedizened."

"Bounties of Zil-e-Subhani are boundless. His Majesty doesn't need anything." Samsam-Daula declared profusely.

"If that were true I would be scattering gold over the head of my lovely queen from your mansion to my palace." Bahadur Shah Zafar quipped merrily. "Come, my lovely Queen, the wedding procession is waiting outside to escort you to your new home.

"The brocaded howdah in which Bahadur Shah Zafar sat with his bride was all perfumed and garlanded. In front of this was the wedding procession replete with music and dancing. Colorful turbans bobbing up and down and dancing girls in layers upon layers of chiffons were creating a collage of rainbows. The studs in their noses and tilaks on their foreheads were radiating their own beams of color against the lights held high by machalchis.

Bahadur Shah Zafar was oblivious to the great show ahead of him, only communing with his newly found love under some spell of bliss and euphoria. Zeenat Mahal was bashful, barely able to whisper *Zil-e-Subhani* against the ardor in his gaze and his gentle caresses. The distance between her parents' mansion and his palace was not too long and the royal cortege was entering the palace grounds.

"You are the queen of my heart and the soul of my love." Bahadur Shah Zafar pressed Zeenat Mahal closer. "Never leave me or I would die." He was kissing her lips madly and feverishly. Totally unaware of the fireworks in his heart and the fireworks exploding outside on the palace lawns to welcome the new queen.

Chapter Three
A Prince is Born

Jahaz Mahal in Mehrauli was hosting Bahadur Shah Zafar and his family. Two happy years of his marriage with Zeenat Mahal and he was the happiest of men despite his grievances against East India Company. More so, suspended in bliss and swoon for the past couple of months since he was blessed with a son by Zeenat Mahal. The newborn Prince, Jawan Bakht, cradled in royal bassinet dripping with laces and velvets was the cynosure of all eyes in this chamber of ivory and damask.

It had been almost a week since Bahadur Shah Zafar's entourage had reached Mehrauli for Flower Festival. Added to the festivities was the official celebration of the birth of Prince Jawan Bakht with fireworks and entertainments. The entire entourage had stayed at Zafar Mahal, but this particular day being the last day before returning to Red Fort Palace at Delhi, Bahadur Shah Zafar had decided to visit Jahaz Mahal where his family enjoyed the informality of carefree abandon. And that's what they were doing right this moment, lounging on velvety davenports or lolling against round pillows in hues of emerald and crimson. One brocaded davenport was Bahadur Shah Zafar's royal seat along with Zeenat Mahal. The shafts of sunlight illuminating the floral arrangements on rosewood tables were further enhanced by the reflection-dance of colors from a pair of chandeliers all aglow with the fire of crystal brilliance.

The younger princes were seated on Persian carpet by the window in full view of the waterfall, feeding the fountains down below in the garden. They were laughing and drinking while reciting poetry and perfecting the art of versification. A stunning view of the garden could be seen from the window right across from the window framing the waterfall and that's where the bevy of princesses were gathered, playing cards. The begums with the exception of Zeenat Mahal had formed their own circle, only the white bassinet separating them from the ever-loving couple as the king and the queen. The warmth of love and serendipity was in the air as poesy and parlance drifted side-by-side, yet a subtle hush pervaded all of a sudden as if the angels stood listening to the silence. Zeenat Mahal's pallor with the glow of marble was making her eyes brighter and more beautiful than ever before as she ripped open the curtain of silence with the spontaneity of fairy godmother.

"Zil-e-Subhani, I have been meaning to ask." Zeenat Mahal asked dreamily. "During our stay at Zafar Mahal, I couldn't help noticing that no Europeans were seen passing through the Gurgaon road?"

"They are not welcome, Beloved, and banished from the precincts of Mehrauli as far as I am concerned." Bahadur Shah Zafar smiled whimsically. "Their own arrogance has become the bane of their exile. British shopkeepers to be precise! While riding close to Zafar Mahal it was customary for them to dismount as a mark of courtesy to me—the emperor tuned king. Since they refuse to practice the art of courtesy anymore, I have bought all the land around here, diverting the main road away from Zafar Mahal so that they could never come close to our palaces or gardens."

"Whether they come close or not, Zil-e-Subhani, they still meddle in our affairs behind the scenes." Ashraf Begum began half cautiously, half apprehensively. "After our dear Prince Dara Bakht passed away, the British Resident became obsessive with the issue of succession of the Crown Prince. Ignoring your choice of the oldest Prince Mirza Quaish and choosing Prince Fakhroo instead. I love Prince Fakhroo equally as other princes, but I don't like the idea of British Resident asserting his authority to choose and decide."

"I don't think that the British Resident had any intention of asserting his right." Taj Mahal Begum was quick to rise to the defense of her son chosen as Crown Prince before Bahadur Shah Zafar could respond. "Prince Mirza Quaish himself was disinclined, didn't want the burden of responsibility. He told me so before he left for Cawnpore."

"Now to think of it I heard conflicting reports from all quarters which need disseminated." Bahadur Shah Zafar condoning the comments of his wives turned his attention to Prince Fakhroo. "Satisfy my curiosity, my beloved Prince, if you will. Did you sign any secret pact with Earl Ellenborough?"

"No, Zil-e-Subhani. I couldn't even think of signing any pact without your permission." Prince Fakhroo lied smoothly.

"Still reports keep coming to me from several sources that you signed or might have signed something to the affect that after my death you would not be recognized as heir apparent to my kingship, but only as a prince and would vacate the palace?" Bahadur Shah Zafar's look was stern and piercing.

"No, Zil-e-Subhani. Yet I have heard such rumors too from Delhi to Agra, to discredit me I suppose, as far as Cawnpore." Prince Fakhroo whipped up another lie.

"I hope what you say is true, my beloved Prince, only rumors." Bahadur Shah Zafar murmured doubtfully.

"Cawnpore reminds me of the recent marriage of a poor Brahmin girl by the name of Manu to Raja Gangdhar the Maharaja of Jhansi." Akhtar Begum tossed this piece of diversion. "A fairytale marriage, Zil-e-Subhani, and she becoming Rani of Jhansi amidst great celebrations, fireworks and cannon firing a salute."

"Not poor by any standards, my Dear." Bahadur Shah Zafar indulged amusedly. "The court gossip gets distorted somewhere along the way. Her mother died when she was two year old. Her father was advisor to Chimnaji Appa the brother to Baji Rao11 — the last of the Maratha Peshwas. When Manu — her real name Manikemika was three year old, Chimnaji Appa died and her father took her to the court of Baji Rao where she was raised as a princess. Now after marriage she is styled as Lakshami Bai. She is the Rani of Jhansi, true, the only wife of Gangdhar since his first wife died a year ago."

"Real or distorted, Zil-e-Subhani, court gossip fails to satisfy my curiosity." Zeenat Mahal chirped happily. "Offering floral fan and floral canopy at the shrine of Qutubddin Kaki I understand since Prince Jahangir was allowed to return home from exile and his mother fulfilled her vow to offer such gifts, but why the same gifts are offered at the temple of Devi Yogmaya?"

"Two more years of court gossip, my beloved Queen, and you would know the answers to everything. All the rites and rituals of the royal protocol, no matter how shallow and impecunious everything has become." Bahadur Shah Zafar sighed reminiscently, his gaze tender and profound. "Since the temple is not far from the shrine, I think I told this to one of my sons before, can't recall when. Well, my father wanted to honor the temple with similar gifts in respect of his Hindu subjects. In fact this is done in the true spirit of Islam that one should not hurt the feelings of the followers of other faiths."

"And what does royal protocol suggest, Zil-e-Subhani, when followers of other faiths hurt us?" Zeenat Mahal challenged.

"Forgiveness is divine, Beloved, if hurt is not too deep." Bahadur Shah Zafar smiled tenderly. "We need to get out of our dark thoughts and bask under the grandeur of Zafar Mahal. We would stop there before returning to Red Fort. I have to show you the new addition in honor of our Prince. A royal balcony called Hira Mahal right across from Moti Mahal in Red Fort. You must see Hayat Bakhsh garden with roses the size of sun-disks—"

A lusty wail from the lungs of Prince Jawan Bakht lured everyone's attention to the bassinet. Bahadur Shah Zafar literally leaped to his feet, scooping his son into his arms and rocking him back and forth until he was soothed.

"Here, Beloved, I have lulled him to sleep." Bahadur Shah Zafar lowered his son into the loving arms of Zeenat Mahal. "I must see my viziers in the garden and then a poetry session perhaps?"

"You can't leave, Zil-e-Subhani, not as yet." Taj Mahal Begum protested. "You promised to tell us about the legend of the waterfall at this Jahaz Mahal."

"Several legends, my Dear, but one would suffice for right now." Bahadur Shah Zafar indulged cheerfully. "The waterfall which you see from the window of this Jahaz Mahal is actually fed by a reservoir named Hauz-i-Shamsi. Iltumish of the Slave Dynasty in his dream saw Prophet Muhammad indicating to him a site revealing the footprints of his horse and instructing him to dig a reservoir to collect rain water. He obeyed and the reservoir was named after him. Later during the period of Lodi Dynasty a retreat was built close to the reservoir for the pilgrims which is now this Jahaz Mahal. Another legend is that Qutubddin Kaki also had a similar dream and since drinking water supply was getting low, he had the reservoir expanded with the result that now we enjoy this beautiful waterfall. Now I must say I have earned the privilege to leave this delightful company." He waved, almost sprinting toward the door lest he be detained.

Bahadur Shah Zafar emerged out on the terrace against the sparkling gurgle of waterfall as if transported to heaven. He looked splendid, swathed in silks with pearls around his neck and his turban glinting multicolored jewels. He stood still for a moment, awed by the beauty of this waterfall as if he had seen it for the first time. Inhaling the scent of Damask roses down below, his feet were guiding him down the lower terrace flanked by fountains. Beyond the symphony of this gurgle and splatter stood the Jharna Pavilion built by his father Akbar Shah. Painted in the color of sunshine this Pavilion was further lit by shafts of sunshine scintillating through neem trees in ribbons of gold. He could see Ahsanullah Khan and Mahbub Ali Khan standing by the pool. They were waiting for the king so that they could commence their afternoon walk, exploring as usual the kernels of wars and intrigues.

"A beautiful day, Zil-e-Subhani, for our last walk here. Tomorrow we would be in Delhi by this time." Ahsanullah Khan swept his arm in a casual curtsy.

"I was just noticing the purity of the waterfall, so crystal-clear and serenading." Bahadur Shah Zafar also acknowledged the curtsy of Mahbub Ali Khan before making this comment. "Serenading some lost beloved, I am not sure who?"

"Serenading the Saint of course!" Mahbub Ali Khan declared involuntarily.

"Keeping at bay the sinners for sure, who are despoiling the peace of this land, already shattered and shuddering against the violence of invasions." Bahadur Shah Zafar Quipped. "Afghanistan. Kabul the Jerusalem of Padishah Babur groaning against the weight of greed-mongers from Russia and Britain." He strolled ahead of his viziers toward the graveled path edged with roses and jasmine.

"Now that Shah Shuja is assassinated, Zil-e-Subhani, peace might return to the land of the Afghans?" Ahsanullah Khan edged closer.

"No peace, I am afraid." Bahadur Shah Zafar appeared to prophesy. "I can smell the reek of death and devastation even in the scented air of this garden. Not only Shah Shuja assassinated, but Captain Burns too by one of the tribesmen. William Machaghten murdered also. Unrest and uprising. British defeated, Afghans exulting. Irony of fates. After William Machaghten's murder by one of the Akbar Khan's retainers, Akbar Khan jeered to the face of a captured British officer, saying: *you will seize my country, will you, you will seize my country?"*

"It is always a lost cause to invade Kabul or any part of Afghanistan, Zil-e-Subhani." Mahbub Ali Khan consoled, keeping pace with the king. "If foreign invaders could study the history of this land, they would know that Khyber Pass is not the gateway to the golden bird of India, but a tunnel of torture and tragedy. No one has ever been able to rule the unruly clans of this land. Though, they are most hospitable when friendly, but if provoked most brutal and unrelenting. Akbar Khan in the spirit of his father Dost Muhammad repossessed Khyber Pass from British soldiers, got Shah Shuja assassinated and brought his father Dost Muhammad back to power. His Baluchi army is gloating over their success, saying that the English being turned out of Afghanistan have eaten dirt."

"Sad and tragic that out of forty-five hundred British force and twelve thousand fellowmen only one man by the name of Dr. Brydon survived during retreat through the snows toward the death-traps of Afghan defiles." Bahadur Shah Zafar commiserated aloud. "Dr. Brydon was severally wounded and utterly exhausted as he rode into Jalalabad, it was reported. The women and children who had survived through the treks of Khurd Kabul defiles were transferred to the care of Akbar Khan." His gaze was absorbing the colors of Bougainvillea as if rainbows had landed on earth in the far pavilions. "Exceptionally tragic such defeats and conquests. Especially, the defeat of the British, considering their magnitude of power, of their superior ships and arsenal."

"More sepoys died than British soldiers during this war of occupation as you know, Zil-e-Subhani." Ahsanullah Khan reminisced aloud. "Before and during the war British forces destroyed many villages, drove off or slaughtered stock, burnt crops and storehouses, chased tribesmen and their families way down the hills to perish. Refugees from Kabul were massacred. The town and fortress of Ghazni was razed to the ground. The bazaar of Kabul was looted and demolished."

"All this happened since Earl Ellenborough replaced Lord Aukland and became the Governor General of pride and tyranny." Bahadur Shah Zafar began regretfully. "This land is being despoiled by the great game of the British and Russia. Both parties condoning the fact that while in the process of killing and subjugating, their chances of being killed are multiplying with as great force as the force of hatred and contempt inside the hearts of the natives. Wasn't Captain Arthur Conolly murdered by the Khan of Bukhara? He was the one who told his superiors in Calcutta that it was feasible for the Russian Army to invade India, either following in the footsteps of Alexander the Great through Khyber Pass in Afghanistan, or else by the example of Persia, using Herat, Kandahar and Quetta as staging posts."

"All that is correct, Zil-e-Subhani, but on a lighter note and quoting Captain Fane we should be more weary of Wahhabis than the British or the Russians." Mahbub Ali Khan chuckled. "Though we should not fear much, they are almost non-existent here. Rather exploring the foreign territory, they are regrouped in Riyadh under the leadership of Faisal Ibn Saud. Riyadh, as the genuine Muslims claim has become the country of the Wahhabis. The stronghold of the fanatics, who claim themselves as true Muslims and everyone else an infidel or a heretic. Promoting their man-made assertion that it's their duty to slay an infidel to earn great merit."

"I don't know what genuine Muslim means! Yet, Wahhabis are very much settled here, even in Delhi, I fear." Bahadur Shah Zafar murmured thoughtfully. "They have very skillfully sidelined Quran's message of mercy, charity, tolerance and forgiveness. Wahhabi is a sect distinct on its own, not even close to any precept of Islam, doling out hatred and hostility to all who don't fit their man-made version of Islam. Distorting the meaning of Jihad and urging their followers to fight, to become martyrs, that way they could go straight to Paradise." His gaze was reaching out to the far pavilion, painted in the color of sunshine. "What were those articles of faith, Ahsanullah, I forget, which Shah Muhammad Ismail wrote—the jihadi, the most devout of all Wahhabis?"

"Those article of faith quite similar to his warring songs which he wrote for his fanatics, Zil-e-Subhani." Ahsanullah Khan began avidly. "He calls his followers the Army of Holy Warriors. His injunctions sort of run this way: *War against any infidel is incumbent upon all Muslims. He who shall equip a warrior in this cause of God shall obtain a martyr's reward. His children would dread not the trouble of the grave, nor the last trumpet, nor the Day of Judgment. Cease to be cowards, good men, join the divine leader and smite the infidel. I give thanks to God that a great leader has been born in thirtieth century of hijra.* By great leader he meant Syed Ahmed, who is no more."

"No wonder, Wahhabis are being denounced as wicked, faithless imposters wherever they congregate." Bahadur Shah Zafar hurried toward the pavilion while admiring the red-dusted path edged by Mulsari trees. "In Bombay, I heard, when the Wahhabis prohibited people from celebrating Prophet's Birthday, they were chased out of town, denounced as infidels. In Delhi also, that was last year, fourteen Mullas issued a fatwa against Wahhabis, denouncing them as seditious hate-mongers. Declaring further that since this particular group of Wahhabis was banished from Mecca and Medina, they came here for worldly riches to cheat and impose upon ignorant Muslims the hateful creed of their own making."

"Wahhabis have banned music too, Zil-e-Subhani." Mahbub Ali Khan added his own snippet of news. "They are also saying, poetry is the work of devil, but I am looking forward to the poetry session this glorious afternoon." He sprinted ahead toward the pavilion of gold and sunshine. "I can hear already the poets gathered there and making merry."

"My father built that pavilion as his lone retreat to escape the hustle and bustle of the Flower Festival, but it is best suited for poetry sessions I am sure." Bahadur Shah Zafar's voice quivered against the weight of nostalgia and sadness. "Poetry is divine, the ripple-dance of music from the throats of the angels." His steps were light and unhurried as he approached closer to the open pavilion.

The afternoon hush outside the pavilion was splintered by the voices of the poets and the trilling of laughter. Inside the pavilion were hum of cheers and cries of ecstasy amidst the bouts of versification. Seated on Persian carpets against pillows of Italian velvet and brocade, a handful of poets were vying for praise, mostly from each other and specifically from the king. Bahadur Shah Zafar was seated on a makeshift throne of green velvet, silver candelabra on a low stool before him his light of inspiration. The rest of the poets had their personal candles in silver candle holders, more for ambience than for serving as the beacons of formality. Though, right this moment a youngest of all poets by the pen name of Azad was being introduced by his father formally.

"My only son, Zil-e-Subhani, and an accomplished poet even at the age of twelve." Maulvi Baqir introduced his son, beaming with pride. "His given name is Muhammad Husain, but he is already known by his pen name Azad amongst his friends since his first poem appeared in Lahore children's periodical by the name of Guldasta."

"Great credentials, Baqir, I didn't know you had a son." Bahadur Shah Zafar applauded, turning his attention to the young poet. "What made you adopt the pen name of Azad, young man?"

"Don't know, Zil-e-Subhani. It sounded good." Azad offered precociously. "Papa told me it means to be free and I love to be free." He lowered his head, awed and flustered.

"Your son is going to be a great philosopher if not a great poet, Baqir." Bahadur Shah Zafar commented after bestowing a smile on Azad. "I hear you are starting a newspaper in Delhi. It would be a great benefit to us and to the general populace. What's it going to be called?"

"Delhi Urdu Akhbar, Zil-e-Subhani." Maulvi Baqir responded passionately. "I have a lucrative business for foreign merchants in Delhi bazaar, but I want to serve the community of Delhi by publishing unbiased news, more in terms of education as well as enlightening."

"A great service indeed if people can have access to truth." Bahadur Shah Zafar commented, becoming aware of the flood of inspiration in the eyes of his poets. "I am a great patron of truth. And poetry is the tongue of truth I can see shining in the eyes of my poets, so we must resume our poetry session." He signaled consent with a wave of his arm.

"With the grace of your inspiration, Zil-e-Subhani, we would resume if you would kindly recite a couplet of your own?" Mustafa Khan Shefta requested on behalf of all the poets.

"My inspiration is cold as a dying flame, but I would recite one couplet." Bahadur Shah Zafar smiled enigmatically.

"In the world of forms I am in human form
But in the world of spirits I am in a different state."

A great applause broke forth, receding to stillness as Mustafa Khan Shefta began to recite.

"Softly blows the autumn blast
The heat inspires the blossoming phase
Even the deserts are garden green
Winsome, beauteous, compelling praise
None is plagued by heaven's blights
The land is one blissful place
The malicious mars has shed his ire
Like Venus soft it now behaves
Restrain your writing, Shefta, hold
Though Muse-inspiring is this vale."

Another burst of applause and Momin sent his quatrain whirling.

"Your arrival has sent them scurrying, otherwise there was
A swarm of despairs around my yearning heart
Momin read that ghazal again which yester night
Had won from audience a soul-stirring applause."

Zauq was next to flaunt his talents before the applause could subside.

"How temperate is this air that in this garden blows
Like the pulse of a man robust, see, it ebbs and flows
Refreshing like the breath of Christ is the vernal breeze
Sanatorium like is the grove with its shady trees."

With a disdainful toss of his head, Ghalib pumped his lungs for the expulsion of his genius, waiting for the applause to subside.

"If there be a Jesus Christ
Let him for my ache provide
Law and scripture could sure be invoked
But that assassin all rules defied
Her gait is like an arrow-flight
Who can in her heart reside
When she speaks, sit tongue tied
O how I prate in frenzy wild
May none make out what I imply
Ignore if someone evil speaks
Do not to evil deeds reply
Restrain the man who goes astray
Forgive if someone errs in pride
Find me the man who has no wants
Who can for everyone provide."

A thunderous applause and Bahadur Shah Zafar with a wave of his arm made a gesture of restraint.

"Before we close this session, let's talk of heart. From heart to heart in tongues of poesy." Bahadur Shah Zafar eased himself up slowly. "Tomorrow we return to Delhi, so make this day worthy of remembrance. A few couplets here and there would suffice, save the ghazals for longer sessions.

"My heart conceals a chiseled diamond, sparkling to the view
Multicolored, multifaceted, flashing different hues"
Ghalib flashed an impromptu couplet.

"Feelings choked within the breast, my life has on the lips arrived

See the state where I have arrived, but you haven't yet arrived."

Momin sang giddily.

"You can't leave as yet, Zil-e-Subhani." Zauq implored, noticing the intention of Bahadur Shah Zafar. "You have to recite one of your poems, old tradition, hard to break."

"Then you have to follow me. For I intend to recite this to the birds on my way to Jahaz Mahal." Bahadur Shah Zafar tossed this comment over his shoulders, reciting.

"I am not a saint-philosopher, nor a tavern-mate
I am God's humble creature, a sinner reprobate
Law is my religion, love, my creed and trait
Call me what you like, O idols—an atheist or a man of faith
I am neither domineering, nor a cringing sort
Nor a singing nettle, nor a flower frail
Like a painted drinker on tavern wall
I am not a man awake, nor a drunkard crazed
I have none to share my grief, no friend, no mate
I'm sorrow's mourner, sorrow mourns my fate
He who once accepts me flings me back in haste
I am a Cain counterfeit in the market place
What should I tell you Zafar, I am what I am
A shoe-bearer of the Prophet, his humble subordinate."

Bahadur Shah Zafar was lost in the magic-mystery of his garden, inhaling deep the scent of roses and nostalgic memories.

The scent of roses was still fresh and nostalgic after more than a year, this time in Delhi as Bahadur Shah Zafar sat with Zeenat Mahal and his daughters in the private chamber of Rang Mahal. Almost one and a half year, now Prince Jawan Bakht was claiming the attention of his step-sisters most adorably, and a bundle of energy he was, royally spoiled. Bahadur Shah Zafar's sons and the husbands of his daughters had gone hunting, so he had decided to spend a quiet evening with his queen and his daughters, forgetting about the issues and concerns of India wading through the tides of invasions and rebellions. Though, such tides had become very much a part of the royal household, luring the interest of Zeenat Mahal and his daughters most specifically. His other wives had lost interest in any kind of political upheavals, abandoning themselves to the sole luxury of relaxation and entertainment.

Zeenat Mahal, perfumed and bejeweled, lolling against a large pillow on the davenport was admiring her step-daughters for their skill in keeping abreast of the news of the bullying British and the sulking rajas subsisting on pensions from British East India Company. Though, her gaze was shifting to her royal husband, happily involved in teaching Prince Jawan Bakht the art of rhythm on his toy drums. The scent of roses from large floral arrangements on brass tables was reaching her and she inhaled deeply, her thoughts languid and fleeting.

"Wars have snatched humor out of our lives, Zil-e-Subhani, but English wit is alive on the streets of London." Rabeya Begum laughed suddenly, exchanging a mischievous smile with her sisters. "Or on the pages of newspaper I should say. A London newspaper, I have heard, has a cartoon of Russian bear looking voraciously at Afghan territory while an equally ferocious British lion tries to stop the bear from reaching its goal. Underneath this the caption reads: *No you don't.*"

"Russia is out of the picture, my Dear, only the Company is adamant upon playing the game of Divide and Rule." Bahadur Shah Zafar watched Prince Jawan Bakht run to his mother before turning his attention to his daughters. "Though, from the corpse-strewn gorges of Kabul River, red-coated myths about the Company's invincibility and its officers' courage are torn to shred. Still, the British keep bullying emirs and rajas out of their states into exiles and annexing their territories to their previously acquired lands of revenue."

"London's new satirical journal Punch, Zil-e-Subhani, makes fun of Earl Ellenborough since he is not humbled by his defeat in Afghanistan." Princess Fatima Sultan flashed her own bulletin of news. "The best is this couplet against him:
Farewell, the plumed troops and the big wars
That make ambition virtue."

"Yes, my Dear, to change the status of Company's humiliation in Kabul to that of prestige, Earl Ellenborough must become the puppet of his own ambition." Bahadur Shah Zafar commented sadly. "And he did succeed in his ambition, annexing Gwalior and usurping the rights of ten year old Raja of Gwalior. His next prey was Sind and to conquer that he appointed Charles Napier. Napier had once denounced East India Company's administration as *leeches sucking the life blood of Indians*, but he is proving to be the most prejudiced of Governor Generals. Advising his colleagues that a British General should never retire in the face of the natives. He too has succeeded in conquering Karachi and Sukkur, forcing Rustum Khan—an emir of suspect loyalty as he believes, to cede some of his territories to the rule of Bahawalpur who has been helpful to the Company during the Afghan War. Well, he has annexed Sind also and allegations are on the rise that British officers have violated emir's harem and have carried away the most attractive of odalisques for their own pleasure."

"Everyone blames Earl Ellenborough, Zil-e-Subhani." Zamani Begum could not be left behind to unseal her own jar of news. "The Punch is quoting the ageing Montstuart in its article. *Earl Ellenborough's behavior is like that of a bully who having been knocked down in a street brawl—Afghanistan, returns home to pummel his wife—attacking Sind.*"

"And yet, Charles Napier is the culprit." Zeenat Mahal broke her silence. "The Punch printed his own confession which he sent after the conquest, a three-letter message to London, *I have sinned.* And Punch also represented him as confessing against the storm of criticism in England of sinning against the emirs by deposing them and seizing their territories. Strange how we all get caught up inside the intricate web of news and intrigues." Her lips parted in a beatific smile. "England seems close when we read about their people in our newspapers and India seems very far when the news from other states reach us. Nawab Wajid Shah of Oudh has married a courtesan, bestowing upon her the title of Hazrat Mahal. Doesn't seem real, more like a myth. Isn't it, Zil-e-Subhani?"

"Nothing mythical about it, Beloved, though the news is quite stale." Bahadur Shah Zafar's eyes were gathering the stars of adoration. "She has already blessed the Nawab with an heir to the throne. The name of their son is Birjis Qadra. Another mythical queen is Rani of Jhansi as you would believe. She is childless as yet, so half mythical perhaps?"

"Not mythical at all, Zil-e-Subhani!" Zeenat Mahal's eyes were lit up with a subtle challenge. She exchanged a meaningful glance with Rabeya Begum who seemed intent and listening while her step-sisters played with Prince Jawan Bakht. "Solid as a rock she is as she was when she was just a little girl. In the court of Baji Rao she acted as a queen of courage while growing up with Nana Sahib and Tatya Tope as her playmates. One afternoon while riding she saw Nana Sahib falling from his horse. He was injured and covered with blood. Witnessing this scene she didn't cry or scream for help, but mounted Nana Sahib on her own horse and brought him into the palace."

"Another story, Beloved, rather this fact." Bahadur Shah Zafar smiled indulgently. "Not only courageous, she was headstrong. Once when Nana Sahib denied her a ride on his elephant, she declared that she would have ten elephants more to each one of his. This prophecy of her childhood came true after she got married."

"Nana Sahib, not only has his elephants, Zil-e-Subhani, but his ambassador of revolution, Azimullah Khan." Mubarak Nisa commented with a tinkling of mirth.

"Azimullah, my Beauty, is no revolutionary, but a lady's man if I may say so in the presence of my wives and daughters?" Bahadur Shah Zafar almost bit his tongue. "Tatya Tope however has a penchant for causing rifts and dissensions."

"A Pashtun by the name of Bakht Khan is gaining rank and esteem in the army of East India Company, Zil-e-Subhani." Princess Fatima Sultan demurred aloud. "Is it possible that we could lure him to Delhi?" Her eyes were riveted to Prince Jawan Bakht in her lap sleeping soundly.

"Alas, my command even over the small army over here is nominal, my Dear. In fact, it's not even an army, but royal guards." Bahadur Shah Zafar eased himself up, beginning to pace. "The glory of the Moghuls is gone. A few rajas who are not sent to exile by the British still extend their hand of friendship to me, chief amongst them, Raja Nahar Singh." He paused, facing Zeenat Mahal. "I almost forgot, Beloved, Mahbub Ali Khan must be waiting for me in the garden. I need to dictate a letter." He turned to his heels, disappearing behind the doors hurriedly.

The most beautiful of palace gardens, Hayat Bakhsh was the abode of Bahadur Shah Zafar where he had strolled with Mahbub Ali Khan before settling in Sawan Pavilion to dictate a letter to Queen Victoria. Amongst others present was George Thompson to witness the dictation of the letter and to deliver it to the Queen. He had come to India on a philanthropic mission as an active advocate to protect the rights of the Indian people. While in Calcutta he had received an offer from Bahadur Shah Zafar to be his agent, so he had come to Delhi posthaste to be the emissary of the King.

Charmed by George Thompson's manners, Bahadur Shah Zafar was feeling at ease to share his concerns and grievances, and postponing the drudgery of dictation. Much had been on his mind lately, including the dwindling of revenues. The expenditures to maintain the royal household were rising and he was constrained to appeal to Queen for funds much to the chagrin of his pride and royal sentiments. Stepping out of his dark thoughts, he was snatching a moment of clarity. He sat inhaling the scent of roses, his gaze reaching out to the square flowerbeds interspersed with watercourses.

"It has been more than five years since I ascended the throne, Thomas, and I am beginning to feel the strain of expenditure." Bahadur Shah Zafar began reluctantly, choking on his feelings of shame and chagrin. "Palace rooms are in dire need of repair. Some of the palace gardens are in utter neglect since the staff of gardeners is small. Well, when my father passed away, Amherst was advised by Lord Aukland that the presentation of one hundred and one trays of presents by the Governor General to be dispensed with. To which I did not agree, so Lord Aukland never presented himself in our court. He proposed an additional stipend of three lakh rupees per anum with the conditions that I forego all further claims of kingship. To which I also declined. I had objected only to the forfeiture of claims of kingship, but the British Government assumed that I had declined the offered stipend. My own funds are depleted due to the flux of more employees and their families. That's why I have decided to send a letter to the Queen requesting increase in allowances."

"I remember, Zil-e-Subhani, your venerable father sending Ram Mohan Roy to the King of England on such a similar mission." George Thompson commiserated with genuine warmth of friend-ship. "I have seen the glorious monuments of the Moghuls, but I am not familiar with Moghul History. Dare I request, Zil-e-Subhani, to enlighten me with a few of the important points concerning Moghul History?"

"Moghul glory is gone, my Friend." Bahadur Shah Zafar sighed relief as if sloughing off all burdens of ceremony. "The beautiful monuments of the Moghuls are falling prey to the ravages of time. Even Taj Mahal needing repair and maintenance. Mostly, Moghul emperors were tolerant and generous in the beginning. Later bigotry and intolerance settled in the courts of the Moghuls, then kindness and compassion again, a strange merging of creativity and destruction. What Tamerlane started as a hurricane of power laced with generosity of spirit by restoring lands to the original landlords, Aurangzeb finished in a flash the liberality and grandeur of decades by his acts of cruelty and hatred. That is the gist of the Moghul rise and its slow, lingering fall."

बहादुरशाह, जफर युवावस्था में (रामपुर—रज़ा लाइब्रेरी का चित्र)

Bahadur Shah Zafar as a young man. The original painting is with the Rampur Raza Library. This picture was published in the Hindi work 'Swatantra Dilli' (Independent Delhi), 1957.

"Tragic, Zil-e-Subhani, sad and tragic." George Thompson murmured with great empathy. "I still fail to understand how East India Company gained so much power in such a vast land as to send Rajas and Nawabs into exile, or annex their territories in Company's name. Claiming those lands as their properties, while forcing the real owners to accept small pensions for subsistence."

"Zakaullah here is a great historian, Thompson, he would gather the pieces of East India Company's power for you in this land of gold and jewels in a few words." Bahadur Shah Zafar smiled, turning his attention to his historian. "Won't you, Zakaullah?"

"At your service, Zil-e-Subhani, but I am not good in presenting the facts succinctly." Zakaullah bowed his head. "And yet the grand presence of East India Company in India can be summed up in this parable of the camel. When a merchant allowed his camel to squeeze his head into the tent against the violence of rain and storm, the camel pushed his whole body inside, shoving the merchant outside to the exposure of inclement winds. In truth, tree of friendship with British began when emperor Akbar the Great granted the request of Queen Elizabeth in permitting merchants to trade goods in India. Later emperor Jahangir granted special privileges to British merchants in trading. The Moghul Empire was in throes of crumbling after the death of Emperor Aurangzeb, that's when East India Company began their crusade of conquest and annexation. The loss of power for the Moghuls began in earnest when emperor Farrukhsiyar granted eight villages to the Company to save—"He paused, noticing the puzzled expression of George Thompson.

"It's time to dictate that letter before I get weary of my own thoughts." Bahadur Shah Zafar bestowed a kind smile on George Thompson before turning his attention to his secretary. "Makhund Lal, dip your pen in black ink the color of my thoughts and your hand would stay steady in rapport with my whole being." He breathed deep before commencing.

"His Imperial Majesty the King of Delhi to her most gracious Majesty Victoria, the Queen of Great Britain and Ireland and their dependencies.

Although from the unfortunate circumstances the flower of my kingdom has faded, and the dominion of this House is placed in your hands and under your Majesty's authority, with the power either to diminish or enhance its dignity, its respect and its glory.

Yet I confidently hope from the love of justice which God Almighty has implanted in your Majesty's noble mind, that the ancient customs and usages belonging to the Imperial family of India will be restored. It is your Majesty's high distinction to be the upholder of the weak and the fallen, and to extend towards such your royal countenance and succor.

I am now old and have no ambition left for grandeur. I would devote my days entirely to religion, but I feel anxious that the name and dignity of my predecessors should be maintained according to the original engagements made by the British government. It is hoped from your Majesty's exalted character for virtue and good faith that your Majesty will in consideration of the friendship which has so long existed between your Majesty's predecessors and this ancient House, command your servants, under whose protection the chiefs of India have placed themselves to give a prompt and just consideration to my claim to an increase of stipend and allowances and restoration of privileges denoting my status and supremacy in India.

In conclusion I have the honor to solicit that your Majesty would be graciously pleased to permit my representative the aforesaid Mr. George Thompson to return to me after explaining my views and receiving your Majesty's reply.

May the blessings of peace and prosperity attend your Majesty's reign." He pressed his temples. "I confer upon you, Thomas, the title of Safru'd-Dawla Musheerul Mulk Bahadur Musleh Jang. Tell your Queen that. May God go with you." His gaze alighted upon the father-in-law of Prince Fakhroo before he closed his eyes. "Please escort Thomas to the palace, Ilahi Bakhsh, and entertain him with a grand feast. I want to stay here a while, then commune with my garden."

Bahadur Shah Zafar kept sitting with his eyes closed even after everyone had left. Seated on his gold chair in utter immobility he was drifting into dreams, neither chasing his thoughts, nor willing to commune with his garden. His beautiful garden right below this pavilion was lost to him. Instead, he was entering a secret, sacred, silvery garden of the soul, surreal and mysterious. Here it was peace, the argent mists soft and gossamer. He was wearing a crown of stars and thinking that he had died. Suddenly, he was torn out of that garden and flung into a hoary furnace of the tortures of the damned. Bodies caked with blood and corpses dangling from the trees. Shuddering and whimpering, he was lifted once again into the white serenity of a silvery garden. His robe was stitched with stars and a crescent moon was lowered over the crown of stars on his head. Surely he was in heaven, sleeping blissfully.

Chapter Four
Festival of Eid

Bahadur Shah Zafar had just emerged out into the courtyard of Diwan-i-Khas, but his thoughts were coasting over the shores of wars and greeds where British were gaining ascendance over the lordships of rajas and nawabs. His gaze was reaching past the gardens down to the river where tents were pitched, hosting motley of stalls to celebrate the festival of Eid. This was the first day of Eid-al-Adha after the yearly pilgrimage in Mecca, and Delhi was abuzz with festivities. Hawkers were selling bangles and henna-painted goats for sacrifice in commemoration of Abraham's act of absolute surrender to God's command to sacrifice his son. As a great reward for his perfect faith, God had sent a ram to sacrifice when he was about to sacrifice his son, and since then this ritual had found a permanent home in the heart of Mecca, spreading from continent to continent wherever the Muslims migrated.

Bhadon Pavilion edged by spruces and entwined with bougainvillea in splashes of purple and orange was coming into view as Bahadur Shah Zafar kept strolling. He could espy Ahsanullah Khan and Mahbub Ali Khan standing by the north wall of the Pavilion under the bower of roses. A thin smile curled upon his lips with a recollection that they were waiting for him as commanded, so that they could accompany him on a casual walk down the river where Eid festivities were in progress replete with dancers, musicians, jugglers and acrobats. His smile was sad and lingering as if imprinting afresh on his memory the zeal of his courtiers which was multiplying as fast as the annexation-mania of kingdoms by the British East India Company. Sadness had become his constant companion since the past couple of years. A subtle realization dawning upon him that British had surreptitious designs to end his nominal rule as they had done with many other kings in India. With this thought simmering in his head he approached closer to Bhadon Pavilion, his viziers coming forward to greet him, avid and smiling.

"Eid Mubarak, Zil-e-Subhani." Ahsanullah Khan greeted happily. "A lucky day, you are the father of another son!"

"Eid Mubarak, Zil-e-Subhani." Mahbub Ali Khan chimed in, smiling broadly. "What did you name your prince born on this auspicious day?"

"Prince Shah Abbas, the most adorable! Mubarak Nisa is the lucky mother, happy beyond measure." Bahadur Shah Zafar's eyes were lit up with a subtle glow. "Eid Mubarak to you both also and may this day prove propitious in dissolving the tides of enmity and unrest in this land already bleeding to death with the arrows of greed and possession by foreign powers." He kept walking, now flanked by Ahsanullah Khan and Mahbub Ali Khan on either side. "All the festivals that we celebrate here should bring us together as one whole, Hindus, Muslims, Christians, non-believers. And yet we are drifting apart. I feel I am an alien in my own country, alienated from everyone, whether friends, advisors or kindred." He espied Ghulam Abbas appearing suddenly. "Ah, my devoted attorney, your wise mother Mubarakunissa might solve this riddle for me, why do I feel so alienated?"

"The breeze of uncertainty, Zil-e-Subhani, my mother would tell you." Ghulam Abbas began with a poetic élan. "Most of the people around here feel the same way I have noticed, and yet they are asserting their wills to practice what they believe to be their privilege and birthright. You might be getting a petition this very day, Zil-e-Subhani, from a group of Muslims to slaughter the cows on Eid, knowing fully well that they are sacred to the Hindus." His kind heart was already rejecting this petition.

"The religion of Muslims does not depend upon the sacrifice of cows." Bahadur Shah Zafar exclaimed with restrained anger. "Islam teaches respect for the religion of others. We live with Hindus and Sikhs and we must respect their beliefs. Jews, Muslims and Christians also must live in harmony, whether in Delhi or in any other part of the world. We should treat everyone with respect, even the ones who earn our anger and disapproval. Especially the ones through whose hands we suffer injustice. Has it already been two years since the British refused to reinstate my allowance as requested by me in my letter to Queen Victoria?" He asked abruptly.

"Your letter, Zil-e-Subhani, probably never was delivered to Queen Victoria." Ghulam Abbas consoled. "Most probably it was cut down by the court of directors. George Thompson as we heard presented two letters on your behalf to the President of the Board of Control. It was reported to us as you know George Thompson's mission fared no better than that of Ram Mohan Roy sent by your venerable father to King George 1V. The fact is that the Directors wrote to the Governor General. *The king having for so many years refused to receive this allowance, it is by no means obligatory to us to renew this offer."*

"The fact is that even in the absence of allowance we have managed to maintain the palace and its grounds in impeccable condition." Bahadur Shah Zafar ruminated aloud, his gaze reaching out to the colorful stalls beyond the palace gates. "Mindset of the British is an open book to me, I can hear them say: *Since palace and gardens are in splendid shape, we don't need to provide any funds for maintenance.* So they withhold the allowance rightfully due to us, collected by them from the revenue of our state. And when we run out of funds to maintain the upkeep of our palace grounds, they would be happy of the excuse they are looking for to dissolve our kingdom. And yet this is the day of Eid and we should be grateful that there is peace in Delhi. So tragic, wars are wreaking havoc in other parts of our empire, ours no more. Many factions and endless frictions, war in Sind, the Sikh wars in Punjab and in several other states, I have lost count." He promenaded past the palace gates into the main road, commenting over his shoulders. "Keep me informed of the outcomes now and then, Ahsanullah, and now is a good time."

All sorts of gifts; jewelry, carpets, jeweled artifacts and paintings just to name a few were housed under colorful tents, attracting wealthy buyers. Though the tide of attraction was shifted toward Bahadur Shah Zafar as soon as he appeared amongst them. He was being greeted most reverently since he was loved by the populace of Delhi, regardless of their race, creed or religion. In return, he was acknowledging their greetings with a wave of his arm. Even when he didn't—absorbed deeply in conversation or simply tired, people understood, bowing double in curtsies along the road or standing there smiling with their hands joined palms upward.

"First Sind annexed, then Gwalior isolated as you know, Zil-e-Subhani." Ahsanullah Khan's impassioned voice was reaching Bahadur Shah Zafar. "Charles Napier defeated the Sindians at Miani and again routed them at Dabo. As for Gwalior, the Maharaja of Gwalior Jayaji Rao Sindia is still a child. His nominal power was usurped by the military party. When the British intervened and defeated the state troops at Majajapur and Panior, they did so on pretext that the British Government is bound to protect the person of his Highness the Maharaja, his heirs and successors."

"Now I remember." Bahadur Shah Zafar stood watching the procession of State elephants decked in cloth of gold with gilded howdahs on their backs. "Those chieftains of Gwalior fighting amongst themselves didn't pose any threat to the British government. When James Outram informed the British government that those chieftains had their own petty grievances and had no intention of rebelling against ruling power of the British, he was replaced by Charles Napier who fought with chieftains with the vengeance of a war-lord."

"The same is true of the first major Sikh war fought on the sacred fields of Punjab, Zil-e-Subhani." Mahbub Ali Khan began with the élan of a war correspondent. "When the second Maharaja after Ranjit Singh's death was murdered, a bloodbath ensued. The heir of Ranjit Singh is still a child by the name of Dalip Singh, his nominal rule contested by the Sikh army called Khalsa. When Khalsa army moved against Gulab Singh who coveted the kingdom of Punjab, British intervened. A costly victory it was for the British at the very heart of Ferozepur. Sikh losses were ten thousand and twenty-four hundred British died. A conclusive, but expensive bid for Lahore was ruled out while the British sued for peace package consisting of an indemnity, partial annexation and reduction in the ranks of the Sikh Army. Kashmir with all its hill country between the Beas and the Indus, in lieu of indemnity, was ceded to British. And yet they sold it to Gulab Singh for three quarters of a million pounds."

"It's all coming back to me now." Bahadur Shah Zafar resumed his walk. "Gulab Singh had started his career as a trooper in the army of Ranjit Singh who had given him the state of Jammu as a reward for his gallantry. Ranjit Singh had offered Punjab to the British, it was rumored. Nothing came of it, but we do know that Gulab Singh is now the master of both Jammu and Kashmir. I am hoping he would keep these states peaceful and prosperous regardless of the diversity of race and religion."

"Peace and prosperity are myths of the past, Zil-e-Subhani, of which past I have yet to figure out." Ahsanullah Khan began pontifically. "The respect for religions is no more. Tolerance for race and religion which endeared British to the local population has been dwindling since the last couple of decades. Can't believe it has been more than a decade since William Wilber Force made those arrogant comments, they are still fresh in my memory. *It is so important to have missionary access over here since our religion is pure, sublime and beneficial, while theirs of the Hindus is cruel and licentious. Their deities are absolute monsters of lust, injustice and wickedness. Hinduism is the most enormous and tormenting superstition that harassed any portion of mankind. Hindus indeed are the most enslaved portion of the human race. To emancipate them from this grand abomination is as much sacred duty of every Christian as emancipating Africans from Slavery."*

"Aside from degrading the religion of the Hindus and the Muslims, the British have improved the conditions of living around here by building roads and digging irrigation channels." Bahadur Shah Zafar appeared to deflect the harshness of such sentiments with a sigh as profound as his thoughts. "The Great Trunk road between Delhi and Calcutta has expedited internal trade. Farmers don't have to depend upon monsoon rains anymore since irrigation channels in Punjab are fed by waters from the Ganges. Benefits outnumber the costs, higher revenues from land taxes. Ignorance of a few earns hatred of many as in the case of religious intolerance. Wisdom of few reaps benefits for all, though rarely noticed or acknowledged. Roads are always here for us to walk on, no one cares who built them. Well, I am digressing. I hear East India Company is planning to build railway lines from Calcutta to Agra, to Delhi."

"Top ranking businessmen are trying to raise money to fund this project, Zil-e-Subhani. Very expensive venture." Mahbub Ali Khan offered hastily, noticing the sullen expression of Ahsanullah Khan. "Just this year, one railway enthusiast from the Company complained to the high officials of his own East India Company that the work they suggest in physical improvement of India is no better than the speed of an ant. Here's his comment which I remember verbatim. *Brilliant as is the Company's prestige which hangs over our Indian empire, it must be confessed that it is still in a state of helpless and discreditable barbarism. Many, many centuries behind the example set by any other nation in civilized history."* He sucked in his thoughts, becoming aware of a few stragglers eager to greet the king.

"I have come to become a Muslim, Zil-e-Subhani." One Hindu man darted forward, prostrating before Bahadur Shah Zafar.

"Begone, begone. You are set in your old ways and can't practice the creed of Islam." Ahsanullah Khan hissed menacingly.

"You are dismissed, Ahsanullah." Bahadur Shah commanded with restrained anger. "Return to the palace posthaste and don't wait on me this evening." He turned his attention to the stunned man who was struggling to his feet. "Here, give me your hand, my good man, and repeat this creed of Islam and you would be welcomed into the fold of Islam." He held the man's hand into his own gently and lovingly. "Now repeat after me.

La illah ill Allah
Muhammad ur Rasul Allah."

The man crumbling under the weight of awe and reverence repeated the Kalima and fled after making a couple of curtsies. Murmuring thanks and choked by gratitude. Ahsanullah Khan, shamed and flustered had disappeared discreetly. Bahadur Shah Zafar's features were washed by sadness as he turned, retracing his steps toward the palace, followed by Mahbub Ali Khan. Clowns and magicians were attracting the attention of all, especially of the families with children, but the king and the vizier were avoiding the crowds and drifting away from the colorful stalls. Both were quiet, both acknowledging the greetings with a wave of their arm. Mahbub Ali Khan was now walking beside the king, his gaze tracing the road back to the palace gates. Bahadur Shah Zafar was contemplating the rise of zeal and bigotry amongst his courtiers, his thoughts turning to Wahhabis.

"The reek of zeal and intolerance I can smell miles away." Bahadur Shah Zafar began poetically. "And yet when the men in my court waft that odor, my mind becomes agitated. Next they would be preaching hatred and sanctioning murder just like the Wahhabis. Though, Wahhabism has run its course in India. Wasn't it during the invasion of Afghanistan when the British succeeded in placing Shah Shuja on the throne, and Wahhabis fought in Ghazni against the British army of sepoys from Bengal and Bombay, dubbed as Army of the Indus? Many were killed and the remaining alive imprisoned. When brought in chains before Shah Shuja, he had them hacked to death with wanton barbarity with the knives of the executioners."

"That is true, Zile-e-Subhani, but Wahhabis are very much alive. Ridiculously deceitful, rather ludicrous in their attempt to raise the banner of Jihad. Which in their terminology means a sacred duty to kill brutally and savagely, proclaiming the sanctity of Holy War.?" Mahbub Ali Khan chuckled in anticipation of sharing with the emperor this bizarre recollection. "Remember, Zil-e-Subhani, a Wahhabi leader by the name of Syed Ahmed who was martyred at the battle of Balakot according to the devout disciples, who mourned him for days."

"Isn't he the one dubbed as Hidden Imam, not killed but hidden from the sight of man?" Bahadur Shah Zafar reminisced aloud. "He was supposed to come out of his hiding after fourteen years and resume the role of preaching—hatred, I presume?"

"The same one, Zil-e-Subhani!" Mahbub Ali Khan declared passionately. "He has returned as prophesied, after fourteen years, yes. Not in flesh or spirit, but in rags of lies. Wahhabi faithful are proclaiming that their Hidden Imam now called Amir-ul-Momineen has come back from the mountains and is summoning the faithful to join him in the just cause of Holy War. Heeding this call were a thousand recruits from Deccan who had arrived in Sittana for military training. Their commander by the name of Zin-ul-Abdin, curious and domineering by nature demanded to see Amir-ul-Momineen. He was informed by Wahhabi Caliph by the name of Qasin Kazzab that he could see the Imam only from a distance, for if he got close the Imam would disappear for another fourteen years. From their camp Zain-ul Abdin and his followers were led up to a mountain overlooking a cave. At the mouth of the cave stood three men dressed in white robes. In the middle was Amir-ul-Momineen, they were told, and the men standing on each side were his disciples to tend to his needs. Zain-ul-Abdin couldn't sleep that night and by early dawn returned to the mountain, followed by a few of his comrades. Compelled by curiosity they ventured close to the three men. Lo and behold, those were not men in white robes, but effigies of goatskin stuffed with grass. Horrified to be fobbed thus, they asked the Wahhabi caliph why he had lied. Qasin Kazzab protested that he didn't lie, that it was truly Amir-ul-Momineen who had performed a miracle by appearing as a stuffed figure. Thoroughly disgusted, Zain-ul-Abdin is now a vociferous critic of the Wahhabis."

"Who would unveil the deception of the Bhils, though they are very much alive and not claiming to be returning from the abode of the dead?" Bahadur Shah Zafar's pace was slackened. "They are still being recruited into Company's army, though they are born dacoits, torturing and burning both rich and poor before seizing their gold and jewels." He was entering the palace gardens.

"This reminds me of a Maharashtra folksong, Zil-e-Subhani, about an elusive bandit chief who was very popular." Mahbub Ali Khan began exigently before the king could disappear inside the palace.

"Raghu raised his revolt
He stayed in the deep hollows of the Konkan
Hid in the mango groves
There was a big gun battle
The rebels fought until they were victorious
And white man's face was smeared with blood."

"Somehow you have the power of refreshing my memory, Mahbub." Bahadur Shah Zafar's feet were leading him toward Rang Mahal. "Raghu was the son of a Bhil Chieftain who was appointed as a police Jamedar in the Company. Another Brahmin Jamedar in the Company had his suspicion that Raghu was leading raids in the neighboring village. After investigation, the police tortured Raghu's family by attaching clipping horns to their breasts and testicles. This started a streak of vengeance with the Government Policemen were murdered, their wives raped. Moneylenders had their noses sliced off. Recently, just this year British officers took this matter into their hands. Raghu's followers were dispersed and he was taken prisoner, tried and hanged."

"Konds of southern Orissa, Zil-e-Subhani, are the ones to be restrained more than the Bhils." Mahbub Ali Khan commented thoughtlessly. "They still believe in killing their newborn daughters. Worse still is their penchant for child sacrifice to placate their gods for good fortune and making the soil fertile. They kidnap children for this religious ceremony, drug them before cutting them up to pieces."

"This brutal custom is declining rapidly and we must give credit to the British general John Campbell." Bahadur Shah Zafar recalled sadly. "In his great wisdom and compassion he sat down with the Kond chieftains, telling them that once British used to sacrifice humans, but at that time they were ignorant. Then he requested them to renounce this evil custom by taking a traditional oath. Which they did, holding a handful of rice mixed with water and soil. Saying: *May the earth refuse its produce, rice choke me, water drown me and tiger devour me and my children if I break the oath which I now take for myself and my people to abstain from sacrificing human beings.* A ray of hope and prayers are our talisman for virtuous living, my good vizier. Now go, enjoy Eid with your family. We will meet tomorrow." His footsteps were guiding him toward the comfort of his palace.

Rang Mahal south of Red Fort Palace was hosting Bahadur Shah Zafar and his royal family this festive day of Eid in a grand style. He was seated on Takht-i-taus—a small throne with dripping velvets and embellished with jewels. His own jewels catching light from the chandelier hanging low from gilded ceiling were changing colors, fiery and brilliant. Velvety davenports were lending comfort to the ladies of the harem. Princes and the princesses lolling against satiny pillows on the Persian rug were admiring the dancing girls with studs in their noses and tilaks on their foreheads. Prince Jawan Bakht barely three year old was trying to imitate the dancers, then skipping around the round pool in the middle of the room fed by the waters of Jamna. Zeenat Mahal was commanding him not to splash the water as was his wont when unwatched. Bahadur Shah Zafar's attention was lured toward his eldest son Prince Mirza Quaish already thirty-three year old, who had begun reciting a poem for the sole delight of his sisters and brothers.

> *"The colonies and foreign governments*
> *Are famous drain for pride and poverty*
> *For gentlemen deficient in their rents*
> *Always in India turn a longing eye*
> *They talk in England of a precious tree*
> *That, but to shake, brings down its fruit*
> *A pagoda tree of Indian gold and jewels."*

Prince Mirza Quaish sang with the élan of a poet star.

"The same pagoda tree which rains gold coins when shaken as Englishmen believe." Was Prince Khizr Sultan's inebriated comment. "And I believe it did exist before the British came. Now stripped naked of its treasures by them, it is shamed into hiding, its beauty ravished."

"You have just turned twenty-nine, my Prince, and still ruled by myths of the past." Bahadur Shah Zafar chided mildly. "Reality is not far from that myth though. Under that pagoda tree if one must believe in that, sit the datura poisoners, and the British know nothing about them. Datura poisoners are people bearing the knowledge of a poisonous plant and greatly skilful in poisoning. They are employed as cooks by the Britons, not even suspecting that they can poison their food if offended. Recently, one such woman who was a cook in Indian household just accomplished that, poisoning her master and disappearing with all his treasures."

"Not half as dangerous as Muslims who are being poisoned by the hateful doctrines of Wahhabis, Zil-e-Subhani." Prince Mirza Mughal only a year younger than Prince Khizr Sultan, tossed his own merry comment "Wahhabis are busy recruiting young male orphans from the poor families and subjecting them to long periods of intensive and exclusive religious indoctrination, while training them as holy warriors to kill all infidels."

"Infidels in all of us, my Son." Bahadur Shah Zafar smiled enigmatically "If we knew its meaning we would kill a part of ourselves most willingly. Infidel in Arabic is Kafir. In Quranic interpretation simply meaning—to cover up the realization of what we are created for. Muslims themselves have forgotten that Prophet Muhammad was sent as a mercy to all nations, that he abhorred war, so how could he sanction killing? The word Umma as the community of Prophet in Medina is derived from the word umm, meaning mother. So Prophet is also like a maternal figure, more like a mother, nursing the infant-like Umma from the breast of his mercy."

"*Fighting is ordained for you, though it is hateful to you.* 2: 216." Prince Fakhroo on the rungs of twenty-seven was quick to flaunt his own knowledge of Islam as if to impress his father-in-law Ilahi Bakhsh.

"At this young age, my Prince, you need a venerable teacher to teach you the interpretations of the verses of the Quran." Bahadur Shah Zafar began thoughtfully. "At the heart of war and peace is this verse which all Muslims should memorize to avoid the evil of warfare. *And fight in God's cause against those who wage war against you, but do not commit aggression. For surely, God does not love aggressors 2: 190.*"

"Eid is the day of joy and celebration, Zil-e-Subhani, and here the conversation is running in rivulets of war." Zeenat Mahal laughed as Prince Jawan Bakht escaped her embrace and bounded off toward the king.

"Here comes my Eid. My reason for joy and celebration." Bahadur Shah Zafar cradled Prince Jawan Bakht into his arms after he jumped into his lap. "No more talk of wars, I promise." He smiled at Zeenat Mahal, his gaze reaching out to caress each one of his wives individually. "Any interesting news that you wish to share with the king, now that even the dancers are taking a siesta, bored by the dullness of our parlance."

"Strange and interesting, Zil-e-Subhani. Colonel Wheeler married Frances—six months pregnant, gasping for breath while walking down the isle." Ashraf Begum chuckled merrily.

"All conversation leads to war, my Beauty." A whimsical smile hovered over the lips of Bahadur Shah Zafar. "Frances, is the widow of Colonel Oliver—her husband who died during the Afghan war. Though he volunteered to fight when all hope of winning was dying. On the battlefield he was heard crying: *Although my men desert me, I myself would do my duty.* Right then, a sniper's ball went buzzing through his brain and finished him off. Afghans then chopped his head off. When they couldn't slip the wedding band off his finger, they chopped his finger too, carrying it along with his severed head."

"How could she, Zil-e-Subhani, only after three months of her husband's tragic death marry another man, and a mother of several children?" Akhtar Begum appeared to question her own astonishment.

"Precisely for that reason, my Dear, to support her children." Bahadur Shah Zafar opined aloud. "Wonder of wonders though. It has been four years since she got married, and you got to know about it recently."

"Great wonder indeed, Zil-e-Subhani, for it takes years for any news to penetrate the harem walls." Taj Mahal Begum teased, stealing a glance at her son Prince Fakhroo. "Prince Fakhroo is studying genealogy of the Moghul emperors and he tells me your grandfather Shah Alam wrote a beautiful elegy after he was blinded, do you remember it?"

"Some of it." Bahadur Shah Zafar murmured. "A great gift of Eid before we go feasting." He shifted his attention of Prince Fakhroo. "Won't you recite it, my Prince, since your memory is fresh due to your recent interest in Moghul History?"

"Yes, Zil-e-Subhani. Right away since I am famished and can't wait any more for the great feast to begin." Prince Fakhroo let his voice ebb and soar.

"Learn that imperial pride and star-clad power
Are but the fleeting pageants of an hour
In the true crucible of dire distress
Purged of alloy, thy sorrows soon shall cease
What, through the sun of empire and command
Shorn of its beams, enlightens not the land
Some happier day, a providential care
Again may renovate the falling star
Again O King raise up thy illustrious race
Cheer thy sad mind and close thy days in peace."

"And to think of it, my unfortunate grandfather was blinded by petty, avaricious man by the name of Ghulam Qadir from the tribe of Rohilla Afghans." Bahadur Shah Zafar's eyes were closed. "Yes, a great feast awaits us in Diwan-i-Am." He opened his eyes, becoming aware of Prince Jawan Bakht missing from his lap. "You have given us a great feast by your sweet recitation, my Son and have earned yet a grander feast." He heaved himself up slowly. "Gifts of jewels and horses, before this day is over."

Chapter Five
Jashni-Holi

Diwan-i-Khas this sultry afternoon was rather cool in comparison with other chambers of the Delhi palace, its velvet drapes and Persian carpets adding the luxury of comfort. Bahadur Shah Zafar was seated on his Peacock Throne in full regalia, flanked by two servants with peacock-feather fans to lend him respite from the weight of crown, jewels and a robe broidered with gold. Time was heavy on his shoulders too, the youngest Prince Shah Abbas now almost seven year old, many moons ahead of the last festival of Eid. At the steps of the throne on either side stood princes, viziers and courtiers with folded hands. This was a small gathering by the express wishes of Bahadur Shah Zafar to assess the past few years of unrest and increased tension between the natives and the British. He had no control over the waves of discontent in India, but he felt he needed to stay abreast of all events in the hope of guiding his people and finding solutions.

"Are there enough vaccines in Karachi to control the onslaught of Malaria?" Bahadur Shah Zafar flung this concern at no one in particular. "I hear many people have died and many more are dying in droves."

"The worst outbreak ever, Zil-e-Subhani." Ahsanullah Khan began histrionically. "I am not so sure about the supply of medicines, but people are dying right and left. More so the British since they have less resistance to this indigenous disease. The last count of death-toll I heard was three hundred and eighty-five, including men, women and children from one regiment alone. Sixtieth Regiment I believe."

"All of us are approaching closer to death, yet sad it is to know that death doesn't discriminate between young and old." Bahadur Shah Zafar couldn't suppress a sigh. "I can never forget the epitaph written by one young husband by the name of Richard Crust whose wife died suddenly.

For in that Orient land, whose annals show
The price paid yearly of domestic woe
Where many a blooming wife and mother lie
Who left their native country but to die."

"Many poets, Zil-e-Subhani, have immortalized such women with praise." Mahbub Ali Khan sought the king's attention. "One of those poems is worthy of your review though I can't recall the name of the poet.

The fair Britain's Isle
When wafted to Indostan's stand
Amidst the sable nation's smile
Like angels from a fairyland."

"Talking about poets, our court poet Ghalib, I hear is arrested for gambling." Bahadur Shah Zafar's thoughts were saddened beyond expression. "To me gambling is not a crime. Most of us gamble away our very lives, more to the detriment of our own selves than committing any social evil in the fabric of life, almost always torn to shreds by inherent evils unnoticed by pious judges. Well, when he is going to be released?"

"As soon as cash is procured for his release, Zil-e-Subhani." Was Zauq's subtle response.

"Ah, the ills of our society! Bribery and bargain, not to mention tragedy and discontent of our times." Bahadur Shah Zafar's gaze was sweeping over his sons as if assessing their character and courage. "Second Sikh war against the British. British emboldened by their victory and Sikhs smarting against their losses. Lord Dalhousie proud and prancing. How he got here and such profusion of warring factions, it's all so confusing. Refresh my memory, Prince Quaish, since you are the eldest, how it all started?

"Despite our religious differences, Zil-e-Subhani, we all, whether Sikhs, Hindus or Muslims feel that our rights/lands are being usurped by the British." Prince Mirza Quaish began obediently. "The feelings simmered and the dissentions began when the British thought they would win the affections of all by simply proclaiming to the citizens that they would be ruled by the best laws, while they would be governed by a Sikh governor, who would rule justly since the English would watch over him. But that didn't win the trust of the general populace. Their skepticism was heightened further when the British Resident Henry Lawrence pressed strict economic restrictions, also reducing drastically the rank and file of the Company forces.

Henry Lawrence then went to London to inform newly appointed governor general Lord Dalhousie that there would be peace in India for at least seven more years. And yet under Lord Dalhousie's strict vigilance troubles began soon after. Mulraj the governor of Multan employed by the administration of Lahore resigned. With his connivance two British officers were murdered, and thus began the tide of great Sikh war. And the rest you know, Zil-e-Subhani."

"Yes, the great war, Sikhs defeated on the battleground of Gujrat. Raja Dalip Singh signing the document of annexation, Lahore ceded to the British and he becoming a pensioner of the British. In addition to the annexation of Lahore, the Raja had to relinquish Koh-i-Noor to Lord Dalhousie." Bahadur Shah Zafar reminisced aloud as if astonished by the thin fabric of his own memory. "What did Lord Dalhousie write to the Secret Committee in London before the war? A secret no more which I can't recall, though. Do you remember Prince Khizr Sultan?"

"A part of it, Zil-e-Subhani. I don't have as great a memory as that of Prince Quaish." Was Prince Khizr Sultan's flushed response. "This is how much I can recall. Lord Dalhousie writing: *I have wished for peace. I have striven for it. But unwarned by precedent, uninfluenced by example, the Sikh nation has called for war. And on my word, Sirs, they shall have it with a vengeance.*"

"Always on a lookout to start war, Zil-e-Subhani." Prince Fakhroo commented to hide his guilt in siding with the British secretly. "After the Multan outbreak Lord Dalhousie also wrote to the Secret Committee: *I have no course open to us, but to prepare for a general Sikh war and ultimately to occupy the country.*"

"Racial hauteur on the part of the British is on the rise and Indian soldiers can feel it, Zil-e-Subhani." Prince Mirza Mughal couldn't stay behind to voice his opinion. "When Multan was under fire, Private Ryder tried to calm two frightened sepoys. One of them protested: *If a ball strikes me and I am killed, you would say, oh, never mind, it's only a black man.*"

"Racial contempt, I should say, Zil-e-Subhani." Azad declared passionately. "I have been researching and the word *nigger* applied to the Indians is appearing in private correspondence amongst the British generals as well as in their private conversations."

"Where would your research lead you, my young Poet, and for what purpose?" Bahadur Shah Zafar asked wearily.

"Leading back to truth, perhaps, Zil-e-Subhani. And for the purpose of enlightenment to understand the covert designs of the alien rulers while they pretend to be courteous."

"And what you have learnt so far?" Bahadur Shah Zafar asked with a sudden spark of interest.

"Early impressions of the Britishers, Zil-e-Subhani, caught by the Indian sailors and later recorded." Azad was happy to empty the quivers of his newly found knowledge. "One sailor wrote about James Walsh as he sailed up to Hughli. He saw flotillas of small rowing boats filled with food sellers and exclaimed: *These people are a race of beings seemingly intended by nature to complete the link between man—the image of his Maker and the tribe of apes and monkeys.* Lord Hasting when he landed in Calcutta said: *The Hindu appears to me nearly limited to mere animal functions, and even then indifferent.* Later he wrote in his journal. *They seem to possess no higher intellect than a dog, a monkey or an elephant.* He also wrote about the sheer number of people on the streets, cooking, eating and defecating in public."

"Sadly and tragically, carrying arrogance on their shoulders they are sure to fall sooner or later." Bahadur Shah Zafar prophesied with a sinking heart. "As far as intellect is concerned, if they had even one grain of it they would not deride the loving, non-judgmental Hindus. There are multitudes, I hear, on the streets of Regency London, if they but choose to look. That would be a humbling experience."

"Gilded with superiority complex, Zile-e-Subhani, they would never know the joy of humbleness." Mustafa Khan Shefta tossed his own poetic comment. "Despite the heavy losses of their men during the Sikh war, they always confronted the Sikhs as if on a parade with colors flying toward the breastworks."

"Someone has to remind them of their bull dog fight at Waterloo." Bahadur Shah Zafar was feeling a hurricane of sadness.

"The British soldiers who won badges of honor at Waterloo, Zil-e-Subhani, have become the envy of soldiers here who are not decorated with any badges." Ahsanullah Khan smiled. One English poet by the name of Charles D'Oyly wrote this verse to arouse the envy of the Company Veterans.

"The colonel looks at the well-dressed lieutenant
With wonder, and the badge of Waterloo
On his young breast conspicuously resplendent

And sighs that all the battles he'd gone through
Should not have gained him some distinction."

"We should join the ranks of the ones to envy the poise and the cleverness of the British." Bahadur Shah Zafar's features were lit up by a pale smile. "They are skilled in making hostility look like friendship and conquest like a favor. And I mean it in a complimentary way."

"The philosopher queen of Malwa, Zil-e-Subhani, by the name of Ahalyabhai Holkar thought otherwise." Azad glowed with youthful pride. "My research goes back more than a century. She warned his people against association with the British, comparing their embrace to a bear-hug. *Other beasts*, she says, *like tigers can be killed by might or contrivance, but to kill a bear is very difficult. It will die only if you kill it straight in the face. Or else, once caught in the powerful hold, the bear will kill its prey by tickling. Such is the way of the English. And in view of this it is difficult to triumph over them."*

"That philosopher queen, my naïve poet, derided Muslim conquerors too and in good conscience I am sure. For quite a few of them demolished the holy shrines as divinely ordained duty." Bahadur Shah Zafar let his gaze sweep over his courtiers, espying Maulvi Wilayat Ali whose eyes were burning with zeal. "Ah, Wilayat Ali, didn't you and your brother start a proselytizing program?" Was Bahadur Shah Zafar's astonished exclamation. "Were you both not arrested by the British officers by inciting people to a religious war and claiming that your deceased leader Syed Ahmed is about to be resurrected, again?"

"Not true, Zil-e-Subhani." Maulvi Wilayat Ali lied blatantly. "Just rumors base and wicked. Even the secretary to the government of Bengal dismissed such rumors with a shrug. However, Zil-e-Subhani, we believe that anyone submitting to the authority of the British has renounced his religion. And anyone failing to heed the commands of God is sure to burn in the fires of hell—"

"Vile teachings of the Wahhabis!" Bahadur Shah Zafar thundered, getting to his feet as if stung. "Hell lies for you outside this hall. Efface yourself immediately before you are dragged into the fires of hell on this earth. And never, not ever step foot in my court." He waved dismissal, his eyes shooting bolts of lightning.

Maulvi Wilayat Ali fled as if chased by demons. Bahadur Shah Zafar trooped past the courtiers, barely acknowledging their curtsies. He was seeking the sanctuary of his harem, still whipped by the fury of his anger. Astonished once more by the precision of his memory that both Inyat Ali and Wilayat Ali were arrested in Hazara a couple of years ago by Harry Lumsden and sent under custody to Patna to stay there for five years. *So they must be ignoring the restrictions and roaming free*, he was thinking, his feet guiding him toward Rang Mahal.

Rang Mahal had disappeared somewhere in favor of Zafar Mahal this year to celebrate the festival of Holi—a Hindu festival symbolizing the commencement of New Year and the season of harvest. Almost a year had slipped past since the effacement of Wilayat Ali and since then Bahadur Shah Zafar had not encountered any Wahhabis in his court. This particular afternoon Bahadur Shah Zafar was in an ebullient mood, he and his family and friends were gathered in Zafar Mahal to enjoy a grand feast and to sprinkle each other with colored water or powder as a part of Holi celebration. The marble floor of Zafar Mahal was already a swamp of yellow, purple and crimson since Begums, princes and princesses were freely indulging in dousing each other with colored rosewater since no decorum was observed on this festive day of colors. Bahadur Shah Zafar was stealing toward the window to admire the swath of roses against the avenues of cypresses. Barely had he arrested the beauty of his garden when a loud exclamation from the lips of his wife made him turn around.

"Look, Zil-e-Subhani." Ashraf Begum sprayed his forehead with a jet of saffron water. "Your forehead is smeared with so many colors you need a thorough wash." She laughed.

"And you, my Beauty, need a change of silks." Bahadur Shah Zafar was quick to release a spray of red water from his sprinkler before she could flee.

"We should stop this madness now. The floor is disappearing in rivulets of colors." Akhtar Begum couldn't help spraying the laughing couple with powdered red-dust.

"Now really, we should settle down for a feast." Zeenat Mahal was too nimble to let the trio escape against her own sprinkler of ochre jet.

"Why I am being sprayed right and left when there is no dearth of royal pranksters in this palace of colors?" Bahadur Shah Zafar made one hopeless gesture against the din of music and laughter. The princes and princesses running and spraying, while squealing with mirth.

"Truly, Zil-e-Subhani, we must stop. I am famished." Taj Mahal Begum implored.

"Yes, time to bathe and dress for feasting." Bahadur Shah Zafar agreed, holding out his hand to Mubarak Nisa who had collapsed on the floor drenched in a rainbow of colors.

The evening still bathed in the colors of festivity was wafting the scent of serendipity as Bahadur Shah Zafar sat with his family to partake of the feast prepared by diligent chefs. A great feast it was with a variety of viands, including twenty-five kinds of bread and as many varieties of rice dishes, and double the amount of desserts garnished with gold and silver leaves beaten thin and sprinkled with chopped pistachios.

Sated with food, music and bouts of festivity, the royal family was sharing bulletins of news with a sense of amusement or indifference. Bahadur Shah Zafar's wives were still teasing him, though spraying no colors, only the colorful jests.

"Now that all five divans of your poetry are published, Zil-e-Subhani, are you going to write more?" Prince Fakhroo asked suddenly with the intention of snatching his father's attention from the protests of his royal wives.

"A poet, always a poet, my Prince." Bahadur Shah Zafar smiled generously. "Can one stop breathing as long as one has the breath left to breathe?"

"Lord Dalhousie almost did, Zil-e-Subhani." Prince Mirza Mughal was eager to share his own bulletin of news. "The Koh-i-Noor diamond which he exacted from Dalip Singh, he finally delivered to Queen Victoria personally. Almost holding his breath, he had confessed, while carrying the diamond from Lahore to Bombay and then on a ship to London. He was heard telling the Queen. *Sewn and double sewn, it was secured around my waist. One end of the belt fastened to a chain around my neck. It never left me day or night.* The Queen was not impressed, it was reported."

"Indians too are not impressed by Lord Dalhousie since he signed a law of Emancipation Act before sailing to London." Prince Khizr Sultan commented. "Under this law no one would be deprived of his inheritance on account of a change of religion. Hindus are very much against this law since they would no longer be able to disinherit their children if they were to abandon their ancestral faith."

"Hindus are already bitter about the European missionaries." Prince Mirza Quaish began thoughtfully. "Religious literature is being distributed openly with the intention of proselytizing. It is unwelcome to many, especially to sepoys and sowars who are being invited by their English officers and exposed to the doctrines of Christianity."

"In earnest, my Prince, I believe the English want to educate, not proselytize." Bahadur Shah Zafar intervened cheerfully. "They have great plans of offering education to young or old, male or female. It would be of great benefit to the general population, in my estimation.

"I have been keeping abreast of news from London, Zil-e-Subhani, and their idea of education is quite different from how you perceive." Zeenat Mahal was quick to join the royal parlance. "An English writer by the name of Macaulay is quoted saying: *If our plans of education are followed up, there will not be a single idolater among the respectable classes in Bengal thirty years hence and this will be affected without efforts to proselytize.*" She stole a glance at her son Prince Jawan Bakht almost eleven now, before continuing. "I am exposing Prince Jawan Bakht to the literature of the west even if it is unpopular around here. I think it broadens the mind."

"It is not the literature of the British, Beloved, that is unpopular, but their policies which antagonize the rajas and their subjects." Bahadur Shah Zafar's gaze was caressing both the prince and the queen. "The policy of Lord Dalhousie for one. His Doctrine of Lapse, whereby the Company could automatically annex the principality of any Indian ruler who died without natural issue. He put this Doctrine into practice a year ago at the death of Sivaji's descendant at Sittana who had left no male heir, annexing his kingdom immediately."

"Jashn-i-Holi is the festival of the Hindus, Zil-e-Subhani, so why do we celebrate it?" Prince Jawan Bakht asked precociously.

"Ah, my young Scholar!" Bahadur Shah Zafar indulged cheerfully. "Celebration is a way of life and my excuse to celebrate any festival adds joy to celebrate life. You are too young to understand the concept of religions. Islam teaches us to honor and respect the religions of others. By participating in celebrations of the followers of other faiths, we honor the spirit of Islam. You would be studying the history of Moghuls soon and I have appointed Hafiz Muhammed as your tutor, though he is a great theologian also, but remember our ancestor emperor Jahangir also celebrated Holi. He named it Eid-e-Gulabi, meaning pink Eid. And now in the spirit of joy let us go for a stroll in our garden Hayat Bakhsh and see if we can discover pink Eid in beautiful blossoms. And don't forget to teach Prince Shah Abbas the lessons you have already learnt." He got to his feet, beckoning all to join him in a leisurely stroll.

Another swift year sucked into the seasons of the past since a leisurely stroll in Hayat Bakhsh garden and this particular afternoon the same garden was hosting poetry recitation. Bhadon Pavilion was the chosen abode where Bahadur Shah Zafar sat with his poets on a palace rug of Persian weave, exquisitely soft and luxuriant. The scent of roses mixed with fragrant blooms from Mulsari tree was permeating the pavilion, making the poets drunk with the perfume of poetry and flowers. Bahadur Shah Zafar was facing the open mehrab and he could see the star-like blooms of Mulsari tree, his gaze reaching beyond and hovering over the array of cypresses. His attention was turned to Ghalib who was obeying the command of the candle before him and reciting ecstatically.

"The object of my worship lies beyond perception's reach
For men who see, the Kaaba is a compass, nothing more."
Ghalib bowed his head amidst the symphony of great applause.

"I am glad you were arrested for gambling, not for heresy." Bahadur Shah Zafar laughed.

"In the Kaaba I will play the conch shell
In the temple I have draped the ahram."
Ghalib spilled one impromptu couplet.

"Now, for sure, you would be imprisoned on the charges of heresy." Azad teased, more so to still his inner rancor against this genius of a poet than to be a part of the revelry.

"I wish I had taken rosary in my hand, put a secretarian mark on my forehead, tied a sacred thread around my waist and seated myself on the banks of Ganges!" Ghalib exclaimed passionately. "That way I would be able to wash the contamination of my existence from myself and be like a drop with the river."

"You would merge with the ocean if you could swallow your pride without hesitation." Bahadur Shah Zafar chided lightly.

"Didn't you refuse a college post, though your financial resources are insufficient, I hear?"

"Yes, I did, Zil-e-Subhani." Ghalib admitted, visibly discomfited.

"What made you decline that post?" Bahadur Shah Zafar asked amusedly.

"My pride as you rightly guessed, Zil-e-Subhani." Ghalib confessed with a bold smile. "And the arrogance of Mr. Thomason, the secretary. It could have been a lucrative job to teach Persian at Delhi College, but when I arrived at the gate I expected Mr. Thomason to come out and welcome me befitting my status. After a long time when he finally deigned to come out, he chortled haughtily that it was appropriate for him to welcome me formally at the Governor's Court, but no such formality was required at the college. I told him that by taking a government appointment I had expected it would bring me greater honor than I now receive, not a reduction in those already accorded me. To which he shook his head, saying: *I am bound by regulations.* I was courteous enough to tell him then, *I hope you would excuse me*, before leaving him standing there perplexed."

"I graduated from Delhi College." Azad seemed awestruck as if humbled by the hauteur of a great poet. "Some of the Shaikhs over there tried my patience while teaching me Arabic and Persian."

"The Shaikh hovers by the tavern door
But believe me, Ghalib
I am sure I saw him slip in
As I departed."

Ghalib's inspiration was fluid it was obvious as he spilled this quatrain.

"The way you are spilling poetry today, Ghalib, it seems you are the master of Urdu poetry." Zauq declared suddenly.

"You are not the only master of Urdu, Ghalib
They say there used to be a Mir in the past."

Ghalib's spark of inspiration seemed inexhaustible.

"Ghalib, pass the candle to Zauq before the wax of inspiration of the other poets melts and disappears." Bahadur Shah Zafar applauded.

"We can see a river in a drop, a barn in a single grain
The whole is a part we can see, a universe compressed in
a lane

Who can strengthen out my life, knotted like a tress
entwined
> *With failures deep from heel to head in our life engrained*
> *The boat of life has arrived at the whirlpool of death*
> *Every breath that we inhale is a fatal gust of windy rain*
> *Our Kaaba is now subsumed in the gem of our heart*
> *Like the whirlpool we should now circle round this fane."*

Zauq moved the candle swiftly in front of Momin before the applause could subside.

> *"Kneeling to the idols, Momin, you have spent your life*
> *How futile to turn a Muslim when your end arrives."*

Momin recited somberly.

"Pray, do not sing of death as yet, you are young still." Bahadur Shah Zafar applauded, his gaze spilling compliments. "Don't be in a haste to pass the candle. Sing of something serene and festive."

> *"What festive scenes my mind recalled that drugged down*
> *my senses*
> *Drunk am I without a drink on this moonlit plain*
> *Lo, at his dying hour he kneels at his idol's feet*
> *Momin has forsaken God, by restlessness deranged."*

Momin was quick to place the candle before Azad, fearing reprimand from the king for using death theme again.

Azad seemed spellbound, and couldn't speak even after the applause subsided. He was feeling bashful, trying to banish the beautiful face of his beloved he had glimpsed but occasionally.

> *"Today a flower must have bloomed afresh*
> *For her face has the freshness of a rose*
> *Angels must be longing to embrace her*
> *To feel the warmth of pure love*
> *Seeking forgiveness from beloved*
> *I dared desire her*
> *This fire of desire alone*
> *Polishing my tears to pearls."*

Azad almost toppled the candle in his haste to place it before Shefta.

"With such a tender piece of poesy, you couldn't be that garrulous editor of Delhi Urdu newspaper as the rumor goes." Bahadur Shah Zafar applauded, showering compliments on this young poet.

"Whatever enterprise you start, be it good or bad
Pursue it with your heart and soul and a determined zeal
Let your body reflect your soul in its subtle, spiritual sense
And your words reflect your meaning, lying deep-concealed"
Mustafa Khan Shefta was as quick as Azad, though steady in his haste to place the candle in front of Bahadur Shah Zafar.

"The brevity of my poets and somberness of their demeanor have robbed me of my own inspiration." Bahadur Shah Zafar laughed before reciting.

"You should have invested me either with a crown
Or wrapped my body in a lowly, beggar's gown
I wish I were turned to dust and strewn at lover's door
If I was meant to be humbled to the ground
If I was endowed with insatiate thirst for love
I wish I were given a life unlimited, unbound
That my heart is rent apart, I do not care
Provided the pillow of your locks serves as its
                                    resting ground
If I am not worthy of the company of the saints
In the revelers' throng at least let my voice resound
Bereft of the Saqi's grace, if I am to burn alone
Make me a tavern lamp, burning at the tavern ground
Everything is always wrong in this mundane world
Such a place had better been a wild barren ground."

Bahadur Shah Zafar's melancholy tones were sucked inside a thunderous applause. "You are generous to the old king." He made a kind gesture. "If there is any news worthy to share we have a few moments before we return to the palace." He invited comments, concerns, and suggestions.

"The kingdom of Jhansi, Zil-e-Subhani, is abuzz with festivities." Mahbub Ali Khan broke his silence. "Lakshami Bai has given birth to a son, naming him Damodar Rao."

"God be praised, an heir to the throne." Bahadur Shah Zafar intoned cheerfully. "One little kingdom where Lord Dalhousie's Doctrine of Lapse won't apply."

"Paradoxically, Zil-e-Subhani, birth and death run parallel, never meeting in twain." Ahsanullah Khan began pontifically. "Peshwa Baji Rao passed away in Bithoor near Cawnpore. His adopted son Nana Sahib has appointed Azimullah Khan as his advisor and secretary. Baji Rao was considered a coward even in his exile. Now people are singing on the streets.

"We emptied the well
And drained the land dry
To grow a tree of thorns
Running, Baji Rao."

"It's not right to think badly of the deceased." Bahadur Shah Zafar intoned sadly. "Peshwa unfortunately was the victim of circumstances. He was born when both his parents were imprisoned by Peshwa's Cabinet. Till the age of nineteen he spent time in confinement along with his parents and he lost both his parents when still in his teens."

"Unfortunate indeed, Zil-e-Subhani." Ghalib commiserated aloud. "His parents were accused of murdering a young Peshwa, their own nephew."

"That nephew was fifth Peshwa, Zil-e-Subhani, by the name of Narain Rao, haunting Baji Rao all his life." Zauq appeared to be jogging down his own memory lane. "To drive the ghost away he built a temple for the priests of Panharpur on a river bank in the town of Maharashtra. The priests succeeded in exorcising the ghost, but it appeared when Baji Rao was exiled to Bithoor. There are many stories concerning this ghost."

"I have heard, but I forget." Bahadur Shah Zafar appeared to contemplate. "Well, was he able to drive away the ghost again?"

"People don't think so, Zil-e-Subhani." Zauq began thoughtfully. "Till the end of his life that ghost stayed with him, though he distributed alms to Brahmins, built temples and bathing Ghats. Performed endless prayers and did penances. Fasted for days and kneeled at the feet of sadhus and soothsayers."

"Sad, passing sad." Bahadur Shah Zafar heaved himself up thoughtfully, his gaze alighting on Momin. "Momin, you still look sad, what's wrong?"

"Nothing, Zil-e-Subhani." Momin smiled. "I am not sad, rather feel peaceful. Somehow I have this feeling that I won't live for long."

"To dispel this doom and gloom, Momin, you must recite a worthy poem before we end this poesy session formally."

"My verse with its magic touch can the dead revive
I have resurrected the name of Jesus Christ
Is this the way to send your wishes through the
rival's missive

Lo, I thank you from afar for such a callous style
Ere, I used the term to suggest her deadly charms
No one knew the name of doom, nor what it implied
There comes to slay me, by hence ye dense despairs
Lest he be unnerved by such a crown in sight
Granted, you gave a harsh reply to the rival's note
But pray, tell me not what his note implied
The bliss of union is separation's recompense
Why do you, O heaven, a new torment devise
Bearing with your wrongs I have spoiled your ways
My doings have undone me, I've now realized."

Momin sang madly and ecstatically.

"Madness of the poets is maddening." Bahadur Shah emerged out into sunshine, leaving behind the Bhadon Pavilion rocking with cheers and applause.

Seal of the emperor in the first year of his reign.

Chapter Six
Weighing Ceremony

The fortifications of Salimgarh outside the palace fortress of Delhi was teeming with guests for Bahadur Shah Zafar's seventy-eighth birthday. He had requested that everyone should dress in yellow for his birthday and the palace gardens were looking like fields of saffron. The small bridge connecting Salimgarh to the palace was hosting a group of dancers, their bejeweled forms in silken splendor reflected in the moat surrounding the bridge, shimmering and shuddering. Bahadur Shah Zafar seated on a grand scale under the noble gateways was being weighed against seven kinds of grain, butter, gold, coral and silver. After this weighing ceremony all these items were to be distributed amongst the poor.

"My head has got used to resting on my love's knees
Propped on a pillow, it never feels at ease."

This couplet escaped Bahadur Shah Zafar's lips as if he himself was its author. Watching bales of grain on the other side of the scale, his gaze was alighting on Ghalib. "More than a year since Momin passed away and my thoughts still wear the rags of mourning for his talent. His poems are still alive in my memory, yet I can't recall how he died. Refresh my memory, Ghalib, while I go through this arduous task of weighing ceremony."

"He fell from the roof of his house, Zil-e-Subhani, and broke his arm and shoulder." Ghalib began with a touch of sadness. "After the accident he predicted that he would die either in five days, or five months or five years. He died exactly five months after the accident."

"Now I recall, there was eclipse of the moon the same year." Bahadur Shah Zafar's gaze was floating over the ocean of his poets and courtiers without seeing. "Even the luminaries mourned the death of that poet."

"He lives in his poems, Zil-e-Subhani." Zauq consoled with a spurt of animation, reciting a quatrain of Momin.

"Accursed by shallowness if I expect
I will win over my love if my rival I deride
For long we heard the name of Momin, today, at last
We actually saw this poet of poets, a name respected high."

"Death is hovering over this continent like a plague. I can smell its reek." Bahadur Shah prophesied suddenly, watching vats of butter on other side of the scale. I don't mean natural death but the death of a nation. Strange this feeling? Recently I learnt what Baji Rao said a few months before his death. *At last I understand the mystery why British are successful in conquering India. They could always rely on the active*
collaboration of thousands of Indians who, for a variety of reasons are willing to cooperate with those whom they see as their masters."

"Baji Rao would have gathered more kernels of understanding, had he lived a few more years, Zil-e-Subhani." Ahsanullah Khan was swift in voicing his opinion. "For both Hindus and Muslims the success in war is a mark of divine favor, as it is for Christians a divine act of providence. Our own people have begun to think that Company's army is unbeatable."

"Our expectations then are making the British bold and boastful, Zil-e-Subhani." Mahbub Ali Khan commented. "At the second Sikh war in Ferozepur, General Gough was heard congratulating his men for having triumphed where Alexander had failed. Though I believe he would be the first one to admit that the price for that victory was enormous, entailing heavy losses of life and armament."

"There is no dearth of armaments for their army." Bahadur Shah Zafar was heaving a sigh of relief to see the piles of coral being removed from the scale to be replaced with the nuggets of gold. "Their latest invention is a mini rifle which can shoot up to a range of thousand yards, swiftly and accurately."

"They may be succeeding in making guns, Zil-e-Subhani, but are failing in their construction projects." Azad was keen to share his own bulletin of news which he was going to print in his Delhi Newspaper. "They are running into debt in building the Calcutta-Agra-Delhi line. Even their own aides-de-camp Charles Napier is protesting that the Company has made very little progress in the improvement of India. He is repeating the sentiment of a railway engineer who had warned him four years ago and is warning him even now. *Brilliant as is the prestige of our Company which hangs over our Indian empire, it must be confessed that it is still in a state of helpless and discreditable barbarism. Many, many centuries behind the example set by any other nation in civilized history."*

"Despite the slow progress of the Company, the Indians are hopeful and applauding the giant projects of the Britishers." Bahadur Shah Zafar heaved another sigh of relief at the replacement of silver after the gold was scooped out, the last precious metal in the rites of this weighing ceremony. "A few years ago an Indian postal official appealed to the general public in this vein: *The honor, the dignity and the glory of the Imperial Britain are vested in this project. A magnificent system of railway communications would present a series of public monuments vastly surpassing in real grandeur. The aqueducts of Rome, the Pyramids of Egypt, the great wall of China, palaces, the monuments and mausoleums of the great Moghuls, not merely of intelligence and power, but of utility and beneficence."*

"A great gift, this sentiment, Zil-e-Subhani, to the swelling self-esteem of the Britain's might and majesty." Prince Mirza Quaish suppressed a derisive chuckle. "Peasant riots are on the rise. Due to drought not much is growing. Hired hands are protesting against the lack of money and justice. Injustice and corruption is running rampant in villages. Local insurgents have taken law into their own hands. Murder comes cheap with a reward of religious merit. People are talking about one holy man who had sought the aid of Mapillas—a secretarian group of poor Muslims, telling them that they would go to heaven if they could murder a Hindu landlord who had evicted a poor tenant. Moneylenders are suffering the most brutal of punishments. One moneylender's limbs were hacked off one by one by the insurgents while they chanted, *four annas, eight annas, twelve annas,* before chopping his head off and saying *good-riddance."*

"Where are the British officers while natives drink the blood of their own brethren?" Was Bahadur Shah Zafar's aghast query as he got down from the scale, squinting against the sudden shaft of sunlight.

"They are busy supervising the torture chambers of their own design, Zil-e-Subhani." Prince Mirza Quaish seemed drunk by his own font of secret knowledge known only to a privileged few. "A sure way of procuring evidence and confession they resort to such punishments as crushing the testicles of the prisoners, pardon my boldness, Zil-e-Subhani. Immersion to the point of drowning is another one, also suspension of arms. Or insertion of a chewing insect into the prisoner's naval. A very common one, the rape of the prisoner's wife in front of him."

"Most bestial and inhuman of tortures! What has the poor wife done to suffer the defilement of her body and soul?" Bahadur Shah Zafar's features were washed by pallor, almost the color of robes worn by the nobles. "A few decades ago, almost thirty years from now—how time defies the dictates of time." He began to stroll toward the garden flanked by two round towers, princes and noblemen following. "Yes, thirty years ago, natives were the ones devising their own methods of torture. Great waves of unrest and turmoil. *Each man according to his own power and influence,* as this saying became popular amongst the powerful and the tyrannous. Suspects were whipped to obtain confession. Notoriety alone was enough to condemn a bandit to death. Patels had the power to flog wrongdoers. And the most hideous of the punishments by the high-ranking Maratha chiefs, sentencing the man to be blown at the mouth of a cannon, or to be trampled to death under the feet of an elephant." His feet were coming to a sudden halt close to the bridge where his own elephant stood garlanded and bedizened. "Ah, my beauty, my faithful one! Didn't I purchase you from Mirza Latif Bakhsh and since then you have become companion of my heart?" He murmured, letting his jeweled hand be caressed by the powerful snout of his elephant Maula Bakhsh.

"Your birthday, Zil-e-Subhani, and you look so sad." Prince Jawan Bakht said precociously. "Maybe poetry would make you happy?"

"No, my sweet Prince, no poetry session today." A spontaneous gale of laughter escaped the lips of Bahadur Shah Zafar. "Music and laughter in the air and the skills of the jugglers and the dancing girls. What else can an old king want from the world?" He stroked the jeweled dagger slung at the Prince's waist. "We would witness the dance of flowers against the gurgling of fountains, my Prince. Explore the circular bastions against the red granite walls and then walk through the arched bridge to return to the palace for a grand feast." He resumed his stroll, Prince Jawan Bakht beside him walking jauntily, joined by Prince Abul Bakr.

"Prince Jawan Bakht is right, Zil-e-Subhani, we should have a poetry session in honor of your birthday." Prince Khizr Sultan proposed, keeping pace with the king to his right, Ghulam Abbas following.

"What's the use, my Prince. Poetry of life being choked here by annexations by the British." Bahadur Shah Zafar's thoughts were crushed by a subtle assault of melancholia.

"A little respite here, Zil-e-Subhani. The attention of the British Government is drawn to our eastern neighbor, the kingdom of Burma and its annexation." Prince Khizr Sultan responded non-chalantly.

"What?" Bahadur Shah Zafar declared involuntarily. His gaze was lured toward the terrace flanked by fountains against the swath of purple and orange in bougainvillea. "The Anglo-Burmese war twenty-seven years ago. The British were victorious, yet they entrusted the kingdom into the hands of Burmese, and now annexation?"

"I thought you knew, Zil-e-Subhani. I was merely commenting." Prince Khizr Sultan looked flustered.

"Of course I know, though I am getting forgetful." Bahadur Shah Zafar admitted reluctantly. "It has been a year since the British stormed the Rangoon Pagoda, occupying Pegu. The big news at that time was that the naval escort to that expedition was Jane Austin's brother introducing English literature. Though details escape me. Won't you refresh the king's memory, my Prince?" His feet were guiding him toward the arched bridge cradling Jamna waters, gilded copper by sunshine.

"You know more than I do, Zil-e-Subhani. I didn't even know about the first Anglo-Burmese war." Prince Khizr Sultan laughed heedlessly. "You are right about the British storming the Rangoon Pagoda. It all started when the English merchants appealed to the king of Ava against incessant acts of atrocity and oppression by their government toward the English investors who were keen on trade and ship-building industry. The king of Ava ignored their pleas and when the English proposed to sign a treaty with a view of stopping oppression, the king refused. That's when the war commenced amidst a flurry of hostilities. The British won and annexed the province of Pegu as their dearly-won portion of British territories."

"The greed and ambition of the Britishers portends gloom and doom." Bahadur Shah Zafar kept strolling, waving now and then at the dancers, musicians and well-wishers. "Annexation of Rangoon is a new beginning, they want to be the masters of the world. I hope Mulla Majasi and his family are safe since they are now settled in Rangoon. I have a feeling we are all going to be sucked into the pandemonium of warring factions. Jhansi annexed too and Lakshami Bai bitter and rebellious. Her husband died recently I know. When did her son die and who did she adopt?" He asked no one in particular.

"Damodar Rao, Rani's son died when he was only four months old, Zil-e-Subhani." Prince Mirza Mughal from behind stepped forward, proud to recall details of two years hence. "Then Raja and Rani adopted Anand Rao the son of their cousin, changing his name to Damodar Rao. Though, Raja of Jhansi never recovered from his grief. After his death, Lord Dalhousie under the protection of his Doctrine of Lapse rejects the legitimacy of the adopted son. Jhansi, you already know, is annexed and Rani is in absolute mood of defiance."

"Another defiant person in the game of Lapse, Zil-e-Subhani, is the adopted son of Baji Rao, Nana Sahib." Prince Fakhroo couldn't be left behind, still feeling guilty siding with the British secretly. "Almost two years since Baji Rao passed away and Nana Sahib is struggling to claim his legacy. Baji Rao, during his exile, used to receive every year a pension of eighty thousand rupees from the East India Company, but after his death all payments ceased. Lord Dalhousie refuses to accept Nana Sahib as legal heir since he was adopted. Nana Sahib is angry and belligerent, demanding the pension late Peshwa used to receive. Now he is sending Azimullah Khan to England to plead his case with the Board of Control or with British Government or anyone who is willing to listen."

"Lords have become beggars!" Bahadur Shah Zafar declared without bitterness. "Since we are wearing saffron robes, might as well hold a staff, get a beggar's bowl and go begging for alms to sustain our tattered empires." He laughed suddenly. "Poor Raja of Nagpur died without an issue too this very year. Quite an insignificant event, not worthy of notice, but noticed by Lord Dalhousie who was quick to annex late Raja's kingdom—one and a half times the size of newly annexed districts in the Punjab." His thoughts were lost in the din of cheers from people in the boat who had recognized the king on the bridge in his regalia of crown and jewels.

"They know it's your birthday, Zil-e-Subhani, and are sending their blessings." Mustafa Khan Shefta caught their warm sentiments before their voices could become clear.

"How very gratifying." Bahadur Shah Zafar murmured gratefully. "Most Europeans used to think that religion, not politics ruled the Indian people. Also that Indians don't care who ruled them—they thought, their own Rajas, Muslims or Europeans? To them, they seemed so jaded and fatalistic in their desires, so could be safely ignored. That was a false judgment. Now Britishers are shocked to discover how bitterly the subjects of even the most dissolute of rulers grieve when Lord Dalhousie dissolves their dynasties."

"They would not be shocked, Zil-e-Subhani, if they could deign to ask any ruling Raja as to the cause of bitterness." Ghalib could not help but share his own portion of wisdom. "They would easily find out that Indians need to have amongst them a figure whom they could revere, a king in their midst and a king from their own people."

"A burden too heavy for any king, old and young if he is chosen to fulfill their expectations while alien forces loom high and mighty." Bahadur Shah Zafar intoned profoundly, leaving behind the arched bridge and entering the palace grounds of Red Fort. "A birthday feast with my family might slough off the burden of such heavy thoughts. "Come, princes, Rang Mahal is the abode of our evening celebration." He beckoned almost cheerfully.

The birthday feast had ended a couple of hours ago, but Rang Mahal was still feasting on music and parlance. Dancing girls too with studs in their noses and tilaks on their foreheads were nimble on their toes close to Nahr-i-Bhisht. Piles of gifts lay neglected at Bahadur Shah Zafar's feet as he sat with Zeenat Mahal on a velvety couch shaded by a gold canopy. Davenports dripping with velvets were occupied by his other wives, perfumed and bejeweled. Lolling against satiny pillows were princes and princesses, jesting and laughing. Brightly lit chandelier under the gilded ceiling was casting fantastic shadows and polishing the jewels of the ladies to surreal radiance.

"What do I hear, Zil-e-Subhani, Americans establishing a Christian village in Farrukhabad?" Zeenat Mahal catching snippets of parlance amongst the princes voiced her own curiosity. "Missionaries from America, encouraging their own kind to inter-marry so that they could breed new Christians for the mission. Is India going to espouse the cause of Christianity and become a Christian empire?"

"Unlikely as it is, Beloved, it could happen, though." Bahadur Shah Zafar indulged amusedly. "It took two hundred and fifty years to convert the Roman Empire and it would take many centuries for India to be converted to Christianity, if ever?"

"It is obvious, Zile-e-Subhani, they are most fertile in breeding and rearing. And if they keep going at this rate, it would be a few years, not centuries before this continent can claim the cross of Christianity." Prince Fakhroo abandoned his discussion with the princes in favor of this interesting topic. "Gathering orphans from the streets, they get them married rapidly, breeding a battalion of workers. In North India, they have even opened a tent factory run by that new breed of Christians. Within a couple of years, they have grossed over sixty thousand rupees."

"Their dedication is commendable though, my Prince." Bahadur Shah Zafar intoned thoughtfully. "When they gather ragged droves of orphans from the roadside, they feed them, educate them and then marry them. There was a hunting ground Rakha in Farrukhabad where they opened a school and a carpet factory. Sad and unfortunate for the missionaries though since most of them get so diseased and debilitated that they die before their missionary duties are fulfilled."

"Their priests and Chaplins and Grecian little churches, Zil-e-Subhani, they survive most admirably I have heard." Zeenat Mahal scoffed with a tinkling of mirth. "Only their wives die young, suffering the ravages of ill hygiene and child-bearing."

"India with its pantheon of gods and goddesses could never embrace any foreign faith." Mubarak Nisa Begum flung this comment with a little toss of her head. "Centuries of Muslim rule and Hindus are still Hindus. Diversity is the creed over here and no one should feel threatened by foreign faiths, not even Muslims."

"And yet they do!" Ashraf Begum began with a sudden vehemence. "Hindus as well as Muslims have begun to voice their fears now that the prime aim of every Englishman is to convert all to Christianity, so that they could rule the entire world."

"Baseless canards, my Beauty. It's not befitting that my wives indulge in such gossip." Bahadur Shah Zafar's tone was rather stern. "In politics one can take liberties, but religion is a delicate subject where one needs to tread with great caution."

"Politics too, Zil-e-Subhani, is a delicate subject since it incites hatred and rebellion." Akhtar Begum sang haughtily, unintimidated by the stern expression of the king. "Nana Sahib's close friend Tatya Tope has become a sworn enemy of the British since Lord Dalhousie has deprived Nana Sahib of his father's pension."

"Many claim to be the sworn enemy of the British, my Dear, but they dare not acknowledge that in the open." A pale smile hovered over the mustachioed lips of Bahadur Shah Zafar. "Another close friend of Nana Sahib, though no friend of the British has agreed to woo the British for reinstatement of funds. Azimullah Khan is his name and he is on his way to London to claim the legacy of Nana's father. The pension which Baji Rao received when he was alive, now truncated, is making Nana Sahib furious, though he feels helpless."

"Such morbid topics, Zil-e-Subhani. Your birthday today. We should be reciting poetry and entertaining happy thoughts." Princess Raunaq Zamani broke her seal of silence.

"Ah, my lovely Granddaughter!" Bahadur Shah Zafar exclaimed cheerfully. "You are right of course. But my poetry sessions are with my court poets. And none over here is ever interested in poetry."

"We are, we are!" Several voices from begums and princesses were raised in unison.

"If you would recite one of your poems, Zil-e-Subhani, it would be your gift to us on your birthday." Rabeya Begum teased sweetly.

"Since I got so many gifts, dear Princess, it behooves me to reward you with something which can't be purchased." He smiled at his daughter before reciting.

"Buried in dust, alas, lies many a beauteous shape
Mirror-like the footprints watch the passing show amazed
See the handiwork of God, His wondrous praise
What varied humans He has made from a fistful of clay
When we saw the spirit divine everywhere preside
The difference between mosque and shrine at once got erased
We depart from the earth loaded with the weight of sins
Setting out for the world beyond, see the baggage that we take

Despite knowing everything, you persist in silly ways
We regret your attitude, your ignorance, O Zafar, bewail"
He closed his eyes, his expression soft and tranquil.

A cheerful applause followed by requests was over-whel-ming Bahadur Shah Zafar as he sat there smiling and demurring.

"One more poem, Zil-e-Subhani, and we would importune no more." Princess Fatima Sultan requested sweetly, knowing that the king would not deny her request since she was the most favorite of his daughters.

"I don't have the heart to deny you anything, my Love, but I would rather spill well-preserved pearls from the songs of my court poets." Bahadur Shah Zafar smiled tenderly. "In the memory of Momin who died young. Here are the precious pearls straight from his heart.

> *"I am afraid of your wrath, for your grace, I pray*
> *I am not scared of hell, nor seek the Elysian gate*
> *How can I stop praying to you for my needs, O God*
> *For in prayer lies subsumed the power of your grace*
> *I should dedicate my merit wholly to the Prophet's gaze*
> *Let my wonder-dazed heart reflect my zeal for my race*
> *Turn me to a dagger sharp, so that by its glint and glaze*
> *I may break into bits, the hearts full of spite and hate*
> *I am a humble slave of the brave Muslim brigade*
> *I intend to rule over the bands of seraphic race."*

"How sad. Poetry makes me weep." Zeenat Mahal murmured, her eyes sparkling with some sort of fear nameless.

"Why, Beloved! Poetry is sublime manifestation of God's own creative energy." Bahadur Shah Zafar caught and held the glint of fear from her eyes into his own. "What is this fear lurking behind your beautiful eyes?"

"Strange feeling, Zil-e-Subhani. I can't explain." Zeenat Mahal was flustered all of a sudden. "For a moment I caught some sort of glimpse of carnage and devastation in Delhi. Then everything vanished in a fog. You were divested of all your jewels and I was wearing only rags."

"Sorry, Beloved, if Momin's poetry evoked such terrible delusions." Bahadur Shah Zafar's look was piercing, his own heart thundering. "We are all tired, it's time we rested." He got to his feet. "Come, Zeenat, we will comfort each other in sleep." He escorted her out gently out of this room toward this vast bedchamber on the west side.

90

Chapter Seven
Mourning at Red Fort Palace

This sultry afternoon the spacious parlor of Moti Mahal inside the Red Fort Palace of Delhi was hosting Zeenat Mahal and Bahadur Shah Zafar. This palace seemed to be mourning like the rest of the palaces in this fortress since the death of Prince Fakhroo and Prince Mirza Quaish, both dying suddenly within a few days apart. But its marble floor furnished with rugs—the finest from Persia and Bokhara was lending the luxury of comfort and coolness. Bahadur Shah Zafar had taken off his turban with jeweled crown which he had worn during the morning ceremony of prayers and was to wear it again in the afternoon during the session with his poets and viziers. He was seated on a davenport, his head pressed between his jeweled hands. Opposite him on velvety couch sat Zeenat Mahal in white silks and adorned with pearls. Her gaze was caressing her king-husband with a mingling of love and sadness. She could neither fathom the depth of his grief, nor of the grief of the grieving queens in Rang Mahal, but her own young heart was longing for some semblance of peace and solace.

"I have never seen you grieve thus, Zil-e-Subhani, though you have lost other children before." Zeenat Mahal sought her husband's attention. "I know losing two sons within a week, it's terrible. Prince Mirza Quaish was quite young when his mother passed away I have heard, so I think now he has joined his mother in heaven. Yet you grieve thus, because you think Prince Fakhroo was poisoned?"

"No, Beloved, no!" A cry of agony escaped the lips of Bahadur Shah Zafar, his jeweled hands falling limp into his lap. "He died of cholera, I know for sure, as did Prince Mirza Quaish. Can't convince Taj Mahal, though. Well, the grieving mother. I have no energy to console her anymore. She has lost her mind it seems. It has been a week since we buried our beloved princes near the shrine of Qutubddin Kaki and Taj Mahal still thinks that Prince Fakhroo is making her suffer the agonies of wait and refuses to come home. I can't endure her grief and the sorrow of my other wives. That's why I don't visit Rang Mahal anymore. I think I have ceased to live."

"How selfish, Zil-e-Subhani!" Zeenat Mahal protested sweetly. "What about me? Prince Jawan Bakht and your other sons and daughters. We all need you."

"You are the reason I exist, Beloved. Without you I would surely die." Bahadur Shah Zafar murmured contritely. "You are so young and beautiful. And so very graciously maintain the aura of freshness amidst all these tragedies. Since Prince Fakhroo's death I see death everywhere. Strange, my heart grieving for deaths yet to come. My court poets too are being snatched by the hands of death. Zauq died a year ago, or is it year and a half?

"Close to year and a half, Zil-e-Subhani." Zeenat Mahal murmured back. "Now I understand, you are still grieving for the poet, Zil-e-Subhani, since I hear you recite his poetry so often."

"Grief piled high over kingdoms dear and lost." Bahadur Shah Zafar suppressed a sigh against one flicker of a wan smile. "I am glad Zauq didn't live to see Oudh annexed, or he would have gone stark mad with grief. He died one year before Lord Dalhousie's masterstroke on the eve of his departure from India when he annexed Oudh. Newly appointed General James Outram condemned the kingdom of Oudh as a den of thugs and sycophants. Though James Outram was ordered by Lord Dalhousie to send an ultimatum to the king of Oudh Wajid Shah to sign over the administration of Oudh to the Company, or the British would take it by force. The king's mother pleaded with James Outram to give her kingly son one chance to rule wisely, but he wouldn't budge as advised by Lord Dalhousie. Depressed as he was, the king wept and pleaded, baring his head which embarrassed James Outram, though he was not moved to compassion. Hazrat Mahal the queen of Wajid Shah urged her husband to disregard the ultimatum for the sake of their son Birjis Qadra—heir to the throne of Oudh. Wajid Shah, heeding his wife's counsel refused to sign over his kingdom to the Company, but it was forcibly occupied and annexed."

"William Sleeman was the general of Oudh before James Outram as I recall, Zil-e-Subhani." Zeenat Mahal reminisced aloud. "Harem gossip, but it's true he was heard saying that the kingdom of Oudh is given up to crime, havoc and anarchy by the misrule of government at once corrupt and imbecile. Also true as he was heard saying that the Government should remove the king's chubby, bejeweled fingers from the reins of power and set up a council of regency with himself at its head."

"Harem gossip or not, Beloved, his claim is refuted by the simple fact that the people of Oudh preferred the slandered regime of the king to the grasping but rose-colored government of the Company." Bahadur Shah Zafar began with a subtle whiff of animation. "The annexation is accompanied by violence and spoliation wholly indefensible. The foundation of all property is unsettled to an extent unheard of under any civilized rule. The landowners are dispossessed. The Company is dealing with the kingdom as if it is not only entitled to its revenues, but to all its property, the spoils of war under their bow and spear. In fact, it is obvious that to them Oudh has become an uninhabited island newly discovered solely for their own pleasure to do what pleases them."

"What else can we expect, Zil-e-Subhani, the British have wired the map of India in one cohesive unit of mobility." Zeenat Mahal consoled smoothly. "Lord Dalhousie alone masterminded the railway lines. New telegraph lines are stretched from Agra to Calcutta to Peshawar. The uniform rate of postage has made people to communicate quicker. Seven hundred and fifty-three post offices in India, a gigantic task."

"Much too gigantic as to undo what they have done with their accomplishments, Beloved." Bahadur Shah Zafar pressed his temples once again as if to refresh his memory. "In the beginning those post offices had supplied free postage stamps to the sepoys which are now being whittled away along with their wartime allowances. To add to the unhappiness of the sepoys, the Company is enforcing the General Service Enlistment Act which requires that they should be prepared to serve abroad, not understanding the fact that crossing the Black Water is forbidden to orthodox high-class Hindus. You don't know of course that during the second Anglo-Burmese war the sepoys were commanded to cross the sea to Rangoon. The Hindus refused of course and their kind general Colonel Tyler informed Lord Dalhousie that in respect of their religion he can't force his men to cross the sea. Lord Dalhousie, in response, as a punishment forced the entire regiment to march by land, not to Rangoon, but to Dacca. Within five months only three men survived, the rest perished due to excessive heat and exhaustion."

"So terrible and tragic, Zil-e-Subhani. I am glad I don't know much." Zeenat Mahal confessed unabashedly. "New policies make me shudder and I have lost interest in politics."

"Poetry is dearer to me than politics." Bahadur Shah Zafar was trying to slough off his sadness. "If events were summed up in poetry, my memory would be revived a thousand-fold. Strange that this poem after the first Sikh war is coming to my mind, reminiscent of the daggers of conceit by British soldiers.

"We lately tamed the Afghan's pride
And now rolls down a fiercer blood
The clarion sounds, the cannons boom—
Unfurl the banner of St. George
Their cry blasphemes the name of God—
Allah, Allah, wild hurrahs
Respond—"

"I like William Thackeray's description of India, Zil-e-Subhani than the poetry of British pride." Zeenat Mahal was grateful of this diversion. "Gorgeous East of Thackeray's genius—a fairytale land where Sultans sit on ivory thrones, fanned by Peacock wings in palaces paved with jasper and onyx."

"While English poets and writers sing of India's fabled riches—though it was rich beyond imagination at one time, its weavers sing of their plight." Bahadur Shah Zafar was holding on to the tapestry of his poems.

"Every jilt of the town
Gets a calico gown
Our own manufactures are out of fashion."

"I fear, Zil-e-Subhani, we would be jilted out of our own royal lineage if we didn't act swiftly." Zeenat Mahal's eyes were gathering clouds of fear all of a sudden. "I know the loss of Prince Mirza Quaish and Prince Fakhroo is still heavy on your shoulders, but we must choose an heir to the throne before the British deprive us of our royal heritage."

"Grief as well as the burden of duty has been heavy within my heart and on my shoulders, Beloved." Bahadur Shah Zafar breathed tenderly. "I have already written a letter to Colonel Frazier appointing Prince Jawan Bakht heir to the throne. He is the legitimate heir, I have stated, gifted with all the endowments, qualifications and virtuous habits necessary for a prince. He has turned fourteen and has obtained complete education under my guidance. In postscript I have written that rest of my sons has no comparison with him, Prince Jawan Bakht alone merits my favor."

"It has been quite a while, Zil-e-Subhani, since the engagement of Prince Jawan Bakht and his father-in-law is anxious to set the wedding date." Zeenat Mahal began reluctantly. "I shouldn't be mentioning it now, but Mahmud Khan has made several trips from Malagarh, expressing his wish to finalize the marriage plans. Prince Jawan Bakht too loves Princess Kulsum and is eager to get married."

"Yes, Beloved, an heir to the throne needs his own heir to the throne, hoping that the Crown of the Moghuls is not snatched away by the British most savagely and blatantly. Settle the wedding date between a week to a month. We can't afford pomp and ceremony since our funds are miserably depleted." Bahadur Shah Zafar donned his turban and crown before getting to his feet, his heart heavy with presage. "Poets and viziers are waiting for me in the Sawan Pavilion and I must not keep them waiting for long. Poetry mixed with politics has become quite pungent to my taste, yet I try to sweeten it with hope, swallowing both bitterness and sweetness." He claimed her hand, kissing it reverently. "You are my sweetness. Stay here, Beloved, till I return." He plodded out of the room, forlorn and despondent.

Evening shadows in Sawan Pavilion seemed to be descending early as Bahadur Shah Zafar presided over the company of his poets and viziers. Sated with the news of unrest and dejection he had resigned himself to listening rather than actively participating. There was no royal protocol in this pavilion, though he was seated on a gilt chair. All ceremony was missing as usual in such a gathering, but more so this evening amidst clouds of uncertainty and hopelessness. Men in plumed turbans seated on Persian carpets were either too drunk with the sense of their own ideation or afflicted with the fever of pessimism to voice any opinion against the dilemma of kings deposed and kingdoms annexed.

"Prince Fakhroo used to give me ten rupees a month to buy fruit for my two adopted boys. Who will give me that now?" Ghalib lamented suddenly, his look glazed.

"So, you are lamenting the loss of funds, not the loss of my prince, my venerable poet." One ripple of a sad accusation trembled upon the lips of Bahadur Shah Zafar.

"That's not true, Zil-e-Subhani, I grieve for the dear, dear loss of both the princes, especially of my royal pupil. A great blow to me personally." Ghalib protested bitterly. "After the demise of Zauq you appointed me as your personal guide and granted me the privilege of tutoring Prince Fakhroo. Eternally grateful I am of such honors, so precious and priceless."

"And yet after the death of Zauq I heard you exclaim, Ghalib. *The Moghul princes gather in the Red Fort and recite their ghazals. The court will not last long many more days. How can it be permanent? Who knows if they will meet tomorrow and if they do, whether they will meet after that? The assembly can vanish at any moment.*" Bahadur Shah reminisced aloud.

"That was when you were ill, Zil-e-Subhani." Was Ghalib's flustered response. "When Zauq was alive, didn't I plead? Look at your slave, my song has all the power of fire. Turn your attention towards me as my skill demands. Treasure me as the apple of your eye and open your heart for me to enter. See my perfection, look upon my skill, my presence alone bears witness that your age excels Akbar's."

"Yes, always in clouds, extolling your own skill and inspiration." Bahadur Shah Zafar commented, rather commiserated. "Your self-worth and self-aggrandizement fetch you nothing but misfortunes. After the death of Prince Fakhroo you were heard saying, *he who appreciated my worth has died.* Well, your fortunes are linked with mine. As long as I live, you will benefit from my favors. After I am gone I don't know who will take care of whom?"

"May you live long, Zil-e-Subhani." Ghalib murmured wretchedly. "I am sending a letter to Queen Victoria. You are going to hear about its contents sooner or later so I might as well reveal those to you now. After praising the Queen I have written that truly great rulers of history rewarded their poets and well-wishers by filling their mouths with pearls, weighing them in gold and granting them villages and estates in recompense. In the same way it is the duty of the exalted Queen to present me with a robe of honor and allot me pension."

"Unfortunately, your request would go unheeded like the requests of others many times before. Even the so-called affable Azimullah Khan failed to secure pension for Nana Sahib." Bahadur Shah Zafar intoned against some burden of sorrow and compassion. "Much like a great adventurer he has returned home a

96

few months ago. Despite his failure he was embraced by Nana Sahib. Chuni Lal here has been keeping abreast of all his moves and he would be glad to relate his adventures to our benefit." He bestowed a kind smile upon the news writer.

"I am surprised to see him sitting here, Zil-e-Subhani." Ghalib was startled by this discovery and amused. "Since he is converted to Christianity, many demanded that he shouldn't attend the court."

"There is no cause for shame for what he has done and he is always welcome in my court and in my palace." Bahadur Shah Zafar's gaze was sweeping over all with a subtle challenge. "Come, Chuni Lal, with all your graciousness, tell us about the adventures of Azimullah Khan."

"Your graciousness, Zil-e-Subhani, has granted me the privilege of staying here and I would be delighted to recount what I can remember." Chuni Lal bowed his head in gratitude. "And if I forget, I know of more who would fill the gaps. Well, supplied with fifty thousand pounds from Nana Sahib and spending lavishly Azimullah Khan couldn't help but attract the elite in London. Was very fortunate in meeting Lucie Duff the wife of the Prime Minister's cousin whose husband served as an usher to the Queen. Lucie Duff, all the newspapers in London boldly write, took Azimullah Khan under her wings and introduced him to great writers like Dickens, Tennyson, Thackeray, Carlyle, Meredith and Macaulay. But before that he had landed in East India House of the Company's Grecian headquarters on Leadenhall Street. He was received by a utilitarian philosopher by the name of John Stuart Mill who was pessimistic about overturning the edict of *no pension*, yet was kind enough to introduce him to Lucie Duff. Azimullah Khan's mission appeared to be a social success as far as his being entertained in the drawing-rooms of London, but it turned to be utter failure in not gaining even the crumbs of any kind of allowance for Nana Sahib. After spending tens of thousands of Nana Sahib's pounds for hiring lawyers, bribing clerks, entertaining dignitaries, or sending gifts of shawls and jewels to the wives of Company's functionaries, he was doomed to failure. He had exhausted all venues of appeal and was constrained to return to his master of dwindling means, no other than Nana Sahib."

"No one can suspect Nana Sahib of dwindling means as long as he keeps entertaining Europeans with the generosity of

Hatim Tai." Bahadur Shah Zafar began thoughtfully. "Not too long ago he greeted one English attorney by the name of Lang on the road with an escort of eight soldiers, their swords drawn, and four cavalrymen making their horses cavort and prance. Later, Lang was treated to a sumptuous feast. Gratefully, Lang would often tell his friends that Nana Sahib never mentioned his own grievances, but did talk of the sad plight of Oudh affair."

"The British though enjoying Nana Sahib's hospitality, Zil-e-Subhani, are not congenial and quite scornful behind his back." Abdur Rahman a new courier from Agra was quick to unleash his bulletin of news. "A couple of years ago when they invited Nana Sahib at the opening ceremony of Cawnpore Telegraph Office, they graciously inducted him into the local Masonic Lodge Harmony. But soon after this they didn't want to be a part of his lavish parties. Whispering behind his back that like all Indian princes he carries the parasitic vestiges of a degenerate past, lazy, dull and useless."

"Every man to his own perception." Bahadur Shah Zafar commented profoundly. "Looking through Azimullah Khan's eyes, British workers or professionals fare not much better than Indian princes. After visiting London with imminent failure in sight he cried prophetically. *If God has chosen Britain to rule the world, why is it entirely populated by shopkeepers, dilettantes, bureaucrats, and their foolish, corruptible wives?* I guess he saw the ghastly conditions of English men, women and children working in the mills and the mines. On his way back from London he stopped at Constantinople, contemplating with dread if the Company intended to displace India's continuity and graciousness and pastoral simplicity with a dark world of gears and roaring engines and blinding fogs, so very thick and poisonous. To allay his fears, he stopped at the battlefield of Crimea, watching the slow return march of tired British soldiers. Wondering this time, where could be the Britain's brave soldiers, their conquering generals and their inexhaustible supply of armaments? Crying in utter hopelessness. *Isn't it sheer brazenness that this mole on the body of man has almost convinced India that its power is infinite and its armies inexhaustible?* And why are you grinning so besottedly, Ahmed Beg?" He asked the newly arrived courier from Mehrauli.

"Pardon me, Zil-e-Subhani, but a strange snippet of conversation between Lang and Nana Sahib flashed through my mind. Though, it's not funny." Was Ahmed Beg's flustered response.

"Nothing funny or lighthearted anymore, but we want to hear it just the same." Bahadur Shah Zafar commanded. "It might fetch a few chuckles if not cheers."

"Might, Zil-e-Subhani, I am hoping." Ahmed Beg obeyed promptly. "One morning Nana Sahib served Lang all English breakfast of Yorkshire pie, anchovy toast, mutton-chop steak, sardines and Forman and Mason marmalade. After breakfast he took him for a drive in Cawnpore in his handsome landau driven by English horses, and guided by two men and five retainers. They had barely driven half a mile when Nana Sahib exclaimed with a sigh. Once I owned a much better carriage than this one, almost worth twenty-five thousand rupees, but I had to burn it and kill the horses. The astounded Lang could only murmur, why? Nana Sahib sighed again, explaining that he had loaned that carriage to a Cawnpore sahib to bring his sick child to Bithoor for a change of air, but the child died. *So the carriage was defiled and I couldn't use it.* Lang couldn't help asking why he didn't give the carriage to a Muslim or a Christian. To which Nana Sahib simply said. *For then the sahib might have seen the carriage in another's possession and his feelings would have been hurt at having occasioned me such a loss.*"

"The sensibilities of a Brahmin are incomprehensible, Zil-e-Subhani." Mahbub Ali Khan chuckled just to please the king. "In his harem Nana Sahib keeps a dancing girl by the name of Bhima and is hopelessly in love with a courtesan by the name of Adala, upon whom he lavishes silks and jewels to win her favor. Though, a couple of years ago he married a Deccani Brahmin girl called Krishna Bhai. Imprisoning her as the gossip goes inside a room with mirrors from floor to ceiling with a trio of Bareilly couches."

"No wonder Indian morality is considered similar to that of the ancient Greeks. Men enamored by enchanting maidens and gods and goddesses weaving spells of wars and amorous seductions." Bahadur Shah Zafar's eyes were lit up with a sudden fire of nostalgic gleam. "During the reign of my grandfather one anthropologist by the name of James Forbes—amazing how I remember this and forget little things of daily occurrence, wrote a report about Indian culture and mannerism. Placing Indians on a far higher plane of civilization than American Indians, praising our native Indians for their accomplishments in poetry, painting and architecture."

"Those were the days of the white Moghuls, Zil-e-Subhani, when British soldiers participated in our entertainments of dancing and wrestling, going from village to village and competing with the best chess players of India." Ahsanullah Khan broke the seal of his silence. "At that time British soldiers could speak our language, attend our dancing parties, went hunting with the rajas and the maharajas, enjoying lavish feasts in their palaces and inviting them to their homes in return. Now the sepoys and the officers can't help but notice that many British officers speak to them as if obliged and don't hide their feelings of impatience, dismissing them rudely and as quickly as possible when there is no more need to talk."

"They don't have the time, Ahsanullah, because they are filling their ranks with Sikh and Gurkha soldiers whose fighting skills are impressive." Bahadur Shah Zafar ruminated aloud. "And yet the fanaticism of the Wahhabis is more noticeable than the rudeness or the indifference of the British. Troubles have been brewing slowly but steadily since the death of Wilayat Ali four years hence. Sittana has become a pothole of Wahhabis where his brother Inayat Ali has assumed the imamship of a Fanatic Camp. His first act of aggression was to seize the fort of Kotla from the king of Amber. Then he started the campaign of preaching hatred against the English whom he calls kafirs—the infidels. News of Wahhabi built-up in Sittana has reached the ears of British authorities in Lahore and Peshawar. Lord Dalhousie before leaving has issued an Act of Amnesty. The fanatics of Sittana are given one month to turn themselves in. If they did so, they would be given ten rupees each to cover their expenses and a safe-conduct back to their homes. If they failed to surrender they should expect no mercy."

"That Amnesty Act is backfiring, Zil-e-Subhani." Azad commenced avidly. "Mullas are angry and defiant since a notice has been issued that any Indian or British subject found in arms would be imprisoned for three years and shackled in solitary confinement. The Mullas have redoubled their propaganda campaign. Circulating the incendiary ode of Niyamatullah which was actually written in twelfth century."

"Pitiful and bizarre since Wahhabis hate poetry and have practically banned listening to music." Bahadur Shah Zafar half groaned, half exclaimed. "What's the ode which has caught their fancy?"

"I have read it so many times, Zil-e-Subhani, I can recite it verbatim." Azad breathed passionately, reciting with great passion.

"Then the Nazarenes will take all Hindustan
They will reign for a hundred years
There will be a great oppression in their reign
For their destruction there will be a king in the west
The king will proclaim a war against the Nazarenes
And in the war a great many people will be killed
The king of the west will be victorious by force
Of the sword in a holy war
And the followers of Jesus would be defeated
In seventeen hundred forty-five this ode is composed
In eighteen hundred fifty-four the king of the west
will appear."

"While Wahhabis are still reciting centuries old odes, Zil-e-Subhani, the Britishers have seized the wind and the wave." Ghalib declared bitterly. "They are sailing their ships under fire and steam. Creating music without the use of mizrab. With their magic, words fly through the air like birds. Air has been set on fire. Cities are being lighted without oil lamps."

"And the fuel of their arrogance is running quicksilver behind the façade of their just laws, Zil-e-Subhani. All beneficial they say?" Ghulam Abbas was ready to attack the guile of the British, equipped with a fistful of rumors. "I hope this is not true, but rumors are rampant that Colonel Frazier has advised Lord Canning that none of the princes should be recognized as heir apparent, least of all Prince Jawan Bakht. He has written personally, it seems, to Lord Canning, that death of Prince Fakhroo five months after the annexation of the rich and independent kingdom of Oudh is a perfect opportunity to prepare Moghuls for the imminent extinction of their line."

"They are waiting for my death, that's quite obvious." Bahadur Shah Zafar got to his feet. "Time for rest and repast. We would meet tomorrow."

"Don't leave us yet, Zil-e-Subhani." Ghalib cried suddenly. "Please recite the poem you wrote after Zauq's death. It would be a talisman to refresh our spirits that we are still the masters of poetry and philosophy, warring with words to win peace, not with swords to woo greed."

"So be it, Ghalib. I too wish to refresh my memory with the gentle-presence of Zauq.

The song-bird of India, my master Zauq
When he took leave of the garden of earth he took
The road to the garden of heaven
If someone inquires about the date of his death, Oh Zafar
Say that Zauq went to heaven because of God's forgiveness
In the year eighteen hundred fifty-five"

Bahadur Shah Zafar plodded past the ocean of cheers as if sleep-walking.

The garden was baring its bosom of beauty and fragrance just for him it seemed, as Bahadur Shah Zafar sauntered toward Rang Mahal, but his mind was communing with his late father. His thoughts were reflecting the poem he had inscribed on the tomb of his father. He could feel the gentle caress of breeze, its very lips murmuring that his words were not erased by the neglect of time.

Akbar Shah who illumines the whole world
Was displayed by fortune like a moon
Zafar has told the date of his passing away
The heaven is the resting place of the noble one
In year eighteen hundred and thirty-seven

Chapter Eight
Fire of Rebellion

Diwan-i-Khas at Delhi this particular evening was dimly lit due to oppressive heat matching the heated discussions of the occupants of the court, rather feverish and tiresome. Bahadur Shah Zafar seated on his Peacock Throne was absorbing all with a sense of foreboding. He had grown melancholy and contemplative, barely noticing two royal servants on either side of him, stirring the air with fans made out of peacock feathers. Three steps down the throne on either side stood poets and courtiers. Bokhara rugs and tapestries adorning the walls seemed more vibrant than before since the hall was packed due to the rumors of sepoys on the verge of sedition against the rule of the British. Scribes, lawyers and historians were a part of this court session, eager and discursive.

"Patna, Lucknow and even in Delhi there are rumors of anger and unrest amongst sepoys against the British. It seems as if the sepoys are ready to overthrow the rule of the Company." Ghulam Abbas was saying.

"If those rumors are true, who could be the ones organizing such a venture on grand scale? Bahadur Shah Zafar emerged from his contemplative state with a dint of inquisition.

"Wahhabis for one, Zil-e-Subhani, have been recruiting and training men to fight the British." Ghulam Abbas was happy to recount what he had heard. "Then partisans and immigrants of Lucknow who have been simmering in rage since their king of Oudh were exiled. Getting wind of the covert designs of various groups and factions, thieves and scoundrels are waiting to be a part of this joint enterprise."

"Wahhabis are the most dangerous of all if the British only knew." Bahadur Shah Zafar demurred aloud. "Although they can be easily identified by their demeanor stern and intimidating. Strange that lacking both intellect and manners those Mullahs attract hordes of zealots who are ready to kill by a mere whiff of their command."

"The Britishers already know, Zil-e-Subhani, since Wahhabis are so vocal about their Sunni Jihad—their mission to kill *infidels* as they deem everyone else who don't believe in their orthodox ideology." Makhund Lal offered his opinion. "Their hotbed of zeal is Sittana where they are constantly in touch with several tribes of Afghanistan.

"This potbelly of intrigues has picked up speed since the beginning of the year." Bahadur Shah Zafar intoned thoughtfully. "So many conflicting news reaching here week after week, month after month. In order to make sense of confusing reports, we must glean facts from rumors month by month to gauge the extent of unrest and antagonism. For the sake of clarity let's explore the month of January, any special events which caused unrest amongst sepoys or general population in India?" He asked of no one in particular.

"I know of one, Zil-e-Subhani." Makhund Lal began exigently before anyone else could respond. "Almost four months now. Yes, it was in the middle of January when Raja Kumar Singh of Patna felt slighted, rather abandoned by the Company though he was always loyal to the British generals. He owned extensive estates in the district of Shahabad, but became debt-ridden due to his own extravagance. The board of revenue of the Bengal Government stepped in to manage his affairs on behalf of his creditors. But the new British Residence Halliday issued an order in January to the board of revenue to stop bailing out Raja Kumar Singh. Since then the Rajput followers of Raja Kumar, noticing the plight of their leader, are simmering in rage to repay the Company with a vengeance of their own as heartless as the decision of the board of revenue to stop all funds to Raja."

"General Halliday! The name sounds familiar." Bahadur Shah reminisced aloud. "Isn't he the one who assured falsely the sepoys of Barrackpore just outside Calcutta that the new cartridges they introduced were not greased with cow and pig fat as suspected by the soldiers? A series of disturbances in Barrackpore due to that, in January I believe. There would have been less objection if the sepoys didn't have to nip off the cartridges with their teeth so that the charge could be ignited by pushing the cartridge down the muzzle of the rifle. But then that's how this new Enfield rifle operates. And then again they could have used some other lubricant, avoiding the sensitive issue of cow fat being abhorrent to the Hindus and pig fat abhorrent to Muslims."

"None of the sepoys believed General Halliday, Zil-e-Subhani. The word being passed from regiment to regiment about the cartridges being greased with cow and pig fat." Zakaullah appeared to be flipping the pages of his own memory. "This event is causing friction even amongst the caste-conscious Hindus. Third week of January, I believe, one low-caste laborer at Dum Dum asked a sepoy for a drink of water from his clay jar. That sepoy being a Brahmin, having just secured his clay jar refused, telling the laborer that it would be defiled by his touch. The laborer was angry, exclaiming: *You would lose your caste altogether, for the Europeans are going to make you bite the cartridges soaked in cow and pig fat.*"

"Well, the reports about sepoys from Barrackpore and their mistrust concerning the cartridges reached us in the first week of February." Bahadur Shah Zafar's thoughts were exploring the heart of next month. "During an evening parade at Barrackpore the sepoys were questioned about their suspicions and misgivings concerning the cartridges. Most of them had answered that they believed the cartridges to be greased with cow and pig fat not only due to rumors, but by the feel of new paper, stiff and cloth-like when they bite it with their teeth."

"In March, Zil-e-Subhani, a strange movement started in Barrackpore and now it has reached all over the North-Western provinces and farther and is still spreading." Mohan Lal the scribe ventured forth to share his own concerns. "It is called Chapatti Movement, but no one is sure what it means. It entails some secret message known only to the ones who distribute those chapattis. Five chapattis exchange hands and the person receiving bakes five more to take those to the nearest village and number of chapattis keeps multiplying from hand to hand, from village to village."

"Strange indeed, this Movement has reached Mathura and Agra, I have heard, yet I fail to decipher its message." Bahadur Shah Zafar's look was distant and contemplative. "A strange flyer was displayed in March also, if I recall correctly. It was only a piece of paper though, depicting a naked sword and a shield, affixed to the back wall of the Jami Masjid here in Delhi. It was supposed to be a proclamation from the Shah of Iran that British expeditionary force had just suffered a massive defeat in Persia and that the Persian army had crossed the Afghan border and was now marching from Herat to come and liberate Delhi from the rule of the Christians. Theo Metcalfe was the one to find that paper, had ripped it to pieces, but somehow its contents were reprinted in the newspaper Siraj-ul-Akhbar, though I never read it."

"March was also the month of madness for one sepoy by the name of Mangal Pande, Zil-e-Subhani." Ilahi Bakhsh couldn't be left behind to share his own memory-book of knowledge. "Mangal Pande of Barrackpore regiment seemed to have gone stark mad when he appeared before his quarter-guard with a loaded musket. He was wearing a regimental jacket, but was barefooted and had donned a dhoti instead of trousers. Shouting invectives, he was urging bugler to sound the assembly. *Europeans are coming here,* he was heard saying. *Why aren't you getting ready? It is for our religion. From biting those cartridges we would become infidels. Get ready. Turn out all of you. You have incited me to do this and now you bhainchutes you will not follow me.* When Baugh and Hewson tried to restrain him, he wounded them both. He would have killed them, had not a Muslim sepoy by the name of Shaikh Paltu restrained him, but he had to let him go for no other sepoys came to his help. Mangal Pande then turned the muzzle of his own gun to his breast, which misfired. The muscles on his neck, chest and shoulders were injured and he fell down prostrate. Though he did not die of self-inflicted wounds, he was tried and condemned to death."

"Reports from Ambala in April mark that month the worst in arson and sedition." Bahadur Shah Zafar's gaze was smoldering with recollections sad and incomprehensible. "The bungalows of European officers in flames. The huts of those sepoys who had used the new cartridge burnt to the ground. Then the tragic events in Lucknow. Hindus becoming more sensitive than ever. When a surgeon Dr. Walter wells at the infantry hospital took a sip from the bottle of carminative without even thinking since he was indisposed, the sepoys raised a cry that this was an insult to their caste since that bottle of medicine had become obnoxious to all Hindu patients. The commanding officer Dr. Palmer rebuked Dr. Walter Wells, smashing the bottle in the presence of sepoys, but that didn't pacify them. Vengeance came in the evening when they burnt down the bungalow of Dr. Walter Wells, plundering the house, though everyone escaped unscathed. In Oudh too, sepoys refusing to bite the cartridges and threatening to murder their officers. Tragedies vast and fathomless."

"The most tragic of all, Zil-e-Subhani, is the recent tragedy of disgraced sepoys at Meerut, all eighty-five of them." Chuni Lal was sealing the month of April with his own bottled up concern. "Those sepoys had refused to bite the cartridges when lined up for a drill. Immediately they were taken off duty and publicly condemned to imprisonment."

"Are they still in the prison?" Bahadur Shah Zafar asked, barely concealing his agitation.

"I haven't heard on the contrary, Zil-e-Subhani." Chuni Lal murmured thoughtfully. "The last I heard was they feel depressed and disgraced. When an officer went to pay their wages, they seemed doleful, rather indifferent. Telling the officer to pay their wages to their wives and the ones not married to some close member of their family."

"Degraded and disgraced for sure, Zil-e-Subhani." Ghalib broke his silence. "I wish it were someone else to relate such sad news. Reports came this afternoon that last evening all those eighty-five sepoys convicted of subordination were brought to the parade-ground amongst other seventeen soldiers as audience. Under a dark sky thick with storm-clouds a sentence was read to them that they were imprisoned with hard labor for ten years. All those eighty-five men were stripped off their uniforms. Their boots were removed and their ankles shackled. Then they were marched off under guard to a new gaol."

"It bodes ill for sepoys as well as for the Britishers, since the sepoys are publicly humiliated in front of their garrison." Bahadur Shah Zafar murmured, his heart somersaulting. "This is not the first time though. Almost a century ago as the history books tell us, on the eve of Buxar Indian sepoys refused orders and were brutally executed by the command of Hector Munro. Then half a century ago before the death of my grandfather Shah Alam, many sepoys revolted at Vellore in Tamil Nadu against a cap-badge of leather—always repugnant to Hindus. Even during the wars in Sind, Burma and Punjab several sepoys protested against the order of traveling abroad, since they firmly believe that they would lose their caste if they crossed the sea. Sad and tragic times ahead. I can smell the reek of danger."

"Such invisible dangers lurking somewhere, Zil-e-Subhani, have no affect on Nana Sahib. He is having a ball, rather hosting extravagant balls at Cawnpore." Azad tried to cheer the king with lighthearted banter. "Just last week he entertained Hildersons and other Europeans to a magnificent ball. Charles Hilderson is a magistrate of Cawnpore and his wife Lydia is an accomplished pianist. Nana Sahib has made a name for himself by entertaining Europeans, who have nicknamed him as the gentleman of Bithoor. He goes riding in Cawnpore, swooning with pleasure when people stop him, praising him for his hospitality to the Europeans."

"The same Europeans, probably, who thrash their native servants if they are careless in performing their duties, even cutting half their wages." Mustafa Khan Shefta scoffed with explicit disdain. "I have heard of one officer who has employed an orderly just for the task of thrashing his other servants. Personally, I have seen two servants sprawled on their mats, covered with plasters and bandages all bloody, moaning without complaint."

Since Bahadur Shah Zafar just gazed ahead of him without speaking, Mahbub Ali Khan tossed his own smoldering comment.

"Inflicting wounds to the servants and treating rajahs with open contempt has become quite common these days. Just last month when an Englishman was leaving for a hunting expedition and was asked if he would wait for the rajah who had offered to accompany him, the Englishman's response was quick and tart. *I should think not. We don't want the beastly niggers with us.*" Mahbub Ali Khan looked shamefaced as if he was the one insulted.

"Thirty years ago, most of the Englishmen had a semblance of respect for both high and low." Bahadur Shah Zafar's gaze was sweeping over the sea of colorful turbans with a keen intensity. "What generated this contempt and arrogance I fail to fathom. Though I too have heard reports of officers under the influence of port and sherry exclaiming. *By Jove these niggers are such a confounded, lazy, sensual set, cramming themselves with sweetmeats and smoking hookahs so viciously that one would might as well train a pig.*"

"This subtle change, Zil-e-Subhani, from that of seemingly kind to this of downright arrogance has been slow and gradual, that's why we have failed to notice it before." Ghulam Abbas began profoundly. "To them, sepoys have become some sort of inferior animals if not contemptible creatures to be sworn at and treated roughly. I have heard the epithets being tossed around, *nigger, saur—pig*, the latter being very offensive to the Muslims."

Before anyone could speak Basant Ali Khan the eunuch trooped into Diwan-i-Khas, sweeping the floor with his curtsies.

110

"Zil-e-Subhani, I am the messenger of happy news." Basant Ali Khan curtsied again. "Prince Jawan Bakht's wife Kulsum Begum has given birth to a healthy prince."

"Happy news indeed!" Bahadur Shah Zafar's sadness was replaced by a subtle glow of joy. "Order sweets for everyone." He got to his feet, waving dismissal. "A delightful excuse for repast and celebration." He strolled past the courtiers amidst a volley of felicitations.

The celebration for the newborn prince were not extravagant, but fetched a few tides of joy to the occupants of the palace. Small baskets of sweetmeats were purchased from the bazaar and distributed amongst the staff of the palace, including guards and servants. All the royal household had gathered at Rang Mahal, feasting and rejoicing. Dancing girls accompanied by musicians had entertained the royal household till midnight. Bahadur Shah Zafar and Zeenat Mahal had retired to their own sumptuous chamber. It was way after midnight before they fell asleep, but Bahadur Shah Zafar's sleep was rigged with dreams most bizarre and astonishing.

Inside the web of his tinsel dreams, Bahadur Shah Zafar was alone and trapped. He could see the waters of Jamna splitting into rivulets of blood and sky raining sparks of fire. Wildfires were raging inside the very heart of Delhi, spreading and swelling into mountains of conflagration. His palace was blackened with smoke, slimy and muddied. Delhi was receding into the bloodied waters of Jamna. The silks on his royal person were turned to rags and not a jewel in his possession to barter for a piece of bread. He was famished and impoverished, fresh dreams converging and licking his face with tongues of fire. Loud, strident voices from nowhere were disappearing into nothingness. Suddenly he was sucked into the furnace of fire, witnessing a pandemonium most terrible and gruesome. Startled to awakening, he looked at the sleeping beauty as his beloved Zeenat, the pandemonium in his head still loud and jarring. This uproar was too real to be encased in a dream state, so he got out of bed, donning his silk robe noiselessly. Gliding close to the window of his balcony overlooking the gilded domes, he could barely make out the forms of few men, making gestures and screaming.

Summoning his personal eunuch Sidi Nasir he dispatched him outside to ascertain the cause of this unusual disturbance. Sidi Nasir returned immediately, informing him that fifteen or twenty sepoys are here from Meerut, very agitated and demanding the King's audience. Bahadur Shah Zafar himself was feeling puzzled and agitated, commanding Sidi Nasir to summon Captain Douglas, instructing him to tell the Captain that he would meet him in the Audience Hall. Zeenat Mahal was still fast asleep, so Bahadur Shah Zafar got dressed hurriedly and came down into the Audience Hall unattended. Feeling giddy and disoriented, he began to pace while waiting for Captain Douglas. Oblivious to the time and surrounding, he kept pacing in this gilded hall, not even noticing the arrival of Captain Douglas when he finally arrived.

"You have never summoned me before at the first streak of dawn, Zil-e-Subhani." Captain Douglas curtsied. "Are you ill? May I call your physician?"

"No." Bahadur Shah Zafar's feet came to an abrupt halt in his act of pacing. "Some sepoys from Meerut. I don't know what they want? Very annoying noise under the window of my bedroom. I have no idea what this commotion is about? If you would kindly find that out for me?"

"I would find out right away, Zil-e-Subhani, and would report to you promptly." Captain Douglas curtsied and made haste, his heart thundering for some nameless reason.

Bahadur Shah Zafar's heart too was thundering, rather somersaulting as he resumed his pacing. A few snippets of his dreams were coming alive with such vivid detail that he was literally horrified as if witnessing the onslaught of violence in broad daylight. So appalled he was by this kaleidoscope vision of horrors that he stood still, not even noticing the breezy return of Captain Douglas.

"No need to worry, Zil-e-Subhani, everything is taken care of." Captain Douglas breathed unconvincingly. "Some thirty to forty troopers from Meerut. I ordered them to depart since they are disturbing you, the King. I also told them that they are very disrespectful, disturbing the king so early in the morning, so they are dispersed. You go back to sleep, Zil-e-Subhani. I will make sure no one disturbs you any more this morning."

"From the window of my balcony, Douglas, those sepoys didn't look friendly. Might as well send a word to Meerut, asking about details and the cause of their appearing in Delhi so early." Bahadur Shah Zafar's thoughts had lips of their own and he didn't know what he was saying. "While you are at it, request royal troops from Meerut, for we have no army here to defend the palace. And order the city gates to be closed and the palace doors to be locked." He drifted toward the staircase as if sleepwalking.

"Yes, Zil-e-Subhani." Captain Douglas curtsied, departing punctiously.

Inside the royal bedroom with canopied bed where Zeenat Mahal sat still with satiny pillows propped behind her, Bahadur Shah Zafar paced slowly and deliberately. Thinking aloud to himself at times or quelling Zeenat Mahal's fears sporadically. The streaks of dawn were now erased by ribbons of gold in sunshine, escaping the latticed windows and accentuating the colors of tapestries on the walls and of the Persian rugs, all silken and exquisite.

"Those were just dreams you dreamed last night, Zile-e-Subhani, nothing more." Zeenat Mahal consoled. "A scented bath would drive away all the demons in your head and you would feel refreshed."

"What horrors! Nightmares of the worst kind!" Bahadur Shah Zafar kept pacing. "Great atrocities, bloodshed. Pillaging and plundering. Fires everywhere. You can't imagine, Beloved, such agony and torment—" His dream-world was shattered by the urgency of appeal in the tones of Ghulam Abbas right outside his chamber door.

"You must come down to Diwan-i-Khas, Zil-e-Subhani. Sepoys everywhere, demanding your audience." Ghulam Abbas' voice was choked with dread.

"How come?" Bahadur Shah Zafar emerged forth dazed and uncomprehending. "Half an hour ago, if I am not mistaken, I sent Captain Douglas with instructions to have the city gates closed and the palace doors locked. He assured me that the sepoys were dispersed before he left."

"They had gone away, Zil-e-Subhani, that's true. But they went to Rajghat and secured a solemn compact with the shopkeepers of Thani bazaar and those are the ones who have helped open all the gates." Ghulam Abbas offered hurriedly. "Please, Zil-e-Subhani, make haste, they have invaded Diwan-i-Khas with their boots all muddied. An unruly rabble they are, might learn discipline under your royal authority."

Diwan-i-Khas, teeming with Indian sepoys and a few royal guards was a rare sight not ever before seen in the annals of history as being invaded by armed, booted, mannerless men with loud voices and rough clothes. Since centuries this hall had maintained its aura of sanctity where decorum and etiquette reigned supreme, next to the king/emperor on the throne. But this particular morning its sanctity was violated by undisciplined, rambunctious men, seething with zeal and anger. Discipline was finally restored as Bahadur Shah Zafar seated himself on his Peacock Throne, wearied and distraught. His appeal for courtesy and silence was met by prompt obedience by the sheer aura of his venerable age and royal bearing. The leader of the sepoys Bakht Khan had taken command, not in the least intimidated by the king's inquisition.

"Zil-e-Subhani, you have already heard about the cartridges being greased with pig and cow fat." Bakht Khan was repeating himself against some flood of feverish refrain. "When the Indian sepoys refused to bite them with their teeth, they were disgraced in front of their comrades by British officers. The ones who refused were stripped off their uniforms, their boots taken off, their feet shackled. They were paraded to the jail and sentenced to ten years of hard labor."

"I know that, Bakht Khan, but you have yet not told me why all these sepoys have come to Delhi under your command?" Bahadur Shah intoned patiently. "Have you abandoned your posts? Do the British officers know?"

"Yes, Zil-e-Subhani." Was Bakht Khan's flustered response. "We have come here to seek protection under your royal guidance."

"Protection against what?" Bahadur Shah Zafar's gaze was stern and piercing.

"Against the British, Zil-e-Subhani." Bakht Khan stood pondering. "We have suffered enough under the brunt of their new laws, injustice, prejudice, oppression. Our religion is being mocked and our culture destroyed. We want your support and leadership."

"You are talking to a king who is more impoverished than a fakir on the streets of Delhi." Bahadur Shah Zafar's heart was swelling with the pain of mad gloating at his own state of false pomp and glory. "I have no treasures to assist you. No troops of my own to protect my palace or even my royal household. At least a fakir doesn't mind begging, I can't even do that due to the curse of my royal pride and false sense of dignity."

114

"We would fill your treasury with gold by collecting revenues, Zil-e-Subhani." Bakht Khan began with a sudden spark of animation. "All our troops from Meerut, Agra and other cities would be gathering here under your royal banner."

"What exactly happened in Meerut which made you come to Delhi. Tell me the truth, Bakht Khan, or leave my palace." Bahadur Shah Zafar commanded, his thoughts feverish and gallivanting.

"You would hear it sooner or later, Zil-e-Subhani, so here it is." Bakht Khan resigned himself to unfold the events of yesterday as succinctly as possible. "The day after our comrades were jailed, we secured their escape at gunpoint. Then some of us set fire to the barracks of the British while they were at church. When they got to know they tried to stop us with threats, but we told them to go away. We didn't mean any harm to them, but we refused to accept them as our masters. Colonel Fritts was shot dead since he tried to shoot us. After we fled, I heard seven more British soldiers were killed and their families. Women and children too, I am not sure how many?"

"You have acted wickedly, so I can't offer you any protection." Bahadur Shah Zafar was stifling his disgust, but his mind was spinning like a tortured globe. "Leave my palace, and seek pardon from the British whom you have wronged."

"Unless you bless us, Zil-e-Subhani, and protect us under your royal banner, all of us are going to be killed by the British." Bakht Khan cried histrionically. "We are being oppressed by the British, our culture and religion usurped by alien rituals and customs. We would be hounded like dogs simply because we refuse to bite the cartridges laced with cow and pig's fat. If you don't help us, we would fall like the flies, our race, religion annihilated. You are our rightful King, Zil-e-Subhani, we would be your obedient slaves, to liberate this country from under the yoke of the British. We proclaim you as our King. Bless us, bless us!" He prostrated himself at the steps of the throne, weeping.

"Bless us, King of Delhi! Bless us, Zil-e-Subhani." Several voices chanted. All sepoys making obeisance and waving their arms with frantic appeals.

Bahadur Shah Zafar was speechless, transported into some world of haze and bewilderment where there were no doors or windows to escape into the light of the universe. One by one

115

sepoys kneeled at his feet and he put his hand over their heads as a gesture of blessing under some spell of daze and self surrender.

"Go in peace. You may stay in Mehtab garden and learn the art of discipline and etiquette." Bahadur Shah Zafar waved dismissal, closing his eyes.

"Zil-e-Subhani, you have just given them the right to fight the British." Prince Mirza Mughal curtsied, uncertain and apprehensive. "Who is going to be their leader?"

"I didn't promise anything. I just gave them my blessings." Was Bahadur Shah Zafar's dazed response. "You can be their leader, my Prince, and train them properly so that they remove their shoes before they come to Diwan-i-Khas."

"Yes, Zil-e-Subhani." Prince Mirza Mughal looked flustered and discomfited.

"So many sepoys already here, Zil-e-Subhani, and more would be coming I heard." Ahsanullah Khan voiced his own concern. "Who would be feeding them?"

"That's their responsibility. I told them there are no funds in our royal treasury, didn't I?" Bahadur Shah Zafar pressed his temples. "I am getting a headache, Ahsanullah, don't bother me with petty details."

"Zil-e-Subhani." Muinud-din Hasan the police officer of Delhi stormed into Diwan-i-Khas, prostrating and gasping for breath. "Sepoys are everywhere. Torching the houses of the Europeans and killing men, women and children most brutally and indiscriminately. They are in the bazaar too, looting and plundering and killing the native shopkeepers. There is chaos everywhere, Zil-e-Subhani, beyond our control. Not enough men to disperse this rabble. Please, Zil-e-Subhani, command these men to desist from killing and plundering."

"And I just blessed them." Bahadur Shah Zafar opened his eyes, which were reflecting the fever of pain and madness. "Maybe Captain Douglas has sent the message to Meerut and we would be getting British troops soon. Why they didn't chase these sepoys from Meerut, I can't understand?"

"Captain Douglas has just been murdered, Zil-e-Subhani." Mahbub Ali Khan was the next intruder entering breezily. "William Fraser too is killed as he tried to lock Calcutta Gate of the palace. Sepoys are on a murderous spree, killing Reverend Jennings and his daughter also."

"A pandemonium, Zil-e-Subhani." Ghulam Abbas even forgot his curtsy as if mad with grief. "Horrible, savage murders committed by Indian sepoys. Infantry regiments of Delhi have joined the sepoys from Meerut and are killing every white male, female or child they can find. Police stations are on fire. Street lamps are broken. Banks are being robbed. In one of the banks one gentleman with two ladies and two children took refuge on the roof, but were bludgeoned to death. It's Judgment Day."

"Makhund Lal, come close." Bahadur Shah commanded his private secretary. "Since no Britishers chased these sepoys, we are not likely to get any help from Meerut. So write a letter to the Lieutenant Governor of Agra if he could send some European troops to Delhi. Also inform him that Indian sepoys after murdering their officers in Meerut have come to Delhi and that I feel helpless in taking any measure against them, since I have absolutely no troops, only royal guards. After the murders of Captain Douglas and William Fraser, no one is safe in this palace." He eased himself up slowly, an impromptu quatrain struggling in his head. "Write this down as a postscript.

"I have reached the last breath of my life
You must come that I may survive
If I no longer survive
What use will be your coming"

He plodded out of Diwan-i-Khas, unseeing. Not even acknowledging the curtsies of his sons and courtiers.

Whose body is this, carrying the corpse of a young prince, becoming emperor then demoted to king. Bahadur Shah Zafar drifted through the gilded halls like a ghost contemplating his past as a collage of memories painful and glorious. *This old body can't carry any more burdens of tragedies. Why is my heart trembling like a leaf and my mind whirling with a dizzying speed, feverish and luminous? I am dying probably, or have died? Such bliss, all agony of the spirit is gone, all torments stilled.* He seemed to be floating in clouds as he sought the staircase to his bed chamber.

Chapter Nine
A Hoary Conflagration

Bahadur Shah Zafar seated inside Diwan-i-Khas on his Peacock Throne with blazing gems looked forlorn and distraught. Amethysts in his crown matching his robe were throbbing like purple wounds, though ropes of peals around his neck were softening the dazzling colors in jewels and silks on his royal person. His pallor was heightened by the feverish glow in his eyes which had grown large and bright within five days since the arrival of sepoys from Meerut. Delhi had become a city of nightmares, ravaged by thieves, zealots and cutthroats. Daily reports of rapine, cruelty and murder had been piling high in the office of Makhund Lal along with urgent petitions for King's perusal. Some sort of pain and exaltation had entered Bahadur Shah Zafar's mind, making it its permanent abode, though he seemed to be listening attentively and commiserating.

"Sepoys are demanding the custody of forty-nine Europeans under your protection, Zil-e-Subhani." Zakaullah was commenting rather than seeking the king's attention. "They say those white folks are their prisoners and they want to deal with them in any manner they deem just."

"And what is just in their perception is nothing but the root of injustice!" Bahadur Shah Zafar exclaimed with a sudden passion. "Murderers all, thirsting for the blood of the hopeless, helpless prisoners. They want to kill them, that much is obvious. First I was virtually the prisoner of the British, now I am a prisoner once again imprisoned inside my own palace by my family and subjects."

"Delhi is in flames, Zil-e-Subhani. Sepoys are torching the houses of all Europeans." Zohur Ali the police officer began exigently before anyone else could speak. "Four or five days ago, can't even remember exactly. Four European gentlemen were concealed inside the home of Muhammad Ibrahim. A group of sepoys raided that house for plundering, and killing all four gentlemen. Close to Ellenborough Tank, another sepoy killed a

European woman trying to escape dressed as a native woman. Indiscriminate killings everywhere and shops are being looted in the bazaars. Anarchy and lawlessness, Zil-e-Subhani. Shopkeepers are pleading for your help and intervention."

"These grievance were addressed I believe." Bahadur Shah Zafar shifted his gaze from the police officer to his vizier. "Didn't I, Mahbub Ali Khan, order Prince Mirza Mughal to take immediate steps to stop this spree of killing and plundering?"

"Yes, Zil-e-Subhani." Mahbub Ali Khan bowed his head, avoiding the feverish gaze of the king. "Astride his elephant he rode through the bazaar, sounding this proclamation that any individual convicted of killing or plundering would be punished severely. Life for life. And for plundering the loss of hands."

"Delhi has become a den of fear and panic, Zil-e-Subhani." Chuni Lal began hastily, for it had become the norm for everyone during the court sessions since the past five days of chaos and confusion. "Shopkeepers have closed their shops, refusing to open until assured of safety for their lives and goods."

"To this affect also, Prince Mirza Mughal sounded a proclamation that shopkeepers refusing to open their shops would be fined and imprisoned." Ghulam Abbas offered this information for the benefit of both the king and the news writer."

"How could they open their shops when there are not enough men to enforce the law?" Mubarak Shah another police officer glowered at Ghulam Abbas. "The other day one of the sepoys went to a shop demanding two pounds of sweetmeats for a pice. The shopkeeper was shocked, exclaiming: *Ah, Mahraj, two pounds of sweetmeat for one pice! No one has ever asked for so much for practically nothing.* To which the sepoy raised his musket and shot the poor man."

"So each sepoy has become a king in his own estimation, a tyrant king for sure. Cruel and heartless!" Bahadur Shah Zafar lamented aloud, his look smoldering with unspent anguish.

"We need brave and honest officers and generals, Zil-e-Subhani, to pound sense into the heads of these sepoys on a mission to loot, murder and destroy." Hasan Askari the Mulla began nervously. "Three days ago a group of sepoys were heard laughing and gloating over their vile bravado in killing Raja kalyan Singh of Kishangarh who had given refuge to twenty-nine European men, women and children. They had stormed into Raja's palace, not only killing him and his family, but all the Europeans. Some other sepoys went to the house of Colonel Skinner, captured his son and killed him right in front of the Chief Police Station. The same sepoys went to the homes of deputy collectors Naryan Das and Ram Charan Das, accusing them of concealing Europeans and plundered their homes. They are also the ones who killed Kazi Pannes and his son for no reason at all. Also two Englishmen dressed as natives were killed by them. Such cruelty and lawlessness, Zil-e-Subhani! Only your authority as a king can tame these savage men."

"No one listens to me! My palace and gardens are invaded by hoodlums, loud and unruly. I have neither the means, nor the power to evict them." Bahadur Shah Zafar's eyes were lit up with sparkling pain from some font of inward torment. "Prince Mirza Mughal, Prince Khizr Sultan, even my grandson Prince Abul Bakr are commanded by me to take charge of the affairs. Daily I remind them that they must take steps to insure the safety of the citizens. Urgently I command and demand that all killing and plundering must stop. They assure me they are doing their best to obey my commands and yet conditions of anarchy and violence are persistent."

"The royal princes are inexperienced I regret to say, Zil-e-Subhani." Ahsanullah Khan began cautiously. "So far they have not succeeded in quelling the rampage of murders. Also the shops in Sabzi Mandi; Teliwara; Rajpur and Mandersa are being looted every night by the Gujars. Gujars have also plundered late William Fraser's house. Taking away all his furniture and tearing up the records of Commissionership and of the Agency."

"That reminds me I had ordered the bodies of William Fraser and Captain Douglas to be buried in a proper graveyard. Report to me, Ahsanullah if my order was carried out promptly?" Bahadur Shah Zafar's gaze was unseeing, his look distant and glazed. "Don't forget to tell other viziers that I have made Bakht Khan general over our soldiers to defend our palace and to safeguard our citizens. Peace comes out of chaos I have heard. Also lull, after a storm, I am hoping."

"Your order was carried out with utmost obedience, Zil-e-Subhani, but the storm is not abating, yet gaining momentum." Was Ahsanullah Khan's rueful response. "Even yesterday a goldsmith killed a man of the same trade against whom he had an enmity. As far as the sepoys are concerned, they are still killing and plundering. Last night, just on a wild spree, a group of sepoys plundered the home of Agha Muhammad Khan, taking away all his jewels and furniture. Also a late night report came that the Magistrate of Rhotak has run away and his treasury is exposed to robbery. Gujars are still—" His commentary was truncated by the breezy arrival of Basant Ali Khan, his face flushed with the Lucifer-charm of humility and subservience.

"Zil-e-Subhani." Basant Ali Khan prostrated himself at the foot of the throne. "Sepoys are demanding the release of the European prisoners in the palace. They want your consent to kill them."

"Consent to kill? Fools and heathens!" Bahadur Shah Zafar was startled to his feet as if stung. "Don't they know killing is forbidden in Islam with the exception of self-defense? And fighting is permitted only if all means of peace are exhausted. These unfortunate prisoners are victims of tragic times and it is our duty to keep them safe until peace is restored." He descended the throne, aiming for the garden, followed by poets and viziers.

Unfortunately for Bahadur Shah Zafar, the garden this precise moment was teeming with rough-looking sepoys, wearing dirty boots, their uniforms unkempt. He seemed oblivious to their loud arguments. They didn't notice the king either, trailed by a scanty entourage. Discovering the king scurrying past them, a few of the sepoys came running toward him.

"Ari Badshah, listen, where is our pay? Who is going to feed us?" One bold sepoy blocked his way.

"I didn't invite you here. You must leave this garden." Bahadur Shah Zafar waved imperiously.

"Look here, King." Another one edged closer, snatching his royal hand. "Your grandson, I hear, has plundered the house of Hamid Ali Khan and is holding the Nawab prisoner in your palace. Is that true?"

"Bahadur Shah Zafar jerked his hand out of his grasp, wincing at this insolence, unable to speak.

"Listen, old fellow, I say!" A young sepoy grabbed Bahadur Shah Zafar's beard. "We are proclaiming Jihad against Hindus, what do you say?"

"Keep your hands away from king's holy beard if you want to keep them attached to your arms." Ghalib humbled the young man with a fierce blow, glaring at him menacingly.

122

"Before King's eyes Hindus and Muslims are equal, you lunatic!" Bahadur Shah Zafar emerged out of his shock, livid and trembling. "And Jihad is inner struggle to fight the evil within you if you only knew." He strode away, numb with grief.

"These sepoys are polluting the city like locusts, Zil-e-Subhani, led by no commander, yet ready to fight." Ghalib murmured as if to himself.

"The skies have fallen down on us
I can no longer rest or sleep
Only my final departure is now certain
Whether it comes in the morning or night"

This impromptu quatrain was Bahadur Shah Zafar's only response, his feet tracing the path to Rang Mahal.

Three grueling days of shock and grief since Bahadur Shah Zafar had escaped the insolence of sepoys in his palace garden and he was still the prisoner of his own grief and shock. Finding refuge in Rang Mahal that day, he had retired for a siesta, not even suspecting the treachery of Basant Ali Khan in league with sepoys. This particular day he was in his bed chamber in the same palace of Rang Mahal, pacing, while Zeenat Mahal lounged on the davenport, thoughtful and apprehensive. Bahadur Shah Zafar's thoughts were tugging at the events of past three days in the ritual dance of circling and stabbing.

Basant Ali Khan after making sure that the king had retired for a siesta, had gone to Gulab Shah, concocting lies most grand that the king had sanctioned the murder of all Europeans. Sepoys were exultant, herding all the prisoners out into the courtyard under the pipal tree and murdering all men, women and children most brutally and gleefully.

"The tragic deaths of the Europeans have left you weak and debilitated, Zil-e-Subhani." Zeenat Mahal began softly. "You must take control over the sepoys. They have proclaimed you king since you are the rightful king and you have the authority to command strict discipline before they go shooting out into the streets, committing more crimes of cowardice and dishonor."

"They already have, Beloved, if you only knew!" A cry of agony escaped Bahadur Shah Zafar's lips. "I have no authority, otherwise, why would I choose to live in this pandemonium of filth and insolence. Have you not noticed hordes of sepoys desecrating the palace grounds with their loud, garrulous presence?" His feet came to a sudden halt by the gilded mirror. He stood watching his reflection—a stranger all bejeweled, eyes smoldering with the fever of madness.

"You must have courage, Zil-e-Subhani, and perseverance." Zeenat Mahal looked baffled, her voice small and pleading. "I am not aware how matters stand. No Britishers have pledged their assistance to support or protect you, so you have no choice but to carry this burden of kingship and assert your authority for the sake of peace and well-being of all your subjects in Delhi."

"My subjects are cutting the throats of each other and sepoys are slitting the throats of the Europeans as well of those who protest against their acts of cruelty and injustice." Bahadur Shah Zafar tore himself away from his own reflection in the mirror and resumed his pacing. "Such cold-blooded murders. Poor Mr. Skinner too, did you know, they dragged him by the hair and shot him."

"You should appeal to the British again, Zil-e-Subhani. Sending details of all the atrocities, maybe they would heed." Zeenat Mahal suggested hopelessly.

"Don't let anyone hear about this, Beloved." Bahadur Shah Zafar groaned suddenly. "Sepoys accused Ahsanullah Khan of siding with the British and almost arrested him. With great difficulty I persuaded them to let him go. If they get wind of what you just said, they might imprison you too. I am already their prisoner."

"Have things come to such a pass, Zil-e-Subhani, that sepoys would dare arrest the king's wife?" Was Zeenat Mahal's shocked exclamation.

"Much more than that, Beloved." Bahadur Shah Zafar stopped in his act of pacing, his look glazed. "I am constrained to go to bazaar myself to quell the fears of the shopkeepers. Urging them to keep their shops open while making promises for the safety of their lives and goods. Not even knowing if those promises would be fulfilled. I am trying my best. And yet the proof of my helplessness—isn't it enough that I am a prisoner in my own palace? Now I must go and face the unruly horde of petitioners or sepoys self-styled as leaders." He drifted out of his chamber, not even noticing the stunned expression of his beloved.

Out in the glare of afternoon sun Mehtab garden seemed desolate to Bahadur Shah Zafar, his look feverish and distraught. In contrast to last few days, there were less sepoys scattered here and there, dozing under the Mulsari tree or simply resting. He was grateful of the peace and quiet all around, noticing suddenly

Ghalib, Mahbub Ali Khan and Ahsanullah Khan standing close to his state elephant Maula Bakhsh which was obviously brought here for his ride to the bazaar. He was barely half way from the trio of men waiting for him when Bakht Khan materialized before him, salaaming him in clear violation of the royal etiquettes.

"Here, Your Majesty, take this sword." Bakht Khan held out his sword to Bahadur Shah Zafar as if talking to an equal. "We have proclaimed Jihad against infidels. In the bazaar if any estranged Hindu complains to you, cut his tongue off before cutting his jugular vein."

"You lunatic!" Bahadur Shah Zafar thundered with a sudden passion. "I can endure the rudeness of the sepoys and their officers, but not their zeal and bigotry against my subjects. You, Muslims are to me like one eye and Hindus are dear to me like my other eye. I would go blind for sure if you lance my eyes with daggers of hatred and ignorance. Remove yourself from my presence. Go, absolve yourself of such vile thoughts." He took one step and was stalled by another rude intruder.

"Your Majesty, we have declared Jihad against the Britishers who have oppressed us for so long." Fazl Haqq appeared beside the shamefaced Bakht Khan like a guardian proud and arrogant. "All Muslims should join in this noble cause of killing the infidels."

"A lost cause already, since corrupted by falsehood and wickedness." Bahadur Shah Zafar lamented, overwhelmed by grief inexpressible. "How Muslims have distorted the very essence of truth. Killing is forbidden in Islam. And Jihad is the inner struggle to fight evil within ones own soul, I am getting tired of repeating this over and over again. Christians are our brethren in faith. People of the Book. Muslims tend to forget that Bible is one of our holy books."

"You don't know how wicked these Europeans are, Your Majesty!" Fazl Haqq persisted, half puzzled, half flustered. "Haven't you heard Lord Canning's proclamation? He is planning mass confiscation of the properties of the ones who don't obey his orders."

"Rumors base and groundless." Bahadur Shah Zafar waved wearily, becoming aware of the trio who had joined them.

"Brahmins are prophesying the annihilation of the Europeans, Your Majesty." Bakht Khan's shame was melting against his inner sense of gloating. "It is exactly hundred years since the battle of Plessey and their astrological charts predict the extinction of

Britishers from India. Besides, Muhammed Sayyid has already raised a standard of Jihad over the roof of Jami Masjid."

"That must be removed immediately the king commands." Bahadur Shah Zafar commanded with a sudden burst of authority. "Report to me that it has been removed when I return from the bazaar." His regal manner brooked no protests as he sailed toward his elephant with unusual alacrity, the trio following.

Capture of the emperor and his sons by William Hodson at Humayun's tomb on 20 September 1857.

"Ah, Maula Bakhsh!" Bahadur Shah Zafar patted the snout of his elephant lovingly. "You are my only loyal and devoted friend." He let himself be assisted in his gilded howdah by Abdur Rahman.

The garlanded Maula Bakhsh had left the garden behind and was now padding along the deserted path of the palace grounds toward the bazaar. Inside the howdah Mahbub Ali Khan was seated next to Bahadur Shah Zafar while Ghalib and Ahsanullah Khan were occupying the back seat. A sepulchral silence had settled over all as if the hearts of all were crushed by the events of the past few days and of this recent encounter with the sepoys. Mahbub Ali Khan was the first one feeling discomfited by silence and seeking king's attention.

"That tragic event at the palace, Zil-e-Subhani, that senseless murder of innocent Europeans has drained you of your will to govern." Mahbub Ali khan commented as if expecting no response.

126

"I am being governed by the servants of the devil, by bigots and zealots." Bahadur Shah Zafar laughed deliriously as if free of all burdens.

"Mrs. Alexander Aldwin with her three children and a native Muslim woman who served them escaped that slaughter, Zil-e-Subhani." Mahbub Ali Khan consoled, his look puzzled and apprehensive. "She pleaded with the sepoys, telling them that she is a Muslim. Even her children knew how to recite Kalima."

"Yes, Muslims also reciting the Kalima and slitting the throats of the innocent men, women and children." Bahadur Shah Zafar's laughter was loud and hysterical.

"Zil-e-Subhani. In these tragic times of conflicting reports and inexpiable atrocities we fail to see the kindness' of few whose hearts are filled with love." Ahsanullah Khan began as if soothing a child. "Here's a report which reached me two days ago. Mrs. Wood and her friend Mrs. Peile escaped Delhi with the kindness of few natives. Dr. Wood was wounded in the jaw at main Guard and was helped by his wife and her friend to reach Karnaul, but their six day escapade was a mixture of cruelty and kindness. They were often insulted and threatened in villages, but then as often cared for by some kind-heated people who concealed them in their homes, serving them milk, bread and curries. Mr. Peile who had been ill, abandoned his bed one evening without leave, had his own lucky, unlucky escapades. Several times he was attacked by sepoys, but escaped. He was robbed of all he had. Some villagers took pity on him, serving him water and sweetmeats. They gave him native clothes, shoes and turban. On his way to Karnaul he was molested by a group of natives who stripped him naked in front of men, women and children. They found only one rupee on him, returned it to him and let him go. In another village he was joined with his wife and Dr. Wood's family. There were almost thirteen Europeans altogether and they were served food by the villagers. On the road again they were attacked by Gujars who robbed them of their rings, studs, watches and buttons, but let them go unharmed. Finally, they did reach Karnaul, half naked, half starved."

"Kindness of few might earn the compassion of many, I am not sure." Bahadur Shah Zafar murmured under his breath.

"Nana Sahib, I have heard, Zil-e-Subhani, is showing kindness to Charles Hilderson, though I doubt his sincerity." Ghalib broke his silence. "He is telling Charles Hilderson that his family is not safe in Nawabganj, offering his wife and two children safe refuge in Bithoor. He says he can hardly believe the rapid turn of events which have left him in shock and he is regretful."

Suddenly, all parlance was truncated. The bazaar teeming with sepoys, merchants, police officers and protestors was coming into view. Abdur Rahman as instructed had started sounding the proclamation that the king is commanding all shopkeepers to keep their shops open and that their safety would be insured. The din of arguments in the bazaar was subsided, though a sporadic burst of complaints were reaching the gilded howdah. The citizens of Delhi loved the king and they couldn't help but treat him with respect and reverence. Complaints, rather petitions were many and while jotting down, Mahbub Ali Khan's fingers were working with the speed of a hurricane, though barely able to keep up with the torrent. Bahadur Shah Zafar was rather feeling giddy and lighthearted, so commanding Abdur Rahman to drive back to the palace. Watching the elephant ploughing its way out of the bazaar, the crowds were thinning, forlorn and dejected. One old man was edging closer to the howdah and pumping his lungs to be heard.

"O, King! How are we going to keep our shops open for business when sepoys come and plunder all, threatening to kill us if we but ask for payment?"

"Who calls me king?" Bahadur Shah demanded suddenly, his eyes shooting flames. "I am but a retired fakir, searching for a place to rest." He relapsed into his former state of inertia and lethargy.

"Zil-e-Subhani, compose yourself." Ahsanullah Khan reached out to feel the royal pulse.

"O King, may I request you grant me a place to stay. Sepoys burnt down my house, accusing me of hiding the Europeans." One middle-aged man pleaded with heartrending despair.

"You can request, my Son, but the king can't even do that, that's his helplessness." Bahadur Shah Zafar appeared to come out of some sort of stupor, straightening his back. "You are asking for a boon from the setting sun on the sky."

The elephant had left the bazaar, no more protests to be heard. Once again there was sepulchral silence inside the howdah, all hearts saddened by devastation in the bazaar. Ghalib's poetic heart was shedding tears of grief, his thoughts whirling back in time.

"Once through the ruined city did I pass
I espied a lovely bird on a bough and asked

128

What knowest thou of this wilderness
It replied, I can sum it up in two words
Alas, alas. "

Ghalib sang as if his heart was breaking.

"Not bad, Ghalib, not bad! As it was a century ago when Mir Taqi Mir wrote that poem. Delhi devastated by Nadir Shah and its citizens massacred." Bahadur Shah Zafar reminisced aloud. "I must be very old, centuries are but a few decades to me and all this devastation seems so remote and surreal."

"Mir Taqi Mir also wrote a sad quatrain, Zil-e-Subhani, after the barbaric invasion of Abdali." Ghalib recited ruefully.

"There once was fair city
Amongst the cities of the world first in fame
It had been ruined and laid desolate
To that city I belong, Delhi is its name."

"Zauq loved Delhi as if it was his Beloved one and only. Once during a poetry session exclaiming: *Who would wish to leave the lanes of Delhi and live elsewhere?*" Bahadur Shah Zafar's voice was choked with memories sweet and nostalgic. "If he were alive he would be asking, who would endure to stay in Delhi?"

"As long as Delhi can endure or repulse the assaults of anarchy or invasion, I would live and die here, Zil-e-Subhani." Mahbub Ali Khan intoned passionately, his gaze welcoming the precincts of the palace with sadness and longing. "Delhi is our home and we need to defend it, heeding the advice of the King of Persia. He has written truthfully, stating: *Englishmen planted their feet in India slowly but diligently. Step by step subjugating all the powerful kings, rajas and princes, and now through Afghanistan they aim to establish their sway in Persia."*

"Anarchy is being caused by our own sepoys." Bahadur Shah Zafar commented, assisted by Abdur Rahman to alight from the howdah. Earlier our sepoys used to complain that they are being harassed by the English soldiers, and now they are the ones harassing everyone, homeowners and shopkeepers, killing and plundering." He plodded toward Rang Mahal, followed by Ghalib, Mahbub Ali Khan and Ahsanullah Khan. "I have lost interest in money and kingship. If this continues I plan to retire to the shrine of Qutubddin Kaki in Mehrauli and then migrate to Kaaba, spending the last days of my life in Haram Sharif of Mecca."

"That would bode ill for your family and for your subjects, Zil-e-Subhani." Ghalib protested earnestly. "May God create a situation in which Delhi is brought to order and may peace return to your court and palace. Earth itself would rise, pleading with the sky if you abandoned us, Zil-e-Subhani."

"Sky is indifferent to the plight of us mortals, my Poet, and earth can't raise its hands to touch the sky." Bahadur Shah Zafar retorted, aiming straight for the gilded doors of Rang Mahal. "Cancel the court session this evening. I need to write some urgent letters." He disappeared behind the doors unceremoniously.

Seated in his library alone and forlorn, Bahadur Shah Zafar was trying to write a letter to Prince Mirza Mughal. He was seated at his rosewood desk cluttered with his poems and journal entries he had not a chance to look at since two weeks. There were some letters also, not sealed as yet, though ready to be delivered personally within the palace to princes or viziers. The pen poised before him, his gaze was scanning greetings to his son, his fingers moving swiftly as he began to write feverishly.

My valiant and illustrious son, Mirza Mughal, you must devise means to safeguard the life and property of our subjects. Sepoys enter and plunder the houses of the inhabitants on false charges that they have concealed Europeans. Despite my urgent orders that sepoys vacate the palace grounds and gardens, they are still there, loud and belligerent. You must force them to leave. These are the places where not even Nadir Shah, nor Ahmad Shah, nor any British Governor General of India entered on horseback. As to paying wages even to the staff of the royal household, there are no funds left in the treasury. The city merchants having been plundered have no longer the ability to provide loans. Wearied and helpless we have now resolved on making a vow to pass the remainder of our days in services acceptable to God. Relinquishing the titles of sovereignty fraught with cares and troubles—

"Zil-e-Subhani, what means this?" A cry of despair escaped Zeenat Mahal's lips. She had crept in unnoticed and overlooking his shoulders had read each word he was writing.

"Beloved mine, I am broken and suffering the agony of the living." Bahadur Shah Zafar pressed his temples, sobbing like a child who would not ever be consoled.

Chapter Ten
Fortress of Despair

Rang Mahal once again was Bahadur Shah Zafar's prison and sanctuary both as he sat writing another letter to Prince Mirza Mughal. It had been a couple of weeks since he had written to him last burdened with grief, and with the flight of time grief had multiplied tenfold. Zeenat Mahal was seated on a davenport against the wall with a gilded painting of Moghul scene depicting court proceedings. She was trying her hand at embroidery, her heart too ravaged by grief and despair. Bahadur Shah Zafar's back was toward her while he sat at his desk absorbed in writing to his son and oblivious to his surroundings. Though seated in the same room of gilt and velvet décor, they both seemed continents apart, immersed in their individual world of inner torment and anguish. Bahadur Shah Zafar was feeling feverish. Even the tips of his fingers felt hot as if they were on fire, so he paused in his writing, his gaze scanning what he had already written.

My Son! It has been fifteen days since I wrote to you last and sepoys still continue to indulge in their old, vicious habits. I had ordered that they camp outside the city and that no one from the cavalry and infantry should go about the city wearing arms. And under no circumstances anyone should oppress or exploit the inhabitants of the city, but do they heed? One regiment is still residing at the Delhi Gate, a second at the Ajmeri Gate and the third one at the Lahori Gate inside the city walls. They plunder the bazaars day and night on false pretense that some Englishman is lurking inside. They enter people's private dwellings and rob them of their belongings most shamelessly. They even threaten to kill the royal servants if they refuse to supply them with the provisions. This being the true state of affairs, how can one possibly suppose that these sepoys desire improvement and welfare of this country? Or even if they attempt to show allegiance to our authority—

Feeling a sudden stab of agony, Bahadur Shah Zafar's sight and senses were caught under some spell of daze and abeyance.

For a moment he just sat there pressing his temples with his eyes closed. Zeenat Mahal happened to look up, her heart sinking against the weight of fear and apprehension. Before she could speak, Bahadur Shah Zafar leaped to his feet with unusual alacrity, not consonant with his age and health.

"What clamor do I hear down in our garden?" Bahadur Shah Zafar's gaze was bright and burning. "Maybe the troops are back from the Ridge, or some ruffians demanding salary. I must go and pacify them." He darted a feverish look at Zeenat Mahal in an act of turning.

"Please, Zil-e-Subhani, don't leave. I don't hear anything." Zeenat Mahal pleaded, hoping that the noise down the palace garden would subside shortly. "And even if you do hear the noise, you shouldn't be confronting those unruly horde of sepoys or merchants. Some of them came here yesterday late afternoon trying to unlock the harem doors, obviously intending to loot, but didn't succeed. Our royal guards who were not there during their attempt to unlock heard about it later and warned me." Her pallor was accentuated by the soft white pearls dangling down her ears and around her throat.

"They did! Did they?" Bahadur Shah Zafar stood there aghast, unable to move.

"Yes, Zil-e-Subhani." Zeenat Mahal's ruby-red lips were parted like a fresh wound, pleading silently with him to stay. "The guards also informed me that they overheard a few sepoys plotting together to kill me, accusing me of favoring the British."

"They dare! Would they?" Bahadur Shah Zafar was awakening to the pangs of pain and reality. "No, Beloved, that could never be." He turned to his heels as if stung, fleeing.

Hayat Bakhsh garden with its stately tower Shah Burj looming over the Mulsari trees was softening the glare of the sun as Bahadur Shah Zafar strode past the terraces toward the scene of uproar close to Sawan Pavilion. Even the gurgling of fountains could not subdue the skirling sounds, though the water channels edged by roses looked serene in contrast to the babel of argument from the lips of the sepoys, rough-looking and belligerent.

"Zil-e-Subhani, viziers and merchants have gathered in Diwan-i-Khas, awaiting your arrival." Mahbub Ali Khan materialized from behind the tamarind trees, his face flushed and his breath labored.

"No court was planned for today due to fighting on the Ridge." Bahadur Shah Zafar kept strolling without looking back. "What is this uproar about? Didn't I issue an order that all palace gardens should be vacated?"

"Yes, Zil-e-Subhani, but this particular group of soldiers have absolutely no manners and understand not the meaning of discipline, a queer lot than the rest of them we have encountered so far." Mahbub Ali Khan stayed a pace behind Bahadur Shah Zafar. "This uproar is about fighting on the Ridge. They are prophesying victory against the British and embroiled in arguments beforehand as to whom they should elect to govern and to collect revenues."

"Goondas governing the hooligans and badmashes looting the treasuries." Bahadur Shah Zafar was appalled by his own vulgar expression, matching the vulgarity of sepoys, though they didn't hear him, still immersed deeply in their heated arguments.

"Zil-e-Subhani." Mahbub Ali Khan murmured in utter misery as he stepped beside the king, becoming aware of Bakht Khan, trooping toward them with the arrogance of a war-lord.

"Mahbub Ali Khan! How did you escape my notice? I should have imprisoned you too since you are engaged in secret correspondence with the British." Bakht Khan declared rudely before turning his attention to Bahadur Shah Zafar. "Zil-e-Subhani, I have arrested your vizier Ahsanullah Khan since he is secretly in league with the English."

"Release him immediately!" Bahadur Shah Zafar's voice was one tremor of a command. "You and your sepoys are doing all kind of evil misdeeds. Falsely accusing my royal staff and the merchants of bazaar, even the rich landlords of misdeeds for the sole purpose of looting and tyrannizing. You, all of you have become just like the thieves playing the policemen."

"How can you say that, Zil-e-Subhani? We are only raising funds to support the army." Bakht Khan seemed to be crumbling against the weight of his own guilt, standing there flustered.

"Funds by killing and plundering!" Bahadur Shah Zafar's eyes were spilling coals of rage and anguish. "Take away all my wealth and the ornaments of my wives for your own purposes, but do not harass my subjects."

"Forgive me, Zil-e-Subhani. We are trying to control the greed of the few, for majority of our sepoys are good, honest men." Bakht Khan lowered his head, ashamed and humbled.

"And zeal of the many goes unpunished." Bahadur Shah Zafar murmured distractedly, ploughing his way toward Diwan-i-Khas. He seemed oblivious to the insolence of the sepoys amidst their own babel of arguments.

Diwan-i-Khas with its openings of engrailed arches was hosting not only the poets and courtiers, but merchants and petitioners. Bahadur Shah Zafar seated on his Peacock Throne inside the rectangular chamber seemed dreamy, rather bewildered. Crowned and bejeweled he exuded the aura of kingship, but his expression was one of self-surrender, his pallor enhanced by the feverish glow in his eyes. Decorum and protocol were missing, yet all present were maintaining a semblance of etiquettes they were wont to practice during court sessions. A great lull had encompassed Diwan-i-Khas all of a sudden. The courtiers and merchants were quiet, but poets were awakening to the sting of optimism and inspiration.

"As my father says, Englishmen are afflicted with divine wrath by the true avenger." Azad was saying in an attempt to dispel the gloom of Diwan-i-Khas. "Their arrogance itself has made them the victims of divine retribution. For as the Holy Quran says, God does not love the arrogant ones."

"What would become of our sepoys considering that verse of the Quran? Their rudeness mixed with arrogance has become highly offensive to us." Bahadur Shah Zafar's gaze was settling on Azad with a quizzical expression. "Canards and ribbons of judgment float freely during the times of wars. Some people swear that when Turks came to India, there were female camels ahead of them upon which rode green-robed riders, but they were vanished from sight instantly. Only the troopers remained and they killed whichever Englishmen they found. Well, Azad, didn't your poem just get published a week ago in the newspaper? A History of Instructive Reversals, wasn't that the title? Won't you recite since the downpour of petitions is silenced for a while?"

"With great pleasure, stilling the agony of my spirit." Azad imbued his response with a dint of enthusiasm.

"Yesterday the Christians were in the ascendant
World seizing, world bestowing
The possessors of skill and wisdom
The possessors of a mighty army
But what use was that

Against the sword of the Lord of Fury
All the wisdom could not save them
Their schemes became useless
Their knowledge and science availed them nothing
The Tilangas of the east have killed them all
And event such as this no one has ever seen or heard of
See how the strange revolutions of the heavens
Open the eyes of instruction
See how the reality of the world
Has been revealed
O Azad, learn this lesson
For all their wisdom and vision
The Christian rulers have been erased
Without leaving a trace in this world"

"The alien rulers are very much present in India, or how else would you explain fighting on the Ridge?" Bahadur Shah Zafar declared suddenly. "I had no idea that the British would attack until three days ago. So sudden this aggression and I am just beginning to learn the details. Gulab Shah informed me that the past week for five consecutive days sepoys under his command have attacked Englishmen entrenched at Meerut since they also have been shooting any native person who happened to pass that way. More details from Sidi Nasir who says General Anson and Henry Lawrence have been planning attack on Delhi for a long time, also securing alliances from the rajas of Sind and Patiala. They were to march from Ambala and Karnaul via Baghpat and join Hewill's troops from Meerut, then march to Delhi. But the sudden death of General Anson delayed their plans. Fighting is still going on as you know on the Ridge opposite Hindan only nine miles from here. You have to compose another poem, Azad, to match the events, predicting results. And what that would be I don't know?" His eyes were sparkling with stark torment.

"I don't know that either, Zil-e-Subhani." Azad lowered his head in utter hopelessness. "Poetry has become a common commodity these days. Every suffered and suffering citizen of Delhi has become a poet, their laments worth praising and cherishing. Many a sepoys are being brought back wounded by swords or gunshots. They are a sight to incite pity, but the natives of Delhi who have suffered through their hands exclaim, *covered with dust they are going to hell.* I have heard some offering thanks to God, saying, *those wicked men, are now decapitated liked fowls.* People on the streets of Delhi would be the future poets of India I think, Zil-e-Subhani."

"To curse, I reckon, not to sing." Bahadur Shah Zafar murmured dolefully. "Won't you say something, Ghalib? You have become reticent of late. Won't you recite or construe a poem to delight our hearts?"

"I wish I could, Zil-e-Subhani." Ghalib's features were washed by pallor and sadness. "The tongue of my poetry is silent, though the lips of my thoughts speak. Lately, my affairs are in the hands of such notorious people as foreign invaders whom destiny has made the model of tyranny. And I speak of no other than the British. Like infidelity they are the embodiment of causes of the world disturbances. They squeeze and while squeezing they look like the habitual tormentors of mankind."

"In every village, Zil-e-Subhani, natives have become the real tormentors to their own kind." Kalandar Khan sought king's attention before anyone else could speak. "Raja Nahar Singh of Bullabhgarh has sent me with this petition. Requesting if you would please appoint some officers to check the highway robberies, for the inhabitants of the village of Pali are on a rampage to pillage and plunder."

"Your petition had reached me earlier if I recollect correctly. That was almost ten days ago." Bahadur Shah Zafar was surprised at his own clarity of recollection, his look piercing. "I did employ five officers who were assigned to arrest and punish the ones involved in those wicked acts of plundering and pillaging."

"Raja Nahar thought you didn't receive his letter, Zil-e-Subhani." Kalandar Khan offered apologetically. "So he sent me with this petition personally since robberies are on the rise on the highway."

"Not strange since my orders are not obeyed and false orders are circulating with my signature forged." Bahadur Shah Zafar appeared to utter a statement, not a complaint. "Much like the past mishap when sepoys attacked the Magazine. I had issued no such orders and their rash act resulted in disaster. The treasury was lost, and who blew up the Magazine, conflicting reports are difficult to disseminate."

"The latest sounds true, Zil-e-Subhani." Chuni Lal began reluctantly. "Lieutenant Willoughby who had posted guards at the

136

gates of the Magazine to safeguard the treasury had given the order to blow up the Magazine. His decision was sudden as a result of sheer panic. Against the last round of firing from the sepoys, one of his civilian clerk was shot through the right arm. Then Lieutenant Forrest was hit by two musket balls, wounding his left hand severely. That was the time when Lieutenant Willoughby gave order to blow up the Magazine."

"Whatever sepoys looted, that money never reached our treasury." Bahadur Shah murmured regretfully.

"Just yesterday, Zil-e-Subhani, another treasury at Mathura was looted." Ghulam Abbas was quick to share his bulletin of news. "Thornhill, the magistrate at Mathura had learned that sepoys were plotting to loot the treasury, so he had the money packed in boxes to be transferred to Agra. Almost half a million silver rupees and ten thousand pounds worth in copper coins. Lieutenant Burton was in charge of loading boxes in the bullock carts. When all was ready he told the native officer to order the guard to drive the carts. *Where*, the officer asked with a smirk. *To Agra, of course*, Lieutenant Burton said. *No, not to Agra*, the officer shouted angrily, turning to the guard. *To Delhi. You traitor,* Lieutenant Burton cried, but before he could protest further, a sepoy stole behind him and shot him dead. Then the sepoys set fire to the building and marched off with the treasure, throwing handful of copper coins to the onlookers. The villagers rushed to the burning treasury to loot the remainder of the silver and copper coins. Quarreling over the loot, wielding clubs and swords. Many were killed and many more injured by falling off roof beams and masonry."

"That money would never reach Delhi, I am certain." Bahadur Shah Zafar prophesied dolefully. "Can't they see how greed is killing them while they are bent on slitting the throats of their own brethren?"

"Greed of the Europeans in the first place, Zil-e-Subhani." Hassan Askari began pontifically. "I met a landowner in the bazaar who was saying, *I didn't object to the English Government at first, but lately it has meddled in everything and have upset all our ancient customs. Besides heavy land revenues and taxes on almost everything, life has become unendurable. It is worse now since village is fighting against village, caste against caste.*"

"Muslims joining their ranks and all on a crusade to kill the Christians." Bahadur Shah Zafar's look was challenging. "Isn't that true, reverent Mulla?"

"Not entirely, Zil-e-Subhani." Was Hassan Askari's bold, yet flustered response. "Many Wahhabis have been gathering under the banner of Maulvi Inayat Ali with cries of *Jihad.* In fact, before the festival of Eid-ul-Fitr on the eastern slopes of Mahaban Mountain. In Peshawar, one regiment of mostly Brahmins was disbanded on the suspicion of revolt, and yet they succeeded in absconding at Hot Mardan and marched off toward the nearby mountains. They were pursued by British troops under the command of John Nicholson, half of them killed. Yet, five hundred of them survived, finding refuge in Valley of Swat. Unfortunately the Wahhabi Chief of Swat, Syed Akber Shah had died recently, succeeded by his brother Sayyed Umar Shah who was not liked by the tribal chiefs. Though he did offer asylum to the fugitives, and yet Brahmins felt they were unwelcome. With the intervention of Akhund of Swat, they were able to depart on amicable terms, half of them finding refuge in Kashmir and the other half joining Inayat Ali in India, always a vocal Wahhabi. Now they are looking up to another staunch Wahhabi by the name of Meer Raz Khan who has seized two villages near the Yusufzai Plain. These are all the reports I have, Zil-e-Subhani, no one here to attest to their validity. As far as I am concerned, Wahhabis are no Muslims."

"Muslims are no Muslims either. Bypassing the injunctions of peace and slitting the throats of the People of the Book, brutally and indiscriminately." Bahadur Shah Zafar's eyes were burning with grief and anguish. "My thoughts are returning to the Ridge. Are we really being attacked by the British?" His look was glazed suddenly. "Two weeks ago, or is it more, I sent a letter to Lakshami Bai to bring her troops here. I didn't hear from her. Did we get any response?"

"Messages get lost in this ocean of chaos and anarchy, Zil-e-Subhani." Mahbub Ali Khan ventured to keep the king abreast of events dark and chaotic. "While the fighting is still raging on the Ridge, Cawnpore is in uproar. There is great fear that sepoys would revolt in the same manner as they did in Meerut. Two weeks ago General Wheeler was commanded to get the barracks ready for refuge and to dig the entrenchment in case the sepoys revolt. Nana Sahib's friend and advisor Azimullah Khan visited those trenches one day when the work was in progress. Noticing crude outbuildings, a lone well and uneven trenches, he could not help ask Lieutenant Daniel, *what is this place?* Lieutenant Daniel had replied, *I am sure I don't know.* To which Azimullah Khan had said, *Fort of Despair I should say. We will call it Fort of Victory,* Lieutenant Daniel had retorted."

"Victory comes at a high price in that region." Bahadur Shah Zafar commented. "That place is hotter than hell, people say and dust-storms so common that the whole sky turns saffron. If anyone needs any protection, it should be against the weather—the major enemy. Where is Nana Sahib? Last time I heard he was perfecting the skill of deception."

"I am not sure, Zil-e-Subhani." Mahbub Ali Khan lost track of his bulletin of news. "He is in Nawabganj, still professing to be faithful to his covenant with General Wheeler. The Collector Charles Hilderson trusts Nana Sahib absolutely as a friend, even considering his offer for a safe passage to England for his wife and children. Strange how he rode into Cawnpore astride a large elephant ahead of a string of more elephants, two brass guns in the rear, four hundred lancers and matchlock men. Riding toward Cawnpore, he and his men encountered Baji Rao's younger brother who had allied himself against Rana with the Peshwa's widows. Nana Sahib's men relentlessly ran that young man and his entourage into a ravine. Waving swords, they warned him that in a few days Nana Sahib would settle with him for good when the Company's Raj would be over."

"Stranger yet, that Charles Hilderson still trusts him." Ghulam Abbas was in haste to untie his own bundle of reports. "Charles Hilderson has installed Nana Sahib in a bungalow across from the treasury. Actually he is in possession of the Magazine and the treasury worth seven hundred thousand rupees."

"He earned that trust by deception I am sure." Mahbub Ali Khan appeared to hold on to the king's earlier comment. "A couple of times he sent his men out to apprehend runaway sepoys from Delhi who had plundered Government money, though those men never returned with any captives."

"At least, our Eid was calm and quiet, already a week gone." Bahadur Shah Zafar sighed.

"Quiet next day after Eid at Cawnpore also, Zil-e-Subhani." Hassan Askari offered, gloating inwardly. "It was Queen's birthday, but General Wheeler decided to forego the traditional artillery salute for fear that troops would mistake it for an attack. They are afraid that sepoys would attack them suddenly. Reverend Haycock over there, I have heard has entrusted his communion plate and altar cash to a neighboring landlord and has moved into the entrenchment. Another European by the name of Peter Maxwell has left his possessions in safekeeping with the natives and has joined others in the entrenchment."

"They can't help but fear, Zil-e-Subhani, since revolts have become very common, rather unpredictable." Makhund Lal seemed anxious to present his report. "Just yesterday there was a sudden riot in Lucknow. One brigadier and three officers were killed. Also European refugees from Oudh are seeking refuge in Cawnpore."

"Cawnpore is a prison, not a refuge, I am beginning to believe after hearing all these conflicting reports." Bahadur Shah Zafar could barely keep his eyes open, seized by a sudden flood of weariness. "Nana Sahib, as the reports keep coming, has covert designs in attacking the entrenchment. He is also in constant touch with Hazrat Mahal of Lucknow with Azimullah Khan as his trusted advisor."

A sudden volley of uproar and commotion was filtering in inside Diwan-i-Khas. Bahadur Shah Zafar had risen to his feet, forcing his eyes open with his innate will to stay alert. All had grown quiet as if expecting a great disaster. This hush was disrupted by the breezy arrival of Sidi Kambar.

"Zil-e-Subhani, British have defeated native sepoys at the Ridge." Sidi Kambar fell prostrate at the steps of the throne. "At the first volley of cannon from the British, and the sepoys turned their backs, fleeing for their lives. The soldiers being brought into your palace gardens are the ones injured yesterday during the fight at Hindan?"

"Where is Prince Mirza Mughal?" Bahadur Shah Zafar asked tremulously.

"He left the field of Hindan yesterday, Zil-e-Subhani." Sidi Kambar lifted his face up, ravaged by tears.

"Were sepoys not under the command of Prince Abul Bakr?" Bahadur Shah Zafar was trying to hold on to the string of recent events.

"Yes, Zil-e-Subhani." Sidi Kambar murmured. "Prince Abul Bakr's heart was stricken with terror, it seemed, as the shells

140

burst and he was stunned by so much bloodshed all around him that he fled as swiftly as the sepoys."

"For the rest of my life I shall live in seclusion of some garden clothed in my winding sheet." Bahadur Shah Zafar murmured back, strolling through the silent files of his courtiers unseeing.

He was drifting away toward Rang Mahal alone and forlorn, not even hearing the groans of the injured soldiers in his garden. A wraith of jewels and silks, he looked more like the ghost of the ages past, as if no blood ran in his veins, only the ether of memories vague and tragic.

Death and tragedy, all illusion. And yet why does this sound real that sepoys have spoilt and wasted all the materials of the Magazine and have squandered all the money from the treasury? Bahadur Shah Zafar's thoughts were gallivanting, his heart on a verge of collapse, and yet he was whipped by his need to be close to his beloved Zeenat Mahal. *Sad and tragic, the fighting on the Ridge would continue until the British troops wend their way to capture Delhi.*

Chapter Eleven
Rocked by Shelling

Seated on his crystal throne inside the central chamber of Diwan-i-Khas, bejeweled Bahadur Shah Zafar looked more like a phantom of the Shakespearean tragedy than the aged king on the brink of collapse. In fact he was afflicted with a touch of senility though he himself was not aware of it, deeming himself the victim of his own moods, ranging from anger to apathy, from sadness to serendipity. Attended by poets, courtiers and a few officers of the sepoys, he had withdrawn himself this particular afternoon into his self-made circle of solitude, though seemingly attentive to the flow of conversation. Almost a month since the Ridge was captured by the British, but they were unable to conquer the city of Delhi against the constant flux of sepoys ready to die and defend. Casualties on the side of the sepoys were enormous, considering a steady stream of soldiers replacing the ones dead or wounded. Bahadur Shah Zafar was awakening to the pathos rife and uncontrollable. Fever and anguish within him seeking company of the dead Sufis.

"I am the devotee of Qutubddin
And dust at the feet of Fakhrudeen
A king I may be
But a lowly servant of Fakhrudeen I seem."

An impromptu quatrain escaped Bahadur Shah Zafar's lips.

"Profound quatrain, Zil-e-Subhani! You are still mourning the death of Mahbub Ali Khan, it's obvious." Ghalib shot an apprehensive glance at Bahadur Shah Zafar. "I can tell since tragedies lure you to the shrines of Sufi poets, seeking inspiration and consolation. Two weeks and two days since Mahbub Ali Khan left this world. Shouldn't the mourning period be over?"

"I am in perpetual mourning, my Friend, for countless dead and for the ones wounded and dying!" Bahadur Shah Zafar declared suddenly. "For unspeakable atrocities and massacres by native people against the usurpers. For vile and atrocious acts of

143

the rich and poor whose hatred for white man looms larger than their love for religions."

"No time for mourning, O King!" Gulab Shah began impetuously. "We need food and ammunition for the safety of our lives and for the safety of Delhi."

"There is no safety for us anymore, anywhere, my Brother." Bahadur Shah Zafar's gaze was feverish and searching. "Ceaseless shower of shot and shell have no eyes and know no barriers. I can't even sit in my favorite garden, or by the pool in Sawan Pavilion, now round shots falling day and night. You say you came here to fight and to drive away the Christians? Can you not do so even so far as to stop this rain of shot and shell falling into our gardens?"

"We can't do that, O King, until we re-capture the Ridge." Gulab Shah glared rudely. "And to do that we need funds, soldiers need to be paid. They can't fight if they suffer hunger and deprivation."

"You will never capture the Ridge!" Bahadur Shah Zafar exploded against one of his rare moods of blistering anger. "All the treasures you looted you expended. The royal treasury is empty. I hear that day by day soldiers are leaving for their homes. I have no hopes of any kind of victory. Tell your men to leave the city, they are harassing my subjects." His very gaze was spilling fire. "Shah Burj Tower destroyed by a cannonball. Our stable boy killed by another cannonball near Lal Purdah. More cannonballs landing close to the harem apartments in our palace. Our Queen's maid Chameli killed by one of those cannonballs. So terrified is my Queen that she has left this fort of horrors and has moved into her haveli in Lal Kuan." Fever had left Bahadur Shah Zafar's thoughts, his features washed by pallor and anguish.

"The Queen at least has a safe place to go, O King! But we can't go anywhere." Gulab Shah murmured obstinately.

"Go now, young man, and appeal to Bakht Khan." Ghalib intervened, noticing the pallor of the king who had closed his eyes. "The King is not well and can't accept any more petitions." He watched Gulab Shah stalk out of Diwan-i-Khas and then vented out his own umbrage at the sepoys. "Every worthless fellow puffed up with pride perpetrates what he will, while men of high rank once in the assemblies of music and wine by the hearth, inhaling the fragrance of roses in fire and delighting in all sorts of pleasures under the bright lamps, now lie in dark cells and burn in flames of misery. The jewels of the city's fair-faced women fill the sacks of vile, dishonored thieves and pilferers. Lovers who never had to face anything more demanding than the perverse fancies of a fair-faced mistress, must suffer now the whims of these scoundrels."

"Poets are still thinking about pleasure and no one to write about Delhi falling to ruins." Bahadur Shah Zafar's eyes were shot open.

"Pleasures are forgotten, Zil-e-Subhani, since bombardment from the Ridge twenty days hence, seems like twenty centuries." Ghalib began with an abrupt animation. "Heavy billows of smoke from the fire-breathing guns and lightning-striking cannons are like dark clouds hanging in the sky and the noise is like a rain of hailstones. Cannon fire is heard all day long as if stones are falling from the sky. In noblemen's houses there is no oil for the lamps. In total darkness they must wait the flash of lightning to find the glass and jug with which to quench their thirst. Amidst this flood of anarchy, brave men are afraid of their own shadows, and soldiers rule over dervish and king alike."

"Atrocities most brutal, every act must find a fit place in our royal records." Bahadur Shah Zafar's voice was a tremor of urgency. "Ill luck has invaded me and besieged me. Sleep is gone, comfort is gone. It is definite I shall die soon, may die next morning or evening. Who would write about these tragedies?"

"May you live and rule to guide us, Zil-e-Subhani. I have already written much what happened in Delhi." Makhund Lal began humbly. "If anyone present is willing to share authentic episodes from other cities I would be most grateful of the opportunity to put that in writing." He sat wiping his jade inkpot with utmost attention.

"Let's begin then, before we fade into dust." Bahadur Shah Zafar half commanded, half demurred. "You all may contribute beginning with leaders, or cities, chronologically if possible. Now is a good time, no strategies to plan, no kingdoms to rule. Besides, I have forgotten much and we all need to empathize with the victims while absorbing the shockwave of realization how cruel human beings can be."

"I have studied Nana Sahib's every move, Zil-e-Subhani, and can relate every event best to my knowledge." Abdur Rahman's voice shook with deep emotion as if he was suffering the torments of the suffered. "In fact, four days ago June twenty-seven Nana

Sahib celebrated his victory over Cawnpore, hosting a grand feast on a plain northeast of Swada House."

"The cries of the dead and dying I can hear, though I have not witnessed their sufferings personally." Bahadur Shah Zafar cupped his ears, his look opiate. "Yes, Abdur Rahman, lend voice to the unspeakable. And Makhund Lal, let not a word escape your pen or memory, in case you have to amend or add more details." He commanded.

"Yes, Zil-e-Subhani, I would do my best." Makhund Lal bowed his head.

"I would try my best too." Abdur Rahman began promptly. "For weeks Nana Sahib had been expecting a wave of unrest and anarchy in Cawnpore much like the ones at Meerut, Ferozepur, Aligarh, Etawah, Mainpuri, Roorke, Etah, Naisirabas, Lucknow, Mathura, so that he could capture Cawnpore, though on the surface professing to be friends with the British, especially with General Wheeler and Lieutenant Hilderson. Since early June he had been noticing the sprigs of rebellion with inward gloating. Three Englishmen were murdered by sowars—the Anglo-Indian soldiers during their journey to Fatehgarh. Lieutenant Fayrer was one of them who had dismounted in a village to quench his thirst when he was murdered by a sowar with a single blow at the back of his neck. His companion Lieutenant Barbour tried to flee, but was hacked to death in his saddle. Another victim of sowar's brutality was Lieutenant Hayes, slashed across the face with an unerring sword. He was unhorsed and died with a heartrending groan, while his companion Lieutenant Carey, fortunately, managed to flee to safety. Meanwhile, General Wheeler hearing of such disturbing news from all quarters and fearing that sepoys and sowars from his regiment too might rise against them, had secured ample provisions in the entrenchment for his British soldiers and their families. Much too soon, General Wheeler's fears proved true. Teeka Singh's garrison was in uproar. In fact, they were feeling angry and insulted after discovering that British officers and their families, without even telling them, had moved to entrenchment. A sense of injury and betrayal had settled in when guns were taken from them and British guards were planning to empty the treasury and to mine the Magazine. The final spear of insult came from General Wheeler's orders that sepoys and sowars come to the entrenchment to collect their pay unarmed and out of uniform. Paradoxically, the first victim of this uproar was a native sepoy of Cawnpore, Major Bhowani Singh, refusing to budge while guarding the treasury for the British. He was knocked down with a sword cut in the back of his head. Mistaking him for dead, the sowars had looted the treasury and had fled, but not before setting fire to the bungalows of the British officers. General Wheeler had then assembled his regiment, telling them that anyone not wishing to serve the Government is at liberty to leave. So most of them laid down their arms and left the entrenchment. The same afternoon a bullock cart was found near the entrenchment with Mr. Murphy's corpse caked with dust and blood. The same day Teeka Singh's regiment had reached Nawabganj to take possession of the other treasury where Nana Sahib had arrived along with Azimullah Khan. Soon, more disgruntled soldiers from Cawnpore had arrived and Teeka Singh was happy to order the gates of the treasury to be thrown open. He was drunk with success, asking Nana Sahib if he was loyal to the natives or sided with the British. To which Nana Sahib replied: *It is perfectly true that apparently I have been the friend of the English and have offered them assistance, but actually I have been long at enmity with them.* Satisfied by this response, Teeka Singh had the treasury loaded on to thirty-six elephants and along with the entourage of Nana Sahib had proceeded toward jail to release all the prisoners. They were jolly marauders, making bonfire of Lieutenant Hilderson's records and setting fire to Magazine and civil establishments. Most of them took the road to Delhi, while Nana Sahib and his men and Teeka Singh and his companions stayed behind to guard the treasure and to complete the destruction of the British bungalows. Remember, Zil-e-Subhani, that sorry rabble as soldiers when they arrived here in Delhi second week of June, clamoring for attention?" He asked as if collecting his thoughts.

"So many of them everywhere, in my palace gardens, I can't recall who came from where?" Bahadur Shah Zafar lamented. "Though I do remember receiving reports that Teeka Singh saluted Nana Sahib as his king. And the king appointed Teeka Singh as his subhedar-major and Twala Prasad the brigadier of his army. He appointed Azimullah Khan the collector of revenues and his brother Baba Bhutt treasurer and head magistrate. Then he claimed a bungalow next to the theatre and started shooting commands. His friend Tatya Tope raised a flag near the old Residency in Nawabganj to mark the beginning of Nana Sahib's rule. Strange, passing strange that I can remember all this, yet daily events of my own palace escape my memory. It's all coming back to me. Nana Sahib's inception of savage commands! His late father's widows were blown to pieces at the mouth of a cannon. Squads of sowars were dispatched to the city to plunder and to execute all the Christians and the natives who were found harboring the Christians. The bungalows of the Europeans were torched. How noble of Nana Sahib to send a letter to General Wheeler that he should expect an attack around ten the next morning?" A ripple of nervous laughter escaped his lips before he continued. "The Church of Christ hit by cannonballs. The Christian families residing at the mission south of Nawabganj herded together and massacred. An Englishman with his wife and child discovered hiding in an abandoned house was brought before Nana Sahib and he ordered them all to be shot. The fate of Nunne Nawab I have forgotten." He sighed, wiping away the bewildered look in his eyes with a perfumed handkerchief.

"Sorry, Zil-e-Subhani, I have no information on that." Abdur Rahman apologized. "All I know is that he was the wealthiest of the rich nobles of Lucknow living at Cawnpore."

"I know a little about the fate of Nunne Nawab, Zil-e-Subhani." Ahmed Beg sought the king's attention. "One young sepoy from Cawnpore told me what happened. First the homes of Nawab's brothers were plundered and they were ordered to serve at Nana Sahib's batteries. Then the back door of Nawab's palace was blown away by a cannon shot, an unruly mob carrying away his lamps, hangings, paintings and furniture. Discovering an old European and his wife with their two teenage children, the men dragged them in front of the Dak bungalow and killed them. They captured Nunne Nawab and his followers and brought them to Nana Sahib at Duncan's house. All of them were imprisoned along with the other exiled functionaries from the court of Oudh."

"My memory is not completely lost." Bahadur Shah Zafar's look was distant and unseeing. "The latest I can recall which might be old by now. A snippet at that I suppose. Nunne Nawab has regained his full authority. He has an army of one thousand Muslim soldiers and a phalanx of coated sowars."

"A fact or a rumor, Zil-e-Subhani, but it is believed Nunne Nawab was coerced into alliance with Nana Sahib in exchange for Cawnpore which Nana Sahib promised him, saying that he would give it to him after he returned from his ancestral capital at

Poona." Azad appeared to jog down his own memory lane for the benefit of Makhund Lal. "At the same time when Nunne Nawab was taken into favor, several Europeans were murdered by the orders of Nana Sahib. Heads of the three officers were displayed in the open in front of Rao Sahib's home in Bithoor."

"A brutal king in name alone." Bahadur Shah Zafar looked at Azad as if commiserating. "You are too young to witness the savagery of the ruling class who have been deprived of authority for so long." He shifted his gaze to Abdur Rahman. "Continue with the Cawnpore story, it might offer us some clues as to the mindset of the deposed kings and rajas."

"Must share this rumor before I continue, Zil-e-Subhani." Abdur Rahman murmured apologetically. "Nana Sahib is proclaimming with the beat of drums that you, Zil-e-Subhani, have conferred titles upon him which the Company had denied him for so long? So he has styled himself as the king of Bithoor and Cawnpore."

"False allegations and counterfeit commands, though where such rumors come from I cannot fathom." Bahadur Shah Zafar waved his arm desperately. "All canards, don't believe a word."

"Yes, Zil-e-Subhani." Abdur Rahman bowed his head again. "Fatehgarh is the next scene of unrest chronologically. Rebellion started in the prison. A British by the name of Teddy Vibrat was hit by a brick by one convict Burriar Singh. Bloody and wounded, Vibrat had managed to control the rebellion by opening fire on the prisoners. Sixteen prisoners were killed and Burriar Singh was executed. Hearing such reports, four American missionaries with their families and neighbors—fearing mass rebellion, had fled Fatehgarh on a boat under the command of Briely toward Cawnpore, not even knowing that this town was under siege by Nana Sahib. Reaching close to Cawnpore they were confronted by countless sepoys with murderous intent. They had no choice but to throw themselves at the mercy of the sepoys. The sepoys herded them together with a long rope, tied their hands behind their backs and took the prisoners to Nana Sahib. Nana Sahib, some profess, ordered the massacre of all prisoners, yet others say it was Bala Rao or Azimullah Khan. But as the story goes, the prisoners were brought to a ditch guarded by sepoys and sowars. Bala Rao was seen perched on a platform quarter a mile north of Swada House to watch and issue orders. Above the din of missionaries praying and children weeping and men shouting, Bala

Rao called out loud. *By Nana Sahib's orders all the Europeans are to be massacred.* The soldiers opened fire and it took them two volleys to still but a few prisoners. Then the sowars skidded down the ditch with swords. Murdering all most brutally and children were dragged shrieking from under the corpses of their parents and cut in halves. Later, the massacre at Sati Chowra, Zil-e-Subhani, and how the besieged were tricked into leaving the entrenchment I learnt from Ahmed Beg. If he could tell the rest, it would be more complete and accurate, for I might forget or misquote."

"So be it, cruelty has a speech of its own which loses its sting when repeated often." Bahadur Shah Zafar appeared to be startled out of his nightmarish reality, his gaze falling on Ahmed Beg. "The task of recounting gruesome details is left to you, my good man, so continue the tale of horrors. And how do I know this is a tale of horrors, because I have heard it in my sleep, waking up trembling."

"Yes, Zil-e-Subhani, I will try my best." Ahmed Beg took a deep breath as if preparing himself for a long ordeal. "Almost twenty days of siege and sufferings of the British inside the entrenchment were horrific and maddening. The onslaught of heat, dust and flies. The wounded groaning from the torment of amputations. Pangs of hunger and thirst. Children dying of hunger in the arms of their mothers, or hit by shrapnel. Odor of sweat and the stench of dead bodies in the nearby well piled high. A few cases of dysentery and smallpox were also reported. One Englishman in the entrenchment by the name of Jonah Shepherd got permission from General Wheeler to venture out to ascertain the condition of Nana Sahib's army, but of course he was captured. The reason Nana Sahib's troops had not come close to the entrenchment was that they feared it was mined. Jonah Shepherd was questioned about this and he lied most convincingly that the entire area of the entrenchment was mined. So Nana Sahib sent a deputation to General Wheeler, proposing that in exchange of surrendering their guns and armaments they would receive a safe passage to Allahabad. Reluctantly and after much deliberation, General Wheeler agreed. He had secured the promise of boats and provisions from Nana Sahib. That's where the horror begins." He took a deep breath. "Horses and elephants were provided for Europeans to ride to Sati Chowra where boats waited for them in their passage to Allahabad. A few wounded were hoisted on palanquins, but there was not enough transport for all. So many of them walked on foot under the scorching glare form the sun. The very first act of cruelty on the land sent a spark of fear into the hearts of the Europeans when sepoys offered to carry a wounded colonel as if to help him, but dropped him on the ground and chopped him to pieces with their sabers, also killing his wife Emma after confiscating her jewels. Down at Sati Chowra with river Ganges at its lowest when the wounded and half starved men, women and children were loaded into the boats and rowed into the middle of the stream, the native boatmen were summoned to receive their pay. So swift was this order and so sudden the commotion that everything seemed to happen in blink of an eye. Boatmen jumped off the boats and made for the shore. A volley of shells was aimed at the boats, cannon fire booming from bank to bank across the Ganges. Boats were aflame and many sank along with their pitiful cargo. Some women and children, their hair ablaze tumbled over the sides of the boats into water. Survivors from the boats were shot mercilessly. Then by the explicit orders of Tatya Tope, sepoys and sowars stormed the shallow waters to finish off the wounded and the stragglers. Blunt swords and awkward blows made many suffer agonies beyond description before they succumbed to death. One reverend by the name of Moncreiff was struck across his neck with a rusted sword. A drummer's face was cut with a knife and his pregnant wife stabbed in the stomach. Another woman in throes of delivery was struck in the stomach, her newborn child cut to pieces on the spot. Georgiana, a teenage girl's head was smashed with a club. Two brothers, five and twelve year old were cut down with sabers. Sepoys tore away earrings from the ears of the women and yanked rings off their fingers already dead or dying in bloodied waters. Seventeen men who had escaped slaughter were captured late in the afternoon. They were brought before Nana Sahib at Swada House and by his orders were immediately executed. Sergeant Matthew was killed while trying to escape into the countryside. Lieutenant Saunders was captured while swimming desperately to get away. He was brought before Nana Sahib, but he had concealed a revolver under his shirt and shot five of his captors before aiming a shot at Nana Sahib. He had no chance though, was quickly seized and then nailed to a plank, his hands and feet chopped off before he was hacked to pieces, pulled by horses in opposite direction. General Wheeler and more men with their families were also captured.

General Wheeler was to be shot by Nana Sahib's orders, but sepoys refused to shoot this kind general. Neither would they agree to shoot Captain Currie. Nana Sahib summoned the Oudh irregulars who were ready to obey his orders promptly. With muskets drawn when Oudh irregulars were about to shoot General Wheeler and other officers, all the wives stepped forward to be shot along with their husbands. All those captives were shot and if they were not killed, their heads were severed with swords."

Bahadur Shah Zafar during his exile by William Hodson. This is possibly the only photograph ever taken of a Mughal emperor.

"The most heinous of crimes where—" Bahadur Shah Zafar's comment was truncated as soon as he noticed the breezy arrival of Inuzzur who had been staying in Cawnpore since the siege began. "Well, my Friend." He paused as if wondering about his new mode of expression, *friend*, which he had adopted lately to address everyone. "How is Nana Sahib comporting after his tyrannous show of great massacre?"

"Celebrating his victory, Zil-e-Subhani." Inuzzur curtsied low. "A proclamation is sounded with drumbeats in the city of Cawnpore, urging the citizens to rejoice and celebrate. His own camp was illumined with mustard-oil lamps while he received a twenty-one gun salute which the British had denied him for almost twenty years. Nineteen guns were fired for his brother Bala Rao now governor general and seventeen for Jawala Prasad, his commander-in-chief. Azimullah Khan was much praised by Nana Sahib who told him that his wisdom alone brought this victory."

"Azimullah Khan who dubbed the entrenchment as the Fort of Despair!" Bahadur Shah Zafar opined aloud as if recalling every detail of the siege which was reported to him earlier. "And yet it turned out to be much worse, the Fort of Horror. Did anyone escape the massacre at Sati Chowra?"

"Only four men, I have heard, Zil-e-Subhani, from the party of one lieutenant by the name of Thomson." Innuzur's voice was heavy with regret. "They had the energy to swim very far, finding refuge in the domain of an elderly Raja Dirigibijah of Moora Mhow, the most powerful of Rajput clans in Oudh."

"Has Nana Sahib filled the house of his prostitute Azizah with gold mohurs?" Bahadur Shah Zafar asked abruptly as if trying to jolt his memory to awakening. "He promised her, it was reported not too long ago, that after his victory he would fill her house with gold mohurs?"

"Victory has gone over his head, Zil-e-Subhani." Inuzzur was quick to share his bag of gossip. "Any spare time that he gets he spends with his concubine by the name of Adala."

"No distinction between reports and rumors these days." Bahadur Shah Zafar eased himself up, his gaze espying Ahsanullah Khan who happened to straggle into Diwan-i-Khas, aloof and distraught. "Any news from the Ridge?" He paused at the steps of the throne as if trying to remember something.

"Skirmishes, if not heavy fighting, Zil-e-Subhani." Ahsanullah Khan curtsied.

"Hopefully, no shells falling on Sawan Pavilion this afternoon. Come." Bahadur Shah Zafar plodded down the middle isle, beckoning Azad and Ghalib to join him. "I have been longing to sit in that pavilion with my poets and courtiers. Alas, no more poetry sessions." He drifted toward the red sandstone pavilion, followed by Azad, Ghalib and Ahsanullah Khan.

"Not a safe place, Sawan Pavilion, Zil-e-Subhani, exposed to shells." Ahsanullah Khan murmured apprehensively. "We should stay close to the walls of the fort."

"Walls are closing in on us." Bahadur Shah Zafar intoned indifferently. "We would take a stroll. My need to fill the gaping hole in my memory is much greater than my need for solitude. A short walk, then I must see my Queen. How long since she left, I can't remember? How my thoughts skip and wander. Was Calcutta also the seat of unrest?"

"A violent outbreak at Lucknow, Zil-e-Subhani, but it was controlled violently also by Colonel George Neill." Was Azad's anguished comment than response? "Colonel Neill was quick to erect gallows and hanged hundreds of suspects involved in inciting riots, including young boys who might have taken part in such revolt. In neighboring villages countless hundreds of peasants were hanged from the mango trees. Some corpses were strung in a way to make the figure eight."

"His atrocities seem to match the atrocities of the sepoys and the sowars." Bahadur Shah Zafar stopped under the Sisal tree, appalled. "And yet sepoys are cruel even to their own kind. Another gaping hole in my memory which I have not plugged yet! Nunne Nawab went through the ceremony of coronation under the threat from sepoys that he would be killed if he did not agree to the rites of the coronation and to protect rebels under his royal banner. Irony of fates and lies grand! After his coronation, the sepoys proclaimed. *The world is God's. The country is the emperor's. The Nawab the ruler is in command."*

"Atrocities grand commencing from the side of the British officers too and that's not a lie, Zil-e-Subhani." Ghalib couldn't contain his own bulletin of news. "In Peshawar forty rebel sepoys were blown to pieces from the mouth of cannon. The rest of the sepoys who tried to escape were pursued and captured. Further, thirty rupees a head were offered to any soldier or civilian who would kill or capture the remainder fleeing. One hundred and ninety-two of them were captured, made to march before the firing squad and shot. A couple of hundred more who were captured later met the same fate. In Lahore, two hundred and eighty-two sepoys who had rebelled at Anjala near Amritsar were executed by the orders of a Deputy Commissioner by the name of Frederic Cooper. The captives were locked up in a bastion and brought out in batches of ten to be shot. Forty-five of them were found dead in the bastion, probably dying of excessive heat, fatigue or suffocation."

"Evil deeds taking root in the soil of all hearts." Bahadur Shah Zafar lamented, his gaze gathering the sprigs of devastation in his garden where shells had blasted the shrubbery and the flowerbeds. "At least the town of Patna was saved from such tragedies since Wahhabis were arrested promptly. Many British officers were loathe to disarm their sepoys, though fearing rebellion. One of the commanding officer Colonel Spottiswood was so distressed that his soldiers would be ordered to disarm, that he committed suicide to avoid witnessing the dishonoring of his regiment he loved."

"Gwalior in arms too, Zil-e-Subhani." Ahsanullah Khan broke his silence. "In the middle of June sepoys from Maharaja Sindhia's contingent poured out of their huts armed with muskets in response to a prolonged high bugle note. The commanding officer was startled from his sleep. Getting dressed quickly and riding boldly toward the horde of madmen he was shot instantly. Then another commanding officer Major Shirreff appeared on the scene, pleading with sepoys that the *Europeans would disarm the sepoys* was just a rumor. To prove his point he moved into their lines. His reasoning didn't even make a dent over the ocean of excitement, so he began retracing his steps holding the hand of his faithful subhedar. Sepoys threatened the subhedar that they would kill him if didn't let go of the Major. Major Shirreff was shot to death when the subhedar ran away. Four more Europeans were killed that day, including a surgeon and a Chaplin."

"Amidst this ocean of insanity I search for the crumbs of goodness to nourish my own sanity." Bahadur Shah Zafar's feet were guiding him toward the royal stables. "Strange that I am the only one who finds these crumbs in plenty to share with others. More strange that my memory doesn't fail in that arena, either. Mrs. Irwin the wife of a lieutenant who escaped the murderous rebels of Latifpur was thankful of the compassion of a Brahmin, offering water from his jug while she lay down to rest. Once again she was met by kindness, saying that she would never forget the kindness of people in another village where they offered her milk and fresh chapattis. She met a young boy who sang her a song about his hope that Feringhis would be allowed to live. She was always on the run, finding shelter in the home of one scribe. When she was captured and imprisoned by the retainers of a Raja of

Banpur, one woman in the palace, taking pity on her, smuggled to her dried fish and fruit."

"Feringhis would live to rule after much bloodshed and devastation, I am afraid." Ghalib commented, addressing no one in particular. "It has been a month since Lucknow riots and somehow details are stuck in my head like a wild creeper most dangerous and overpowering. Muslims pouring out on the streets under the standard of the Prophet. Attacking Christians, grain-merchants and shopkeepers, breaking into their premises, looting and ransacking. Smashing earthenware pots, tearing down mat doors, slitting open sacks of flour and beans and spilling their contents on the floor. Amongst the mob some superstitious dolts had brought a buffalo head garlanded with white flowers at the gate of the royal palace. And a few others had fetched dolls dressed up as European soldiers, slashed with sword cuts. The same soldiers who were hanged on the gallows near Machi Bhawan. Such insanity and madness!"

"No less insane the efforts of Martin Gubbins while fortifying his house against the rebels." Azad laughed all of a sudden, a nervous, unhealthy laughter. "He emptied his library shelves to fill up holes in his defenses. Discovering that his Lardner's Encyclopedia could stop a musket ball after passing through one hundred and twenty pages."

"A genius I should say!" Bahadur Shah Zafar's feet were coming to an abrupt halt by the stables where royal retainers groomed his horses. "I wish I can devise a plan to prevent the plundering of Delhi. Just yesterday five men disguised as native infantry of the Company had gone about plundering the homes of the citizens of Delhi. Insanity and madness indeed. I need rest. Well, my friends, go home. I need to see my Queen." His gaze was already arresting the royal groom. "Come, Allahdad, get my mount ready. I would ride alone to the haveli of my Queen."

"Zil-e-Subhani." Allahdad protested. "The streets of Lal Kuan are not safe.

"No place is safe, my Friend, not even one's heart from the shafts of hatred and vengeance. You may follow me." Bahadur Shah Zafar waved impatiently, his gaze shifting to his companions. "Don't look so dejected, you may keep me company too, my poets and vizier." He let Allahdad help him into the saddle of his Arabian steed.

Evening had descended too quickly for Bahadur Shah Zafar as he sat with Zeenat Mahal in the central pavilion of the haveli called Nagina Mahal. They had just finished their dinner served to them in the private chamber of the Queen with rich tapestries and velvet hangings. Prince Jawan Bakht and his wife had just left to practice archery in the courtyard of Farash Khana. Bahadur Shah Zafar and Zeenat Mahal were sitting together, watching from latticework window the marble fountain, its cascading waters falling like gold beads, polished by dusk. Zeenat Mahal was unusually quiet, but Bahadur Shah Zafar was talkative as if to escape his inner torment lest he be choked with grief. At the moment in response to Bahadur Shah Zafar's feverish complaint against Nana Sahib, Zeenat Mahal had started talking about the young playmate of Nana Sahib, Rani of Jhansi.

"Rani of Jhansi is no less guilty than Nana Sahib, Zil-e-Subhani." Zeenat Mahal began placatingly. "Lakshami Bai as she is called has taken up arms against the British, as you well know. Though, after the massacre by sepoys of European garrison."

"We are all guilty in the eyes of the oppressed and the oppressor, Beloved." Bahadur Shah Zafar's thoughts were wringing themselves free from the fever of anguish. "No one really knows for sure what happened at Jhansi. Initially, a battalion of sepoys had captured the Star Fort along with the treasury. The British forces had fled, seeking refuge in the fort. Rani had promised safe passage. The British troops and their families were to be spared in exchange for the Fort of Jhansi. And yet, without her knowledge or consent, the rebels slaughtered the fugitives brutally and mercilessly. Even the well-disciplined troops of Gwalior have risen against the British, while the Raja of Gwalior, I hear, is prostrate with grief."

"Begum Hazrat Mahal has taken matters into her own hands and is laying siege to Henry Lawrence's garrison in Oudh, Zil-e-Subhani." Zeenat Mahal was overwhelmed with fear all of a sudden, spilling out her own bulletin of news with a great animation. "She is mocking the British for their claim to allow the freedom of worship. *How can people believe that religion will not be interfered when sepoys are required to bite cartridges greased with pig and cow fat. They are destroying the temples of the Hindus and mosques of Muslims on the pretense of making roads. But they are building churches, sending clergymen into the streets to preach Christian religion. Paying people stipend for learning English.*"

"To counter that, Beloved, Wahhabis are adding flint to the seeds of rebellion by their own fire of zeal and ignorance."

Bahadur Shah Zafar appeared to be swept by waves of despair amidst his stormy thoughts. "They are waving the banners of Jihad, martyrdom. The imbeciles, causing rifts between Hindus and Muslims. Jihadis they call themselves. People of Delhi are already disgusted by sepoys within the city walls. Those sepoys are unpaid, hungry and violent, and the citizens of Delhi are in no mood to accommodate several thousand more fanatical, holy warriors. Oh, Beloved!" He exclaimed suddenly, becoming aware of the glints of fear in her eyes. "Why I am talking about this? I came here to comfort you and be comforted. I am old. Trying to fight the curse of senility, that's it. And yet my heart is young and loving. I fear for your safety. What will happen when I die. Prince Jawan Bakht so young, his son Prince Jamshed Bakht not even a year old and Kulsum Begum pregnant again. What would you do, Beloved? Have you heard the poets of Delhi, the insignificant wretches writing mocking verses?

"The batteries have no strength left
Pray for the safety of life, O Zafar
The sword of India has become cold."

"No one can harm you, Zil-e-Subhani, as long as I live!" Zeenat Mahal declared with a sudden burst of anger and passion. "I would protect and guard you as long as I live."

"Ah, Beloved!" Bahadur Shah Zafar held her close, his eyes stinging with tears. "You are my anchor and heart's desire." He got to his feet abruptly. "I must rest. Suddenly feel over-whelmed with fatigue." He hurried out of the chamber lest he bathe her hands with tears.

Inside the solitude of his gilded bedroom, tears flooded freely from the eyes of Bahadur Shah Zafar and he fell asleep quickly, feeling light and cleansed. Beautiful dreams of youth and splendor were soon replaced by nightmares most wild and horrific. He was snatched from his throne and tossed on a bed of straw. No palace, no gardens, no servants. He could hear a cacophony of voices, calling him murderer, then the curtain of hoary silence was lowered. His bed was hoisted up, suspended in the air. He could see Jamna and Ganges the color of blood, vultures flying overhead. Heaps upon heaps of corpses everywhere and men dangling from the trees, some mere skeletons and others with limbs charred or mutilated.

Mercifully, he was transferred to another place, impoverished, yet tranquil. Lying on a coarse bed with white sheets, he could see Zeenat Mahal squatted on bare floor. She had aged all of a sudden. No jewels adorned her and her dress was as coarse as the white sheet under him. Their eyes met and his heart was caught in pincers of agonies indescribable. The ocean of sadness in her eyes had whipped his very soul to shreds.

Beloved mine, precious love, tell me it's not true? Where are we? Beloved, pretty Zeenat, my dove, awaken me from this nightmare. He was murmuring in sleep. *Where are my sons, our daughters?*

Chapter Twelve
Festival of Flowers

Sawan Pavilion in Red Fort of Delhi this sultry afternoon was hosting the emperor and his poets and viziers. Bahadur Shah Zafar was bejeweled, his purple robe newly stitched for the festival of Eid-ul-Adha. Though there were no celebrations, only the drone of fears and proposals and recollection of events dark and dreadful. Lately, Bahadur Shah Zafar's moods had been dark too, but a little light had crept in into his heart where his newly born grand-daughter slept peacefully whom he had named Raunaq. Prince Jawan Bakht now was the proud father of two children, Prince Jamshed his first born and Princess Raunaq the newborn. But his joy and pride were tarnished by the rust of wars and uncertainties. It had been month and a half since Bahadur Shah Zafar had a nightmare at the haveli of Zeenat Mahal and that nightmare appeared to be unfolding day after day in a most uncanny fashion.

"Your ban on slaughtering the cows at least has made our Eid peaceful, Zil-e-Subhani, despite the clouds of war hovering over the Ridge." Mufti Sadruddin strove to cheer the king who was sinking slowly inside a pool of melancholia.

"The clouds of war are not hovering over the Ridge, my good Friend, but looming close over here." Bahadur Shah Zafar failed in his attempt to smile. "Though, I am grateful no cannonballs are falling in my garden today. As to the ban on slaughtering, no one listens to me any more. Since I couldn't lock up the Jihadis, I had to lock up the cows. I must send a note of thanks to the head of police who offered shelter to all the registered cows in the city's central police station. Rather you convinced Jihadis, and I am wondering how you convinced them not to slaughter cows on Eid?"

"No easy task, Zil-e-Subhani." Mufti Sadruddin smiled wryly. "I hired a charming man of noble character Maulvi Sarfaraz. He persuaded Jihadis that slaughtering cows and eating beef on Eid is not prescribed by any tenant in Islam. They can very well eat goat or camel meat and not offend their neighbors."

"The same neighbors who did cut the throats of five Muslim butchers accused of killing the cows." Azad scoffed, addressing no one in particular.

"Don't be in a haste to deride our Hindu neighbors, my young Poet." Ghalib chided. "For two and a half months now Jihadis are the ones looting the entire city of Delhi. Thanks to the injunctions of Zil-e-Subhani, we have some semblance of peace."

"There is no peace in Delhi, my Children!" Bahadur Shah Zafar exclaimed, waving his thin arm, his look feverish. "Sepoys have been killing and plundering both Hindus and Muslims. I wish I had the means and the authority to check their wicked acts, causing death and destruction. Neither do I have treasures, nor a kingdom. Always a Sufi at heart I wanted to sit in a corner in search of God with a few people around me, eating my daily bread. Now the great fire that was lit in Meerut has blown over to Delhi and it has engulfed this great city in flames. It seems I and my line is destined to be ruined. The name of the great Timuirids would soon be destroyed. These faithless sepoys have rebelled against their masters and have come here for shelter, they will all be gone before long. They have been unfaithful to their own leaders, what can I expect of them? They have come to ruin my house and once they have ruined it they will flee. Then the English would cut off my head and those of my children and they would display them on top of the Fort. They would not spare any of you. And if any of you are saved, then remember what I am telling you. Even when you take a morsel of bread, it will be seized from you and the noblemen of India will be treated like base villagers." He stopped as abruptly as he had begun, panting for breath.

"Zil-e-Subhani, Zil-e-Subhani." Several voices rose in protest, unable to voice their concern.

"A day of reckoning! We should talk about the great atrocities and assess the course of future." Bahadur Shah Zafar resumed with an unusual spark of animation, his gaze lowering a feverish gleam. "Some sort of catharsis to purge clean our hearts of all grief. No more poetry sessions to lighten our hearts. Inspiration is congealed by the cries of the dead and the dying. By enacting the horrors of the past month we might be able to avert the current of future tragedies."

"The worse has happened and the worse is yet to come. That's the litany repeated by many over here, Zil-e-Subhani."

Ghulam Abbas took the lead to unburden his own heart of grief, knowing that no one in Delhi could celebrate this festival of Eid amidst the volcano of death and devastation. "Riots everywhere, murders and massacres. Prisoners blown away from the mouth of a cannon. The same day as of the massacre at Sati Chowra by Nana Sahib, riots at Fatehgarh had intensified and sepoys had opened fire on Fatehgarh Fort. Great slaughter followed, many sepoys as well as Englishmen were killed. Next day the Englishmen secured boats to escape to Cawnpore along with their families, not knowing about the great massacre by Nana Sahib who had settled himself in his new headquarters at the old hotel of Cawnpore. Learning of the Englishmen's boat approaching the village of Fathehpur, Nana Sahib's batteries opened fire across from his palace at Bithoor. A few of the men were killed by a swarm of villagers and the rest taken captive. Wounded and bleeding the prisoners were loaded into bullock carts and transported to Azimullah's house in the old Residency. A few days later the men were executed by the orders of Azimullah. The ones escaping the first volley of bullets were mercilessly slaughtered by the butchers. The women and children were imprisoned in Bibigarh. Three officers, Smith, Goldie and Thornhill were spared their lives and kept as hostages with the promise of securing evacuation of Allahabad. Now the atrocities by Englishmen, Zil-e-Subhani, if someone else has the heart to jump into this pool of catharsis?" A great sigh escaped his lips as if his heart was breaking.

"The pool of catharsis is crimson by the blood of the victims, Indian or English, the same blood, the same life force. Hearts have become callous. Minds gone stark mad by blind rage." Bahadur Shah Zafar moaned. "Yes, anyone brave enough to exhume the valley of death?" His feverish gaze was a beacon of woe and challenge.

"Highlanders have dyed the heart of mother India with the blood of the sepoys, Zil-e-Subhani, as a token of vengeance." Ghalib began pontifically, unable to contain the flood of misery and despair. "These frock-coated Victorians dubbed as Highlanders have descended upon India like the vultures of vengeance. Under the command of Colonel James Neill Indians are hanged on trees along the road to Benares. Villages upon villages are plundered, then torched and if anyone tries to escape the flames they are shot to death. Retribution at Fathehpur was terrible. Indians were flogged, then hanged, their bodies dismembered. This time under the orders of General Havelock, his soldiers singing in drunken revelry.

"With our shot and shell
We made them smell hell
That day at Fathehpur."

"Wasn't it at Fathehpur that Tatya Tope went tumbling down, his elephant shot by a Highlander, though he escaped unhurt?" Bahadur Shah Zafar's mind was blocking the gory details which were sure to be repeated and would haunt him till his dying day.

"Yes, Zil-e-Subhani, but Tatya Tope managed to flee, while General Havelock marched on to Cawnpore with the hope of saving the lives of the prisoners at Bibigarh." Zakaullah began quickly, more so to lessen his own burden of shock since the events of past week than to console the king almost insane with grief and hopelessness. "Anger and desperation are compelling everyone to flee to safety. Learning of General Havelock's victories and march to Cawnpore, Nana Sahib suspecting spies in his camp ordered the cutting of nose and right hand of any English writing Indian with the exception of Azimullah, of course. Next the three hostages Smith, Goldie and Thornhill were shot to death. Immediately after that Nana Sahib ordered the slaughter of prisoners in Bibigarh. He appointed Hussaini Khanum the begum in-charge for the extermination of the prisoners. She was waiting for such a day and ordered sepoy guards to drag the prisoners out and shoot them. But their leader Yusuf Khan refused, saying that he would not kill women and children. Calling him a fool and a coward, she ordered the sepoys directly. When the sepoys asked the prisoners to come out, they would not budge. Taunting and jeering once again and threatening Yusuf Khan with the punishment of hanging, she ordered them to shoot all the prisoners inside the house. Fearing for their own lives the sepoys obeyed, aiming their guns at the prisoners amidst the din of women and children screaming and trying to shrink away from doors and windows. The first volley of shots killed but a few and the sepoys backed away, replaced by a second squad. They emptied their muskets into the air and staggered back, unable to endure the cries of the wounded and the dying. The Begum cursed and taunted again and again, but the sepoys moved away shamed and silenced. Yusuf Khan saying, *let Tatya Tope kill us, but we have had enough.* The Begum then called her lover Sarun Khan to finish the slaughtering. He hired a horde of butchers, handing them the swords. Five butchers began this dark deed by stabbing, hacking and mutilating like the reapers, wading through a pool of blood. Cries of the children were heartrending, trying to evade the blows of swords, many were suffocated to death under the skirts of their mothers. Morning after the night of this massacre when bodies were hauled out to be thrown into the well, some surviving children maddened by this horror were running in circles as if to ward off blows. Soon, their heads were decapitated by the butchers and they were joined with their families in the deep of the well." He lowered his head, his breath labored.

"Ah, how one lives to breathe the foul air of torment and tragedy." Bahadur Shah Zafar groaned. "That same evening I heard Nana Sahib left Bithoor on his chestnut horse. And what followed, does anyone have the heart to recall and disseminate?"

"Only for the sake of posterity, Zil-e-Subhani, where history blunts the sword of vengeance. Hoping that it is blunted enough so that this age of horror ceases to exist." Was Hasan Askari's distraught expression, his eyes ready to drain blood from his own bleeding heart. "General Havelock's soldiers drunk with grief what they encountered at Bibigarh went on a rampage of vengeance in Cawnpore. They stormed into the shops and homes of the Indians in a mad fit of plunder and rapine, sparing neither sex, nor age, yielding to no pity and not abstaining from any crime. Sepoys as well as civilians were dragged in droves to the gallows. Prisoners were flogged before being hanged. Beef was forced down the throats of the Hindu captives and pork down the throats of the Muslims. Brahmins were smeared with their own blood before being hanged by the sweepers. After General Havelock left, Colonel Neill took the reins of vengeance. He commanded that all Brahmins would be buried and all Muslims burnt. Introducing a *blood licking law*—that blood on the floor of Bibigarh was not to be washed, but cleaned up by forcing the natives to lick it from the floor. The captive sepoys were to lick blood from the floor of Bibigarh while being flogged and then hanged afterwards. Anyone refusing to lick blood was lashed so repeatedly and—"

"No more, no more! Judgment Day is nigh." Bahadur Shah Zafar closed his eyes. "Men blown to smithereens from the mouth of the cannon. Siege of Lucknow more horrendous than the bombardment at Cawnpore. Hazrat Mahal still holding?"

"Holding strong, Zil-e-Subhani, since the populace of Oudh has crowned her son Birjis Qadra as the king of Lucknow." Makhund Lal appeared to commiserate rather than share this information. "Though skirmishes resulting in deaths are reported. The British General E.R. Rees writes. *The natives we don't count. We feel their loss is nothing very great, but it pains us all to hear a poor European being knocked over.* As to the massacre in Cawnpore, three days after that people noticed a partial eclipse of the sun, saying. *The devil's wind has not yet ceased to blow. There would be more massacres, horrors, famine.*"

"Famine of love in the soul and arrogance of the invaders!" Bahadur Shah Zafar's eyes were shot open. "What pains me the most is how the Europeans are addressing the natives. *Black-faced curs; fiendish niggers,* besides—"

"Zil-e-Subhani!" Sidi Nasir appeared suddenly, staggering. "The British launched a massive attack and the sepoys are crumbling against that assault, dying and fleeing." His breathless confession had thrown a curtain of silence over all.

"Zil-e-Subhani. I have six thousand warriors under my command and with your permission I would send them toward the Ridge to fight the British." Zohur Ali ripped open the curtain of silence, waving his arms, his eyes shining with a desperate appeal.

"How could your handful of men dislodge the British, my Friend, when ten times their number has failed?" Was Bahadur Shah Zafar's feverish exclamation. "It is the end of August, the month of Flower Festival. We would go to Mehrauli to celebrate, right now!"

"Zil-e-Subhani, Zil-e-Subhani." Several voices protested in unison.

"How could you, Zil-e-Subhani, when Delhi is under siege?" Was Ahsanullah Khan's stunned expression.

"We are not the besieged, but laying siege over the Ridge, you must stand corrected, my wise Vizier! They have captured the Ridge, true, but are the victim of their own victory. Can't even come out of their stronghold to capture Delhi" Bahadur Shah Zafar's look was glazed, but the tone of authority in his voice brooked no further protests. "The Flower Festival with all its pomp and pageantry. Flower fans and garlands of flowers to be offered at the temple and the shrine." He got to his feet under the spell of unusual vigor and determination, turning his attention to his attendants. "Abdur

Rahman, go post haste to the haveli and bring Queen Zeenat Mahal with you with all due propriety. And you Ahmed Beg, look to the preparation of flower fans and garlands and flowers stitched in sheets for offering. All must be done by this evening. The most important of all, you Inuzzur are in charge of the mounts, we leave early this evening." He turned with the intention of leaving, but stood there suspended, the glazed look in his eyes replaced by a feverish glow.

"Just to get away from this morbid state of affairs, Zil-e-Subhani. Are we a part of this pleasant excursion?" Ghalib asked skeptically.

"Of course, my poets and viziers. We would have poetry sessions. Sufi music and songs under the canopy of starry skies." He turned to his heels, color rising to his gaunt cheeks and feverish glow in his eyes deepening.

The evening had descended early, it seemed, without pomp and pageantry as Bahadur Shah Zafar had dreamed or expected. The saddest of evenings, Ghalib had thought while accompanying royal pilgrims on the way to Mehrauli. Rather, it was a mournful procession with no fanfare of dancing girls and acrobats as was customary when there was peace and prosperity, but only the music of cannon shots in the distance. There was dearth of flowers too since most gardens were neglected during this pandemonium of killing and plundering. Only a couple of flower fans were hastily assembled and a few garlands. The age-old offerings of four-poster bed of flowers and waves of flowers on silken sheets were missing. The ladies in palanquins escorted by princes on caparisoned mounts were commencing this journey with heavy hearts, so was the king on his lone mount, bemoaning the absence of festivities in the bazaar.

Bahadur Shah Zafar was still shielded by some spell of dream-reality, but feverish strain had left him and he had grown quiet and contemplative. He and his entourage had left through Delhi Gate, halting briefly at Humayun's tomb and then proceeding straight toward Mehrauli. Bahadur Shah Zafar was oblivious to the poets Shefta and Ghalib riding beside him and they too were lost in their lone contemplations, merely the scepters of someone's imagination if anyone chanced to watch them this sepulchral evening. One flower fan and a garland were offered at Yogmaya Temple followed by a simple repast.

Now the machalchis were lighting their torches as the procession headed toward the shrine of Qutubddin Kaki. Something hoary and subliminal was in the air as if some evil was lurking against the dark shadows, but not a soul was to be seen for miles at this hour of the night.

Azad along with Prince Jawan Bakht and Prince Shah Abbas were night escorts riding beside the palanquins, but their young hearts were heavy with the weight of premonitions. A gibbous moon had sailed above the white clouds, scudding along over the highway to starry heavens. In the distance, Jungli Mahal was coming into view, lit only by moonbeams. To Prince Jawan Bakht, this palace looked haunting and menacing, but he suppressed that feeling.

"Are the Begums going to rest here in this palace, Zil-e-Subhani, while we continue our journey toward the shrine of Qutubddin Kaki?" Prince Jawan Bakht asked, his heart dithering.

"Might as well ask the Begums, my Prince." Bahadur Shah Zafar began somnambulantly. "Though this palace looks dismal. No colorful lamps or rich carpets to welcome us." He sighed, the Scythian night within him more terrible than this unwholesome, unwelcoming island of darkness.

"I don't want to be robbed of the privilege of making offerings at the shrine of Qutubddin Kaki." Zeenat Mahal chimed in, peeking out of her palanquin.

"Thank you, Beloved, for saving me the trouble of making a decision." Bahadur Shah Zafar sighed again as if alone with his beloved in this dream-world. "We should dismount here and walk to the shrine."

A sad and solemn procession of the royal pilgrims had reached the shrine of Qutubddin Kaki on foot as if ready to offer their lives if peace could be ensured. Abandoning their palanquins, the ladies had succeeded in infusing light-hearted gaiety to this strange whim-caprice of the king. Torches of the machalchis were adding great charm to the moonlit night, highlighting the grand gateway to the shrine. Shafts of moonlight scintillating through the marble screen of Moti Masjid not far off, was enhancing the ritual of offering flowers and garlands at the shrine. After that ritual all stood in reverence, praying silently until Bahadur Shah Zafar announced over his shoulders.

"The ladies would rest at Jungli Mahal while we would go to our Amarian picnic spot at the mango grove."

"Not at Jungli Mahal, Zil-e-Subhani!" Zeenat Mahal protested. "We would stay at Jahaz Mahal as we always did before."

"Then we must commence our poetry session in Jharna next to Jahaz Mahal, Beloved." Bahadur Shah Zafar's heart was awakening to the pain in living. The mockery of his impoverished circumstances landing upon his awareness like an avalanche. "The purity of that waterfall is crystal-clear, and it seems to serenade some lost beloved. Mahbub Ali Khan, may his soul rest in peace, once in response to one of my comments said that these falls serenade the saint. I am hoping damask roses are still in bloom." He dared not meet anyone's gaze lest he weep. The enormity of war with all its atrocities and absurdities crushing his poetic spirit into pincers of agony."

Dawn was emerging pale and crimson, much like the freshly spilt blood. Poetry session had lost its sting of mad versification and was on the verge of expiration. It had been hours since the ladies had sought the comfort of sleep in Jahaz Mahal. Jharna was not the royal abode of the king and his poets, but the mango grove with rich carpets under their feet and a canopy of stars overhead. Machalchis of course were vigilant, entranced by the downpour of inspiration, so replete with grief and lamentations. Shefta's voice was swaying on the last rungs of recital, his look opiate and distraught.

> *"Who has lived in peace on this wasted hearth*
> *The rose lies lacerated, restless blows the breeze*
> *All are subsumed in Him, but He stands unique*
> *The glass inheres in the mirror, the mirror*
> *   retains its entity*
> *What matters is the substance, not the surface show*
> *If the mirage effaces the wave, it serves no need*
> *We do not see a whiff of breeze, nor a rose-scented sweet*
> *In our days of restlessness, we keep an even keel*
> *What is so surprising if the masks are many-hued*
> *They assume the color and shape, depending*
> *   on the sites they see*
> *The object and its qualities thus mutually correlate*
> *As the sun and its rays, springing from the*
> *   brightening east*
> *Once again we long to taste music sweet and*
> *   rapturous wine*
> *For long we have lived a life of abstinence complete."*

"Food for my soul, this poem of yours, Shefta." Bahadur Shah Zafar complimented, his gaze arresting Ghalib. "One last poem, Ghalib, and then we all must woo sleep."

"Maybe the very last, Zil-e-Subhani." Ghalib laughed histrionically.

"Again the vernal reign arrives
The sun and moon survey the sight
How the earth is beautified
From end to end the earth presents
A challenge to the starry skies
Pressed for space, the expanding green
Turned to moss, no water lies
To see the verdure decked with blooms
Narcissus has been blessed with sight
The air breathes the breath of wine
A stroll, the bliss of wine provides
Why shouldn't Ghalib, the world rejoice
The saintly king has got alright."

"Sublime, sublime! Saints and sinners in all of us." Bahadur Shah Zafar heaved himself up slowly. "Farewell to the night, yet dawn is bidding us to sleep. You all go, seek the comforting abode of Jungli Mahal. I must seek solitude before I retire."

"One last poem from you, Zil-e-Subhani, before we grant you the privilege of solitude." Was Ghalib's nostalgic appeal.

"I have forfeited all privileges, my Friend, already." Bahadur Shah Zafar's bruised heart was uttering these words, not his lips.

"What on earth did we see
Dream-like seemed the world indeed
Though man is but a clod of earth
A water bubble it turned to be
Unnumbered beauties though we saw
But none like you on land or lea
Swell thee not, O bloated bubble
Suddenly would burst and cease
The heart before that fatal glance
Is like a victim, arrow-seized
Though we mingled ourselves in dust
The dust of His feet we couldn't be
Give your heart to none, O Zafar
Faithless is all the world you see."

Amidst half applause and half protests, poets had retired along with the machalchis. Bahadur Shah Zafar was left alone, grateful that his wish to be alone was honored. He had begun to stroll on the familiar paths, awed by the beauty of sunrise so very fresh and sparkling. The crimson streaks were blending with the purple ones and he thought those were large gashes, big wounds from the hearts of all victims so brutally tortured, mutilated and slaughtered. His own soul was swollen much like a purple wound, and he kept drifting under some spell of peace he had not experienced for so many years. Something noble and awful had touched his soul, had given it strength to embrace his sufferings. Fatigue had left him and he had that uncanny feeling that his old heart was infused with some strange energy which was making him leap and dance, though his senses were suspended in a daze.

The scent of damask roses was in the air and Bahadur Shah Zafar inhaled it deeply, his senses reeling against the onslaught of memories which seemed so real. The path which he had taken toward Jharna edged by neem trees on both sides was decorated with silk pennants, his very sight was playing tricks. He thought he was entering the familiar bazaar of festivities, athletes and acrobats whirling and twirling their Bhutans. Musicians and dancing girls and soldiers in uniforms, all were a part of this Flower Festival. He could feel the shower of silver coins and flowers over his shoulders, the poets and the viziers cheering. Suddenly all music had stopped, the chain of his reveries broken. He stood under the Mulsari tree in perfect immobility. Another spell of dream-reality was invading his solitude, so very alive and surreal.

He was in this garden of the Festival of Flowers, but it was not a garden. He was caught in a whirlwind of mystical journey, his soul entering a realm unknown where prayers of the mortals find fulfillment. And yet again, it was a fragrant garden, its beauty ravished for the sake of offering royal gifts at the shrines of the saints and the pundits. Garlands upon garlands were piled high at the gate of Yogmaya Temple and at the shrine of Qutubddin Kaki. Flowers tracing mosaic patterns on hand-held fans and four-poster bed of flowers decked with intricate designs of roses and marigold was coming into view. His hands were reaching out to touch and feel the vibrant colors in flowers, but he was slumping down, his eyes closed and dreams unfolding in rivulets of blood.

Yes, the mystical journey had ended, the garden was no more. He was the prisoner of time, exiled into an alien world. The face of cruelty, dark as death was everywhere. His sons were killed, his palace ruined, his jewels confiscated. He was drifting deep into mists gossamer where there were no pains and no sorrows. He indeed had taken a last walk in his garden and would never celebrate another Festival of Flowers. Something was wrong in the picture of his dream. He was returning to this garden, his last mystical encounter with loss, grief, disbelief. A light drizzle had awakened him from the dream-state of his nightmares. And yet he was sleepwalking toward Jahaz Mahal, drunk with grief and hopelessness.

Chapter Thirteen
Shattered Star

Bahadur Shah Zafar, the ill-starred king of Delhi was seated on his Peacock Throne, alone and forlorn. He was bejeweled and richly appareled. Almost two and a half weeks since his return from that capricious journey to Mehrauli and he was whirled back into the reality of siege and waves of atrocities. Paradoxically, reality had escaped him and he had begun to hallucinate half the time, half mad with grief and shock. Even this particular day, reality had eluded him. He had taken great pains in dressing up regally as if he was getting ready to preside over his court. No court in session and no one attending on him, he had begun writing letters to his sons. He had been writing since hours, not even aware that now it was late afternoon. Princes, even Zeenat Mahal had checked on him now and then, all returning to their private asylums against the weight of their own inner misery and torment.

Prince Mirza Mughal had returned to Diwan-i-Khas with the intention of seeking advice from his royal father, but noticing a clutter of letters over the carpet he had slumped at the foot of the throne dejected and overwhelmed. Bahadur Shah Zafar was still writing, oblivious to the presence of his son, his own form sculpted into gold by chunks of sunlight filtering through engraved arches. This rectangular central chamber itself seemed polished with gold, accentuating maroon carpets against the beams of sunlight. Ironically Prince Mirza Mughal had picked up randomly a letter which was addressed to him and he began reading it, distraught and frightened.

My son, let it be known that when the sepoys first came to me, I told them plainly that I possessed neither soldiers, nor money to help them, but that I would not hold my life dear if it were any use to them. They promised to lay down their lives in the attempt to carry out my orders and in showing me allegiance. So they were permitted to stay here, though they were ignorant and unacquainted with court etiquette. Now many days have passed, but they continue to indulge in their vicious habits. They don't carry out my commands. I ordered them to encamp outside the city, but I find that one regiment is residing at Delhi Gate, a second one at the Ajmeri Gate and a third at the Lahori Gate right inside the city walls. I think I wrote about this to you several months ago, and yet I don't know if you received my letter. Well, they come riding on horseback into the palace courtyard improperly dressed. Even though whenever an officer of the British Government came into the palace grounds, he dismounted from his horse at the gate of Diwan-i-Am and proceeded on foot. Moreover the sepoys plunder the bazaars day and night on false pretense that some Englishman is hiding inside. They dash into the homes of innocent people and go killing and plundering. They break open the locks and even carry away doors and the shutters. If they do not desist from this shameful behavior and don't obey my orders, I would retire to the shrine of Qutubddin Kaki and sit there as a fakir. My son, you must not take this lightly on account of my old age and feebleness. I cannot bear all this weight on my shoulders. And it is no easy matter to rule such people and— Prince Mirza Mughal stopped reading, cupping his head into his hands. He couldn't speak or move, his heart a floodgate of anguish and presage. Unable to contain the flood of sorrow, he exclaimed suddenly.

"Zil-e-Subhani, what are you writing? I have read one letter, it has nothing to do with the present. What you are writing now pertains to four months hence. Right now we are on the brink of annihilation."

"There is no present, only past and future, my Son." Bahadur Shah Zafar appeared to awaken amidst some ocean of profoundest deeps, his look wild and piercing. "What was then is now!" His eyes were lit up with a mad glint. "Didn't the sepoys come to me demanding money? They were hungry they said. I could only offer them forty thousand rupees, but they were not satisfied, clamoring for more. Then I brought out all the crown jewels, even the jewels of the begums, asking them to take those if that would assuage their hunger. What surly lot these men are, steeped deep in violence, yet ashamed to accept pebbles of the earth from the king?"

"What was then, Zil-e-Subhani if you can't recall was the rain of bullets on the royal palace and on the streets of Delhi. The breeching and cracking of the ramparts. The bombardment over its

174

gates, the battering of its bastions." Prince Mirza Mughal began with a dithering heart. "Not to mention heaps of dead bodies on the streets and the wounded groaning for medical assistance. Now the British are not far from the gates of Delhi. Now is not then, but now, we the besiegers have become besieged."

"How very admirable of you, my Son, to remind the king." Bahadur Shah Zafar laughed hysterically. "The British are already in Delhi. Qudsia Bagh is theirs. They are guarding the Kashmiri Gate, the Lahori Gate—how much blood spilt on the steps of the Jami Masjid?"

"Bakht Khan is still defending the city of Delhi, Zil-e-Subhani. If we don't fortify our—" Prince Mirza Mughal was distracted by the breezy arrival of Prince Khizr Sultan.

"Zil-e-Subhani, Bakht Khan just arrived. Probably the bearer of bad news. Ilahi Bakhsh wanted to talk with him, but he stormed past him and has shut himself up in his private quarters." Prince Khizr Sultan's own expression was one of utter dejection, his gaze shifting from king to the prince.

"Misfortunes upon misfortunes. Since he came here, he has brought nothing but grief." Bahadur Shah Zafar's look was distant and feverish. "To feed him and his insolent rabble, even the silver of my howdah and royal plates are minted into currency. Nothing is left, this useless life—" His thoughts were truncated by the arrival of his grandson Prince Abul Bakr.

"The begums are requesting your company at dinner, Zil-e-Subhani." Prince Abul Bakr appeared to shrink against the feverish glow in the king's eyes.

"Dinner, no, my Child, we would have a feast tonight!" Bahadur Shah Zafar declared with a sudden burst of animation. "To celebrate life. How often I have offered my life?" He paused, noticing the reluctant approach of Ghalib. "Ah, we would have a poetry session right here. Yes, Ghalib, my sons, they write poetry if you didn't know. Yet, they pretend I don't know."

"Zil-e-Subhani." Ghalib curtsied with his usual flair for decorum. "Poetry indeed, Zil-e-Subhani." He abandoned himself at the foot of the throne where all three princes had managed to huddle together. "I have ceased to write poetry since a bomb destroyed the gunpowder factory in Gali Churiwallan, killing five hundred people. Sepoys, in return, as you know, Zil-e-Subhani, are accusing Ahsanullah Khan of treason and have destroyed his mansion." He sighed, his face ravaged by grief. "How can I forget the great mansion of Ahsanullah Khan which in beauty and ornament was equal to the painted palaces of China? After looting the roofs were torched. The great beams and the inlaid panels of the ceiling were reduced to ashes. The walls were completely blackened by smoke. It seemed, in grief, the mansion wore a black mantle."

> *"Do not be misled by the fortunes the skies may bestow*
> *The treacherous skies entangle*
> *In anguish and torment*
> *Those they formerly laid in the lap of love."*

Bahadur Shah Zafar recited this quatrain which invaded his thoughts suddenly, the fever in his gaze abating. "Didn't you write this, Ghalib?"

"Can't recall, Zil-e-Subhani." Ghalib murmured evasively.

"Can't recall, don't remember! Mad litany of sad times." Bahadur Shah Zafar murmured back. "And yet how can one forget facts staring us in the face. No one is interested in defending Delhi, neither Hindus, nor Muslims. They sit in their homes, playing cards or drinking. General Nicholson I hear is shot by a cannonball in the left of his arm?"

"The sepoys fled, Zil-e-Subhani, against the heavy assault under the command of General Nicholson." Prince Mirza Mughal broke the seal of his silence. "The British soldiers discovered a large stock of wine and got drunk, it was reported."

"Yes, that was when Captain Hodson lamented aloud, Zil-e-Subhani. *Our troops are utterly demoralized by hard work and hard drink.*" Prince Khizr Sultan offered his own morsel of news.

"Ah, that cruel, vicious Captain Hodson!" Bahadur Shah Zafar rose from his seat as if stung. "His troops are rightly named *Plungers.*" A wave of shock passed through his spine like a sharp knife. "Didn't he burn twenty-five sepoys alive?"

"Who is counting, Zil-e-Subhani!" Ghalib began exigently. "Countless hanged or slaughtered. A just act of vengeance they say, for what sepoys did to the British. Now Earl Ellenborough is suggesting, I hear, that all males of Delhi be castrated and this city named as Eunuchabad."

"Delhi the beautiful! Its beauty marred and gouged." Bahadur Shah Zafar lamented aloud, oblivious to the presence of others. "Has it come to such a pass? Is this the end? Delhi in utter ruins, its poets and artisans mocked and mutilated. Would they

176

rather not choose to be blown from the mouth of a cannon than to be castrated? Didn't the Wahhabis request to be blown at the mouth of cannon than to be hanged on the trees?" He paused, his eyes sparkling with madness as if his heart was on fire. "And all this since sepoys invaded our palace and gardens. Without my knowledge they killed, plundered and wielded the whips of anarchy. Even imprisoning whomever they wished at the dictates of their own whims. Extorting forcibly whatever sums of money they thought fit from merchants and appropriating such exactions to their own private purposes." His gaze was arresting the slow approach of Bakht Khan who looked haggard, his shoulders sagging.

"Zil-e-Subhani." Bakht Khan muttered weakly. "The conditions on the Ridge are deteriorating. We are losing ground. Troops are disheartened and leaving."

"I do not care who goes or stays!" Bahadur Shah Zafar exploded with a sudden burst of anger. "I did not ask anybody to come here and I do not stop anyone from leaving. You were the one who brought destruction over the heads of Nimuch troops through your own sense of pride and your obsession to claim victory all by yourself. Didn't you?" He demanded.

"Not true, Zil-e-Subhani." Bakht Khan was transformed from that of a proud general to a lowly suppliant, crumbling against the weight of his own guilt. "Since the siege train came to the rescue of the British troops, they have grown very aggressive and their supply of ammunition is inexhaustible."

"You should take responsibility for the disaster of Najafgarh, Bakht Khan." Bahadur Shah Zafar continued relentlessly. "At a critical moment you withheld support from Sudhari Singh, the commander of Nimuch troops. That's the reason they suffered defeat. You didn't accept his suggestion to advance and encamp across the canal. And when the British guns bombarded the grounds where Nimuch troops were encamped, you didn't come to their defense."

"Torrential rains demoralized the Nimuch troops, Zil-e-Subhani, but that is in the past." Bakht Khan shook his head vigorously in an attempt to drive away the demons, it seemed. "I have come with a suggestion. Delhi is be taken in a few days I am afraid. Your life is not safe here. When the British come here they will take all you have and will kill you and your family. Come with me to the mountains. We would rally great forces and defeat the British."

"I have been wearing the shroud of mourning since you came here and have been always ready to expire. It would be better that you kill me!" Bahadur Shah Zafar's eyes were sparkling with anger and madness.

"How could you say that, Zil-e-Subhani? You are that candle of universal light which would keep India intact against British invasions!" Bakht Khan declared with a sudden passion and maddening fury of his own state of helplessness. "Your ancestors faced bigger setbacks than this, yet persevered. Padishah Babur often had to escape surrounded by his enemies. Emperor Humayun went into self exile in Persia to insure safety for his life and for his family. And yet the Moghul Empire flourished and the legacy of the Moghuls stayed. Come with us, Zil-e-Subhani, our army would protect and safeguard you and your royal family."

"I am thinking of going to Humayun's tomb. If you don't find me here in the palace, come to Humayun's tomb and we would talk then." Bahadur Shah Zafar muttered distractedly. "Now leave, I am tired. Must rest, think."

"Yes, Zil-e-Subhani." Bakht Khan murmured as distractedly as the king before plodding out, almost colliding with Ilahi Bakhsh on his way out.

"I overheard what Bakht Khan just said, Zil-e-Subhani." Ilahi Bakhsh curtsied hastily, his expression flustered. "There is no place Bakht Khan's troops could hide and put up a fight against the British. I beg you not to heed the offer of Bakht Khan to go somewhere under the protection of his troops already dwindling in numbers. You and your royal family would not withstand the assault of heat and rainy season is on its way. The best way to deal with this situation is to befriend the British. I myself would arrange with the British to secure the promise of safety for you and your family. No harm would ever come to you and your family."

"No harm would ever come to us. We are of royal blood and strong in faith." Bahadur Shah Zafar got to his feet with an astonishing surge of alacrity, giddy with the fever of anguish and madness. "Tomorrow at the stroke of midnight, we are going to attack the Ridge, I myself would lead. A proclamation to this affect is to be issued by the beat of drums to the populace of Delhi this very evening. We would gather at the Kashmiri Gate and when we attack, victory would be ours. Britons would flee, never to come back and harass us."

"Zil-e-Subhani." Ghalib protested, getting to his feet stunned.

The princes were in utter shock, springing to their feet in unison, standing there appalled and speechless.

"Don't just stand there and gawk, Ilahi Bakhsh. Go, summon Kali Khan and entrust him with this proclamation." Bahadur Shah Zafar commanded.

"Yes, Zil-e-Subhani." Ilahi Bakhsh stalked out of Diwan-i-Khas, deflated and apprehensive.

"Don't bother to come and see me tomorrow, Ghalib." Bahadur Shah Zafar sauntered past all, unseeing. "Go, finish your diwan of poems." He left Diwan-i-Khas, forgetting about his proclamation, it was obvious.

The proclamation was sounded after all, but Bahadur Shah Zafar was not there to honor his decision by his presence. An evening of fear and presage, followed by nightmares had rendered Bahadur Shah Zafar more vulnerable than ever before, and he had decided to leave the sanctuary of his own Fort. Afflicted with the fever of madness after he had left Diwan-i-Khas, a barrage of reports had begun to filter into the palace that British soldiers had concealed themselves inside the houses nearby with the intention of attacking the Fort. Fever of madness still coursing through his veins, his sleep was rigged with nightmares most horrific and excruciating. Blood was everywhere in his dreams. Royal blood churning before his eyes in fantastic ripples and streets of Delhi carving rivulets of blood, bright and crimson.

Crimson dawn with omens dark had jolted Bahadur Shah Zafar to a rude awakening. Nightmares had heightened the fever of his madness to such a pitch that he had herded his royal household together. Announcing that they were leaving the Fort right away, taking refuge at the tomb of Humayun against the imminent assault of the British.

The streets of Delhi were deserted when the royal entourage left the Red Fort. To Bahadur Shah's feverish awareness, Delhi seemed to be cloaked in mourning as if dreading some terrible misfortune which could not be averted. Though leaving the palace in utter haste, Bahadur Shah Zafar had not neglected to carry with him the palace diary, a reliquary from Prophet's beard and three sacred hair of the Prophet in a box. These relics had been in his possession as a sacred trust from father to son in the House of Timur since fourteenth century. He had deposited all these relics at the tomb of one Sufi by the name of Nizamuddin Auliya in the care of Shah Ghulam Hasan before proceeding to the tomb of Humayun.

Standing at the eastern gate of Humayun's tomb, Bahadur Shah Zafar with a sudden clarity had remembered about his mock proclamation. Also recalling with much regret the absence of Bakht Khan who had come here telling him that his proclamation had gone into affect, but since the king was not there, the crowds had dispersed. Bahadur Shah Zafar kept standing at the eastern gate, peering out into darkness, envisioning the scene of his conversation with Bakht Khan who had begged him to come with him to Lucknow with his band of troops waiting at the River Side, but he had declined.

What would I do in Lucknow? Bahadur Shah Zafar's head was spinning like a globe, muddied and bloodied. *Why did I leave my palace? Why I am here at Humayun's tomb?* He leaned his head against the grilled gate, overwhelmed with grief and confusion. *Where am I? Where is Zeenat, my princes, princesses?* His eyes were closing and the ground slipping out from under his feet.

The night was silent and menacing, but Bahadur Shah Zafar was oblivious to his surroundings. The wind was whispering to him dolorous secrets through the swishing of neem trees and yet he couldn't hear anything. His gaze was riveted to the sky studded with stars, a crescent moon embedded in there like a sharp bow, waxen and luminescent.

Suddenly, Bahadur Shah Zafar was sucked into another plane of dream-illusion where nothing existed but his senses gone numb. He didn't know where he was. Delhi was a distant dream. He was tossed into a void, divested of royal robes and crown jewels. Alone and forlorn, imprisoned in an alien land, he had even forgotten his own name. He was on his deathbed, Zeenat Mahal watching him. His lips were forming words without sounds, a song rippling in his head.

I am not the apple of anyone's eye, nor the joy of any heart
A handful of useless dust, no purpose I discharge
I've lost my strength and shape, I am severed from my friend
I am spring of the garden, laid waste by fall
I am a friend to on one, nor a foe to aught
I am the star-crossed fate, I am the ruined resort
Why should someone sing my dirge, or come to lay a wreath
I am the tomb of helplessness, better left in dark

I am not a lilting song, which others may hear or heed
I am the wail by severance caused, a cry of anguished heart
Bahadur Shah Zafar was gathering pearls of poetry in tears in dreams. He had slumped to the ground in a royal heap. His body was leaning against the gate and jewels on his crown throbbing like purple wounds against the canopy of white stars.

Autograph of His Majesty Bahadur Shah of Dehlie.

29ᵗʰ April 1844.

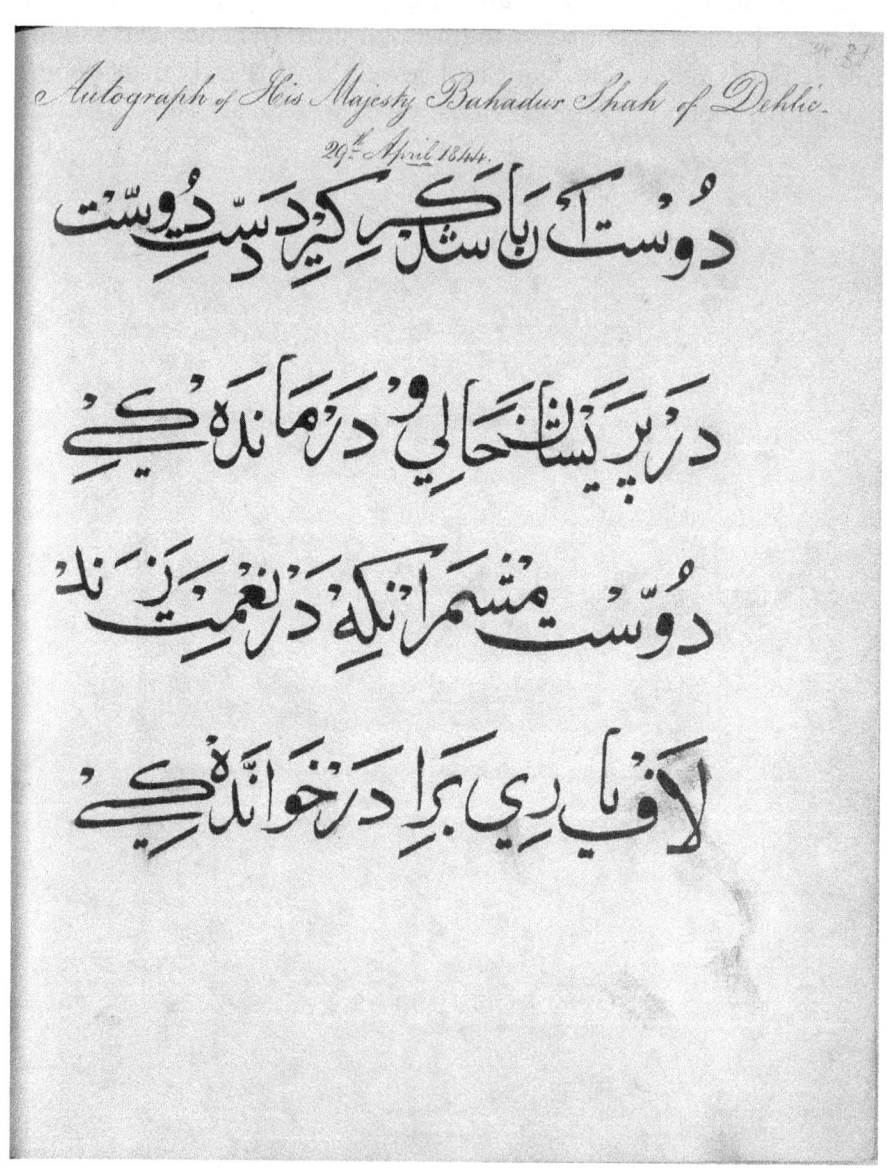

دُوست آرا باشلا کجر کرد دست دُوست

در پریشان حالی و درماندہ کے

دُوست مشمار آنکہ در نعمت زنند

لاف یاری برادر خواندے

Poem written by Bahadur Shah, dated 29 April 1844.

Chapter Fourteen
Sacking of Delhi

Delhi was burning this morning, pillaged and plundered. The streets were littered with corpses and rivulets of blood streamed through the homes of the victims in wake of British troops marching toward Red Fort. They didn't know that the king had fled the night before. Madly drunk with the loot of the liquor and pugnaciously drunk with the poison of vengeance, they were on their grand mission to capture the king and his royal household. Even a brief eclipse the evening before had not deterred them in killing indiscriminately. So determined they were to reach the gates of city that they had engaged in hand-to-hand fighting when other means didn't prove successful. Captain Hodson was indefatigable, though the dwindling groups of sepoys were proving to be tireless fighters. General Nicholson was already injured in the arm while commanding, more hurt by the drunken revelry of his soldiers than by his own physical wounds. General Wilson was appalled by the suggestion of General Nicholson who was contemplating retreat.

Far from retreating, British troops were advancing toward the Red Fort from their front-line position close to the ruins of the Delhi Bank. The spiked guns were lined up in front of the palace and the explosion party dashed forward under cover of fire to drop powder bags under the gates. In contrast to facing great difficulties while capturing Kabul Gate, Lahori Gate and Kashmiri Gate, there was virtually no resistance at the palace gates. The palace gates were blown open quickly and the British took possession of the palace. Only a few men were found hiding within and they were slain indiscriminately. A great cheer could be heard ricocheting through the palace halls, while the British victory flag was hoisted over the ramparts of the Red Fort.

The city of Delhi, already ruined and plundered and submerged into rivers of blood was given to looting afresh by the orders of General Wilson, sanctioning the killing of all natives they could find. And that's what the soldiers precisely did, returning to the houses where the rich merchants sat behind closed doors. Sat shivering with fright at the barbarity of the British assaults against their men, women and children, murdered in cold blood or slaughtered brutally like animals. Chandni Chowk once again was the scene of horror, violence and carnage where a few hours ago one-eyed General Theo Metcalfe's forces had fended off the axes and swords of the natives. The natives of course were hacked to pieces as they tried to flee pell-mell through Kabul Gate or Lahori Gate. After this pandemonium of mass slaughter the streets and bazaars of Delhi were soon deserted.

Looting more liquor from the stores and getting grandly drunk, the British soldiers were on a mission of indiscriminate violence, killing all who dared show their faces on the streets. Men were being shot, hanged or bayoneted with a surge of glee and self-gloating. From all quarters, entire families trying to escape from the city were rounded up and executed in a ditch outside the city gates. Amidst the corpses littered on the streets were women with their throats cut from ear to ear, most probably by their own fathers or husbands against fear that they would be captured by the British. Though the ones surviving were not only captured by the British, but killed, their gold ornaments torn out of their ears and throats. The plunder at Kashmiri Gate swelled to a mountain several feet high. Silver and gold coins, jewels and jewelry boxes of exquisite designs and broaches carved out of solid gems of rubies and emeralds. So great and precious were these treasures that there were fights amongst the British soldiers while dividing the spoils, those fights ending even in bloodshed.

The palace of Bahadur Shah Zafar too was thoroughly looted and ransacked by the regiments of General Wilson, Captain Hodson and General Theo Metcalfe. Gold mohurs, strings of pearls, necklaces of gold studded with rubies, diamonds and emeralds. Plates of silver and gold and boxes and vases inlaid with precious gems. Silks and tapestries, even a silk robe of the emperor with verses of the Quran woven into its fabric. Royal wardrobe as well as royal furniture were seized with great greed and stowed away. Chests with koftgari designs, tables and chairs with gold marquetry. Fans of ivory, swords and daggers with jeweled hilts, cashmere shawls, gold bangles and gold-filigree ornaments.

General Wilson had made himself at home in Diwan-i-Khas. Seated on Peacock Throne he proposed a toast to Queen Victoria. *God bless the Queen!*

"We would have a grand dinner this evening right here in Diwan-i-Khas to celebrate our victory." General Wilson proposed another toast amidst cheers from his officers and soldiers. "We would torch the whole city of Delhi and erase it from the map of this earth." He sang gleefully.

"I would not suggest such a drastic measure, General Wilson." Edward Vibrat drank heavily. "I have seen enough horror in less than an hour. Almost forty defenseless people shot in cold-blooded murder by Turkman Gate alone."

"If not the entire city of Delhi, then anything within the radius of five hundred yards should be demolished as a celebration of our hard-one victory." General Theo Metcalfe suggested hilariously.

"Only to demolish Jami Masjid and Red Fort would be enough to mark the inception of celebrations." General Nicholson croaked against the assault of pain in his thigh—the gunshot wound he had received but yesterday in addition to his wounds in arm and left hand. "I wanted to witness the fall of Delhi and now I can die in peace."

"We should spare Jami Masjid and the Red Fort." General Wilson proposed thoughtfully. "It's enough that our soldiers are dancing jigs inside Jami Masjid and Sikhs are lighting victory fires next to the mosque."

"The celebrations would not be complete without the jigs of vengeance, General Wilson." Fred Maisey boasted drunkenly. "Fourteen hundred Delhiwallahs were slaughtered in Kucha Chelan. Why, because Nawab Ali Khan resisted the plundering and shot three British soldiers. Then began the spree of mass murder. Haveli of the Nawab was blown asunder. People were bayoneted and when our soldiers got tired of this sport, they rounded up the survivors, ordered them to march toward Jamna. Then lined them up below the walls of the Fort and shot them."

"Such a shame that amongst them were poets, painters, philosophers and calligraphists." Fred Roberts raised a mock lament. "I felt no pity for them though, but my heart sank when an old grey bearded man was brought and shot most savagely."

"We can't find the king and his family anywhere, General Wilson." Edward Campbell stormed into Diwan-i-Khas breathless. "We have searched everywhere, Diwan-i-Am, private apartments, arcades and cloisters, even the harem quarters and the inner courtyards. Not a trace of the royal family—" He couldn't finish, becoming aware of the slow approach of Ilahi Bakhsh.

"I know where the king is." Ilahi Bakhsh caught the attention of everyone with his air of mystery and smugness. "The king and his family have retired to the tomb of late emperor Humayun. General Bakht Khan was also there, begging the king to go with him to Lucknow along with his troops. I have persuaded the king otherwise and have made sure that he doesn't leave with Bakht Khan. Since I am in secret communication with Ahsanullah Khan, he has sent me a message that the king has declined the invitation of Bakht Khan, and the general has left along with his troops. State jewels of the king are with the queen Zeenat Mahal. She is with him and so is his royal family."

"Let me go, General Wilson, and capture the king!" Captain Hodson appealed suddenly.

"Very dangerous expedition. I cannot allow." General Wilson demurred.

"Our victory would be incomplete if we didn't capture the king and his family." Captain Hodson persisted.

"Why don't we send Maulvi Sarfaraz and Ilahi Bakhsh to test the mood of the king if he is ready to surrender?" General Wilson was thoughtful and concerned.

"Captain Hodson should be allowed to go with them, General Wilson, that's only fair." Neville Chamberlain appealed on behalf of the Captain who looked crushed and flustered.

"Alright." General Wilson agreed reluctantly. "Let Maulvi Sarfaraz and Ilahi Bakhsh proceed first. Captain Hodson, you follow a little later and maintain a considerable distance between you and those two men. Take a small force of few soldiers with you. Go at your own risk and don't beg me to come to your rescue."

"Thank you, General Wilson." Captain Hodson almost collapsed with relief. The fever of vengeance rising inside him on the brink of explosion.

The afternoon scudded by islands of luminous clouds seemed surreal as Captain Hodson dispatched Punjabi irregular cavalry under the command of Ilahi Bakhsh and Maulvi Sarfaraz toward Humayun's Tomb. Unable to contain himself of the excitement and burning with the ardor of vengeance, he started soon after toward the marble Tomb with fifty of his soldiers. Half way to Humayun's Tomb, he could see Ilahi Bakhsh and Maulvi Sarfaraz, followed by their cavalry riding back toward Delhi.

Captain Hodson was greatly distressed upon learning that while on their way to Humayun's tomb, Ilahi Bakhsh and his men were attacked by a party of sowars who had killed four of his escorts, wounding their horses. Much to the chagrin of his own pride, Captain Hodson was able to persuade the retreating cavalcade to follow him and finally they were on their way to the Tomb in white marble. The clouds had grown thick and dark as they approached closer to Humayun's tomb. A storm was brewing within the hearts of men, it seemed, and within the hearts of nature. Reaching closer, Captain Hodson could see that a great crowd of guards and courtiers had taken shelter within the walls of the garden tomb.

Facing the white domes of the Tomb, Captain Hodson stood vigilant with his sword unsheathed, his troops waiting behind him as grim as the dark clouds above. He had already sent Ilahi Bakhsh and Maulvi Sarfaraz inside the chamber of the tomb where the king had lodged himself along with his family. They were entrusted with the message that if the king came out and surrendered peacefully, he and his family would not be harmed.

Inside the spacious chamber of Humayun's Tomb, Bahadur Shah Zafar was pacing under the spell of agony and disbelief. Suddenly he stopped in his act of pacing, glaring at both men, his eyes shooting coals of accusations.

"You stopped me from going with Bakht Khan." Bahadur Shah Zafar held Ilahi Bakhsh under the pincers of inquisition. "If the British have nothing to do with me then why are they here to arrest me?" His fever of madness was returning. As Ilahi Bakhsh didn't respond, hanging his head in shame, Bahadur Shah Zafar darted a scorching look at Maulvi Sarfaraz. "Mullas, for truth, have been the ruin of religions and empires. Go, Maulvi Sarfaraz, tell Captain Hodson that if he means what he says, then he should come to me and tell me the same thing face-to-face."

"Yes, Zil-e—" Maulvi Sarfaraz couldn't speak, fleeing against the fire of grief and madness in the eyes of the king.

This anguished scene was re-enacted again as Maulvi Sarfaraz at the entrance of the white Tomb entered, followed by Captain Hodson. Bahadur Shah Zafar peering through the door waved away Maulvi Sarfaraz, his gaze piercing the very soul of Captain Hodson.

"Are you Captain Hodson?" Bahadur Shah Zafar asked suspiciously.

"Yes, my name is William Hodson." Captain Hodson responded stiffly.

"If you are Captain Hodson then I want to hear form you the promise that you delivered to me through Ilahi Bakhsh."

"Be assured, O King, there is no danger to your life and your family if you come with me peacefully." Captain Hodson was feeling proud of this glorious lie, adding. "You would not be subject to dishonor or personal indignity."

"This satisfies me." Bahadur Shah Zafar almost collapsed with grief and exhaustion. But he stepped out bravely, lowering a command over his shoulders for his queen and princes to follow.

Palanquins were procured for the king, queen and Prince Jawan Bakht and they were escorted toward Delhi under the strict vigilance of the British guards. A wheeled carriage was waiting for the older princes, Prince Mirza Mughal, Prince Khizr Sultan and for king's grandson Prince Abul Bakr. Well-wishers of the king and a few stragglers had lined up on both sides of the street, watching the king in custody with great sorrow, but dared not lament or protest in presence of the British soldiers armed with rifles. At Captain Hodson's orders the palanquins had to be at least one mile ahead of the carriage before it could be driven toward Delhi. The carriage too was guarded and yet Captain Hodson had stayed close by lest the princes try to escape.

A hoary sunset flanked by luminescent clouds was hovering over the palanquins, wending their way past Lahori Gate toward Chandni Chowk on the road to Red Fort. Captain Hodson had commanded that route so that the citizens of Delhi could see that their king was under arrest. Though, there was virtually nobody to witness this portrait of sorrow. The streets were silent and deserted. There were no merchants sitting in the bazaars. No strings of camels or bullock wagons toiling through the city gates. No passers-by in the thoroughfares. No men talking by the doors of the houses. No children playing in the dust. No women voices from behind the screens. The path was littered with corpses and broken furniture. Ashes were still black by the open hearths and animals were roaming free without their masters. The houses were burnt or shattered by cannon shot and fragments of shells were scattered amidst corpses gouged and scarred by crows and jackals.

None is left now for you to kill with your coquettish sword
Unless you bring them back to life and then kill them again

188

Bahadur Shah Zafar's mind, with astonishing clarity was chasing that fleeting memory of tragedy and massacre a century ago by Nadir Shah. Within only a span of few hours Nadir Shah had accomplished the task of such a great massacre that a petitioner had cried before him, reciting that couplet which was now eluding the captive king. Instead he was transported into the time-bubble of his last Flower Walk to the shrine of Qutubddin Kaki in Mehrauli, his soul flooded with the sweetness of Sufi music. Barely noticing that he and his queen and their prince were escorted into the haveli of Zeenat Mahal in Lal Kuan, received by Kendal Coghill as prisoners. Double sentry was posted at the doors of their chamber. *Old pig!* Bahadur Shah Zafar could not help hear that epithet hurled after him by Kendal Coghill before the door was locked shut after them. *This old scoundrel!*

Another epithet was tearing open the rags of his memory which Captain Hodson had grunted under his breath before he was assisted into his palanquin.

Captain Hodson was now with the young scoundrels, the same epithet which he had flung at the king now swimming in his head, though he didn't voice it at the princes while riding beside their carriage most regally and haughtily. The streets were still deserted as they neared the city gates, guards surrounding the carriage on all sides while riding jauntily. Delhi Gate was coming into view and Captain Hodson's mind aflame with the fever of vengeance was suddenly snapped to action, as he commanded over his shoulders.

"We need to halt right here." Captain Hodson waved his colt revolver. "Macdowell, stop the carriage and order the princes to get out." He leaped down from his horse with the alacrity of a young man.

Against the glow of twilight the princes looked pale as they got out of the carriage, but they were unafraid since Captain Hodson had promised them safety and respectful treatment. Contrary to their trust and belief, the princes were ordered by Captain Hodson to stand by the wall of Delhi Gate and remove their shirts. Their jeweled swords were seized by the guards.

Though puzzled, the princes could not help but comply against the fiery gaze of Captain Hodson. The twilight appeared to crack on the horizon, carving pink streaks as the princes stood there naked waist up, their jewels throbbing with the pulse of their own subtle breath. A sepulchral silence had fallen over all, the guards standing there vigilant and speechless. Captain Hodson stood facing the princes, his eyes lowering coals of hatred.

In a flash Captain Hodson poised his colt revolver before him and began firing. Swiftly and precisely he shot point-blank until all princes fell in their own pools of blood. Prince Mirza Mughal was the first one to fall, shot through his heart, blood spluttering out of his chest like a gurgling fountain. Prince Khizr Sultan fell next, shot in the neck, his whole frame shuddering before he fell to the ground with a heartrending groan. Prince Abul Bakr the grandson of the king was the last one to die, suffering the agony of death before another shot could still his suffering.

"Remove their bloody signet rings and turquoise armlets from their stinking corpses as our reward of victory." Captain Hodson croaked with great pleasure. "Sever their heads and present those to the old king as our Nazr which he has been missing for the past few years." He jumped to his horse, riding through Delhi Gate as the king of the winds.

The rightful, unfortunate king of Delhi imprisoned inside the haveli of Zeenat Mahal didn't know about the tragic fate of his sons and grandson. He was aware of his own tragic existence though, sitting in a room stripped bare of all amenities with the exception of one coarse sheet between him and the bed. He too was robbed of all his jewels, even his silk robe taken away, replaced with a white robe of cotton. Zeenat Mahal and Prince Jawan Bakht were separated from him in another chamber of bare necessities, their jewels too confiscated by the greedy guards. Bahadur Shah Zafar sat hugging his knees, the trauma of his tragedy holding him impaled to the mercy of shock. Suddenly, the doors to this bare chamber were thrown open and Edward Campbell stormed in, carrying a tray laden with severed heads of the slain princes.

"Your Majesty." Edward Campbell mocked, lowering the tray beside the bed on the floor. "This is your long-neglected Nazr we had stopped presenting."

"Thanks to Allah!" Bahadur Shah Zafar's numb senses were awakening to the fire of madness. "The descendants of Timur always come in front of their fathers in this brave way." He couldn't take his gaze away from the beloved faces splattered with blood.

"Your brave descendants, old King, are going to delight us for days." Edward Campbell laughed boisterously. "We are going to impale these heads over the walls of Delhi Gate as our trophies of victory." He picked up the tray and stalked out of the room, banging the doors shut behind him.

Bahadur Shah Zafar sat there stunned, his heart somersaulting in throes of grief wild and excruciating. Slowly and involuntarily, tears began trickling down his white beard, wetting his white robe. He had not ever known such agony before, the lava of pain congealing his anguished heart and the volcanic eruption within his mind hot and searing. His very soul was broken and shattered. Nothing was left of him, but absurdity of illusions. He was drifting into dreams which had nothing to do with him, but with a world alien to his comprehension.

The king was inside Diwan-i-Khas. Everything was familiar, yet nothing belonged to him.

No, nothing is familiar.

Bahadur Shah Zafar's thoughts were asserting.

Diwan-i-Khas looked more like a church, some sort of service being conducted there with all due propriety. His dreams were taking him on a stroll through the bazaars of Delhi. Khas bazaar was no more. Kharram bazaar had disappeared. There was nothing left but dust and rubble. Gallows were being erected on Chandni Chowk. Jamna Bridge of boats was destroyed and the path to Flower Walk had disappeared like a dream.

Dreams were merging into dreams and a tunnel of future was sucking Bahadur Shah Zafar into its awful horrors he had not ever witnessed before. Gallows were not only being erected on Chandni Chowk but everywhere and citizens of Delhi were being herded in droves to be hanged. Actually, it was horrific to watch those men dangling and being kept alive while the British soldiers stood there puffing on their cigars and laughing.

Pandies hornpipe. We got to see them dance before they die.

The voice was that of General Theo Metcalfe, watching his soldiers devise means of hanging their victims in figures of eight. Down the street dead bodies were strewn in every direction and the wounded suffering death-throes of agony most pitiful and horrible.

The white ghost of Bahadur Shah Zafar in dreams was fleeing this horrible scene and seeking the sanctuary of Red Fort. Trooping through the ruined gardens of the palace, he was entering Diwan-i-Khas. Peacock Throne was there and the gilt chairs were occupied by British judges and lawyers, it seemed. Something strange was happening there, Diwan-i-Khas was transformed into a court house and some sort of court session was in progress, it was obvious. He could see an old man lying on a bare bed being prodded ruthlessly. A sudden realization was dawning upon him that the old man was he himself robed in white muslin, no jewels adorning his royal person. Jolted out of this nightmare Bahadur Shah Zafar sat upright on his bare bed. Paradoxically the nightmare was receded into the tunnels of his subconscious. He was awakened by rude noise of the opening and shutting of the doors.

A British officer on duty had entered imperiously, followed by two English sentries, armed with bayonets.

"You wouldn't be needing these." Edward Campbell tossed king's gilt slippers to the floor, laughing contemptuously. "Get up, old king, and bow to us, as you used to demand from us." He edged closer to the bed.

Bahadur Shah Zafar sat there stunned, his look glazed and uncomprehending. He didn't know where he was or what was happening.

"Get up, I say, and pay respects to us with great humility." Edward Campbell demanded, tugging at the king's white beard.

"Where is the buck antelope of my queen, so gentle and magnificent?" Bahadur Shah Zafar whimpered deliriously. "It is time to feed the pet tiger of my Zeenat Mahal. He must be fed."

"Bloody interesting!" A volley of mirth escaped the lips of Edward Campbell. "Your niggers are being hanged and fed to the dogs and you are concerned about the pet tiger of your wife." He staggered away, drunk with the fever of hatred and vengeance.

Bahadur Shah Zafar was drifting into the bowers of nightmares once again, his head lolling to one side and his lips trembling. He was sighing and groaning as if horrific scenes were unfolding behind the closed shutters of his eyes. A low moan and a slight tremor and something within him were awakening to the poetry in life so brutally ripped apart by the gusts of tragedies. His lips were moving, his voice clear and doleful.

> *Not worth narrating is Delhi's tale*
> *It will make us weep and wail*
> *Such palaces have the raiders razed*
> *Which were a sight to see and praise*
> *None is left to tell this tale*
> *Except Zafar, the unfortunate.*

Chapter Fifteen
Mock Trial of the Emperor

Almost bent double over a brass basin, Bahadur Shah Zafar sat retching violently, supported by Ghulam Abbas on his bed with a dirty blanket. He had been imprisoned in this bare room of Zeenat Mahal's haveli for more than six months now and his health had deteriorated considerably. Since the past couple of months he had been subjected to the rigors of trials under British Law, neither understanding the barrage of charges against him, nor comprehending the mockery of such proceedings. He had grown daft for sure. Paradoxically, he knew that, but he had neither the will, nor the strength to defend himself against base accusations. Occasionally his mind would awaken to inspiration, even during the trial sessions when he would find some comments both absurd and amusing, and his dull eyes would light up with the fire of rage and repartee.

Right now hunched over his bed in his white muslin tunic and skull cap, Bahadur Shah Zafar was a pitiful sight to behold, though his retching had subsided. Ghulam Abbas wiped the king's lower lip which seemed to hang down over his toothless gums and his heart lurched with compassion for this old man who was once an emperor. *Now an ex-king, not even that but a state prisoner in a wretched state*, Ghulam Abbas was thinking. Bahadur Shah Zafar took a sip of water offered by Ghulam Abbas and crashed upon the bed exhausted. His eyes stinging with pain scanned the bare room while his hands stroked absently the wispy white beard almost touching his stomach.

"Fetch my hookah." Bahadur Shah Zafar groaned suddenly.

"It's being refreshed, Zil-e-Subhani." Ghulam Abbas could not help but maintain this decorum of speech. His thoughts in perpetual revolt against the appalling conditions in which the king lived and suffered. Considering, the emperor's ancestors were the ones who had granted boons of free trade to the merchants of London and now the same traders had dared imprison the last of the Moghul emperors, subjecting him to the degradation of poverty and contempt."

"Zil-e-Subhani." Bahadur Shah Zafar repeated wretchedly. "I am but a slave. A handful of dust to be sprinkled over the waters of Ganges. Fetch me something to write with, my mind is swollen with this sudden flood of inspiration."

"Would you kindly dictate, Zil-e-Subhani?" Ghulam Abbas requested gently. It would be easier. I wouldn't miss a word."

"You are right, my fingers won't obey." Bahadur Shah Zafar conceded. "My arms are eaten up by sores, lack of water and proper bathing. My hands are weak and bony. Are you ready, my devoted Friend? This deluge of inspiration would kill me if I didn't drain it quickly."

"Yes, Zil-e-Subhani." Ghulam Abbas settled himself on a low stool beside the bed. He dipped his pen in the inkpot, straightening the creases of rough paper with the other hand.

"Give it to Zeenat Mahal after you have written it. She longs for the feast of poetry. This inspiration once I dreamed in my dream, so very familiar, maybe I did write it somewhere?" Bahadur Shah Zafar's eyes were lit up with the fever of inspiration.

"I am no one's light of love, nor the light of desire in any heart
Worthless as a handful of dust, no joy I can ever impart
With no music of hope to share, why should anyone take delight in my song
My wounded heart cries for love, to that voice of despair in spring I belong
Separated from my beloved, my youth and beauty despoiled
I am that harvest of spring which autumn destroyed
I am not anyone's beloved, nor a rival worthy of hate
That ill-starred lover I am whose heart is broken by fate
Why should one send flowers, or recite Fatihah on the death of this slave
I have become a tomb of despair, why should one light a candle on my grave."

He coughed, pulling close the soiled sheet over his shoulders. A thin smile hovered over his lips as he noticed Ghalib straggle into the room. "I see ghosts and apparitions often. Are you real?" He asked, his gaze bright and dreamy.

"As real as this tragic world permits me the luxury of appearing and disappearing, Zil-e-Subhani." Ghalib offered a low curtsy beside the bed, smiling at Ghulam Abbas who procured for him a stool to sit. "Before your last trial I am granted permission to visit you. How many countless times I have tried you could never guess. Even now I am not here and no valid sanction exists. I might be an apparition if that suits the present rulers. Most of them don't know I am here."

"Yes, forty-two times I have counted of my *mock trial*, which might be real under the auspices of British jurisdiction. Though they have counted these sessions as twenty-one times?" Bahadur Shah Zafar murmured, his look puzzled. "We are having a poetry session, won't you join?"

"With great pleasure, Zil-e-Subhani, before I get evicted." Ghalib began exigently as if afraid to be thrown out of this bare room into the streets equally barren and desolate.

> *Every armed British soldier*
> *Can do whatever he wants*
> *Just going from home to the market*
> *Makes one's heart turn to water*
> *The Chowk is a slaughter ground*
> *And homes are prisons*
> *Every grain of dust in Delhi*
> *Thirsts for Muslims' blood*
> *Even if we were together*
> *We could only weep over our lives."*

"Tears and tragedies. Death and betrayal. Anything else to share?" Was Bahadur Shah Zafar's nostalgic appeal. He seemed indifferent to his ailment and impoverishment, his gaze dull and unseeing.

"A tale of love and fidelity, Zil-e-Subhani." Ghalib began feverishly. "The day British moved into your palace, your favorite elephant Maula Bakhsh and your horse Hamdam refused to take food or drink. A mahout who took care of both these animals reported the matter to Lieutenant Saunders. To test the validity of this claim Lieutenant Saunders ordered rich food for Maula Bakhsh, which he tossed away angrily. Lieutenant Saunders was so dismayed that he commanded the elephant to be auctioned. When Maula Bakhsh was sold to a grocer for one hundred rupees, the mahout said. *O Maula Bakhsh, you had been all your life the emperor's pet, now as ill luck would have it you have been sold to a grocer.* Hearing this, Maula Bakhsh grunted loudly and died. Your

195

horse Hamdam was found dead the same day, Zil-e-Subhani. I heard this from Zaheer Dehlawi."

"Poetry in death! We would have poetry session after all in Diwan-i-Khas." Bahadur Shah Zafar's eyes were attaining the luster of madness.

> *"Many kings of might and majesty have been in this world*
> *What powerful armies of different kind did they possess*
> *At last they left this world and departed alone*
> *Where is Darius, where is Alexander, where is Jamshed*
> *O Zafar, bearing good deeds which might remain*
> *Nothing will survive in this world."*

"The light is gone out of India!" Ghalib lamented suddenly. "This land is lampless. Countless millions have died and amongst the survivors, thousands are in jail. Many of my friends have been killed. I am left alone to mourn for so many. Allah, when I die, not a single soul would be left to mourn for me."

"Only Prince Jawan Bakht might be left alive to mourn for me, or maybe Prince Shah Abbas." Bahadur Shah Zafar intoned with a sudden clairvoyance. "Twenty-nine of my sons shot to death. Even the younger ones, Bakhtawar Shah only eighteen, and Mirza Meandoo who had just turned seventeen this year. Slow, lingering deaths, I have heard. Was it Captain Hodson who took pleasure in making them suffer?"

"Captain Hodson, I forgot, Zil-e-Subhani. He was just killed today. That's why I made haste. The main reason, and then looking at you—" Ghalib almost choked with grief, becoming aware afresh of the impoverished state of this ailing man who was once an emperor. "He was killed in action at the Begum's palace outside Lucknow, but not before he had taken part in looting Lucknow, second only to the sacking of Delhi. Besides amassing great treasures, great atrocities were committed with a sense of gloating. People were dragged out of their homes, stabbed and bayoneted and then thrown into fire to be burnt alive. Rooms after rooms were searched and victims slaughtered until there was no one left to be killed. Begum Hazrat Mahal fled while fighting. No one can find her, she is known to have vanished in the Nepalese wilderness."

"Ah, wilderness in hearts!" Bahadur Shah Zafar declared poetically. "Every tree in Delhi lopped off. Houses leveled to the ground, or their burnt walls rigged with holes. Ruin and devastation everywhere. Skeletons bleaching under the sun. The smell and—"

His thoughts were disrupted by the breezy entrance of Kendal Coghill.

"Who gave you the permission to come here?" Kendal Coghill demanded of Ghalib.

"Does anyone need permission to enter a prison voluntarily?" Ghalib quipped.

"Watch your manners!" Kendal Coghill grunted menacingly. "Are you a Muslim?"

"Half." Ghalib muttered laughingly.

"What does that mean?" Kendal Coghill suppressed an oath under his breath.

"I drink wine, but I do not eat pork." Ghalib intoned nonchalantly.

"Your insolence would cost you your head." Kendal Coghill couldn't help but laugh.

"My head has a price. Severed from its shoulders, it would cost the executioner his own head for killing a famous poet." Ghalib hissed arrogantly.

"We have no use for poets in this war of vengeance." Kendal Coghill waved impatiently. "You better leave and dare not come back. I have my orders to shoot."

"It would be difficult to obey such orders since almost everyone has left Delhi." Ghalib murmured in response, returning his attention to Bahadur Shah Zafar. "Goodbye, Zil-e-Subhani. It's unlikely that I would ever see you again." His voice was choked. Noticing that the king had drifted into his own world of half bliss, half oblivion, he plodded out of the room. Painfully aware that for the first time in his life he had neglected his usual curtsy to the king before begging leave.

Kendal Coghill stood watching the king in contemplative silence. A shadow of annoyance crossing his brow as he shifted his attention to Ghulam Abbas.

"Make sure, your Ex-king is in a fit state to understand the proceedings of the trial this afternoon." Kendal Coghill resumed his tone of authority. "Don't let him relapse into one of those passive moods on the verge of senility." He stalked out of the room.

"Zil-e-Subhani, how I am to defend your case?" Ghulam Abbas got to his feet, wringing his hands and expecting no response.

"Allah's truth! No defense needed to proclaim one's innocence!" Bahadur Shah Zafar exclaimed suddenly, his eyes lit

197

up with the awareness of pain and recollection. "Get ready to write down my defense while I dictate." His voice was strong as if all illness had left him, though he closed his eyes.

"Yes, Zil-e-Subhani." Ghulam Abbas claimed his usual seat, retrieving his papers and inkpot.

"Write every word, Ghulam Abbas, even when I hold you witness in my thoughts for the sake of summoning my clarity of vision." Bahadur Shah Zafar opened his eyes, a spark of pain and madness returning to his gaze as he began to speak. "You were there when I begged the sepoys to go away. Leave my palace and gardens I told them. I never sanctioned the death of William Fraser or any Britishers for that matter. As regards to the orders given under my seal and under my signature are false accusations. The day sepoys invaded my palace, I became their prisoner. They had my seal impressed on the outside of the empty envelopes unaddressed. There is no knowing what papers they sent in to those or to whom. They used to accuse my servants of sending letters and keeping in league with the English. The officers of the army went even so far as to require that I should make over my queen Zeenat Mahal to them, that they might keep her imprisoned, saying that she maintained friendly relations with the English. All that had been done was done by the sepoys, I was in their power. Disgusted by their actions and by the impoverished state of my life I even told the sepoys that I would don the garb of a mendicant, retire to the shrine of Qutubddin Kaki and then to Mecca. The sepoys utterly lacked all kind of manners, were negligent of conforming even to the simple protocol of etiquette, didn't even offer the mandatory curtsy and didn't remove their shoes when entering Diwan-i-Khas. Making use of my name, they murdered English men and women, tyrannized over my servants, plundered and murdered the merchants of Delhi—" His thoughts were disrupted by the arrival of his servant and by a sudden fit of coughing.

Inuzzur was carrying a tray consisting of poor meal and a jug of water. Ghulam Abbas was quick to hold the water of glass to the lips of Bahadur Shah Zafar as he lay there spent and exhausted. Prince Jawan Bakht had slipped in, watching his father relapse into peaceful slumber. The tray of food lay neglected while the Prince and the lawyer sat whispering as was their wont when the king slept and they had a few moments of venting out their anguished concerns.

It was late afternoon when Bahadur Shah Zafar was hoisted inside a palanquin and carried toward Red Fort for the last day of his trial. His palanquin was heavily guarded by British soldiers. Accompanying this procession were Prince Jawan Bakht and Ghulam Abbas. Though ill and distraught, Bahadur Shah Zafar was painfully aware that his usual route of journey through underground tunnel from his queen's haveli was abandoned this afternoon in favor of open roads leading to residential areas and markets.

Anguished awareness was Bahadur Shah Zafar's only companion, his gaze barely touching the destruction of the vegetable market. Mounds upon mounds of ruins were coming into view, houses collapsed or burnt walls rigged with grape shot or musket balls. Drifting in and out of fresh shock and rising bewilderment, Bahadur Shah Zafar's eyes were pouring mists of tears over two large gallows in the Chandni Chowk.

This devastation equally horrific as at the time of Nadir Shah's invasion. Bahadur Shah Zafar's thoughts were fluttering over the ruins like a wounded bird. Aloud his lips were lowering the appeal of an anonymous British poet whose words had reached him like the whiff of cool breeze to extinguish the fire of vengeance.

> *"Upon the wretched slave thy vengeance feast*
> *There stop, let not his guilt thy manhood stain*
> *But spare the Indian mother and her child."*

Giddiness and delusion were Bahadur Shah Zafar's companions now as he became aware of the precincts of Red Fort. His mind's vision of beauty and splendor of these surroundings was crushed by a sudden realization that nothing seemed familiar anymore, offering not even a hint of former wealth and grandeur. This was not his palace. Where were his beautiful gardens and courtyards? All he could see was ugly barracks teeming with British soldiers.

Ah, the splendor of Diwan-i-Khas! I am home again. Bahadur Shah Zafar's thoughts were chirping under the cloud of great delusion.

Seated couchant against huge cushions on his bamboo bed in white muslin robe, Bahadur Shah Zafar seemed to cherish the familiar grandeur of his Diwan-i-Khas. A Pashmina shawl was draped around his shoulders, his hands clutching the silk scarf which he was reluctant to let go even in his sleep.

Diwan-i-Khas at least was not despoiled. Engrailed arches over the central chamber appeared to embrace the magnificent floral designs inlaid with jewels. Gilded ceiling and marble pillars were greeting Bahadur Shah Zafar with utter devotion. Upon the Peacock Throne sat Major Harriat the Deputy Judge. Two gilded chairs were placed to his right and two on his left, occupied by Major Palmer, Major Redmond, Major Sawyers and Captain Rothway. The hall was packed, abuzz with cheerful arguments, but suddenly Major Harriat's voice rose above all, summoning the court to session.

In a flash Bahadur Shah Zafar was hurled into voids terrible and excruciating. He was transformed from that of an emperor to an abject slave. This was not his home, but his prison. That Peacock Throne upon which he sat and held court was usurped by some man alien and ruthless. This hall where men curtsied and sought his audience was now teeming with men rude and mannerless.

The trial had begun with all the fanfare of a protocol in the British court, but Bahadur Shah Zafar sat indifferent to the proceedings. Most of the time he was listless and occasionally occupied himself by wrapping the silk scarf around his head and feeling its softness with a dint of pleasure. A spark of awareness or recognition would alight in his dull gaze at some question by the judge or by some account of a witness, but then he would relapse into lethargic abandon. Many flames of reflections which his unseeing gaze had entertained were lodged in his thoughts like the coals of bewilderment as he sat listening, half dreaming, half absorbing.

Ghulam Abbas had been called on the witness stand, plied with several questions, but the one registered by Bahadur Shah Zafar was: *Were the women and children murdered by the consent of the Prisoner?* Ghulam Abbas had replied: *I have no further knowledge on the subject beyond what I heard from Ahsanullah Khan who said the king had prohibited the slaughter, but unavailingly.*

Ahsanullah Khan was recalled as a witness with a question. *Did the native newspapers urge the necessity of a religious war against the English?* Ahsanullah Khan replied: *That no such article was printed in any newspaper.*

Witness Jat Mall was questioned. *Were any guns fired as a token of joy upon the arrival of rebel troops from Meerut?* His response was: *No, I heard none.*

Captain Theo Metcalfe was presented as a witness with a question: *Short time before the outbreak in May, was there any paper stuck up on the walls of Jami Masjid with a proclamation from the king of Persia?* Captain Theo Metcalfe replied: *Yes, it was a dirty piece of paper with one naked sword and shield depicted on the right side and the same pair on the left. The proclamation from the king of Persia urging the followers of Prophet Muhammad to join with him in extirpating the English infidel.*

Hasan Askari was brought to the stand and interrogated. *Did you ever tell the king that you had a dream about a hurricane from the west coming upon India? Devastating the land, though the king would be lifted above the flood to annihilate the English?* Hasan Askeri denied the charge saying: *Allah knows I never had such a dream. I have no faith in dreams.*

Chuni Lal is brought to the witness stand: *Did you witness any procession made by the king on an elephant of state?* Chuni Lal boldly confessed. *No, I did not.*

Lieutenant Saunders takes a stand as a witness. *Was there any limit to the prisoner's armed retainers?* Lieutenant Saunder's response: *The prisoner requested Lord Aukland to be permitted to entertain as many men in his service as he deemed proper. The Governor General granted him permission that he could entertain as many men as he could pay out of his allotted income.*

Makhund Lal is brought as a witness. *Was it generally supposed in the palace that Hasan Askari had great influence over the king?* Makhund Lal testifies: *Yes, not only in the palace, but throughout the city also. It was generally known that Hasan Askari and Mahbub Ali Khan exercised great influence over the king.*

Captain Martin takes the stand. *Did you observe any difference in making complaints about forcible deprivation of their religion between Hindus and Muslims?* Captain Martin's response. *Yes, the Muslim sepoys laughed at such an insinuation, but the Hindu sepoys complained in reference to losing caste.*

Witness John Everett. *Are you aware whether any persons in the military service of the Company were ever solicited to go over to the king?* John Everett replied briefly. *Not to my knowledge.*

Bahadur Shah Zafar had grown oblivious to the trial as it dragged on, witnesses appearing and disappearing as phantoms in a play. The insolence of the members of the trial commission and the British witnesses toward Bahadur Shah Zafar was compensated by the profound respect of the native witnesses. Without exception, all of them before taking the witness stand would first approach the king's bed with hands clasped, bowing reverently and addressing him as the Ruler of the World.

Ruler of the World, fortunately or unfortunately was neither aware of the devotion of his subjects, nor of the insolence of the invaders. After all the witnesses had testified, Major Harriat had announced that the charges against the prisoner would be read aloud. Major Palmer was appointed to read the charges and he began pontifically.

"The Prisoner is charged that at various times between the tenth of May to October first of the year eighteen hundred and fifty-seven, he did encourage, aid and abet Bakht Khan and other native commissioned officers of the East India Company's army in the crimes of mutiny and against the state." Major Palmer was about to read the second charge when Bahadur Shah Zafar's eyes were shot open and he sat upright suddenly.

"Mutiny! Now that's an interesting word." Bahadur Shah Zafar exclaimed with unusual fervor. "How can a king mutiny against his own subjects? I am the king, have never been the subject of East India Company. How could I be guilty of anything? East India Company is the guilty party, revolting against a feudal superior to whom it has shown allegiance for nearly a century. The absurdity of this trial. Have you cleared away the skeletons of my subjects littering the streets of Delhi? The domes and minars of the city riddled with shell holes—" He almost collapsed over his pillows exhausted.

Diwan-i-Khas was swathed in a curtain of sepulchral silence as the members of the trial commission sat there gawking and speechless. Outside the hall some mad poet had begun to chant the familiar refrain written against the British soldiers during the early weeks of rebellion.

The idiots' stood gazing while the cities were blazing
And all they could do was gibber and gape

A few shots were heard and chants were silenced. Major Palmer had regained his composure and continued dutifully to finish reading the charges against Bahadur Shah Zafar.

"The Prisoner is charged with encouraging Mirza Mughal his own son and inhabitants of Delhi and of North-West Province of India to rebel and to wage a religious war against the state." Major Palmer was taken aback as Bahadur Shah Zafar's eyes were shot open once again.

"How could a religious war be proclaimed by a Muslim king when majority of his subjects are Hindus and Sikhs?" Bahadur Shah Zafar's lips were trembling, his eyes now hermetically shut.

The hall was plunged once again into a vacuum of silence so profound that no one dared breathe. The air itself felt heavy with sadness, yet Major Palmer managed to resume with an air of detachment.

"The Prisoner being subject of British Government, in Delhi or thereabout, acted false and became a traitor against the State, proclaiming and declaring himself the reigning king and sovereign of India." Major Palmer paused but briefly before continuing exigently. "The Prisoner is accused of becoming accessory to the murder of forty-nine British men, women and children on the premises of his own palace."

Major Palmer finished reading all charges, his expression taut and wearied. The air was charged with sadness once again and Diwan-i-Khas appeared to melt against this pressure of silence. All eyes were turned to Bahadur Shah Zafar whose eyes were open, but he was lost in a world of his own, wrapping the silk scarf over his head in a playful manner, oblivious to his surroundings. Major Harriat cleared his throat before presenting his own closing speech.

"I have endeavored to point out how intimately the Prisoner as the head of Mohammedan faith in India has been connected with the organization of that conspiracy, either as its leader or its unscrupulous accomplice." Major Harriat paused, becoming aware of the smoldering gaze of Bahadur Shah Zafar fixed on him. He cleared his throat once again and continued. "After what has been proved in regard to Mohammedan treachery. Is there anyone who hears me today can believe that a deep-planned and well-concerted conspiracy had nothing to do with it? If we now take a retrospective view of the various circumstances which we have been able to elicit during our extended inquiries, we shall see how exclusively Mohammedans are in all the prominent points attached to the case. A Mohammedan priest, with pretended visions and assumed miraculous powers! A Mohammedan king, his dupe and his accomplice. A Mohammedan clandestine embassy to Mohammedan powers of Persia and Turkey. Mohammedan prophecies as to the downfall of our power. Mohammedan rule as the successor to our own. The most cold-blooded murders by Mohammedan assassins. A religious war for Mohammedan ascendancy. A Mohammedan press unscrupulously abetting. And Mohammedan sepoys initiating the mutiny. Hinduism, I may say, is nowhere, either reflected or represented. Also Christianity, when seen in its own pure light, has no terrors for the natives."

Bahadur Shah Zafar dozed off while the judge and the trial commission retired to decide on a verdict. They didn't have to retire, for the verdict was pre-planned as everyone knew, for soon they returned. The verdict was read by Major Redmond quickly and dispassionately. Bahadur Shah Zafar was unanimously declared guilty of all and every part of the charges prepared against him. He was sentenced to be transported for the remainder of his days, either to one of the Andaman Islands or to such other place as may be selected by the Governor General in Council.

Bahadur Shah Zafar seemed indifferent to the verdict, lost in his own quiet contemplations. He was still struggling with his scarf playfully as he was being transported into his palanquin. On his way back to the haveli, his mind was playing tricks, juggling his thoughts like cannon balls and being witness to the expulsion of events which had nothing to do with the horrors of the trial or awful sentence.

He could see the dazzling colors in jewels described to him by Abdur Rahman—the great loot by English Prize Agents. Gold jewelry of exquisite design and precious stones. Rubies, pearls, emeralds and diamonds, some as large as hen's eggs. Gold chains, necklaces, ornaments and gold bangles piled high in mounds with the glitter of sunshine. The sunshine was whisked away from his thoughts all of a sudden, as he remembered another scene described by Ahmed Beg. Roistering through Nana's menagerie, British soldiers had carried off two bulldogs, an enormous squirrel and a wandering monkey that later took to leaping from tent pole to tent pole in Cawnpore camp. The squirrel died in Shearer's keeping and the monkey was dispatched to London Zoo.

A sharp pang of realization was dawning upon Bahadur Shah Zafar of the awful sentence, as he became aware of the haveli with its gate of red Kota sandstone. His palanquin was lowered in front of the iron-studded doors and he could hear the voice of Lieutenant Saunders issuing orders to take him into his lone cell of a prison inside the haveli of his own queen.

The queen was with him. A reality or phantasmagoric dream? The events were shifting in such a succession with lightning speed that he felt spent and exhausted. The mortal wound of his painful sentence had broken his heart so brutally that it lay within his breast mangled and bleeding. He could see Zeenat Mahal beside his bed, pale and crestfallen.

"I am exiled, Beloved. I don't know where they would send me." Bahadur Shah Zafar could hear his own words as some distant echo from the bottom of a dry well.

"I would go with you, Zil-e-Subhani. Wherever you go, I go." Zeenat Mahal consoled bravely.

"Ah, Beloved, I knew!" A flood of tears was pouring down Bahadur Shah Zafar's eyes in a torrent. "Remember the first time I set eyes on you I wrote a couplet?"

"How could I forget, Zil-e-Subhani?" Zeenat Mahal's own eyes were gathering mists of tears as she recited.
"Beloved mine, how my heart is robbed of its peace
That from the prison of beauty it seeks no release."

"Ah, Beloved." Bahadur Shah Zafar kept weeping like a child, nostalgic and brokenhearted. "Our poetry sessions against the marble fountain here and your Nagina Mahal. The huge banyan tree under which we sat and laughed. Drummers announcing your arrival here when your palanquin was brought from Red Fort, and the servants saluting you—" His maudlin tones were truncated by the rude interruption of a British soldier carrying impoverished meal on a steel tray.

"And now, Zil-e-Subhani. This food, not even fit for the dogs." Zeenat Mahal's patience failed after the soldier left. Her voice choking against the burden of wretched grief and misery.

"Yes." Bahadur Shah Zafar began knotting the silk scarf between his fingers, an impromptu couplet pouring down his tear-streaked lips.

"The crow enjoys meat while the Phoenix has to live on mere bones
What justice, there is no comparison whatever between crow and the Phoenix."

His eyes were closing.

Bahadur Shah Zafar was slipping back into the world of his nightmares where pomp and pageantry of the past was sucked into the furnace of blood and devastation. His features were contorted and his hands clutching the silk scarf. The severed heads of his sons were visiting him again, their eyes bloodshot and their lips trying to form expressions. He was hurled into voids, under him his beloved Delhi burning. One hoary blaze had carried him away to some land alien and inhospitable. He was ill and dying, Zeenat Mahal beside him old and wearing rags. He was sleeping, breathing hoarsely, dreaming dreams.

Chapter Sixteen
Exile to Rangoon

A spacious room in Nagina Mahal was hosting the royal family for the last time before their journey in exile to Rangoon. No remnants of royalty were visible on any members of the royal household since they were dispossessed of all jewels and rich gowns. Bahadur Shah Zafar was wearing a robe of coarse cotton, his queen too robbed of all jewels was dressed in white muslin. Almost seven grueling months of captivity since the king was sentenced to exile and finally their destination for exile was decided. At first they were about to be sent to Andaman Islands where most of the rebels were exiled, but Rangoon was chosen as a safe and expedient location.

All members of the royal household, including the servants were assembled in this one room stripped bare of all fineries. A mournful cortege it was, waiting to embark on their journey to a far off land, alien and probably inhospitable. Bahadur Shah Zafar on his bed with thin mattress looked utterly broken, his hookah beside him neglected. Zeenat Mahal was a portrait of sorrow, but maintaining a dignified demeanor so as not to add more despair into the hearts of king's children and grandchildren. Besides, she was determined to keep her husband as comfortable as possible and to share the weight of his pain and grief with love and indulgence. Already, she was excruciatingly aware of her husband's frail constitution, his mind on the verge of senility. But she could never deny his bouts of inspiration and introspection and strove toward keeping his genius alive with the pulse of empathy and encouragement.

Prince Jawan Bakht seemed resigned to his fate, absorbed in playing with his two year old son Prince Jamshed Bakht. His wife Kulsum Begum beside him looked dejected, oblivious to her daughter sleeping in her lap—Princess Raunaq almost a year old. Hafiz Muhammad the tutor of Prince Jawan Bakht sat huddled in one corner on a bare bed made of jute, almost falling asleep. Prince Shah Abbas, utterly devoted to the king, sat close to his bed in case the king needed assistance. Abdur Rahman sat in one corner, totally dejected. Ghulam Abbas was not seated too far from the king on an armless chair, beside him his mother Mubarakunissa, both whispering so as not to disturb the repose of the king.

Zeenat Mahal's servants, Ishrat, Sultani and Raheema were sitting on the floor at the feet of the queen, their eyes now and then touching the bare legs of the chair upon which the queen sat, its velvet ripped and discolored. Inuzzur, Bahadur Shah Zafar's faithful servant stood in attendance by the bed, while Ahmed Beg sat by the door, waiting sorrowfully for the inevitable journey to commence. The number of people waiting for the dark journey was thirty-one, not including the children.

"Rani of Jhansi is calling me, where is she?" Bahadur Shah Zafar was jolted out of his nightmares. His red-rimmed eyes were searching the faces, lit only by the chill of October this early morning.

"Alas, Zil-e-Subhani. It has been four months since she was killed at Marur near Kotah-ki-Serai close to Gwalior." Was Zeenat Mahal's involuntary response. "She was fighting against the army of Sir Hugh Rose when shot dead by a soldier."

"Ah, now I can follow my dreams!" Bahadur Shah Zafar sat up suddenly, Inuzzur supporting his back with a pillow. "I saw her dressed as a Maratha horseman. She was wounded by a trooper of the Hussars. She fired at her assailant, but missed, and he in turn shot her dead. Can still see the glittering of her jewels."

"Those jewels disappeared quickly I am sure, Zil-e-Subhani." Zeenat Mahal muttered bitterly. "As did the jewels of Nawab Jhajjar, in addition to his being fleeced of his riches by Captain Hodson several months before he was killed on a battlefield while still looting."

"*Brutal Muslims*, isn't that what the British call us?" Bahadur Shah Zafar's gaze was feverish and unseeing. "*Brutal Muslims and sensual Hindus in their mad desire insulting, torturing and raping the English women before killing them?*"

"The enquiries have been made on such charges and British know by now that no English woman was raped or tortured prior to murder." Ghulam Abbas' voice appeared to come from the well of his own misery and hopelessness.

"Innocent people still being hanged in dozens." Prince Jawan Bakht commented absently. "A soldier from Bombay crying before he was hanged. *We are your children, do with us as it may seem best to you."*

"They have yet to do their best considering what their priests are saying." Mubarakunissa Begum broke her silence, almost whispering. "I have heard that Canon Stowell speaking from the pulpit cried angrily. *This is the revenge I covet that every idol should be cast to the moles and bats, every pagoda changed into a house of prayer, every mosque converted to church."*

"And the hymns most wholesome floating around!" Prince Jawan Bakht laughed half deliriously, half hysterically.

"O may their blood by Satan shed
Our holy watchword be
In turning by Thy spirit led
A pagan race to Thee."

"No wonder the British let Chunna Mal buy my Fatehpuri Masjid." Zeenat Mahal lamented low, noticing with relief that Bahadur Shah Zafar had dozed off. "My beautiful mosque Zeenat-ul, Masjid sold to a baker."

"That's not all, dear Mamma, this, your beautiful haveli of Lal Kuan is going to be occupied by Theo Metcalfe as soon as we leave this very day." Prince Jawan Bakht could not help but comment as if wading through his own ocean of pain and despair. "He is the one who went on a shooting spree, erecting gallows everywhere he went and hanging any Delhiwallahs who crossed his path."

"Why must you remind me that?" Zeenat Mahal declared rather irately. "His name alone strikes terror into the hearts of people. Ishrat heard from someone that one day a jeweler came to offer his wares to Mrs. Garstin, who thinking he charged too much, said, *I would send you to Metcalfe Sahib.* The man was so terrified that he fled leaving his treasures behind."

"Nana's head! Where is Nana Sahib?" Bahadur Shah Zafar bolted upright out of another nightmare. "I saw Nana Sahib fleeing headless."

"He is very much alive, Zil-e-Subhani. Hiding somewhere in Nepal." Abdur Rahman's heart was reaching out to the old king in compassion. "A ten thousand rupee reward is set on Nana's head by Lord Canning. But people are heard saying, *no one can set a price on Lord Canning's head, because his head is empty and worthless."*

"Azimullah Khan, Tatya Tope, where are they? I was chasing them in my dreams too." Bahadur Shah Zafar's look was feverish, his gaze restless.

"They are hiding somewhere, Zil-e-Subhani." Hafiz Muhammed commiserated aloud. "Tatya Tope, I hear, is contemplating guerrilla warfare.

"Hazrat Mahal, fleeing. I see her in my dreams too." Bahadur Shah Zafar's voice was but a feeble lament. "I am chasing her deeper and deeper into Nepalese wilderness. Her husband still in exile in Garden Reach? Where are we going—"

"To the Bridge of Boats, Ex-king." Charles Saunders appeared suddenly, intercepting king's low lament.

"The boat of life over the bridge to death." Another low lament escaped Bahadur Shah Zafar's lips, his eyes hermetically shut.

The morning sun against cool, crisp sky over Delhi was gilding the Moghul arch of Lal Kuan haveli to gold as the cortege of the exiles assembled on the backyard of Nagina Mahal toward Farash Khana. Iron-studded wooden doors of Zeenat Mahal's haveli were shut forever for the royal family as they were getting ready to commence their journey to Allahabad, then to Calcutta and finally to Rangoon. Bahadur Shah Zafar seemed alert in his palanquin over the bullock carriage, his deep-set eyes reaching out to red Kota sandstone walls with nostalgic desperation of the senses marred by tragedies. His gaze was shifting toward the Banyan tree with sorrow so palpitating that it appeared to envelop the sky and the earth in one anguished embrace.

Bahadur Shah Zafar could feel that his heart was left bleeding over the steps of Zeenat Mahal's haveli as his carriage rolled onto the street amidst the mournful cortege flanked by squadron of lancers. He was attended by his sons Prince Jawan Bakht and Prince Shah Abbas. Zeenat Mahal and other wives of the king were in the second carriage. The third carriage hosted other members of the royal family, including servants and the children. Following these carriages were five magazine store carts filled with male and female attendants of the king and the queen.

Stupor and delirium of the past few months had left Bahadur Shah Zafar in utter hopelessness as his carriage rolled through the Lahori Gate. From his palanquin, his gaze was sweeping down over the ruined city of Delhi as if searching for some signs of life. To his shocked awareness, Delhi was no more, but a desert of charred bazaars, bullet-riddled houses and not a soul to be seen on the streets of devastation. Red Fort was barely visible against the gray structures looking like barracks. Rang Mahal was not there, only brick and mortar with chunks of marble gleaming in between. Hayat Bakhsh garden and Mehtab garden were nothing, but mounds of mud and debris, no flowers, fountains silent and muddied. Gilded domes had disappeared, Red Fort too vanishing like a dream as Bahadur Shah Zafar closed his eyes, the weight of grief his bliss and oblivion.

A dismal evening scudded by pink clouds in Allahabad was hosting the Moghul exile in their old fort, now captured by the British. It had been more than a month since their journey from Delhi via Cawnpore and they had been treated well by General Ommaney. There was one mishap on the Bridge of Boats though where one of the store carts housing Bahadur Shah Zafar's ladies of the harem was almost drowned into the waters of Jamna, but saved most skillfully. The rest of the journey toward Allahabad had been comfortable and uneventful. Their bivouacs along the way were amply furnished with strong tents and there was great supply of food and blankets. For the first time they had boarded a steam train, puffing away with a whistle while the band played, *the Englishmen on the platform.*

Bahadur Shah Zafar had been ill and distraught on the last stages of the journey. Becoming aware afresh in Allahabad of the ruined and fire-blackened bungalows and the burnt-out police-stations, a grim reminder of the Delhi devastation which had become a part of his suffering savage and bottomless. Even now in this room of the old fort stripped bare of tapestries he lay on his cot in utter misery. Puffing on his hookah occasionally he was watching the royal trio with lacerating compassion, his queen and his sons, Prince Jawan Bakht and Prince Shah Abbas. Suddenly the memory of devastated Delhi was crushing his thoughts into pincers of agony and his lips could feel the scalding downpour of an impromptu couplet.

"Delhi was once a paradise where love held sway and reigned
But its charm lies ravished now and only ruins remain."

"Delhi might yet be restored to peace, Zil-e-Subhani." Prince Shah Abbas consoled while ruminating aloud. "At least the wholesale destruction of Red Fort is checked by Henry Lawrence. Both Jami Masjid and palace walls are intact. Alas, too late, he couldn't save Abarabadi Masjid and Masjid Kashmiri Katta. Sufi shrines, including the shrine of Sheikh Kalimullah Janatabad are leveled to the ground. Beautiful palaces are gone too, as well as the gardens." He couldn't continue, noticing a sudden fever of anguish in the gaze of the king.

"Gardens efflorescent with the buds of death." Bahadur Shah Zafar commented, his gaze holding and beholding stark torment in the eyes of Zeenat Mahal.

"Henry Lawrence is trying to amend the situation in Delhi, Zil-e-Subhani." Zeenat Mahal's torment was replaced by the light of love and concern for her husband. "He has written a letter to the House of Commons, stating. *I have seen things which would make me suppose that instead of bowing before the name of Jesus we are preparing to revive the worship of Moloch.*"

"More so the worship of Queen Victoria, dear Mamma." Prince Jawan Bakht began caustically, practicing his usual flair for drama and absurdity. "We have been told that this very day, preceded by fireworks, military salutes and thanksgiving services, a proclamation has been read out in every station in India that East India Company is abolished, replaced by British Government in Queen's name."

"By her orders then we drift toward alien shores." Bahadur Shah Zafar murmured to himself. "All thirty-one of us if I am not mistaken."

"Only fifteen are going, Zil-e-Subhani." Zeenat Mahal murmured back. "Some of the begums and attendants want to go back to Delhi." She was becoming aware of the slow approach of General Ommaney.

"Are you ready to travel again, Ex-king, to Calcutta, this time?" General Ommaney asked genially.

"In my life's journey I have not traveled that far, my good Friend." Bahadur Shah Zafar's voice was toneless. "Now I must journey far to the valley of death. Though, the citizens of Delhi don't have to journey far to reach there."

"Our Queen has offered amnesty to all whoever didn't take part in killing the Britons." General Ommaney commiserated quickly. "Also proclaiming that religious tolerance would be observed and ancient customs respected."

"The slaves of her will would drift where she commands." Bahadur Shah Zafar murmured again. "Where we are going?"

212

"From here we go to Mizarpur and then take steamer Thames to Calcutta." General Ommaney intoned promptly, noticing that the king had relapsed into his usual state of oblivion if not self-surrender.

Another month of tiresome journey in which steamer Thames due to engine malfunction was replaced by steamer Koyle and the party of exiles had reached Diamond Harbor in Calcutta on one of the December evenings, cold and blistering. Tents were set up as a night bivouac since they were to resume their journey next day early in the morning. Despite woolen robes and Kashmiri shawls, Bahadur Shah Zafar was feeling utterly miserable as if ready to expire. Attended by his sons Prince Jawan Bakht and Prince Shah Abbas, he was craving for more company which came his way by the kindness of General Ommaney. General Ommaney genuinely loving and caring trotted into the tent with the sole intention of offering comforting words to the royal prisoner who was a stranger to such discomforts since all his life he had lived in luxurious palaces, enjoying his palace gardens and poetry sessions.

"Bloody awful weather, Ex-king, but we would be boarding a ship early in the morning. Hopefully, we would have kerosene stoves at our disposal." General Ommaney chirped genially.

"Morning. Wither we go?" Bahadur Shah Zafar's features were washed by a flood of sadness so propound that his very eyes were turned to beacons of tragedies.

"Initially, it was decided that we go to Cape, but now Burma, to Rangoon. Only four or five days of journey." General Ommaney consoled. "You and your family would be comfortably lodged once we reach Rangoon."

"How many of my family are coming with me?" Bahadur Shah Zafar seemed to be stuck in the mode of inquisition.

"Fifteen in all, Ex-king." General Ommaney murmured thoughtfully. "Thirty-one in all started from Delhi, but half plus one have decided to return to Delhi."

"A wretched lot with a wretched king—once an emperor who would dare choose exile?" Bahadur Shah Zafar lamented suddenly. "Is there peace in India? Rani of Jhansi already dead. What is the fate of Tatya Tope, Azimullah Khan?"

"Tatya Tope still fighting a guerilla campaign in Sagar and Narmada, Ex-king." General Ommaney began with regret and sadness. "A melancholy sight, burnt bungalows, blackened walls, charred timbers, broken gates. Trees knocked down, stripped bare of leaves and branches. Azimullah Khan is on the run since the defeat of Gwalior."

"What became of Ahsanullah Khan?" Bahadur Shah Zafar appeared to flip the pages of his own memory book.

"Sadly and regretfully, Ex-king, Ahsanullah Khan is lodged in the stables of his own mansion." General Ommaney offered reluctantly.

"*Where is Delhi now?*" Bahadur Shah Zafar quoted Ghalib with a cry of agony. "Ghalib wrote to me before we left. *Delhi meant the Fort, Chandni Chowk, daily bazaar near Jami Masjid, Jamna Bridge of Boats, Flower Walk. These five things which kept Delhi alive have lost their limbs and luster. Khas bazaar, kharram ka bazaar disappearing in dust. Entire villages, large havelis, razed to the ground.*"

"Everything would be restored, Ex-king, reinvented, in time." General Ommaney murmured evasively. "Too many deaths already and mountains of destruction." His voice was choked against the fever of misery in the eyes of the king.

"Death is a boon to the ones who suffer." Bahadur Shah Zafar's feverish gaze was lit by poetic inspiration all of a sudden.

"I have been so afflicted that I do not fear to die
If I were to die I would be saved from grief
My life, O God, is a heavy burden to me."

He closed his eyes, his features washed by ghastly pallor.

Morning had arrived much too quickly, bleak and ominous. Conveyed in the Soorma Flat in tow of the Koyle Steamer, the royal cortege was taken on board on ship Meckanzie—Her Majesty's good ship of war. The main deck was crowded with household furniture, live and lifeless stock in the form of cattle, goats, rabbits, poultry and bags of rice and lentils. Bahadur Shah Zafar was conducted to the deck below, collapsing immediately upon a couch of pillows and cushions which his attendants had arranged for him, swiftly and devotedly.

The ship Meckanzie steamed away down the Hughli toward Rangoon, while Bahadur Shah Zafar drifted in and out of nightmarish reality much like the waves, restless and turbulent. Many deaths were housed in his frail body. Death of kingdom and royalty. Death of intellect and inspiration. Death of hope and heritage. And most painful of his deaths, the death of his soul, still lingering in his body like a ghost of the ages past, gathering a host of demons for one last accolade.

Lies, all lies, Bahadur Shah Zafar's soul protested feebly. *You didn't love anyone and no one loved you. How stark and painful is this stab of truth. Now can you let this realization dawn upon you that how intensely you wanted to love and how grandly you failed amidst the rocks of rifts, expectations and disappointments? Can you let go of this realization which is holding you in pincers of grief that how passionately your loved ones pretended to love you and how magnificently they succeeded in living this lie, never fearing that one day you would see through their façade of deception.*

That day has come, Bahadur Shah Zafar's soul was dying once again in throes of agony. He was a mendicant, drifting along on the face of this earth without a staff and a beggar's bowl. Alienated from man and God, he could see nothing but the face of ugliness, its eyes bulging with the light of hatred and vengeance. In his dreams he was journeying back in time, watching Prince Jawan Bakht getting married, remembering with astonishing clarity the news he had received the very same day that British troops along with their regiment of Sikhs had invaded Rangoon.

The entire bulletin of news was impressed in his dreams like an open scroll. After British naval artillery had breached the stockades and the Burmese troops had been driven back towards Mendlay, Prize Agents had been let loose to loot the shrines and to smash the sacred idols to gather gems. Much later it was reported that European artillery-men had sold in great numbers the silver images and jars of rubies that were found inside the shrines. One party of looters had even tunneled deep into the foundations of Shwe Dagon Pagoda, determined to find thick cladding of gems that legend said had been buried there since centuries. Regiments of Sikhs were happy to camp in the desecrated courts of Shwe Dagon.

Now the cousins of Sikhs probably lighting cooking fires in the arcades of Delhi Jami Masjid, Ghalib had written, Bahadur Shah Zafar's thoughts were a jumble of recollections in dreams.

Bahadur Shah Zafar was jolted out of his dreams by loud voices from the upper deck. The ship was docked at the muddy brown waters of the swampy tidal creeks bordering Irrawadely Delta and into the Rangoon River which had been since the past five days of damp, blistering weather collecting stormy whirlwinds.

Carried on a palanquin to the upper deck, Bahadur Shah Zafar could see the great golden spire of the Shwe Dagon Pagoda rising up above the thick tropical greenery of the riverbank.

The shore was teeming with gawkers, a large group of Natives and Europeans waiting to have a glimpse of the royal prisoners. They were to journey toward their quarters prepared by the Commissioner from Pegu by the name of Major Phayre. General Ommaney with great difficulty had succeeded in dispersing crowds from the port fringed with toddy palms and crowded with paddle steamers, rafts of teak logs and junk-like Linow fishing boats with their billowing sails. Yellow-robed Buddhist monks with their wooden begging bowls and peaceful demeanor caught Bahadur Shah Zafar's attention and a stab of agony ripped through his heart, reaching up to his brain with a fever of stark torment. An impromptu quatrain danced in his head with the fire of vengeance and he closed his eyes shuddering against the weight of misery and fright.

"Oh, I wished to live and die in Medina's sacred earth
Rangoon becomes my last resort, my hopes are crushed
Instead of Zam Zam water I drink my life-blood
I have a few days to live, come ere my life has fled"

216

Chapter Seventeen
Swan Song of Bahadur Shah Zafar

It had not been a few days, but four years of misery and deprivation and Bahadur Shah Zafar still clad in his death-wish lay on his bed, suffering agonies of the mind, flesh and soul in Rangoon. For the past few months he had been ill and delirious, subsisting on broth. His throat was sore due to excessive coughing and at times he could barely breathe. Today his breath was somewhat normal, his voice returning along with his sense of clairvoyance. This bleak November afternoon his intuition was heightened with a subtle flash of certainty that he was going to die, if not after dusk, then certainly late at night before dawn. After a violent bout of coughing, he was lying down on a bare bed with only a thin sheet under him and an old pillow to support his head. His eyes were closed, his thoughts gallivanting.

For the first and a half year in Rangoon, Bahadur Shah Zafar along with his family and attendants had lived in wretched conditions. Major Phayre was not in the least prepared to receive the royal prisoners. He had secured only two small rooms near the Main Guard in new cantonment of the area just below the Shwe Dagon. One room was allotted to the king and his queen. The other room was shared by the princes and their families. The attendants were housed in tents, outside of which were made cooking arrangements. By the kind persistence of General Ommaney a new house was built for the royal prisoners within a few yards away from the Main Guard. So after one and a half year General Ommaney was able to personally transfer the king and his family to the newly built house. This task accomplished, he had returned to Delhi, leaving royal prisoners under the care of Captain Davis.

Not a big house, but it had four rooms. One for Bahadur Shah Zafar and another for Zeenat Mahal. Prince Jawan Bakht and his family occupied one, and a separate room was assigned to Prince Shah Abbas and his mother Mubarak Nisa. Before leaving General Ommaney had described to Bahadur Shah Zafar the town of Burma with all its manifold features, artifacts and attractions which unfortunately he was never going to see or dream about seeing. And yet he was now dreaming about those sites through the descriptions provided by General Ommaney.

Burmese architecture of the town with its tiers of gilded spires and finials and flying eaves. The Buddhist monasteries with their massive bells and winged gryphons, their giant Buddhas and Bodhisattvas. Their carved wooden struts and bamboo partitions and cane latticework. Their stupas and pilgrimage sites. The silken Litamein wraps and sequined parasols of the women and pasoe sarongs of the men. The gold lacquer work and delicate decorative pottery. The strange form of the Lle-yin bullock carts with their finely woven bamboo roots and floral side panels. The music of the street bands. The calm, blue lakes that once belonged to the Burmese kings.

A sudden pang of grief mingled with nostalgic memories pierced Bahadur Shah Zafar's thoughts with the impact of a sharp blade. He lay awake, bleeding internally in mind and soul. His eyes were still closed and he didn't know Zeenat Mahal had stolen in, making herself comfortable on the reed mat beside his bed. His thoughts were shaking like reeds, gathering gusts of inclement winds and raising bootless cries amidst hurricanes of tragedies. Something inside him was sundering and splitting, raining tears of poetic inspiration which had eluded him for so many years. One ball of excruciating pain was exploding inside the very core of his brain and he didn't even know that words were tumbling down his lips in a torrent of grief indescribable.

"In this ruined garden of a world my heart has taken flight
Wonder if anyone can find rest in this transient bazaar of sorrow
A long life of four days I begged as my newly wedded bride
Two passed in longing, two in conflict spent between today and tomorrow Sweet hopes, grant me a last boon, leave this heart of strife
Stricken with grief, no room left for more pangs of agonies grand
How tragic is Zafar's plight in this prison of life
Even death denies two yards of burial ground in sweet homeland"

"Zil-e-Subhani!" Zeenat Mahal cried hopelessly, feeling his pulse. "May I call Mulla Majasi?" She hastened to jot down the poem lest she forget.

218

"What need, Beloved?" Bahadur Shah Zafar's eyes were shot open. "Won't you stay with me and talk about our beloved Delhi? You still get news, I don't know how, but you do. What became of Hazrat Mahal? Nana Sahib, Tatya Tope, Azimullah Khan?" He asked painfully, trying hard to expel his feeling of nausea.

"What need, Zil-e-Subhani, I say the same." Zeenat Mahal tucked the dirty paper under her shawl, the poem lacerating her heart afresh. "And yet to humor you, I must share my news with you. Hazrat Mahal after her defeat in Oudh has taken refuge in Nepal, Bahadur Jang finally giving her asylum. Nana Sahib after his defeat at Cawnpore is disappeared into oblivion. Maybe in Nepal, died of fever, some say. Tatya Tope, I think I told you was arrested a year after our exile and executed. Nana's nephew Rao Sahib also captured and executed, not long ago this year. Azimullah Khan as the rumor goes, also died a year after our exile, of fever while wandering in the country of the Nepalese Terai."

"Poor Nunne Nawab, banished to Mecca." Bahadur Shah Zafar intoned weakly. "Was it last year—" He was gasping for breath amidst a fit of coughing.

"Let me fetch you chicken soup, Zil-e-Subhani." Zeenat Mahal supported his back, rubbing it vigorously.

"No." Bahadur Shah Zafar cried chokingly. "Stay, Beloved, don't leave me." He pleaded, his cough subsiding.

"You need rest, Zil-e-Subhani, and nourishment." Zeenat Mahal murmured, helping him lay on his back gently.

"I have been resting for years. Now my soul needs rest. Eternal rest." Bahadur Shah Zafar lamented low. "I have been famished for news from Delhi. My nourishment is your sweet voice, the sound-smell of Delhi, doleful or heartrending, it doesn't matter. Ghalib, he writes to Prince Jawan Bakht. When was it that he wrote last? Didn't he say: *A man cannot quench his thirst with tears? You know when despair reaches its lowest depths, there is nothing left but to resign oneself to God's Will. What lower depths can there be than this that it is the hope of death which keeps me alive. My soul dwells in my body these days as restless as a bird in a cage.* Ah, poetry sessions. Red Fort. Where is home?"

"No more, Zil-e-Subhani, no more!" Zeenat Mahal cried distractedly. "Delhi no more, I can't recount. No use. Much too painful—"

"I would talk about Delhi. Pain is an antidote to pain." Prince Jawan Bakht who had been listening in the doorway made his presence known, pale and distraught. "Delhi and Ghalib, the only entertainment for Zil-e-Subhani, no matter how stark and painful. Home is no more, Zil-e-Subhani. Red Fort is reduced to grey British barracks. Your Naqqar Khana where the arrival of ambassadors from Isfahan and Constantinople was announced by drums and trumpets is now the quarter of British staff sergeant. Diwan-i-Am is converted to a lounge for officers. Your private entrance is a canteen. And Rang Mahal, whatever is left of it, serves as an officer's mess. Mumtaz Mahal is converted to a military prison. Lahori Gate is renamed Victoria Gate. This magnificent structure now housing a bazaar for the benefit of Fort's British soldiers. Our floating pavilion in red sandstone tank is used as a swimming pool for the officers. No flowers or fountains left in Hayat Bakhsh garden, but newly constructed latrines." His voice was choking, so he began to pace nervously.

"Zil-e-Subhani is ill, growing weak day by day, barely able to even swallow soup." Zeenat Mahal murmured, watching her son apprehensively. Her gaze was returning to Bahadur Shah Zafar who appeared to be resting, his eyes fluttering open.

"Weak flesh, still holding on to the strength of the soul." Bahadur Shah Zafar's feverish gaze was shifting from Zeenat Mahal to Prince Jawan Bakht, following him in his pacing. "I want to hear Ghalib's voice, what does he say?"

"*Alas, my dear boy*, Ghalib writes to me and his friends, Zil-e-Subhani." Prince Jawan Bakht reminisced aloud, still pacing. "*This is not the Delhi in which you were born. Not the Delhi in which you got your schooling. Not the Delhi in which I spent fifty-one years of my life. The area between Rajghat facing on to Jamna and the Jami Masjid is without exaggeration a great mound of bricks?*"

"How are my people in Delhi? Are they living in peace?" Was Bahadur Shah Zafar's cry of hope against hopelessness.

"They are driven out of Delhi, Zil-e-Subhani. Living outside the city on ridges and under thatched roofs, in ditches and mud huts." Prince Jawan Bakht appeared to recite like a parrot, while Zeenat Mahal sat there wringing her hands. "They want to return. Hindus are slowly being readmitted into the city. Muslims are still banned from within the walls. Delhi is empty, grass-grown streets mark the uprooted houses and shot-riddled palaces."

Prince Jawan Bakht was leaving as quietly as he had entered. Zeenat Mahal was cradling her head into her hands, grieved beyond consolation. Bahadur Shah Zafar was drifting back into his haven of dreams or nightmares. Two hot, scalding tears were rolling down the cheeks of the exiled queen, she too was welcoming the bliss in sleep and oblivion.

A pale smile was hovering over the gaunt, wrinkled features of Bahadur Shah Zafar as if he was having peace-loving dreams. Which in fact was the truth. He was young, admiring his reflection in the full-length mirror in gold frame. Dreamy in dreams he seemed fascinated by his red lips half parted as he kept standing there twirling his mustache, his face clean-shaven. He thought he looked younger than his twenty-nine springs and vulnerable in his full regalia of purple silks with a matching turban. The mirror was catching shafts of sunshine from the large window in the back and the ropes of pearls in his turban and around his neck down to his waist were illumined, vibrant and glowing. He was turning away from the mirror, trooping out of this luxurious room, down into the palace gardens. Hugging the trees, the flowers and the fountains in his thoughts. Happy and carefree, he was standing there, just watching golden orioles and paradise flycatchers. Hovering over the flowerbeds were butterflies in pairs, going in circles as if mating in the air and laughing.

How long did Bahadur Shah Zafar dream happy dreams and when they were merged with fogs of tragedies he had no idea until he felt choked by anguish in dreams and in reality. Something inside him was constricting and expanding. He was being sucked into a dark tunnel, invaded by all sorts of foul worms and orange scorpions. His flesh was attacked by an army of ants and a cloud of bees hovering overhead were aiming to sting. A loud groan escaped his lips as if he was caught in a whirlwind of death throes.

"Zil-e-Subhani!" Zeenat Mahal was jolted to a rude awakening.

Searching in the dark for a flint to light the lantern, she almost tripped over a wooden stool. As soon as she succeeded in lighting the lantern, she could see Bahadur Shah Zafar laying there ashen and breathing hoarsely. Prince Jawan Bakht and Prince Shah Abbas had just trundled in, bleary-eyed and bare-footed while Zeenat Mahal stood in one spot, motionless and speechless. Both the princes were kneeling beside the bed, Prince Jawan Bakht feeling the king's pulse while Prince Shah Abbas massaging his feet.

"Water." Bahadur Shah Zafar could barely speak as if a big wound was slashed open in his sore throat.

Prince Shah Abbas was quick to procure a tumbler of water, out of which Bahadur Shah Zafar could swallow only a few sips, a major portion of it dripping down his chin. The glint of fear in his feverish gaze was dissolving, replaced by some semblance of peace which his loved ones had not ever seen before. A small cough and he cleared his throat, his gaze sweeping over all with a dint of sadness so profound that no words could ever convey such deep silence laden with hopelessness.

"Awful night. What time?" Bahadur Shah Zafar's eyes were gathering rills of pain, the knowledge of death in there dark and shuddering.

"Way beyond midnight, I am sure, Zil-e-Subhani." Prince Shah Abbas yawned before returning the tumbler beside the carafe on the lone shelf.

"My last wish, rather request. I want to know if the pulse of poetry and inspiration is returning to Delhi." Bahadur Shah Zafar's eyes communing silently with Zeenat Mahal were almost shining with some inner light of foreknowledge he could neither share, nor expound. "What says Ghalib?" His gaze was shifting to Prince Jawan Bakht while Zeenat Mahal lowered herself on one low stool, distraught and apprehensive.

"The hour is late, Zil-e-Subhani. You need rest." Prince Jawan Bakht coaxed, resting his arm over the edge of the bed.

"My last wish, my Prince, won't you grant?" Bahadur Shah Zafar pleaded, childlike, his eyes lit up with flames of impatience.

"Yes, Zil-e-Subhani. Just this one last time. I am sleepy, though." Prince Jawan Bakht was trying to discipline his thoughts. "Ghalib doesn't write to me anymore, or maybe his letters don't reach me? And the news which I receive are years old, most probably. Yes, I do remember now, Ghalib did write to me, this was the last letter I guess. *Libraries have been looted, its precious manuscripts lost. Colleges demolished, the most famous one Rahimiyya auctioned off to one baniya by the name of Ram Das who is using it as a storage place.* Ghalib says he can't find a single book-binder, bookseller or a calligrapher in the entire city of Delhi.

There are no poets left here, he laments. *Where is Mammun? Where is Momin Khan? Where is Zauq?"*

"Zauq." Bahadur Shah Zafar's voice was tender all of a sudden as if he was tasting the sweetness of this name on the lips of his memory. "How well I remember that when someone suggested to Zauq that he would prosper much more if he went to Oudh. His response was a couplet in return."

"Do you remember that couplet, Zil-e-Subhani?" Zeenat Mahal ventured, watching Bahadur Shah Zafar close his eyes.

"Yes, clearly and gratefully, Beloved." Bahadur Shah Zafar's lips were trembling.

"Oh, Zauq, who would wish to forsake
The alleyways of Delhi and go elsewhere"

He opened his eyes. "Now go to your room. I want to sleep, eternally." His eyes were drooping shut.

No one left the room, Zeenat Mahal cradling her head in her hands again. The princes chose to lie down on the reed mats stacked for royal attendants, in case Bahadur Shah Zafar needed their assistance during the night. Bahadur Shah Zafar was sleeping, breathing laboriously and groaning occasionally. The queen and the princes listened with bated breath, knowing not if he was in pain or the usual victim of his nightmares. The king was in a world of his own, alien to the creatures of this earth rooted solid to the ground of joys and sorrows. He was swathed in ghastly pallor, his features shrunken and cadaverous. And yet there was some sort of peaceful aura, hovering over his bony, listless frame. The same aura of peace was enveloping the royal trio, offering some shade of comfort in their hour of loss and grief yet to be experienced.

Bahadur Shah Zafar was experiencing the bliss of freedom from the dungeon of life. He was standing at the gates of death. Suddenly the doors were flung open. He had come home. Returned to the beauty in living. Rivulets of sunshine from nowhere were flooding the scenic splendor of a sacred garden. White purity of the mountains with the warmth of marble was reaching down to caress the mirror lakes, reflecting rainbow-clouds sailing in islands soft and glittering.

Inhaling deeply the scent of roses and jasmine, Bahadur Shah Zafar was floating down the familiar paths where he was nurtured from childhood to youth, on to the ripe old age. Memory was his guide, shuddering like the white disk of a sun, into which he was sucked like one moth to a flame. And yet he was cradled into the loving arms of peace, the serenity of the garden down below his home. The long-lost paradise of eternity in eternal living.

The fragrance of homecoming was teasing his senses. The serpentine valley under him lifting its arms up to receive him body and soul. He had fallen into the welcoming embrace of the cosmos, singing the song of love, peace and harmony. An indescribable sweetness of a kiss was upon his lips, his heart wafting the fragrance of flowers he had not ever seen or smelled. And yet again he was lowered into the heart of one rose garden with a shower of rose-petals over his crownless head. In the distance he could see the Flower Walk of his heart's delight. Perfumed breeze was carrying him in its arms on the road to Mehrauli. Qutubddin Kaki himself was welcoming him, wearing a robe of rainbows. Rainbows were draped over his head too and trailing behind him in long braids. Rainbows gliding higher and higher and splashing the sky with rainbows upon rainbows.

"As sure as I am of the rainbows behind the clouds, I see a loving God whose boundless love embraces all!" A cry of agony and ecstasy was wrenched out from the very depths of Bahadur Shah Zafar's soul, wounded and bleeding. "Yet the ones blinded by the virtue of their vice in cruelty, hatred and tyranny shun this light of love as they would shun the shadow of death." His eyes were sparkling, holding beacons of anxiety, impatience, anticipation. "Summon the whole family. Friends and attendants. How many?" He closed his eyes.

An eerie curtain of silence was drawn over this room as Bahadur Shah Zafar lay there breathing heavily. This curtain of silence was ripped open by a sudden fit of violent coughing, though his eyes remained closed. Prince Jawan Bakht was trying to pour water down his father's throat, but it only dribbled down from the sides of his mouth, offering no relief. Prince Shah Abbas had rushed out of the room to awaken the handful of royal household and attendants. Slowly and quietly they were streaming into this sick chamber, which looked crowded.

Prince Jawan Bakht's wife Kulsum Begum was the first one to come holding the hand of Prince Jamshed Bakht barely six, drowsy and stumbling. Their daughter Princess Raunaq almost four was still sleeping, carried by Raheema. Prince Shah Abbas had returned, followed by her mother Mubarak Nisa. Mulla Majasi

224

looked like he was sleepwalking, dragging along his grandson Muqaddam who was a couple of years younger than Prince Jawan Bakht. Ghulam Abbas had trundled in as if under some spell of daze, posting himself beside the bed of the king dreamily. The attendants were the last one to enter this room, squatting themselves at the foot of the bed humbly and reverently.

Another fit of violent coughing with guttural sounds from within and Mulla Majasi helped Bahadur Shah Zafar sit straight, rubbing his back vigorously. Prince Jawan Bakht was trying to pour water down his father's throat once again. Bahadur Shah Zafar's eyes were shot open, his gaze fluttering over the faces with a scorching intensity. Some sort of surreal sparkle was emanating from his eyes, his gaze lingering over Zeenat Mahal, his sons and grandchildren. His coughing had subsided and Prince Jawan Bakht stood wiping his father's mouth with the corner of the bed sheet.

"Ghalib is mourning the death of all his poet friends. I can hear him." Bahadur Shah Zafar murmured suddenly, his voice barely audible and his eyes shining with a gleam of madness. "Didn't Ghalib say, *Allah, Allah, I am mourning thousands. When I die, who is left to mourn me?* That's what I say, Allah, Allah, Allah." His body went limp into the arms of Mulla Majasi. He lowered the king's head over the pillow gently, tears welling into his eyes on the brink of a storm.

A loud lament broke through the lips of Zeenat Mahal as she sat there screaming and sobbing hysterically. Prince Jawan Bakht and Prince Shah Abbas rushed to her side, trying their best to comfort her, but she remained deliriously loud and inconsolable.

Captain Davis arrived suddenly, obviously awakened by the noise and commotion, hastily dressed, it was obvious. His eyes were polished like the blue marbles and his hair was in disarray. The scene before his eyes was one of woe and tragedy. The imprint of grief was written all over the faces of everyone, grim and tear-streaked. Even the children were weeping, frightened and bewildered. Captain Davis's presence alone was enough to cure the hysterics of Zeenat Mahal, who now sat there sobbing quietly. He stood there still, studying the faces and then threaded his way toward the bed, his eyes meeting the doleful gaze of Mulla Majasi.

"So the Ex-king has passed away." Captain Davis murmured, averting his gaze.

"Yes." Mulla Majasi could barely murmur back, tears streaming down his cheeks and wetting his white beard.

"His body must be interned immediately." Captain Davis intoned indifferently. "I have ordered lime and bricks and the spot is chosen for internment." He sauntered out of the room, deep in thought.

The death chamber was plunged in complete silence, with the exception of quiet sobbing, or an opiate cry from the lips of a child. No one dared speak. Mulla Majasi bent down to imprint a kiss on the brow of Bahadur Shah Zafar. He seemed not to be looking at this meanly clad figure on a bare bed, but envisioning the emperor as he had seen him so often in purple robes of silk, jewels blazing in his crown. He almost collapsed on the floor, recalling the glorious day of Bahadur Shah Zafar's marriage to Zeenat Begum, his head resting on the bed close to the listless arm of the dead king.

"Yes, here lies the last of the Moghul emperors ever to rule the gold paved streets of India, in rags and poverty, exiled from the world of grief and devastation." Mulla Majasi's voice sliced through the thin fabric of air like a sharp knife. "And there expires the glory of the Moghuls, remembered only by the legacy of their grand poetry and marble monuments. Red sandstone only the dregs of time, not ever to be kneaded into the dough of glorious art and nonpareil architecture. The poets are silent."

Bibliography

Dalrymple, William, The Last Mughal, Penguin Books, India, 2007

Burke, S. M, Bahadur Shah, Sang-E-Meel Publications, Pakistan, 1996

Lane-Poole, Stanley, Low Price Publications, India, 1903

Amini Iradj, The Koh-i-noor Diamond, Roli Books, India, 1994

Fraser, George MacDonald, Flashman in the Great Game, Alfred A. Knopf, Inc, USA, 1975

Farwell, Byron, Armies of the Raj, W. W. Norton & Company, London, 1989

Hibbert, Christopher, The Great Mutiny, The Viking Press, USA, 1978

Husain S. Mahdi, Bahadur Shah Zafar, Aakar Books, India, 2006

Ward, Andrew, Our Bones are Scattered, Henry Holt & Company, USA, 1996

Kanda K. C, Bahadur Shah Zafar and his Contemporaries, Sterling Publishers, India, 2007

James, Lawrence, The Making and Unmaking of British India, St. Martin's Press, USA, 1997

Dunbar, Sir George, History of India, D.K. Publishers, India, 1936

Srivastava A. L, The Mughul Empire, Shiva Lal Agarwala & CO, 1998

Garret, H. L. O, The Trial of Muhammad Bahadur Shah, NCA Publications, Pakistan, 2003

Allen, Charles, God's Terrorists, ABACUS, UK, 2006

Dalrymple, William, White Mughals, Harper Perennial, London, 2002

Keay, John, India A History, Grove Press, USA, 2000

Table of Contents